GHOSTSPEAKER CHRONICLES

Books 1-3

PATTY JANSEN

Capricornica Publications

GET FREE EBOOKS

JOIN MY NEWSLETTER

RECEIVE THIS STARTER PACK FOR FREE

Visit pattyjansen.com
to sign up for Patty's mailing list. You get four ebooks for free!

WHISPERING WILLOWS
LOESIE'S STORY

THE RIVER behind Granma's house runs deep. The water's like a vat of dirty milk, all murky, with eddies and floating sticks that twirl and twirl downstream.

From the top of the dike, with only green fields and willows around me, I can see the other side—just. Maybe I could make out a person if they stood on the bank, but I's not sure 'cause no one ever does. The other side is Burovia and them's bad as they come, at least so says Granpa in between stuffing his pipe and stripping willow twigs.

No one with half a brain would try to cross the river. No one ever could.

Except the man and his enormous horse.

I were cutting willow switches, and then I seen them in the middle of the water. Two heads, a black horse's and a man's. It seemed the horse was walking-like, on the bottom, but I don't know's the river has a bottom. But whatever it were doing, the horse were coming straight for me.

I hid in the tree, which were pretty silly-like, 'cause a willow's no leaves in early spring.

The man didn't see me, or he pretended he didn't see me as much as I pretended to be a bird. Or something.

He had hair red as a fox, all curly, and the bit below his shoulders were wet and dripped water onto his jerkin.

The horse—it were huge, with a long mane and masses of fluff around hooves big as Ma's milking bucket. It were noisy-like, snorting and blowing and grumbling.

The stranger sat straight on the horse's back, no saddle, and grabbed a breath of wind in his hand. He whispered into it, and let it go. *He were using magic.* His eyes met mine and my cheeks glowed like they was on fire.

He kicked the horse's sides and rode off. The orange spot that were his hair got smaller and smaller amongst the grass and the buttercups.

🌀

Annette looked at me, eyes wide like a rabbit's just before it got clubbed.

"I don't believe you."

I shrugged. Annette's pale hands never stopped weaving willow twigs in-out-in-out around the leads. Apple baskets we was making, not that I'd a clue what city people want with those, seeing there's no apple trees in the city, but Granma said make apple baskets, so we made apple baskets. For taking to market, you know.

"I seen it."

"No one can swim the river."

"He did."

"Then where is he now, that man of yours?"

Heat flamed in my cheeks. "He lives in the reeds and he keens for me. He be hiding."

Annette snorted. "There was never a man. You and your stories, Loesie." She tamped down the woven twigs with a piece of wood.

I said nothing, taking one lead twig after another and weaving them around the edge of the basket so it made a thick braid. The willow twigs sang out to me, showing me the fox-haired stranger and his giant horse. His eyes met mine and inside me something stirred I couldn't begin to describe. I never met anyone else who knew about magic.

"You know my ma says I got to take my vows next time we're at church? She says I'm too old for stories."

I pretended to be busy with my basket. I hadn't taken my vows, and I weren't going to, much as Granpa suddenly seemed keen. But the triune of the Spirit, the Ghost and the Holy God could go fishing as far as I's concerned, because the church said there weren't any magic. It was just that city people didn't believe what they couldn't see. That's why they made statues of the triune, hideous three-headed things, painted in colours and glittery-like. As if something with three heads could exist.

"They's not stories I tell, Annette. I seen the man. He were crossing the river, and then his magic told me to come to him, you know. His hair's soft like a newborn lamb's."

"You didn't really touch a man, did you, Loesie?" Annette's eyes were wide.

"I did. It's just as true's I sit here talking to you." It were such fun, telling Annette stories.

"Hush. Just keep quiet about those things, or my ma won't let me come anymore. I don't want that, Loesie. You're my only friend."

"No," I said. "I's not telling anyone." Of course I wouldn't. Granma would send me to bed without dinner.

"Good," she said, and then her eyes glinted. "Can I see him?"

Annette and me went down to the river, but of course the man weren't there. I told her of the great black waterhorse and with each word I said, the horse grew until it was so tall there were no way the man could get on its back. Never mind, Annette listened.

"Do horses have magic?"

"Horses don't. Waterhorses do. They have hooves that turn into duck's feet when they get into the water."

"Wow, a magic horse." Annette stared at the far bank of the river. The breeze stirred her straw-blond hair, and the soft light made her eyes baby-blue. She were pretty, Annette, in all the ways I were not.

"This man, do you think he was a foreigner?"

"Of course he were. He came right from the Burovian king's castle."

On winter nights, the farm hand Ko would tell stories of the king, who could change into a bear and would rip the throats of the men who didn't please him, and that were just his own men —imagine what he would do to us weak Saarlanders and our gibbering priests.

Annette shivered. "What do you think he was doing here?"

"Spying on us, of course."

Annette clamped her hands around herself. Sometimes I felt sorry for her, only sometimes, though. Most of the time I just told her stories, and laughed at how she believed I knew everything. Never mind it would only last until she made a good match, and no man wanted me.

At dinner time, I had to hear all about it.

After Granma told me to leave my clogs by the door, and *wash your hands because they're dirty, girl,* I found Granpa sitting at the table glaring at me. That's when I knew something were up. Granpa don't look at me like that for nothing.

I sat down meekly and he said the daily prayer. Something about the Spirit giving us life and the Ghost taking it away and the Holy God keeping our souls in his heart. He murmured words like I's never heard him say on the farm, and I guess he don't know what they mean either. City words-like.

Granma had her hands folded on the table. Ma held hers on her lap because they was all brown, the kind of dirt you can't wash off, from the cows. Ko had taken off his cap. His hair stood up straight, like straw in the barn, only dirtier.

We was never praying kind of people before Annette and her ma come back from the city with all their ideas about what's right and proper. I didn't think Granma and Granpa believed in the triune, but they's good at pretending while the neighbours was watching. Ko, you see, works for them, too.

While Ma ladled soup onto our plates, Granpa began. "Pier were here this afternoon." His words was stiff with meaning.

You see, Pier and Granpa . . . let's say they didn't get along. At times when Granpa thought I weren't listening, I'd heard him talk about "that stiff-face" and his "mad sister" from town. The mad sister would be Annette's ma. She'd lost her husband, see, when he'd gone off in some war to fight, at least that's what Annette says, but I don't believe her. I think he's died of some silly disease-like and she's ashamed to say. The people of Saarland don't fight, they trade. The king's got no army to speak of, even me knows that.

Anyway, Granpa were saying that Pier had stepped inside Granpa's house, and that were something. It said: this is important, Loesie. You better listen.

"Pier said you'd been telling Annette stories again."

"I . . ." The stupid cow! Tell me I weren't to say anything, but blab to her own family instead?

"No, I don't want any more of this kind of trouble. Waterhorses and magic! What were you thinking, Loesie? Didn't you learn anything from the time her ma called you a witch?"

"Granpa, the man and the horse were real. I seen them." Besides, if seeing things in willow wood made a person a witch, I *were* a witch.

"I know." But his eyes said he didn't believe me, or at least he didn't want to, and at the moment that were pretty much the same thing. "I want no more trouble with Pier, Loesie. I've half a mind to send you to church school to make a lady out of you."

The wind whistled around the corners of the church and whispered magic into its willow wood. Giant black horses and fox-haired strangers. The meeting of gazes across a river bank. The priest stood at the church doors, his mouth open in a chant, but the magic went straight through him.

I woke up sweating under too many blankets, while my breathing filled the dark. The wind howled around the corner of the house, wolf-like. With such strength, it must have a lot of stories to tell. Of black horses, knights with shields and swords, dark castles and deep forests. Listen as I might, I could not hear them, but I knew the fox-haired stranger could. And I wondered what he were listening to.

❀

As punishment, Granpa sent me to prune willows upriver.

That were a long way from the farm, and the path were all muddy-like from last night's rain. Half the morning were gone by the time I got there, ducking lapwings who thought I were after their eggs. Stupid birds.

Here, the water churned softly around a bend. There were no sound except sometimes a fish leapt out of the water and landed back in. *Splash*. It were frightening until you got used to it. A moist wind whipped hair into my face, a mere ghost of last night's gale, all its stories swept out to sea.

I took my ladder, propped it against a tree, stuck my saw in my belt and climbed. Last time Granpa cut these branches were five years ago, and they had grown lush and thick. Just right for apple baskets. Whatever city folk needed apple baskets for.

When I put my hand on the first twig, I heard a harsh shout. I no longer saw the willow's misshapen trunk, but a line of men coming down the opposite bank. One of them unslung an enormous bow from his shoulder, nocked an arrow and loosed it. The arrow flew across the river, trailing a thin rope. It thunked into the wood of a nearby tree.

The man waded into the river, and swam, a small head in the churning water. He clambered onto the bank hanging onto the rope. His arms was freckled, his hair curly and dark. He yanked the arrow out of the tree, and pulled at the rope. He pulled and pulled until something else came out of the water—the end of a thick rope, which he dragged to the tree and tied it around the trunk.

Then the other men splashed into the river, their horses blowing from the nostrils, keeping their necks straight so their heads stuck out of the water. The last horse were without rider. The rope stopped them drifting with the current.

There was at least twenty of them, clambering onto the river bank. They wore breast-plates, and swords, massive bows across muscled shoulders. The freckled man jumped into the saddle of the riderless horse in a single leap.

With them came three animals like I's never seen before. Big, long-haired and shaggy, with a pointy nose that wriggled and little piggy eyes. They crawled up the bank awkward-like, on their flat feet. But as soon as they come on top of the dike, they was off with great speed. A young calf with its mother were no more than a game for them, bellowing and gurgling in bloody death.

Someone yelled. A man stood on the path with a wheelbarrow full of fat cheeses.

Annette's granpa? What were he doing here? He'd gone to market this morning.

The freckled stranger drew his bow and said hissing words that floated from his mouth, mist-like, and wrapped themselves around the arrow. Willow wood, it were. It sang through the air and hit the old farmer in the chest. His body twisted, turned brown and rough, sprouted branches, and next thing there were a willow in the field.

The freckled man spread his hands, snagging tendrils of wind between his fingers. There were *magic* in the air. Pictures. Men on horses wielding swords. A holy man shouting. The freckled stranger hissed sibilant words and the army surged forward. They wasn't just men, they was demons, with snarling faces.

He laughed and looked at me. For a fleeting moment, I saw the face of a different man, one with fox-red hair.

I gasped and almost fell down the ladder.

Looked around.

Green fields, reeds and meadows. A swan grazed by the river bank. The river stretched out on both sides like a silver ribbon, with all its murky eddies. Completely normal-like, with no archers and shaggy brown animals. No magic arrows.

But reeds on the bank was pushed aside. There was hoof marks in the sand. On the trunk of a tree clung a clump of fur with hair as long as my hand, thick and dark brown. And a willow stood in the middle of the paddock, a wheelbarrow next to it, empty.

They's took the cheese.

❁

When I came home, Ko were just letting the cows out of the milking paddock. One after the other, they ambled into the sunset, their stupid noses in the grass.

He grinned at me, the sunlight catching his sail-ears. "Seen any more waterhorses, Loesie?"

I stomped into the barn and dumped my bundles of twigs. It were already half-dark, and I couldn't see much in that musty cobwebby place, other than Annette's unfinished basket. She hadn't come today. Silly me and my stories. Silly Annette for believing everything I said.

There were a snort.

A horse stood in the corner, tied to a ring in the wall.

The black horse.

The fox-haired man—he were here! I ran outside.

Shadows moved against the light in the kitchen. Annette were in Granma's vegetable garden, peeking into the window.

My stranger were at Granpa's table, eating a bowl of soup. He sat with his back straight, looking around like he's owned the place. Ma stood at the stove, stirring the pan. She were giving him dirty glances-like as she don't trust him. Granma were sitting in the corner in her rocking chair, knitting. Granpa sat at the other end of the table, his hands folded on the table, as if he were praying.

"Isn't he handsome?" Annette said in a voice like I's never heard from her, bewitched-like.

"Annette, go home, these strangers is no good."

She whirled at me, her cheeks red. "What do you know about that? Telling stories again? You just want him for yourself, don't you?"

"No. These men's dangerous. They's bringing an army of demons—"

"Shoosh, Loesie, before you talk any more nonsense. Have

you seen his *water horse*? Your granpa has it swimming in the cow's trough."

I said nothing. Glared into the room without seeing anything. Then I turned to the door. "Like I care if you don't believe me! I's going to warn Granpa."

As I went in, Annette looked at me and there were something in those blue eyes that I never seen before. I knew that things'd never be the same.

The stranger's voice were deep and rumbled like the growl of an angry wolf, or how I thought it'd sound, not like I's ever seen a wolf, but that's what the willows tell me about wolves.

He were now standing, having tipped the contents of a leather pouch on the table. Gold pieces! He counted out three and gave them to Granpa, who picked them up and tried to bend them. Like they would. Always seemed too eager to take visitors' money, Granpa were.

"We'll tell you when we seen something strange," Granpa were saying. "Loesie, this traveller were just telling us how he's looking for bandits."

"I seen something strange," I said. See? He were not a bad man. Nothing to do with the demons. "There was men crossing the river. They's had brown demons, all shaggy-like, and one of the men changed Annette's granpa into a tree."

"Oh, Loesie, stop telling stories," Granma said, looking up from her knitting. "Their granpa has gone to market. He won't be back until tomorrow."

"But I seen it."

The man nodded, a smile on his face. His eyes met mine. They was golden brown, like the freckles on his nose and his cheeks. Freckles must be common in the lands across the river.

He called up a breeze. It tickled my skin as it flowed past me, and I could see that even though I weren't seeing things on the air, he were. Of what I'd seen when the willow spoke to me. Magic were speaking to magic.

He traced his finger across the ticklish skin under my chin. "Fiery girl you have here, Anton."

His speech were like city folk's, in which Granpa's name floated like a turd in a scented bath, but I's just making that up, 'cause I seen a turd plenty times, but I never seen a scented bath.

My skin crawled with his touch, goosebump-like. I wanted to hit him, I wanted to throw myself in his arms. I believed him; I didn't believe him. His eyes spoke of danger.

Without a word, the stranger gathered his bag and strode to the door, leaving behind a deafening silence.

"Here be dinner, Loesie," Ma said.

I sat down and took my spoon, blowing steam off the soup. The willow wood table sang the stranger's touch. *Trustmetrust-metrustme.*

"Handsome fellow," Granpa said, glancing at me, rubbing his gold pieces.

Ko went out to feed the cows, Granpa had to bring in hay, and when I finished eating, I said I needed to lay out my twigs. I'd already done that of course, but my mind were clouded with men on giant horses and their brown shaggy demons. Glistening arrows and huge swords, whispering magic to the air.

The sun hung low on the horizon, an orange ball in a grey sky. Shadows of the cows crept over the field, ghost-like, many times longer than the animals was tall.

The windows of Pier's farm glowed golden in the setting sun. The vegetable garden were empty; Annette must have gone home for dinner.

There was voices in the shed. For a moment I thought it was Ko and Granpa, but then I remembered they was in the field. It were a woman's voice I were hearing.

Annette.

They stood in the corner of the shed, next to the horse.

He leaned lazily against the wall, having drawn her so close she might as well be lying on top of him. He stroked hair out of her face with his right hand. His left hand rested on her back. There were magic in the way he looked at her, the way he spoke soft words, his lips almost touching her ear.

I ran out of the barn.

The night were full of thunder and magic rumbled in the storm. I swung Granpa's axe, chopping gauges in soft willow wood. With every chop, I felt the pain. Magic being chopped out of me. Pain were good. I wanted pain; I wanted blood on my hands, on the chest of Annette's pale dress. Her screams pierced the night. She were the tree, or the tree were her. Supple branches reached to strangle me.

I woke up when someone banged on the front door. Hard. Thunder boomed. Noise filled the night.

Granma stumbled from the bedroom, lit a candle and went to open the door. A gust of air blasted in, almost as furious as Pier's voice. "Where is Annette?"

The candle threatened to flutter out.

"Pier, it be the middle of the night. Why would Annette—"

"Last I saw her she were walking to your barn. To finish her baskets, she said. It's that crazy girl of yours, isn't it?"

Granma backed away. "Look, Pier, I don't know—"

"Where is Annette?" He almost screamed.

Granpa hustled him inside.

He poked the fire in the kitchen, but it cast little more than meagre warmth. I sat, shivering, in the chair furthest from it. If something had happened to Annette, it were my fault.

The door clanged open and Ko stomped in, wearing a raincoat and carrying a lantern. "We's going to look for her. Where were she last? In the barn?"

I nodded, and thinking of that scene made me want to strangle her.

"I be coming." Granpa threw on his coat and lit the lanterns that hung in the hall. All that time he didn't look at me.

When they had gone, I rose from the table. "I'm cold. I'm going to wait in bed."

Ma said softly, "Don't be afraid. Granpa and Ko will find her."

But I didn't go to bed. I slipped my warm clothes over my nightgown, opened the window and climbed out.

The barn were empty except for stacks of apple baskets and bundles of willow switches. I knelt and touched the wood, but all I saw were Annette and the stranger *kissing*. Why did Annette always get everything that were mine? I ran back to the shed door.

Flashes of lightning showed Granpa and Ko along the road with the plough horse. They was going the wrong way, the wooden handle of the pitchfork told me that.

I sneaked up the dike to the other side. Here, a patch of grass were trampled. In amongst the reeds, I found Annette's long-sleeved dress, ripped and stained with blood.

I called, "Annette?"

No reply.

Rain drizzled on me. The river and the fields was all dark and still. No Annette.

On the bank of the river stood a slender willow I never seen before.

No, Annette!

As soon as I put my hands on the trunk, screams filled my head. Pale arms flailing, hands clutching for purchase in the grass, scratching his back, pulling at his hair, screaming, *Stop, stop!* Her pain became mine. His grunts filled the night.

"Annette!"

Then there were a deep man's voice, growling, wolf-like, behind me. "I give you credit girl. You are not half as stupid as the rest of them."

The fox-haired stranger held my wrist in an iron grip.

"You . . . you killed her."

He shook his head, glanced at the tree. "She lives."

"Let me go! Let me go!" I tried to pull my arm free.

He turned me around to face him.

I looked into the eyes of death, expecting . . . I don't know what. His hands ripping my dress. The pain of a stab to the chest, icy cold as he held me under water.

But he did none of that.

He bent forward and pressed his lips to mine, forced his tongue into my mouth. Hot, hungry. Magic reached out to magic. My heart thundered crazy-like in my chest. The moment lasted a few gasping breaths, but I wanted it to go on forever, ride his horse and share his bed. I'd take the pain, for I were sure he would hurt me, even though I understood that willow magic stopped him changing me into a tree. I deserved pain; I wanted it. I had betrayed my family. He could have me, as long as nothing happened to them. I wanted to tell him, but no sound passed my lips.

He laughed. "You thought there was no price?"

I raised my hand to my throat. *My voice?*

"I cannot let you tattle to anyone. It was my brother and his men you saw, scouting for the army. I have a war to fight."

He let go of me and swung himself onto his horse. Blew his magic into the wind and left me with my soundless tears.

I stumbled over the dike, but all I found on our farm, and Pier's, was whispering willows.

INNOCENCE LOST

Book 1 of the Ghostspeaker Chronicles

PATTY JANSEN

CHAPTER 1

J OHANNA SASHAYED down the church aisle towards the open doors that beckoned her to freedom. Her clogs clonked on the wooden floor, clop-clop-clop. With each sway of her hips, her skirts swished around her ankles, and her plait swung over her back, free of the bonnet.

Outrageous. Improper.

Poor girl, needs a mother. Look at her clothes. As if her father can't afford anything better. He's giving her far too much freedom.

She knew the whispers of the merchants' wives, the not-quite-nobles and other hangers-on of the Saardam gentry, and all the others in the pews. She knew the rules of the church about women, *that they should dress modestly and not show any exuberance or draw attention to themselves.*

There would be hell to pay for this later, but today, she didn't care.

On second thoughts, coming to church wearing her clogs instead of her proper shoes was probably not her smartest idea ever. But she didn't want to get her best shoes dirty. Of course she had a second-best pair of shoes, but even her second best pair of shoes was too good for the markets, where farmers cast their scraps on the ground and their pigs and cows and chickens left their business, and where the cobbles were always covered in slimy mud.

Indeed, the daughter of a merchant who hoped to attain noble status wasn't supposed to go to the markets. One had *servants* for the purpose.

Not that she cared about that either. Because, for once, the weather gods smiled on Saardam, bringing out the colours, the paint on the merchants' houses, the red of the roofs, the blue water in the canals, the brilliant green of the leaves on the trees, the yellow of the cheeses on the market stalls, the blue and white shirts of the cheese sellers. Had she ever noticed how many weeds grew between the pavers in the street and how brightly yellow the dandelions bloomed? Did she remember how blue the sky was and how white the clouds?

She stopped at the church door, drinking it in.

She called it *freedom,* now that the boring part of the day was done.

The sunlight was kind even to Nellie, with wisps of flaxen hair peeking out from under her oh-so-proper bonnet. Her eyes were clear and blue and her skin was like the velvet bottom of the neighbour's baby, so much prettier than Johanna's. Those cheeks now flushed with red as she caught up with Johanna at the church doors, bowing and apologising to all those who had nothing better to do than complain.

She whispered, "Mistress Johanna, you aren't wearing your proper shoes."

"Aren't I?" Johanna lifted up the hem of her skirt, letting the sunlight fall on her clogs. Pretty ones, these were, too, with painted patterns and made from willow wood that sang its stories to her whenever she wore them. Happy stories, of fat cows, green pastures, and peace.

"Your shoes were in your room. I put them there this morning."

"Oh. I must have missed them."

She clonked down the church steps, clop-clop-clop on the wood. Clop-clop-clop down the new stairs of the new entrance porch with its Lurezian woodwork and stained glass windows. Clop-clop-clop onto the cobbled street.

See me? I'm wearing my clogs to church. If there is any such thing as the Triune—which I doubt—He will love me or hate me with my clogs just as much as with my shoes.

"Come, let's go!"

Nellie sighed and rolled her eyes. She did that a lot lately.

Frivolous, they called Johanna, and said she needed a man. But have you ever noticed how marriage takes the life out of a woman's eyes?

She slid into the crowds of the markets, the servants, shop-keepers and common people buying their daily needs: bread, butter and cheese; potatoes, fish and—shudder—cabbage.

"Good day Mistress Johanna, good day, Nellie," said Leo Mustermans, standing behind his stall. He wore his Market Day best, a hose that was grey and less patched than what he usually wore when lugging cheeses from the sloops in the harbour. He did well enough; under his golden hair he had a round face, now sweaty and squinting into the sunlight.

"Beautiful day today," Johanna said. "The cheese will be good this summer."

"That, it will be, Mistress Johanna. Though the cheese will get sweaty if the breeze doesn't pick up."

She laughed. She wanted to say, *Just like you* but Leo would laugh, because he was that kind of man, and others would know what she'd said and next thing *that* would be added to her list of recent sins.

"It's good quality cheese, the kind the Estlanders like." He looked like he wanted to add something about Johanna's father buying his cheese and selling it to Estland, but he didn't. She was a frivolous *girl* after all and one couldn't possibly discuss business with a girl. Fancy that.

Then he asked, "You're all excited for the king's ball?"

Johanna laughed but her good mood fled the instant he mentioned the word "ball". Why did they always have to ask about that? As if it were the only thing that mattered for a young woman in Saardam: to be invited to the royal ball. She said through clenched teeth, "Our family is not important enough to go to the ball."

"I'm sorry to hear that."

"Don't be, because I don't want to go."

"But you should be invited, Mistress Johanna. You'd be pretty enough to turn all the noble boys' heads, and brainy enough to outsmart them all."

She laughed, the sound again hollow. "Thanks for the flattery, Leo, but no thanks. I'm glad I don't have to go." It was not like the noble boys *wanted* brainy girls.

"It's a pity. The rumour goes that the king will announce a surprise for the citizens of Saardam."

Johanna had heard that, too, whispered to her by the wood of the pews in the church. She stifled a wave of suspicion and dread. Last year, the king's surprise had been his donation of the statue of the Triune to the Church. The thing was so big that it had come on a river sloop pulled by two full teams of sea cows all the way from Lurezia. The blocks of the statue had to be dismantled even further before they fitted through the church door.

She hoped the surprise would be nowhere as extravagant as that. And that it would be something that people could use. She heard the Burovian king had paid for a new concert hall, and that Lurezia now had a building dedicated to the study of the skies. Why couldn't King Nicholaos give something like that? "I'm sure we'll hear about it soon enough."

"That is true. We will, Mistress Johanna." He nodded. "Have a nice day."

"A nice day to you, too."

She walked away from the stall, running her fingers over the wooden planks of the trestles groaning under the weight of his cheeses, big, fat yellow ones. The willow wood brought images of grazing cows and green fields to her mind—buttercups and dandelions, and stacks of drying hay.

"He *is* right, you know," Nellie said in a soft voice once they were in the next aisle.

"What?" Johanna frowned at her, still thinking of green meadows and fat cows.

"You *should* be invited to the ball. Your father is important enough. He's certainly wealthy enough."

"Oh, pfaw, Nellie. He's a merchant. Haven't you noticed how much the nobles get out of their way to put us in our place? I'm glad I don't have to go and that's the truth of it. Do you see me dancing and twirling in frilly dresses? Do you see me walking up the steps to the palace with half of Saardam gawking at me and gossiping about what I'm wearing? I can just about hear their voices already: 'She *is* very coarse, isn't she?' and 'Goodness me, who did her hair?' or '*What* is she wearing?' "

"They are doing that already." Nellie glared pointedly at Johanna's clogs.

Yes, she got the point.

Clearly scenting blood, Nellie stuck her nose in the air. "It would be a good opportunity to show that you're a real lady. It's not too late for you to find a good husband—"

"Nellie, have you noticed that as soon as a woman gets married, she dresses 'proper' and suddenly loses her youth and her sense of fun? Well, I have no intention of becoming like that."

"You can still be a fun person when you're married."

"Show me a woman who managed that, and I will believe it."

She glared at Nellie and Nellie glared back.

In her eyes Johanna saw the frustration of years of waiting, the embarrassment of watching her mistress do things that made her cringe. Johanna's father employed Nellie as a personal maid and companion, but she wanted to be the maid of a household, a servant to the man Johanna was yet to marry, and a governess to the children Johanna didn't have.

You're twenty-four, mistress. It is beyond time that you were married.

Why did discussions always come back to that old subject?

It was getting very tiresome.

She continued from stall to stall, across the cobbled pavement, sliding her hands over the wood and hearing in the wood's essence the conversations of men who had put out the trestles early this morning, the voices of the merchants as they arrived, the gossip, the people who were always late paying, the liars and cheats, who married whom, who cheated with whom, that sort of thing. She listened to the talk of merchants, about accounts, about imports, the sort of news she would relay to her father.

Then Johanna came around a corner and found a stall with

stacks of baskets of the type that were woven from willow twigs. Her heart leapt. Loesie was here.

Johanna hadn't seen Loesie since the pale beginning of spring. She lived with her grandmother on the flood plains of the Saar River that looped around Saarland to form the northern border with the kingdom of Estland and the eastern border with the barony of Gelre.

Nellie had seen Loesie, too, because she touched Johanna's arm. "Please, Mistress Johanna, it's time to—"

"I need a basket for my embroidery things."

"But you hardly ever do embroidery, Mistress Johanna."

"That's why I need a basket—to keep it out of my way."

"But you have a room full of baskets. A basket for your wool, a basket for your laundry, a basket for your winter blankets . . ." She counted on her fingers. "I could scarce find room for another one."

"I am sure you can find one that is broken."

Johanna progressed to the stall, Nellie hobbling behind her, protesting that Johanna never broke any baskets. She felt sorry for Nellie; only sometimes, though. On second thoughts, Nellie was a nice girl, but she really needed to stand up for herself more, even against her mistress. Especially against her mistress, because she took advantage of it.

Having felt Johanna approach, as Johanna knew Loesie would, Loesie rose from behind a pile of baskets.

And there the day turned not-so-very-good at all.

The young woman in the stall was no longer the one Johanna knew as her friend, no longer the vivid, laughing, large-eyed creature that people in town called a witch when they thought Johanna wasn't listening. No longer the figure that inspired fear in Nellie and the ship's boys who sneaked around trying to steal from the stalls.

This pale shell of her friend was like a ghost. Her mist-grey eyes were wide, her skin so pale it was almost translucent. A black dress hung off bony shoulders, and a black scarf covered her limp, grey-brown hair.

As Loesie recognised Johanna, her face split into a grin, but it was more like a grimace. Her cheeks were death-pale.

Johanna ran to her, simultaneously horrified and revolted. "Loesie! What happened to you?"

Her arms closed around Loesie's shoulders, and at the same time, a shudder of cold went through her. There was no meat on Loesie's bones at all. "A sickness? Death in the family?"

Loesie only looked at Johanna.

"What happened, Loesie? Where is your grandmother?" But it was clear that she had come alone. There were not as many baskets as usual and the stall was rather messy.

Loesie's lips opened, but her mouth made only a kind of *ghghghgh* noise from the back of her throat. She lifted her hand up to her neck. It sounded like she had a turnip stuck down there.

"You can't speak?"

She nodded.

"You have a disease?"

She shook her head. Her eyes bore a glazed expression, as one—Johanna shivered—one touched by magic.

Of course the Shepherd in church said there was no magic, and that's what the people wanted to believe. The Church had no control over magic, because magic flows where magic goes, in the wood of the willow trees, in the wind and in the water. Magic didn't happen for everyone, and certainly didn't answer to priests and their prayers.

So magic or no, Johanna knew not what else to call it, but it hovered in Loesie's eyes sure as she could hear willow wood speak.

Johanna dug under her apron, trying not to notice how thin Loesie was and how ill her grandmother's dress fitted her, and how her skin had paled until it looked like she was a corpse that had floated in the water for days. She took a bag of biscuits out of her pocket and slipped it into Loesie's hands. She scrunched open the paper.

"Go on then, eat them. They're good. Koby made them."

With her bone-thin fingers, Loesie broke a piece off a biscuit and popped in her mouth. She closed her eyes as she chewed, then she smiled. Johanna put her hand on Loesie's shoulder.

"Tonight you should sleep in Father's sea-cow barn. You'll be warm there. I'll bring you some food, right?"

She nodded.

From the corner of her eye, Johanna could see Nellie fidgeting.

Yes, yes, I know I came here to buy a basket. Let's choose a basket, then.

She ran her fingers over the rim of a coarsely-woven laundry basket. The stripped willow twigs made her skin tingle. She heard laughter, sloshing of water around a boat, the voices of a young man and a young woman. She pulled away and reached for another basket. Those twigs gave her no more than the soft lowing of cows. The next thing, a footstool made from willow twigs, contained a male voice, which said, "You know, one day in spring a flood will come and all this land will be under water."

A boy responded, "Can't we stop it?"

"No, son, it needs to happen. It's part of life."

Johanna withdrew her fingers. She'd heard all these voices before. They came from twigs cut from willows around town.

Loesie rummaged under her table and pulled out a few more baskets, none of which were in the shape of anything that Johanna could remotely use for storing embroidery.

She glanced over her shoulder at Nellie, who scrunched her hands up before her, white-knuckled, and who was studiously avoiding gazes from genteel citizens, glances that said, *You should tell your mistress not to involve herself with such questionable people.* Poor Nellie.

Then Loesie pulled a square basket that had been at the bottom of the pile and held it out to Johanna, uttering more *ghghghgh* sounds.

"For me?"

She nodded, her eyes vivid.

The moment Johanna touched the woven twigs, she heard the most bloodcurdling scream she had ever heard in her life. A woman. It was night and the pale moonlight wasn't strong enough to show what was happening. There were men's voices, too, rough and . . . foreign. The sound of galloping hooves, and a low, guttural, demonic roar. Some kind of creature bounded through tall grass. All Johanna saw was a silhouette, pushing aside tall grass and leaves that occasionally reflected the moonlight like silver. The creature ran flat-footed, was long-haired, and had small, rounded ears and a long snout, like a hunting dog, except it was much bigger than that.

She dropped the basket, goose bumps crawling over her arms. "Where . . ." She gulped for air. "Where did this wood come from?"

Loesie thudded her hand on her chest.

"You cut it?"

She nodded.

If she cut it, it must come from somewhere close to her grandmother's farm. Johanna bent to pick up the basket, and used her apron to touch the wood. The messages in the wood faded the more people touched it.

Did that poor screaming woman survive? What was that dreadful roar? What was that creature? Willow tales were always true. If that's what the tree had seen, then that was how it had happened.

"Loesie—was this at your grandmother's farm?"

She nodded and mimicked fighting.

"They're bandits? Coming into Saarland?"

She nodded again and then formed her hands into claws and mimicked a roar.

"And demons?"

Loesie nodded again.

Except the kingdom of Saarland had been at peace for many years. There had not been any marauding bands of invaders for a long time. Certainly not magical ones.

Johanna wanted to set the basket down, but Loesie gestured for her to keep it and pointed across the marketplace.

"You want me to leave?"

"Ghghghghgh!" She shook her head and pointed more strenuously.

Nellie reminded Johanna, "We should be on our way, Mistress Johanna. We have to be back for midday—"

"Cowpats, Nellie, we have plenty of time."

Nellie's cheeks darkened. "Mistress Johanna. You shouldn't

say such . . . things. And in the marketplace, too, where everyone can hear it, mind you. What is your father going to say when he hears—"

"Stop it, Nellie, before I say any worse words. My friend needs help. That's much more important than what people think of me."

Then, spotting the crest of Saardam above the entrance to the council chambers, she realised what Loesie had been trying to say. "You want me to tell someone, like the mayor?"

She nodded, her eyes wide, while she gripped Johanna's arm. *"Ghghghgh!"*

"Yes, I will." Though what she would tell a mayor who went to church every day and didn't believe in magic she didn't know. She could just about see the man's face, over his hideous ruffled collar. *The wood told you there are bands of rogues about?* "If I'm to make a convincing story, I need to know who these men are and where they are now."

Loesie made a sweeping motion with her hand.

"Everywhere?"

She nodded.

Johanna looked at the peaceful market scenes, the cheese merchants, the fabric sellers, the turnip farmers, all people she knew reasonably well. No one she didn't.

"Here?"

Loesie made a sound of frustration. "Ghghghghgh!"

"In the city?"

Loesie pulled her arm again, placing her hand flat on her chest. Then she pointed at Johanna.

"Yes, I promise I'll tell someone."

CHAPTER 2

WHATEVER HAPPENED to the nice day?

Johanna left the markets with no idea what she was going to do about the promise she'd made to Loesie. She couldn't just walk into the mayor's office and tell him about the magic warning.

The mayor went to church and took the Shepherd's teaching *very* seriously. A few weeks ago in church, the Shepherd Romulus had given a sermon that condemned magic in the strongest possible words. Johanna could still hear his voice. *There are those who adhere to the dark crafts of old, from quacks who tell the people lies about treatments that do not work, and fortune-tellers who take your money for deceit and extortion, to those who try to do evil. They tell you they see things on the wind or in the wood. These are lies. At best, the dark crafts are a fallacy. At worst, they are evil.*

He let his words echo through the church.

Then there are those, at the pinnacle of all evil, who willingly engage in the black arts that are the domain of the Lord of Fire. Those who seek to possess other people, those who speak to ghosts, and worst of all, those who try to raise the dead.

A kind of shudder had gone through the congregation at those words.

Johanna remembered sitting in her pew with her hands clamped between her knees, feeling like the Triune itself would burst through the ceiling of the church and point a great shining light at her. A big voice would boom through the church, *Here is a sinner and a witch and yet she sits in our church every day and she shares our meals. Who knows what she reads about you when she runs her hand over your dining table?*

It was at times like this that her father's words haunted her: that she didn't belong in this church—which she knew because she didn't really believe in the Triune—and that she should stop going to it.

But the church was useful. The benches made of willow wood were full of stories, which they released to her at the touch of her hands. They taught her many things she would never have known otherwise.

And everyone went to church. Everyone of her age at least. It was new, it was a good thing for the citizens, because the Verses taught that people should be sensible, compassionate, honest and frugal, all things that the Lurezian culture that had gripped the nobles of the city was not. Of course the nobles and those who wanted to be nobles disliked the Church's teachings against blatant displays of wealth.

There was just that little problem about magic and the way the Shepherd portrayed all magic as black and evil. One day, Johanna had told herself, she was going to show the Church that magic was mostly used for good. But that day hadn't come yet and each day the Church's teachings against magic intensified.

Increasing numbers of people, like the mayor, believed in the evil of magic. That was because many had never seen it.

Many, many people couldn't see things in willow wood, or hear voices on the wind, and therefore, to these people, this magic was something dark and evil. They liked what the Shepherd said about magic: that it was the mark of the Lord of Fire and those who practiced it were disciples of that evil force.

For Johanna, there was no right or wrong about magic. Magic just was. The wood showed her what the wood had seen. It re-played those images until the magic ran out. There was nothing evil about it, nothing that she could control. The magic was in the wood. She was simply there to see it.

But because the Church and the Shepherd had become

popular—and because the king went to church—it meant that if she needed to warn people, there was no way that she could do so with Loesie's story alone.

She couldn't tell anyone of the bloodcurdling scream from that woman or the demons, because she couldn't explain how she had seen them.

A plain warning that *some people crossed the river* would not bother anyone, because people in the border regions crossed the river all the time. Yet if Johanna spoke of the demons, they'd say that this was a hallucination by an unstable woman, unmarried and *frivolous*. The Church would consider *her* evil, too.

But she knew what the wood had shown her was true.

Who could these invaders be?

Saarland had been at peace for longer than Father had been alive.

She didn't *think* the royal family had offended anyone. They preferred trade with the neighbouring countries. Father's sloops, the *Lady Sara* and *Lady Davida* and the smaller ones, went up and down the river all the time. Father met with the Estlanders at Aroden castle and went as far as the rapids where the Saar River came down from the mountains in Westfalia, far beyond the borders even of Gelre. He'd never said anything about threats or bandits. It just made no sense.

There was only one thing to do: she needed to find out if someone else had seen anything.

Johanna said to Nellie, "You go ahead. Tell my father I'll be home soon."

"But Mistress, what are you going to do? It's almost midday." And midday was dinner and heaven forbid if she was late for that, even if only with her own father. *Do you ever not think about what's proper, Nellie?*

"I won't be long. There is something I have to do right now."

"Your father will be so angry if you're late. And what with you wearing your clogs to church—"

"Please, Nellie." Johanna held up her hands.

"Your father wants me to keep you—"

"Out of mischief and on the right path, yes. I'm not going to do anything silly. I just need to talk to someone."

Nellie glared at her and an unspoken warning hung between them.

It had something to do with the time last month that Johanna had borrowed a looking glass and wanted to see how the Moon would take a bite out of the Sun, as Jan Dieckens, who was the lighthouse keeper but who spent a lot of time looking at the stars, said.

But it happened at dusk and the sun was so low that Johanna couldn't see it from her bedroom widow, or the garden, so she'd climbed up on the roof through the attic window in the drying room. Before going out there, she had taken off her dress because it was too cumbersome for climbing on roofs, right?

But it so happened that her father had wanted to see her, and not finding her in her room, he had asked the servants, and none of them knew where she was. Then they all started looking, and getting more concerned until the gardener—a man no less—found her on the roof wearing only her drawers. What a scandal that had been!

"Please yourself, Nellie. You can go home, or you can come with me, but I am going. And the sooner I go, the quicker I'll be back." She turned and walked away.

Nellie ran after her. "Where are you going?" The words *to the roof in your drawers?* hung in her voice.

"To Father's office."

Nellie's eyes widened. Apparently she had expected something entirely different. Some of the tension went out of her posture.

The merchant office of the Brouwer spice merchants was along the harbour, in one of the stately buildings on the quay. The front window looked out over the harbour, and the ships, the sails, the masts and the activity that came with the many different kinds of ships.

There were big sailing vessels that went over the ocean, which went to places as far as the Horn and beyond, and brought back exotic spices and silks. There were the trusty river barges such as Johanna's father owned, which lay, ugly and plain, side-by-side in the glittering water of the harbour. A ship's boy was jumping from one boat to the other. A couple of quay workers were unloading fat cheeses onto a cart. With their greenish hue, they were Estlander cheeses, made from sheep's milk. That was what Father did: he took the exotic spices and silks to the inland cities of the east, and brought back their cheeses and dainty cabbage sprouts. He'd said not long ago that the company had enough money to invest in a seafaring vessel, but no one would dream of setting sail without guards to protect the vessel against pirates on the open ocean, and mercenaries did not work for common citizens. And the nobles wouldn't accept Father as one of them.

It was all very silly and frustrating.

A few herder boys in rowing boats were taking a group of sea cows across to the barns on the other side of the harbour. The sunlight glistened on the animals' hairy backs. They could probably already smell the cabbages and carrots in the water. The Brouwer Company's barn was somewhere amongst the boathouses perched on stilts over the water. This was where Loesie would sleep. Johanna would come back tonight and check on her.

As she squinted into the light, she noticed that there was an unusual sloop in the harbour. With its dark-painted sides and large cabin, with real glass windows and red curtains, it didn't look like a cargo ship. In fact, it looked like some rich person's private ship.

A few men sat on the deck of the *Lady Sara*, the Brouwer Company's flagship, smoking and drinking coffee, and waved as Johanna passed.

"Good morning, Mistress Johanna."

She stopped. "Good morning, Adrian. How's business?"

"We delivered the cheese to the Hendricksen warehouse. The *Lady Davida* should be back tomorrow with the wheat."

"Make sure the hold gets cleaned out properly. The *Lady Davida* will be taking a shipment of fine food to Estland, and I'm sure Lord Aroden won't like finding weevils in his biscuits."

"Sure, Mistress Johanna." Adrian snorted, no doubt thinking of *that* weevil incident.

She nodded at the black barge. "Do you know who that ship belongs to?"

"The black one?"

"Yes. Whose is it?"

"Don't know, Mistress, but I wager it's someone important. They arrived last night and there was a big to-do with folk on horses and carriages. All of it after dark, mind. Didn't see who came in, but it musta been important. Master Willems saw them too and said they might be guests for the royal family."

Oh, that dratted ball again. Now there were important *foreign* guests, huh? Wonder what outrageous things they would be wearing?

Pardon the sarcasm.

She looked at the boat and its immaculate shiny deck and she couldn't begin to figure who this important person would be. She would have recognised the Estlander flag if they were people from the Estlander royal family. But it wasn't the Estlander family standard. It was a blue flag with a small yellow emblem in it that depicted something complicated, like a flower or a frilled dragon, but was too far away for her to see.

"What company does that flag belong to?"

He shrugged. "Something Burovian. Heard a rumour that it belonged to some religious order's sanatorium. Dunno if that's true, mind . . ."

That didn't sit well with her. The Church—a religious order —a sanatorium. People from a Burovian religious order invited to the ball? King Nicholaos had become so obsessed with religion recently—religion which forbade magic. Magic, which she could not help having. Church, which she attended because everyone did, but where she didn't completely feel at ease.

She shivered. "Thank you, Adrian."

He waved and she continued on to the office of the Brouwer Company. The bells above the door clanged as she stepped inside, onto the familiar wooden floor where she'd played as a child, the familiar desk, now empty, where the office clerk usually sat, and the shelves with samples on the back wall. Even the smell was familiar. Tobacco, curry, nutmeg, cinnamon.

Nellie followed her and closed the door, shutting out the harbour sounds.

Master Willems, fresh-faced and red-cheeked, in black overdress and white ruffled shirt, came out of the door to Father's office.

"Good morning Mistress Johanna. Good morning, Nellie."

It was still morning. Only just.

He must have been ready to go out to the Church midday service because he held a thumbed copy of the Book of the Triune in his hands. He was Reader at church and would stand to the side of the altar and read out passages of the Verses.

"I haven't finished the Pietersen account yet," he said. "I'm sorry, I know I promised your father but I've been—"

"I didn't come for the Pietersen account. I want to talk to you."

"Oh?" He raised one blond eyebrow. One corner of his mouth quivered. He wasn't handsome, exactly, but trustworthy and dependable. If it hadn't been for his piousness, Johanna might even have liked him. "Me? Well, Mistress Johanna, I'm not sure that I—" He looked more puzzled now.

"It's about the wind."

"What wind?"

His face went blank, but by the way he gripped the edge of the table, Johanna figured he knew what this was about. He looked from her to Nellie, as if he wanted to say, *how much does she know?* and then jerked his head at the back office. They went inside, leaving Nellie in the front room.

Inside, by the hearth, big velvet-covered chairs took up most of the space. Account books lay in tottering piles on the heavy wooden desk in the corner. This used to be her father's desk, but her father hardly came in anymore, preferring to do his work from the comfort of his chair by the fire at home.

The air in the room smelled of fresh tobacco and an array of spices that were laid out on the table. He must have had a visiting buyer this morning.

Johanna sat down in one of the chairs, Master Willems in the other, smoothing the folds of his robe. He still held the Book of the Triune, and clutched it to his chest, nervously.

They sat there in silence for an uncomfortable moment before Johanna asked, "Have you seen anything on the wind lately, Master Willems?"

He froze, the book of the Triune in his hand. She had never spoken of magic, much less that she knew he could read wind magic from the way he stood at the end of the pier, letting the wind buffet him.

He pursed his lips, and eyes looked at her as if she was something disgusting washed up on the shore. "Of what do you speak, Mistress Johanna?"

He knew very well of what she spoke.

Johanna spoke in a low voice. "This can stay between us. You and I both know I have no great love for people who sow fear amongst the citizens for something they have no control over. The magic is in the wood and in the water and the wind. We do a lot of good with it. To blame those who can see it is not fair, and I cannot believe that any benevolent deity would agree to shame law-abiding citizens."

He gulped a few times.

She continued, "I do not care what you believe privately, but for the safety of our country, tell me if you've seen anything."

"Why . . . why should I have seen something . . . if I could see . . . things on the wind?" He wiped sweat from his upper lip.

Johanna put her newest basket on the table.

"Touch the willow wood, Master Willems. Can you tell me if you see anything?"

He did, and shook his head. "Do you see something. . . ?" His voice was no more than a whisper.

Johanna nodded. "I got this basket from a seller at the markets. I've known this woman for some time. She is a bit odd and she gets teased a lot, but she can also see things in willow wood. This morning when I saw her, something dreadful, something I think is dark magic, struck her mute—"

"That's because she is an evil practitioner of magic!" He held up the book, as if using it to ward off evil that emanated from Johanna.

"Oh, cowpats!"

His eyes widened. His mouth quivered. He looked like he wanted to say something about language, but couldn't possibly offend the daughter of his boss.

Johanna went on, "The woman gave me the basket. This is

the only way she could tell me what happened to her, or what happened at her farm. See, this is how 'evil magic' is used for good, because she can't read or write."

"And, pray, Mistress Johanna, what happened at the farm?"

Johanna had to bite her tongue not to lash out at his pious tone. "That's what I'm not sure about. The wood tells me . . . there are men on horses coming this way. I don't know who they are. Estlander bandits on our borders, perhaps. They have magicians. They have demons. Big, hairy, flat-footed creatures with snarling teeth and strong jaws."

He stiffened, then snorted. "No demons exist. They're a myth perpetuated by the Lord of Fire in order to strike fear into the congregation. The Church of the Triune seeks to exterminate those folk rumours. These are foolish girlish dreams that you're seeing."

And he, of all people, believed this? "Have you ever seen a bear, Master Willems?"

He met her eyes squarely, but said nothing. He hadn't.

"I have." She thought of the sad creature she'd seen in an Estlander market, chained up to a tree. A bear in its natural state was just a dangerous creature, but those with bear magic could turn it into a demon. That was what the rumours said at least. "I'd be glad to be proven wrong, Master Willems, but what I saw looked very much like demons. I simply wondered if you had seen something similar, because if you have, other people need to know. We should warn the king, or the guards, or whoever will listen. This has nothing to do with dreams. The wood always speaks true. I suspect the wind always speaks true as well. We see the images; it's up to us to ascribe meaning. The basket seller Loesie lives in the Bend, which is where she cut the wood. If the Bend has been invaded, the bandits will be in the marshes and may not be spotted until they're almost in the city. So, I ask again: have you seen anything?"

"No." The denial came too quickly, too defensive. He was sweating and gripping the book with more force than necessary.

"Master Willems, please. There could be trouble on the way."

"The wind does not speak, Mistress Johanna. And you would do well not to mention these things anymore."

"Well then," she said, rising from the chair. "I leave it up to you. I was worried by what I saw, and if you are concerned as well, you don't have to tell me, but do tell someone. Write an unsigned letter, if you are too scared."

"I'm not scared, Mistress Johanna. I will fight this evil magic in all the ways I can."

She left the office more worried than she'd been coming in. And she still had no proof of any trouble that the mayor would believe.

CHAPTER 3

W HEN JOHANNA and Nellie got home, the hallway was filled with the smell of cooking. As they took their coats off in the hall, Koby was just coming up from the kitchen carrying a tray of bowls and terrines.

Johanna followed her into the dining room.

Father already sat at the table. He nodded briefly to her as she sat down.

While Koby ladled soup in their plates, they started their usual talk about business and accounts. Father asked if Pietersen had paid yet, which Johanna informed him he had not, and then he said he'd chase it up. He mentioned that he had heard that Octavio Nieland was interested in buying bigger boats and going into ocean trade. There had been talk of forming a group, because the palace guards were obviously not going to protect the ships, but there would need to be money invested in protection and men and weapons. Anglian ships were in strong competition with the Saarlander ones. They always looked to steal the best trades and more than one skirmish had been fought over trading partners or safe anchorage. Also, there were many strange folk out beyond the Horn. Far Eastern ships with their red, square sails sometimes came all the way to the southern Lurezian coast. They sold silks and spices, but they spoke strange tongues and no one knew much about their rulers or whether they might be hostile.

Father scoffed, tucking his napkin into his collar. "Frankly, I don't understand why the investors tolerate Octavio Nieland, because he upsets everyone with his improper manners. He's too much of a pinchpenny to contribute much to the guards so they're not going to be interested in defending his ships. Have you heard about the time when he accidentally asked a Lurezian duchess to share the bed with him?" He chuckled.

This was Father in his element: ridiculing Octavio Nieland, who was a few years older than Johanna, had recently taken over his ailing father's company and belonged to the noble class that Father so wanted to join but probably never would.

"He meant to say join him on the couch, of course, not the bed. She was most upset, and he did not end up getting the contract that he went to Lurezia to negotiate."

Of course Johanna already knew that through the church gossip. It was amazing what those wooden benches told her, and the story might not be quite as Father told it. The gossip told her that the lady had been flirting, as Lurezians were bound to do.

"My point is, dear daughter, that the boy is not suited to negotiating delicate contracts with foreigners. He will make blunder after blunder and will create a bad name for Saarlander merchants. We could easily step in and show those people that we can be serious about business without offending everyone and making enemies in important places."

Except that Father could not buy any ships outright because, as a non-noble, he couldn't hire guards. He could only invest his money in other people's ships, and he was too stubborn for that.

"Sea trade will be more important than river trade. I predict that the Far Eastern traders will come into harbour soon enough. We don't want to appear weak—"

That reminded her— "Do you know, by the way, whose dark-coloured sloop is in the harbour? Someone coming to the king's annual ball, I heard."

"I don't follow gossip, you know that, daughter. You might be better off asking your people at church, hmm? All they seem to do is gossip."

Father, please. Koby was still in the room. She went to church. He often said these things just to rile her.

There were voices elsewhere in the house, Nellie letting someone into the front door. A male voice.

"I don't understand why you keep going to that church. That Shepherd is a gibbering idiot. Have you ever heard of such thing as the Triune? A three-headed monster that's supposed to do good on the earth in the name of God. And then they say that they don't believe in magic. Three-headed monsters."

"They are symbols."

"That's not how that dressed-up clown explained it to me—"

"Father!"

"He is a dressed-up clown, and a gibbering idiot, and I'll say so however many times I please in my own house. He was talking real monsters, and believing what he said, too. You know that three-headed monsters can't work? Each head has a mind of its own, and there is no one head to decide which way the monster is going to go if all three want to go in different directions."

He snorted.

Johanna managed to bite her tongue.

A discussion about this was pointless, and they'd had so many of these discussions already. It never got them anywhere.

"Everyone goes to church. People stick out when they don't. People talk about them."

"Octavio Nieland doesn't go."

"He's one of the few. He sticks out, but he doesn't care because he's Octavio Nieland." Also because he belonged to the nobility. He looked down his nose at something like the Church that was born of the common people. The Shepherd was said to have been a poor man, walking from town to town and helping people where he could, and it seemed King Nicholaos understood the commoners better than the nobles did. Johanna disliked many things about the Church, but this wasn't one of them.

"Daughter, you lack the most important ingredient of a believer: belief; and one day that's going to break you up."

He might be right, or he might not. She'd worry about that when the problem came up.

They ate in silence for a while. The big clock against the back wall went tick-tick-tick.

Why did he infuriate her so much lately?

Father put his spoon down and looked at her in a self-important way. "Anyway, daughter, about the ball. It seems I have received an invitation after all. You will be going with me—no, don't look at me like that. It's time that you started behaving a bit more like a lady."

"Father, the ball is in two days' time. I have nothing good enough to wear." If she was to walk up the palace steps under the eyes of all those in Saardam who cared about fashion, even her best shoes wouldn't be good enough, because they were serviceable, not fashionable. Father didn't like to spend a lot of money on clothes, not even hers. She felt the same.

He smiled. "We will have to fix that, then. You'll soon find that you have a visitor coming here who will help you solve that problem."

"You're getting a dress made for me? Now? Don't you want me to do the accounts?"

"Forget about them for these two days." He rose from the table, looking at her with that *you're my little girl* look that he'd used since she was little. "For once, I want you to look your very best. I have to go now. Business calls. I believe my visitor has already arrived."

And he was out the door.

Johanna stared after his back. That had to be the first time that he'd told her to take time off from the accounts. Was there something wrong with him?

When she went into the hall, Father's visitor was already in Father's study, having left behind a scent of tobacco and spice that lingered in the hallway.

She heard a voice in the room. Not Father. Not Captain Pieters of the Brouwer flagship, the *Lady Sara*. Not master de Waard, the manager of the warehouse. Not Jan Hendricksen, one of Father's best customers. Not that annoying Octavio Nieland either, or his elderly father.

An unfamiliar coat hung on the stand. A man's coat. Black. A very finely-made one with a very small pin on the coat's collar: the rooster, the symbol of the Carmine House.

What in all of heaven's name would Father have to say to the royal family?

In the stairwell, on the landing halfway between the ground floor and the second floor, was a little door that led into a low-ceilinged storeroom that had been built between the floors. The servants used this to store items of furniture that they didn't use anymore, or spare plates or tableware that didn't fit in the cupboards. This room was directly above Father's office.

Johanna paused at the stairs, looking carefully if anyone could see her. Then she opened the door quietly, went in and shut it again so that it became dark and stuffy inside. In the little cupboard-like space, she wriggled off her shoes and carried them in her hand while she very slowly climbed up the couple of steps to the room. The steps were odd, at an angle, and uneven. They were made of rough wood that creaked badly unless you were very careful and very slow.

The storeroom was barely tall enough for her to stand in. Father would have to bend his head to avoid hitting it on the ceiling beams. There was a window in the far wall. Half of it vanished below the floor and the bottom part of it was the window in Father's study below. The light that shone through silvered items of furniture covered with sheets and various boxes and crates. One of them had Estlander writing on it. It had belonged to Johanna's mother, Lady Sara Aroden, a minor duchess of the Estlander court.

The sound of father's voice drifted up through the floor-boards. Johanna sank to her knees, trying to make not the slightest of sounds, and put her ear to the floor. It was very dusty.

Father was speaking. ". . . We can provide loans, certainly. But I don't know that we have the capacity to do what you ask."

Johanna held her breath. Her nose tickled with the smell of wood that hadn't seen a mop for years.

"I'm not sure I understand your problem. I hear the Brouwer Company is one of the most profitable in all of Saardam." She didn't recognise the voice of this man. He was not the royal family's buyer, who sometimes came to get Estlander cheeses, which was how the Brouwer Company got its royal-approved seal.

Father said again, "That may be as it is, but I still like to invest my money wisely, in a way in which it will see us get returns. I frankly cannot see what this loan is going to do in my favour. And for what, precisely?"

The man from the court coughed, the wet phlegmy cough of a smoker. He said something that Johanna didn't catch, except that it was about the good of the country and something that needed to be defeated.

Johanna's heart thudded. Did the royal family know about these demons crossing the river?

"Drink?" Father said.

Johanna heard him open the door of the cabinet that held the pretty glasses. There was the chink of glass on the metal tray and the glug-glug of brandy being poured.

The silence was uneasy. She hardly dared move, even though her nose was starting to get very itchy and her knees were sore from kneeling on the rough wood.

"You live well, Dirk," the visitor said. "You have all you want —no, don't say anything. I know you want noble status. I know you want it mainly so that you can provide for your daughter by marrying her off well, and that you're waiting for this to happen before she marries."

What?

Father replied, but Johanna didn't hear it because her heart was thudding so loudly.

The man said in reply, "That can be arranged. I will even see to it personally."

"It's starting to sound like blackmail to me. Pay up and you can have what you want."

"No, no, we need people like yourself. We want you to invest in our country."

Father snorted. "The kingdom charges enough taxes to pay

for its army. What is wrong with the current size of the army? We're at peace, are we not? Why doesn't the king invest in it, if he thinks it's that important?"

"The king has already invested a considerable amount—"

"In an army?"

"The king looks after the spiritual wellbeing of the people."

"Building churches is investing in the country?"

"The king has made the Church his first priority."

A silence fell. Johanna could just about see Father sit behind his desk swirling his brandy, giving the man a suspicious look. Father was also too smart to voice any of the colourful thoughts he had about the Church.

He said, "Do you have any of the nobility investing in this new army?"

Oh, that question struck home. It said, *Does the nobility still trust the king?* Johanna could almost feel the tension in the room.

The man went on, sounding uneasy. "There have been . . . problems. Not everybody is as lucky as you, Dirk. Many of our merchants have been shunned by buyers across our borders. They don't make anywhere near as much profit as you do."

"It has nothing to do with luck. Before you say any more about luck, you can have all the luck in the world. I would have my wife still around over any luxury I've amassed in my life. I've worked hard at this business and even harder not to offend anyone with ideas. That's why I've done well. I don't play games and I don't judge. And now if you want to get back to our business—"

There was a small squeak from behind Johanna. A shaft of light fell into the room from the hallway.

She turned around and gasped.

"Mistress Johanna!" Nellie stood at the bottom of the steps, her mouth open in shock. "You're eavesdropping on your father? That's terrible!"

"Shhhh!" Johanna rose and tiptoed out the room back into the stairwell and shut the door behind her. On the stairs, she slipped her feet back into her shoes.

"Mistress, aren't you too old for this sort of behaviour? It's bad enough for children, but a lady your age should definitely know better—"

"Father's got a visitor from the court. They're talking about . . ." But she wasn't sure if she should tell Nellie what they were talking about. If what she heard was right, and she understood it correctly, the palace was in financial trouble and the nobles didn't want to support the king, and the king thought that a threat to the country was strong enough to warrant a bigger army.

She shivered, seeing men on horseback and demons. Did this mean that the king knew about the demons?

Nellie said, "Anyway, I came to look for you because you have a visitor."

CHAPTER 4

NELLIE PRECEDED Johanna into the formal room to the right of the main entrance. The door was opposite Father's study, whose door was still closed. A smell of smoke seeped into the hall. She also smelled perfume that definitely didn't come from Father's visitor.

Johanna went into the formal room and found that her visitor was Mistress Daphne, the Lurezian seamstress. She waited, primly seated on a chair next to the hearth. She was perhaps ten years older than Johanna, tall and elegant, a dark-haired southern beauty. Today she wore a plain working dress in moss green with little edges of lace at the sleeves. She might not look spectacular, but as far as fashion went, she was the best of the best. She knew how to dress to look elegant and not take any attention away from her well-heeled clientele.

"Good afternoon, Mistress Johanna." She rose and bowed.

Her face was prim and stiff, but Johanna didn't miss the faint twinge of disapproval and her glance at Johanna's house shoes and plain dress. Johanna cringed. In the eyes of this woman, she was as a dirty riverboat to the owner of a large seafaring ship. That was her life: plain, serviceable, sensible.

"I am here to arrange your dress," Mistress Daphne said. "Your father wants me to supply you with a dress that will make you look like a princess, so he said. I heard that he was so lucky as to get a last-moment invite to the ball at the palace tomorrow night." Mistress Daphne said all this with a prim face, as though she clearly despaired at the prospect of making Johanna presentable. "I told him that it would be impossible to have a gown made, but I always have a couple of sample gowns that I can adapt, so you may yet be in luck." Mistress Daphne picked up a pile of boxes she had brought. "You have little enough time to choose, so we better get started now."

Johanna glanced at the strange curly writing on the side of the boxes. She was pretty sure, from the lessons Father had made her take, that it was Lurezian. Each box was a work of art in itself, made from fine board, with carefully painted patterns and held closed with a coloured ribbon.

Mistress Daphne picked up the first box, set it down on the couch, pulled the ribbon and took off the lid. Inside lay a shimmering dress in vivid blue, all lace, frills and ruffles. Johanna saw noble girls walk the streets in dresses like this sometimes—that airhead Julianna Nieland for example—and thought they looked like sugar cakes.

Mistress Daphne held it up.

"Oh, it's so beautiful!" Nellie said. "Try it on, Mistress Johanna."

That thing? She'd look like a dressed-up troll. Frills and ruffles were for shapely girls, but courtesy of her mother's Estlander blood, Johanna was tall for a girl and didn't have much shape, unless you counted "barge pole" as a shape.

"I'm not sure about the colour," she said, eying the other boxes and hoping they contained something less frilly.

"Blue is all the fashion this year," Mistress Daphne said, running an experienced and critical eye over Johanna's long legs. "If you would just try it on, I can guarantee you will look stunning in this dress. This is a very special one I had shipped straight from Lurezia. It's from the modistes of the House of Giron, their latest design collection."

It meant nothing to Johanna, and worse, she couldn't get excited about it. She pretended to look interested, but just couldn't pretend any longer. "Can I see the other ones?"

Mistress Daphne seemed disappointed, but did open the

other three boxes she had brought: two of the dresses were frillier than the blue one, and one of them was even pink. The third one was a dark red, rather plain number. Plain and simple, like her.

"I like that one the best," Johanna said.

"Well then, let's try it on."

Mistress Daphne laid the dress out while Johanna took off her overclothes, placing her house shoes discretely behind the couch, and hoping no one would say anything about them.

Mistress Daphne came to help her into the dress, doing up the countless fiddly little buttons on the back.

"This itches," Johanna said. "And it's too loose."

"I know. We can fix that." Mistress Daphne took a box of pins and started pinning the sides of the bodice together.

"You look so pretty," Nellie said.

Johanna snorted, standing there with her arms spread. She didn't *want* to look pretty. All those noble girls would only gawk at her. She understood that Father wanted to go to the ball because there would be foreign people to talk business, and of course he couldn't go alone, and he had no handy widow friends to accompany him, so she would have to do. But it would be terrible, and boring. And no one would want to talk to her.

"There are rumours Prince Roald is to attend the ball," Mistress Daphne said at her back.

"Is he really?" Nellie said.

"That's the rumour. There was a Burovian ship in port this morning that's said to have brought him, but it arrived late last night and no one saw the passengers disembark."

"I saw that ship." Johanna remembered the sloop she'd seen in the harbour, the sleek one with the cabin and the red curtains.

Prince Roald, really?

"It looks like the King is trying to keep it a surprise," Mistress Daphne said, in a conspiratorial tone. "I've heard it said that, last night, the Shepherd even locked the church doors when the royal family came in for prayer, so that no one would see the prince."

Johanna wondered where Mistress Daphne got that information. Did she see things in willow wood, too? Surely Johanna could have told if that was the case. The gift of magic wasn't common in Lurezian people anyway.

Nellie's eyes were wide. "Does that mean Prince Roald is cured?"

"That depends on what's wrong with him," Johanna said. There were rumours about that, too. That the king didn't control his son's tempers and had sent him away so that he could be disciplined and taught manners by monks, or that the prince had some incurable illness.

"Sickly children will often end up growing into healthy adults," Mistress Daphne said primly. "Given plenty of food and fresh air."

Whatever she knew about it, not having children herself. "Roald is past childhood." Johanna was born in what was termed "the prince's year" and she was reminded often enough that she was fast getting too old to be married. Roald was a month older than she was.

"Maybe the king has decided that Roald is well enough to take his position as crown prince," Nellie said.

"It's not as if he's got another option. With Celine—"

"Mistress Johanna, why do you always have to think the worst of people?"

Johanna turned around to face Nellie. "I don't, providing those people do their job. If King Nicholaos chose to make his second child his heir, then there must have been a reason for it. If he chose to send Roald away, even after Celine's death, there must be something going on. Roald is his only remaining child. Why hasn't he been at the palace learning how to rule the country? There has to be a reason. And I'm not sure if I like it. If Roald was too ill to learn, then why hasn't one of the King's cousins come to take Celine's place? That's all I want to know."

"Stand still," Mistress Daphne admonished, her mouth full of pins.

Nellie blushed. "You mustn't speak of the king like that, Mistress Johanna."

"Tell me then what else I should think. I'm worried. The royal family is small. If Roald can't do the job, then one of his cousins should. King Nicholaos is not getting any younger." Or, for that matter, any saner. Rumours about how much money he gave to the Church were hard to miss. And the conversation she had overheard in her father's room only added to her worry.

Neither Nellie nor Mistress Daphne dared venture a further opinion. They all knew why none of the other royals had helped out. None of Roald's cousins lived in Saardam and Johanna was sure any of his cousins would be deeply unpopular with the genteel folk of Saardam.

Bah, nobles.

Mistress Daphne finished pinning up the dress and stepped back, looking Johanna up and down.

Johanna cringed. She hated it when people judged her looks, and those dresses made her resemble a dressed-up garden rake.

Mistress Daphne wheeled the mirror across the room, that one where Johanna could almost see her little fingerprints on the glass and hear her mother say, "Don't touch," in her Estlander accent. She'd been four or five then.

The young woman that looked back at her in the mirror didn't seem familiar. The dark dress made her look stern, and the parts where Mistress Daphne had taken in the sides the skirt didn't sit properly. She tugged at it.

"That will be fixed," Mistress Daphne said. Judging by the small shake of her head, she didn't seem to like the result.

To be honest, Johanna didn't like it either. The sleeves were long and tight, the neckline was high, and the dark red made her look very old.

She admitted defeat. "I guess I should try a different dress?"

Mistress Daphne sighed a little happy sigh. "Your exuberance does not deserve something so . . . dour. You are not a matron; you're a maiden."

"Did I mention I don't like wearing frilly dresses?"

"You are truly different from the other girls, Mistress Johanna." Johanna didn't know if that was meant as an insult or a compliment. Probably both. "Given approval by their fathers, the other girls would choose the frilliest, the finest dresses I have. Will you just humour me and try on the blue one?"

"Yes, try it," Nellie said.

Johanna eyed the box, still open, on the table. Horrible. Frilly. Like a sugar cake.

She didn't want to go to the ball. She hated pomp. But going to the ball was obviously important for Father. She let out a frustrated breath. "All right."

Mistress Daphne undid all the fiddly buttons and helped her out of the red dress into the blue one. The colour was exquisite; she had to hand it to the weavers and their experimenting with exotic ingredients. The fabric was a material that looked to her like silk, but Mistress Daphne said it was something called taffeta, a material that was much stiffer than silk and allowed the puffed-up sleeves to stay puffed up by themselves. The bodice was embroidered with tiny beads and silver thread.

"Hold your hands up, Mistress Johanna."

Johanna did and Mistress Daphne tightened the lace at the back. The bodice drew tight around her waist.

"Does it have to be so tight?" She put her hand on her side. Her hand met taut and stiff fabric threaded with whalebone straps to keep it in place. The top of the corset squeezed her breasts so that they were pushed together in a way they normally weren't. And very *visible*. Johanna put her hand on the bare skin of her chest.

"I modified the dress. The Lurezian version has a much lower neckline, showing more skin, but the palace wouldn't approve of that at all."

"Even more skin?" Johanna could see right down into the slit between her pale breasts where sunlight never came and where her skin was free of freckles.

"Yes, sometimes you can even see the indecent parts—who are you taking to the ball, Mistress Johanna?"

"I presume I'm only there so Father doesn't have to go alone."

"Pfaw, don't be silly," Mistress Daphne said around the pins in her mouth. "You should look at every young man there. You are not getting any younger."

Except they would all be nobles and would look down on her, not to mention insufferable bores who could only talk of the latest spoils of hunting expeditions. Johanna would be required to talk to the even more boring women, who only cared about who wore what.

Mistress Daphne stepped back. "Now, how is that, Mistress Johanna? Of course, you will have to do your hair, and add jewellery."

Nellie looked dubious. "It does show a lot of skin."

Mistress Daphne dragged the dressing mirror across the floor. Johanna had been right: This dress did make her look like a sugar cake. She pulled at the frills on her shoulders, secretly wishing they'd all come off.

Mistress Daphne nodded. "Don't you think that looks much better?"

Johanna turned around in front of the mirror. Frills everywhere, even on her back. It was horrible. But she had to admit that this dress fitted better. And in a rebellious way, she liked the low neckline. The bold colour made her eyes come out. The dress was a bit rebellious against everything. A bit like wearing clogs to church. The Shepherd told the flock in church that women had to cover up and be modest. The same Shepherd who said that all magic was evil.

"Don't you think it looks gorgeous on her?" Mistress Daphne said.

Nellie nodded. "You look like a princess, just like your father wanted."

"You think so?" Johanna looked at Mistress Daphne.

Some part of her still hoped that either of them would say that she couldn't possibly wear this in public.

They didn't.

Mistress Daphne nodded appreciatively. "It looks very good. Julianna Nieland tried it on, but she was too short to wear it."

And with that, she sold it. Johanna would do anything to annoy Julianna Nieland.

CHAPTER 5

MISTRESS DAPHNE packed the other dresses away, and then got into taking serious measurements. Johanna stood barefooted, with her hands spread wide, while Mistress Daphne put pins on every panel of the dress, until Johanna wondered if there would be anything left of the original design when she finished. Mistress Daphne and Nellie talked about fashion and fabrics, and Johanna was keen to be let out of the pincushion prison.

There was the sound of voices in the hall, and then at the door. Father's visitor was leaving, and it frustrated her that she still had no idea who he was. A bit later, she heard the distinctive tread of Koby coming up the stairs, and then the sound of the tableware cupboard being opened and plates being put on the table. She'd been locked up in this room talking *clothes* all afternoon.

"I think dinner is ready," she said. She wanted to be out of that dress. She needed to go to see Loesie as she promised. Loesie would want to know what Johanna had done about her warning, and she couldn't tell her any good news. *I spent all afternoon being measured for a dress,* or *No one would believe me,* wouldn't be statements Loesie understood. People from the land never questioned wind magic and willow magic. That was also why

Johanna liked Loesie: because she didn't have to explain her magic or apologise for it.

"It's done," Mistress Daphne said, and she started unlacing the back of the dress until Johanna could step out. "I'll work on this, and have it ready for you tomorrow night."

After stiff fabric and all those pins, Johanna's old clothes felt like a comfortable blanket. She felt like she never wanted to take them off again, never mind what people said about them.

She left Nellie and Mistress Daphne to their gossip and went into the hall.

The smell of tobacco and spice still lingered in the air. The door to Father's study was open, but there was no one inside the room. The black coat with the Carmine House pin was gone from the coat stand. A fire burned low in the hearth and the scent of brandy and tobacco lingered.

They called this the Green Room. On one side, there was a table surrounded by chairs with silk cushions. The entire left-hand wall was taken up by a glass-fronted cupboard with shelves full of books. Most of those were Johanna's, bought for her by Father on his travels. Above the hearth hung a portrait of Johanna's grandfather.

Father himself sat at the table in the dining room, while Koby ladled soup in a gold-rimmed soup plate.

Johanna took her place opposite him and Koby came to fill her plate, too. Leek soup. It smelled heavenly. "Thanks, Koby."

Koby nodded and walked out, leaving behind a woolly sort of silence that stretched while they both ate. He had changed into the comfortable woollen vest which his sister Aunt Dianne had knitted for him. His short beard was now more grey than blond, and the hair that he so carefully combed over his bald spots hung down his neck in a greying ponytail.

"You sorted yourself out with a dress?" he asked. "I presume you've seen Mistress Daphne?" So, he wasn't going to tell her who the mystery visitor had been.

"I have."

"Has she made sure you got something pretty?" The wrinkles around his eyes crinkled with a brief smile.

Johanna shrugged. She wanted to show her displeasure over

his avoiding the subject of the visitor, but he would probably get angry with her. "I got a dress."

"What colour?"

"Blue." The dress would probably turn a few heads, even if only Julianna Nieland's.

"I trust she'll have you looking like a real lady."

"Don't you start, too, Father."

"It's becoming more important that you take life a bit more seriously, young lady."

Something about that remark made Johanna shiver. He wasn't going to talk about this getting married thing, was he? "How did you get an invite to go to the palace?"

"It was a stroke of luck," he said, thoughtfully spooning soup out of his plate. "Mind you, I'm not going for fun. Most of the ball will be to conduct business."

"Did you apply to the council of nobles again?"

He put his spoon down, and seemed to deliberately avoid her eyes. Eventually, he said, "No. As long as the old Nieland is alive, there's probably little point in trying that avenue again. But, there may be another way."

"Another way into the nobility?"

Koby came in with a tray that contained gold-rimmed platters with carved duck and mash gravy, and another platter with sliced bread. Father said nothing while she set the things out on the table.

He spoke again only after she left. "This is not common knowledge, so I prefer you told no one about this—"

"Do I ever gossip about things you tell me?" He infuriated her so much. The twists and turns he took, the avoidance, the right angles in his conversation. Why couldn't he just talk straight?

He sighed. "Prince Roald is back, and will be confirmed as the king's successor at the ball tomorrow night."

"Tell me something new. He came on that Burovian ship that's still in the harbour, didn't he?"

Father smiled briefly. "I should have known that you were smart enough to figure it out."

"Is he cured?"

He flicked his eyebrows and continued eating his soup, in that infuriating way he would go silent when she most wanted him to speak.

The old clock on the wall went tick-tick-tick. Next to it hung a portrait of an elegant brown-haired woman. She wore a beautiful green dress—buttoned up to the neck—and a string of pearls. Lady Sara Aroden, Johanna's mother. How would she have coped with Father's infuriating silences?

Eventually he said, "Prince Roald will assume his duties as of tomorrow night." As if she had asked nothing.

"What was wrong with him? Why has he been away for so long?"

Father held up his hands. "Johanna, none of this is meant to be public knowledge. There will be royal announcements about this at the ball, and you will be there to hear it from the king's mouth."

She restrained a snort. As if the king would tell the good nobles all the details about his family. If he hadn't done so when they first decided to make Celine the crown princess, he certainly wouldn't do so now.

"Why were we invited?" Mother and Father had been to these balls at time, but usually that was because of some business thing, like that time when Father had opened up trade with the lands beyond Estland and some of those people happened to be guests at the palace.

Father gave a half-smile. "The Brouwer family seems to be going places, after all." He put his spoon down.

Johanna sensed the importance of his words. "Is this about the visitor you just had? He was from the royal family, wasn't he?" Just what was Father getting into? *There were other ways?*

Other ways of what? Was he buying his way into the nobility? Wait.

The crown prince was back to resume his duties. The prince was twenty-four. His duties would include finding a wife and getting busy with producing an heir.

She and Father looked at each other and she saw in his eyes that he knew what she was thinking.

He nodded, slowly. "King Nicholaos has issued a call for all ladies of good standing to attend the ball for a dance with the prince."

Johanna opened her mouth—

"No, Johanna. Do your old father a pleasure and for once do as I say. The king has fallen out badly with most of the city's nobles. Many of those so-called nobles don't even have half the capital that we do. You are the most eligible lady from the new merchant class."

"You have got to be kidding! I thought you wanted me to look after the company."

"I do."

"How could I do that if I'm choking in ruffles and court ladies?" And she'd just asked Mistress Daphne for that ridiculously frilly dress.

"My guess is: better than if you marry Octavio Nieland."

"But . . ." Johanna stopped there. "Octavio Nieland?"

"Yes. He's been in my office several times to ask for your hand in marriage."

"But why? The Nielands hate us!"

"They only hate what they can't get. The best way to stifle a competitor who frightens you is by marrying into their family."

"But . . ." The Nielands were nobles. The very ones who scorned Father. Why did he involve himself with them?

"Johanna. He's very insistent. You amuse him, he says. He wants a strong woman who is able to look after his affairs when he goes to sea. I'm not going to be able to say no to him indefinitely. Not if there is no other option."

No other option?

She had assumed that he had been happy enough not to let her marry. Not Octavio Nieland, not anyone. She'd just continue to do the work he'd been doing, without the need for a man. She'd shown him that she could do it.

One thing she hadn't considered: he saw her marrying to the advantage of the company. Tears of anger sprang to her eyes.

"I thought you loved me," she said, her voice unsteady.

"I do love you, and that's why I'm trying to get you the best I can negotiate. The prince desperately needs to marry. At the ball tomorrow night he will be presented with Saardam's most eligible ladies. I've negotiated one dance for you with him. The court adviser who was just here has let me know that the king looks favourably upon you. Take the opportunity to present yourself well and he may want to see you again. It seems fortunate, perhaps, that King Nicholaos has made a lot of enemies amongst the nobles with his insistence on church donations. We are successful, and the royal family wants support from successful traders, and they desperately need an heir from a family that goes to church. We can provide those things."

He thought of the rest of her life like that? Something to be bartered?

Johanna rose from the table, throwing her spoon down. "I'm not hungry anymore."

"It upsets you."

"Of course it upsets me." She tried very hard to keep the anger out of her voice, but didn't succeed entirely. "How can you just drop this on me like that?"

"Just one dance, Johanna."

"And what if he likes me . . . or what if he doesn't? Would you honestly expect me to marry Octavio Nieland after all the bad things you said about him?"

"I don't want you to, no. But if you don't marry and I die, our wealth goes to my useless cousin. I want that even less than I want the company to go to the Nielands."

"Do I get a say in this?"

"I've waited years for you to have a say. You don't look like making up your mind any time soon."

"I don't want to get married. Look at the girls who used to be my friends. Claire got married. I never see her anymore. Does she even leave the house? Augustina got married, and her husband won't even let her do any shopping. Willemina got married and she's got so many children that she has no time for anything else. They never go out. They rarely talk to me anymore. Does that look like fun?"

He slammed his flat palm on the table. "This is not about fun!"

The explosion of his voice shocked her into silence.

He took a deep breath, nostrils flaring and went on, "You are behaving like a spoilt child. I'm thinking I've waited far too long already. There is a lot more to marriage than two people. It's about their families and their combined wealth and business."

"*You* married for love." Not only that, her mother's parents had let their daughter go off with a foreigner.

"I was extremely lucky."

Johanna, on the other hand, was in danger of becoming an old spinster, and at this point in time, she was just a piece of property to be moved around for maximum gain.

She got that message loud and clear.

"I won't be around forever, and I worry about what would happen to you if you don't have a family—no, don't tell me that you're happy to run the company by yourself. I know you are, and I know you're capable, but things don't work that way in this world, do they? No one will do business with a woman who runs the company by herself. And it's getting worse because of that stupid Church."

Johanna looked down, tears pricking in her eyes. She knew, and had always known. The world was changing. It had no room for happily unmarried women.

"Please, Johanna. One dance with him. Chat to him. Try your best. Because I wouldn't give my company to Octavio Nieland over my dead body."

After one long stare, Johanna left the room without speaking.

CHAPTER 6

I N THE SUMMER the nights were long, and after that disastrous evening meal, Johanna slipped down the stairs into the servants' quarters. The house staff, Koby, Nellie, the gardener, all sat around the kitchen table. The sounds of spoons clinking against plates drifted from the room, as well as talk and laughter. Johanna always felt a bit jealous hearing them chat and laugh. She wished she could join them and laugh with them instead of having to suffer Father's long silences.

She slipped into the pantry and grabbed a half-cut loaf of bread and a piece of soft cheese, which she put in a basket.

Then she went out the back door into the garden with its pebbles and neatly-clipped bushes. The roses were very prolific this year and the scent of the flowers hung heavy in the summer air.

Johanna walked past the garden house—where her grandparents from Aroden used to stay when they visited, but that was now full of old furniture—and out the back gate into the street.

Passers-by greeted her, but she was too absorbed in her angry thoughts to take much notice of them.

Prince Roald!

What was her father thinking? As if anyone would take her seriously when she came to dance with the prince. All the noble girls would laugh, and the prince would know her for what she was the moment she opened her mouth.

Even if the prince was the most dashing, romantic young man, it would not work. Princes did not marry merchant daughters.

She was more concerned about what Father had said about Octavio Nieland. Octavio was the biggest piece of arrogance in the Saardam gentry. When he set his sights on something, he usually got it, in his unforgiving and blunt way. She did *not* want to marry Octavio Nieland.

The harbour was quiet at this time of day, with the boats dark and locked up. All the ships' boys had gone home, the wind had calmed and the only sound that disturbed the silence was the slap of waves against ship hulls and the creaking of planks or boards.

The Brouwer Company's sea cow barn was at the end of the quay, behind a couple of warehouses and behind where the boys had moored the *Lady Sara* now that the hold was empty.

Johanna walked past the large warehouse doors where her footsteps sounded loud. A cat stalked along the wharf, waving the tip of its tail. A couple of deck hands were still talking somewhere. She could hear their voices although she couldn't see them, the sound echoing weirdly here.

The dark Burovian sloop that had brought Prince Roald from wherever he had been still lay moored at the quay, giving up none of its secrets. Prince Roald? Really?

Johanna didn't remember him very well, because even before he left, he rarely came outside. Part of her hoped that he'd come back healthy, as a handsome young man who would fall in love the moment he saw her. Yeah, like that was going to happen. Like she even wanted it to happen.

She opened the door to Father's barn and stepped into its inky darkness. Something rustled in the corner.

"Loesie?"

"Hmmmm."

Johanna turned up the wick on the oil lamp that always burned in the corner. By its measly light, a sea cow rose to the surface of the water and cast a baleful look at her. Its eye, brown and mournful, looked surprisingly human. The surface of the water looked oily, with a mess of cabbage leaves floating around. Ripples disturbed the surface where the other cows were. Also, occasionally there would be a trail of bubbles escaping from the animals' pelts or other places.

On the right-hand wall the harnesses hung on hooks, with thick oiled leather straps that held the pack to the front of the boat on the upriver runs. Underneath the harnesses was a workbench and tools for repair.

Johanna put the basket on the bench.

"I've got bread and cheese for you."

Loesie came out of the darkness. In that horrible black dress and her translucent pale skin and eyes so wide that the whites showed on all sides, she looked like a wraith.

She snatched the bread and held it to her chest like a treasure needing protection. She shuffled aside, like a mangy dog afraid to be hit.

"Loesie?" A chill went over Johanna's back. She was no longer sure that it had been a good idea to come here alone.

"Ghghghghghg!" Loesie darted forwards and grabbed the basket. She snatched the cheese and bit into it.

While she chewed, she put her hands on the handle of the basket. She closed her eyes and let the magic of the wood flow through her. She opened her mouth and uttered a soft cry. A pale white dribble of half-chewed cheese ran down her chin.

"Loesie, what's wrong?" The chill that Johanna had felt earlier grew into a blizzard.

What sort of dark craft did it take to put a spell this strong on a person? What else had been affected other than Loesie's ability to speak? How could she know that Loesie wasn't leading her into a horrible trap? She'd heard the stories of people turning other people into diseased ghosts. The stories about madmen who devoured blood or human flesh *were* stories, weren't they?

Loesie's eyes opened as slits of pure white. She tilted her head to the ceiling of the barn and swayed from one foot to the other while uttering a low moan.

Johanna backed away.

No, definitely not a good idea to come here.

Loesie came towards her, holding out the basket. "Ghghghghghghgh!"

She tried to push the basket into Johanna's hands, but Johanna wanted nothing to do with it anymore.

"Keep away from me!" Johanna's back bumped into the barn door. She lifted the bar, pushed the door open and ran.

Johanna ran down the wharf, past the dark shadows of boats. Her footsteps sounded loud on the cobbled ground. The cat she'd seen earlier gave a surprised meow and skittered out of her way, into the open door of a warehouse.

There was a light within and a few deck hands were inside, moving barrels. The warehouse belonged to an Estlander merchant but long-time citizen of Saardam, Master Deim. Those Estlanders had odd customs, still working after dark. They must have received an important shipment.

Johanna didn't want the men to see her, because they'd ask what she was doing here. They'd see that she was upset. They would discover Loesie and the state she was in. They might even tell the mayor, or the king's guard, and instead of going to the ball, Johanna would be spending tomorrow night locked up in a cell. No one still did witch burnings anymore, did they?

She ran past the entrance when the men's backs were turned. She ran past the other warehouses and the forbidding walls of the King's guard armoury, where the single guard on duty followed her with his eyes.

She stopped in front of her father's office, catching her breath. The windows were dark. Of course Master Willems had gone home long ago. He was the only one she could talk to about magic, and even he avoided the subject. She couldn't go and see him at home, because his father would be there, and he was with the Church. Visiting him at home would be inappropriate.

Then what?

Panting, she looked back over the wharf, past the warehouses, the ammunition depot and the barn and the *Lady Sara*. There was no movement on the wharf.

Johanna wiped her face, seeing Loesie's wild expression when she closed her eyes, that dribble of half-chewed cheese down her chin.

Had she been wrong to shelter someone who was clearly possessed by evil? And was Loesie now trying to make her a victim as well? Was Master Willems right in saying that nothing had happened upriver? Could Loesie possibly have imbued the wood with the images for the evil purpose of seducing Johanna into the influence of evil?

She shivered.

Loesie, as Johanna remembered her, was a kind young woman. Yes, she was a bit odd, and loved scaring people with her strange tales of creatures that came out of the river next to her grandpa's farm, most of which were stories she made up.

Loesie loved playing pranks. She'd tell an outrageous story and see how far in she could get before her audience understood that she was telling them fibs.

But this . . .

Looks like reality caught up with the prankster.

White eyes, a dribble of milk-like fluid from her mouth—that was how scholars identified people who were possessed by demons.

Her little voice of sanity said, *It was only half-eaten cheese.*

But what about Loesie's eyes? They had definitely turned all-white, without irises.

Johanna wanted to run home and forget that all this had happened. She wanted to burn the basket that Loesie had given her and that sat on the chair by the window in her room.

Then again, Loesie was always a bit strange, but kind-hearted. Loesie would never harm anyone.

A little voice inside her said, *If Loesie had turned into a demon, then the evil would have taken complete possession of her and would not have taken only her voice, right?*

Coming from a farm, Loesie wouldn't read or write. Her voice was the only way in which she could warn people.

The question remained: how much of the real Loesie was still in there?

What to do, what to do?

Whatever happened, she couldn't abandon a friend, because

no one else would help her, but she couldn't handle this alone either.

Johanna had started walking again. She came past the harbour-side bars where the sound of yelling male voices spilled out. Through the windows, she could see patrons sitting around tables served by the young man who was the son of the owner. A single dark-haired woman sat on one of the tables. Johanna knew her, too.

Helena had come to Saardam as First Mate's pet aboard one of the southern sea's vessels. After two months at sea, her belly started swelling. She drank a concoction that was supposed to rid her of the child, but it had made her so ill that the First Mate ditched her as soon as they came into port. Helena managed the rooms upstairs, where a never-ending line of sailors were keen to part with their hard-earned money to spend some time with any of the young women Helena had plucked off the streets in towns along the Saar River. She also knew which men were out of work and was a good contact for hiring deck hands.

Johanna crossed the markets where the trestle tables had been packed away until the next market day. On the far side, the belltower of the church reached for the heavens, like a dark shadow against the sky. A light was on in the porch, flickering with the breeze. Hadn't the Shepherd Romulus said that the church doors were always open?

Johanna hesitated, looking around. Apart from the church, the other main building at the markets was the market house. During the day, its front and side doors were open, and merchants would bring in their wares to be officially weighed by market officials. At night, the doors were closed. Few private houses surrounded the markets, and in those that did, the curtains were closed over the windows. Something rustled in the shadows that might be a mouse or a rat, or one of the cats employed to catch those pests. There were no people in sight.

Quietly, Johanna walked up the church steps into the darkness of the porch, into the glow of the flapping flame of the storm light that hung on the back wall of the porch, and pushed the door open. It creaked.

It was not completely dark in the church either. Oil lamps

set in sconces on pillars that supported the roof spread an orange glow just strong enough for her to see the aisle. Candles burned at the altar.

Her footsteps sounded hollow in the large space and for once she was glad that she wasn't wearing her clogs.

The church was a reflective space, with simple glass windows, plain pillars and plain wooden pews. The only thing that had any prominence inside the building was a large statue at the front. The three-headed demon stood on its hind legs, with its front legs slightly in the air. It had the body of a strong dog, with muscular legs and shoulders. The three heads were those of an emaciated ghost, a dog and a man. Father was right: it was a hideous thing, but it was meant to be: it symbolised the ugliness of human emotions the Church sought to change.

There were footsteps at the back of the church and a man in a simple robe dissolved from the shadows. Shepherd Romulus.

"Can I help you, child?"

"I . . . um . . ." There was no going back now.

He came towards her in the aisle. From close up, under the candlelight, he looked older than he did in the service. He wore his customary brown robe, a simple garment without any embellishments except the white knotted cord around his waist. He had grey hair cropped short and a short beard, also grey. His green eyes were kind, but surrounded by a spider's web of wrinkles.

"You look disturbed, child."

You would, too, if you'd seen a person possessed by evil. But she said only, "I came here to pray."

He smiled. "You're in the right place for that. Do you want to pray together?"

That seemed like a good starting point. Better than the question she would have to ask later: *What can I do to exorcise a demon from my friend?* Because that question would mean acknowledging that magic existed, or maybe even that she had magic.

Johanna sat next to the Shepherd in the front pew, directly opposite the giant statue of the three-headed Triune. The light cast deep shadows over the dog face that jutted out above her. An angry and snarling thing it was, depicting the evil Spirit in the Triune. The head of the Ghost was on the far side of the statue, a long-haired man with hollow eyes, and the middle head embodied the Holy God, a man with a kind face and a short beard. He looked a bit like King Nicholaos, although she'd seen children clipped on the ear for saying that.

The Reverend folded his hands in his lap and neither of them said anything for a while. The calm beauty of the place soothed Johanna's rattled mind. The wood under her hands showed images of people filing into the church and taking place in the pews. See? There was nothing to panic about. There might be demons and bandits on horseback in the border regions. They might even be on their way to Saardam. But the city was strong and the king's guards would deal with them. She ordered her thoughts into a couple of perfectly rational questions.

"I seek advice about a friend," she said when the Shepherd raised his head.

"Is this a friend who has strayed off the right path?"

"A friend who is possessed." Did she see him do a little double take? "She has lost her voice and her sanity, and speaks gibberish. Maybe she's trying to tell me something, but I can't understand her."

He gave her a thoughtful and calculating look. "Does she roll her eyes and secrete fluids?"

Johanna nodded, and the chill of seeing the white slits of Loesie's eyes returned.

His expression went hard. "She is possessed by evil. Any such should be banished from the city."

"She's my friend. She frightens me, but I have to look after her or no one else will. I don't think she has anyone left in the world. I know her as a kind person, and this is not her fault. Please tell me how to help her."

He turned around and fixed her with his green eyes. "Your heart is kind, sister, but playing with evil will beget more evil. You can pray for her, but the evil of magic is strong. You should not get further involved with her."

"Should I let her die then? She can't look after herself like this." It was a wonder that Loesie had even made it to the markets.

"Your friend is already dead. All that's inside her is the spirit of evil." He folded his hands before his chest as if in prayer.

"She tries to talk to me. She recognises me."

The Shepherd put a hand on her shoulder. "Sister, I see that this upsets you. But demons take on the memories of human bodies. They seek to seduce us with something we want, maybe the voice of someone long ago deceased. Take it from me: most likely, this demon has killed your friend already."

Johanna again heard the penetrating woman's scream that Loesie's basket had played back to her. She didn't *think* it was Loesie's voice, but from that sound, it was hard to tell.

"If, however, your friend's soul is still alive, the demon will leave after it has completed its task. For that reason alone, it is better not to stay close to her."

"You're sure?" How could he know all this? "Have you seen this happen?"

"It's written in the Book." He reached in the pocket of his robe and drew out a well-thumbed copy of the Book of the Triune. With a pale-fingered hand he leafed through the pages. His fingers trembled.

"Ah, here it is." He pressed the book open and read. "Two days after the encounter on the road, Coran woke up one morning, speaking in tongues. No one in his household, not even his dear wife, could understand what he said. They were afraid and went into the church for guidance, but the Shepherd was not there, since he had gotten up at dawn to spread wards around the edges of the village. When they returned home, Coran was gone as well, and the villagers reported seeing him wander around the fields that surrounded the village for days. Although he had no weapon, his hands were covered in blood. He would not reply if they spoke to him, and would not look them in the eye. His eyes were rolling in his head and when he tried to speak, milk-like fluid would leak from his mouth. After four days, the madness vanished from his eyes, and he came back home, clean and washed. When his family asked him about his absence, he said that he had seen much evil and would never speak to a demon ever again. The next day, the neighbour who had been cheating found his prize cow dead in the paddock, ripped to shreds."

Johanna knew that passage. It was a metaphor for a man learning his lesson after trying to make financial gains at the expense of his neighbour. It held no authority on the subject of demons.

She clenched her hands in her lap, biting her tongue in frustration. There was so much she wanted to say about magic, that it wasn't always evil, that it belonged to objects and not people, that some people couldn't help being able to see it. That you were born with it and it was not something you could choose to engage in, or, for that matter, disengage from. But this was probably not the right time.

"Who is this friend of yours, pray?"

"Someone I know from the markets." She also couldn't say why she knew Loesie—because they both had willow magic, because she had felt the magic in Loesie that first day she'd met her at the markets as a little girl. "She comes in from the eastern border. She's seen evil things that are coming this way. She may be possessed, but her mind is still fighting the demon. I don't believe that she's evil. And I don't believe that the demon has taken her over completely. I want to know how we can get rid of the demon and restore her speech."

The Shepherd's face became a closed mask. "You're asking for someone who can perform an exorcism. The Church does not provide these people. Exorcisms are quackery that most likely make matters worse than they are. Demons are manifestations of the Triune. They are repelled by prayer, not by fake magicians with horseshoes, goat's blood and other items that wouldn't look out of place in the Lord of Fire's dungeons."

Johanna had never seen an exorcism and had no idea how it was done or if it was effective, but she didn't believe him anymore. He didn't care about Loesie.

What was more, she suddenly had an irrational desire to get out of there. This church was not a place where she could get answers. This Triune was not her friend.

CHAPTER 7

JOHANNA SPENT most of the night worrying about Loesie and what to do. She could only try to imagine how scared her friend must feel, and this made her more determined to ignore the Shepherd's advice to stay away from her. She couldn't leave Loesie to her own devices, *especially* not now.

When Johanna came into the barn the next morning with breakfast, she found Loesie sitting on the side of the walkway, dangling her legs over the water. For a moment, it looked like she had been cured, but when she turned around, her eyes were still wide. She looked so thin and sickly.

Johanna knelt and put down the basket with food at a safe distance, never losing sight of Loesie. "I've brought you eggs and bread, a piece of ham, some butter and cheese."

Loesie dragged the basket over.

"Do you need any more help? I can get you onto the river barge so you can go back home."

"Ghghghghghgh!" Loesie shook her head.

"You don't want to go home?"

"Ghghghghghgh!" More headshaking.

"You can't go home? Where is your family?"

"Ghghghghghgh!" Loesie made a sideways motion in front of her throat.

"Killed? All of them?"

She nodded. Her eyes glittered.

Johanna still hesitated to come any closer. The voice of the Shepherd said in the back of her mind, *They seduce us with what we most want to see.*

Loesie folded her hands in her lap. A tear ran over her cheek and hung at the angle of her jaw. Her shoulders shook.

"Just be strong, all right?" Johanna said. She wanted to hug Loesie, but at the same time, she could *feel* the magic that seeped from her friend.

"I'll come back, I promise. I'll find someone who can—"

"Ghghghghgh!" Loesie pointed out the open door of the barn.

There was a lot of activity of boats in the harbour. From here, you could see the far side of the quay where freight was being unloaded. The Burovian ship still lay there, all the windows and doors closed.

The space where the *Lady Sara* had been yesterday had now been taken by the *Lady Davida*. Adrian walked on the deck.

"What is it, Loesie? What did you see?"

"Ghghghghghgh!" She pointed, but Johanna couldn't make out what she was pointing at. The *Prosperity*, one of the barges belonging to Master Deim, one of Father's friends and competitors, was just coming in. Jakob, Master Deim's sea-cow handler, yelled something to Adrian and Adrian laughed so loud that the sound carried all the way across the harbour to the barn.

"I don't know what you mean, Loesie. I see nothing unusual."

Loesie bent her fingers so that her hands resembled claws and mimicked attacking.

"I don't see any demons," Johanna said. "Why don't I come back this afternoon and bring a slate so that you can draw what you mean?" She should have thought about that earlier.

"Ghghghghghhgh!" Loesie mimicked attacking.

"Yes, I understand."

"Mmmmmmmm!" Loesie shook her head, spreading her hands in a gesture of frustration.

"I'll bring a slate, I promise."

❀

IT WAS ONLY after she had left the barn that Johanna remembered that she had to go to that dratted ball tonight—how could she ever have forgotten that? Maybe she could have some time before leaving?

This stupid ball would be so embarrassing, with her as a dressed-up sugar cake a thousand times less elegant than the girls to whom nobility came as second nature.

She could already hear the scorn as soon as she walked up those palace steps.

She should have stayed with the sea cows.

That dress would have looked nicer on a bitch in heat.

That would be unbearable. She wished the whole thing was already over. Of course the royal family would have no real interest in her. What was Father thinking?

She could, of course, refuse to go, or refuse the dance her father had brokered with the prince, but he was right about one thing. Octavio Nieland should not get the business. Those ships were going to remain under the Brouwer flag.

When she came home, she met Nellie walking up the stairs carrying a box with a ribbon that would contain the dress Mistress Daphne had adjusted.

"You're just in time for dinner, Mistress Johanna, and then we should get ready."

What, already? What about Loesie? "But the ball is not until tonight."

"Yes, and that will be only just enough time to get everything done."

"The whole afternoon?" But the horrible realisation sank in. Last time she'd gone to a formal occasion—her cousin's wedding —she had also spent ages sitting in her room being primped up by Nellie.

"We need to do your hair, your powder, your jewellery." Nellie counted off on her fingers. "We have a lot to do. The coach comes at six. You have to be ready by then."

But, I promised Loesie . . .

There was no point in resisting. Whatever needed to be done needed to be done.

First Nellie started on Johanna's hair, combed, braided and fluffed it up so it would sit neatly under the beaded hairnet that used to be her mother's. Nellie took forever putting it up in a pile on her head.

Koby brought some tea and biscuits. "Don't eat too much, Mistress. It will look rude if you don't eat at the banquet, and people will gossip."

"People find the silliest things to gossip about."

She gave Johanna an exasperated look.

Then the dress. Nellie helped her do up all the fiddly buttons and hooks and laces at the back.

Nellie brought the pretty box that sat on the dressing table in her bedroom, mostly untouched. Inside, gold and silver chains, gemstones and strings of pearls lay draped over a bed of red velvet. Most of these had been her mother's, pure Estlander silver with precious stones. Johanna felt like a fraud trying on the different pieces. Her mother had been a minor royal, and Johanna was nothing but a fishwife in comparison. She didn't want to meet prince Roald. She knew of the balls, of the infighting between the royal families of neighbouring kingdoms, of the gossip between nobles, and wanted no part of any of it.

Johanna chose her mother's silver necklace with its huge ruby pendant. It lay cool against her skin in the hollow between her breasts.

"Isn't this a bit scandalous?" Johanna asked, putting her hand on the skin of her chest. *So much* skin. Since when had the open and low-cut dresses become the fashion?

"Not if we make your skin all nice again." Nellie draped a cape over Johanna's shoulders to protect the dress from powder. She already had the powder box out, tut-tutting at Johanna's expression. "If you covered your hands in gloves and used an umbrella when going out, you wouldn't get all these horrible freckles and you wouldn't need so much powder." She dusted powder over Johanna's face.

The smell made Johanna's nose tickle.

Then Nellie took the cape off, brushed some hair off the

dress and declared Johanna ready to go. She caught sight of herself in the mirror. That young woman in the blue dress with her hair curled and piled in a bun and covered with a gemstone-studded hairnet didn't look like her at all. In fact, she had to move her hand and turn around a fraction just to make sure.

"You look so elegant, Mistress Johanna. You're sure to turn the heads of all the young men at the ball."

Johanna felt like rolling her eyes.

She rose, and found that with the dress' hoops, she could no longer see her feet. When she had tried on the dress with Mistress Daphne, that hadn't been so important, but now Nellie had to help her down the stairs to make sure that she put her feet on the steps.

Father waited in the hall, dressed in his best silk shirt with ruffled collar and the magnificent purple cloak he'd bought on one of his recent travels. Apparently it was dyed with the pigment of thousands of snails. His hair was tied at the nape of his neck, and he had trimmed his beard. He wore his watch and gold chain and enough perfume that she could smell it halfway down the stairs.

He stared at her, his mouth open.

When Johanna joined him, she noticed a glitter in the corner of his eye.

"You look so much like your mother," he said, his voice unsteady. He cleared his throat and went on, "We went to the ball together a few times. I would be waiting here and she would come down just like you. Looking beautiful. You should wear pretty dresses more often."

Johanna felt uneasy and didn't know what to say. She'd just spent the entire afternoon hating getting dressed up. If it pleased Father, why did she complain?

The rattling of wheels on cobblestones, and the clip-clop of a horse's hooves, drifted in from outside.

"There is the coach." Johanna was glad to break the silence.

He offered her his arm. They left the house and went down the steps and into the street, where people stopped to look. Even though he greeted the people politely, Johanna could feel, beneath his clothes, that Father was nervous, maybe even more so than she was.

She knew the cab driver and his magnificent black horse.

"Good evening, Master and Mistress," the man said. He held the horse by the reins and patted its flank. The animal breathed out through flaring nostrils, tossing its head.

"Nice weather today," the man said.

"That, it is," Father said.

Indeed the sky was cloudless, though less clear than the previous day. The first stars were already visible.

Father helped her up into the cab with the awkward hoops in her dress, climbed in himself, and the driver shut the door while Johanna and her father sat down, facing each other. The driver then walked past the cab and jumped onto the driver's seat. The cab wobbled under his weight and a moment later jerked forwards.

Father stared out the window, pulling at his ruffled sleeves.

"We are not in any kind of trouble, are we?" she asked him when the silence lingered.

He sat with his hands interlaced, elbows leaning on his knees. "We are not, but Saarland is, or, more precisely, the royal family," he said in a low voice. "Johanna, please don't speak of this to anyone else."

"What sort of trouble? Is Estland making threats? Or Burovia?" Most of the inland nations envied Saarland's position, because of its harbour city and the river trade. There had been plenty of threats in the past, but Saarland had been at peace for a long time. She remembered the visions in the wood. Demons crawling through the marshes, unseen to the unsuspecting citizens of the city.

"No threats, as far as I know. Not that sort of trouble." He paused for a bit, looking at the streets glide past out the window. "Or, not that kind of trouble initially."

Why didn't he just say what was going on?

His eyes met hers. Johanna felt chilled with the seriousness in his expression. "The envoy from the King came to us for financial help."

So she'd heard that right. Eavesdropping was really a most useful thing.

"And you named your price for the Brouwer Company's financial assistance, which was to get me into the palace?" Those words sounded so strange in her mouth.

"No, Johanna." His eyes met hers; then he looked down. "Or maybe yes. One dance with the prince only. There will be others. It still remains the King's choice. But there are a number of important things in your favour: Roald needs to marry as soon as possible. There really is no time to waste. Dare I say the king has already wasted too much time? Secondly, the king has expressed displeasure with the way many of the nobility ridicule the Church and the way he's spent money on it. Most of the nobles are not in his good books."

Not without reason.

"Thirdly, he'll want a woman who goes to church. I think you would be perfectly suited. The royal family doesn't need a pretty princess; they need someone with some common sense in a position where they can make hard decisions. King Nicholaos doesn't seem capable of making these decisions anymore."

"No more wasting money on statues and religious buildings, huh? How does this help the company?"

"You will inherit it and it will remain under your control . . . if you were to be chosen. The queen is the only woman who can inherit in her own right."

"I'll marry the prince, just like that?" She couldn't even believe she was saying this. Why would the royal family have any interest in her?

Father looked at her; there was sadness in his eyes. "Daughter, we need to be strong. Our country needs us. You need to be strong and look after the company. But you can't do it too openly. I wish there was a world where a woman was not bound to her father's or husband's wealth, but there isn't. I can't change that for you."

Johanna looked towards her knees, under the hoops of the frills. She was angry, angry as she hadn't been for a long time. Angry with herself that she'd been so stupid to expect a free life.

She let a long angry silence pass, but, being who she was,

couldn't stay angry for long. There were worse candidates for potential marriage, and even if, as was likely, nothing came of it, she could still say she'd danced with the prince. But the bubble of laughter that rose in her—why on earth would the prince want to dance with her?—quickly evaporated when the coach passed the markets and she remembered Loesie and the demons.

"Did the king say why he wanted to have a bigger army?"

"He wouldn't divulge what happened and why, but the king seems to have deeply upset a Burovian religious order."

"The one that owned the boat and the sanatorium where Roald was?"

"I'm not sure. No one has gone into details about it."

"Does this order belong to the Church of the Triune?"

He held his hands up. "I don't know. What I'm telling you is what the envoy told me. I'm sure there is a lot more to it, but this is all I know. Although I'm guessing you already know a fair bit of it." He met her eyes squarely.

Blood rose to Johanna's cheeks. Outside the cab, the driver yelled at the horse.

"Really, Johanna, if you're going to snoop in the store room, you need to be a lot more careful. You weigh a lot more than when you were eight, you know."

She ignored that comment. "The king wants to put together an army?"

"He is afraid. It seems he did something that made the members of this religious order exceedingly angry. That wouldn't have been such a problem had the order not had strong ties with Baron Uti of Gelre. I understand he is exceedingly angry as well, although he has not publicly expressed his displeasure. Baron Uti is also a guest at the ball. He has probably been invited as a gesture of reconciliation, but the king's envoy let slip through that they don't expect much in the way of negotiation."

"And the king has ignored the army in much of his spending recently," she added.

Father nodded, gravely. "Since Celine's death, the king has lost his grip on pretty much anything, including finances. He's been so consumed by grief that he's spent vast amounts on churches—as if that's going to bring her back—and not enough on things that matter—no, and before you say anything, Johanna, churches do not make any money; they sponge off those who are willing to give it. That could be because they have a lot of money, or because they are somehow deluded that giving to the Church will help them. I suspect the Shepherd promised King Nicholaos salvation for his stricken family, and the king was too addled by grief to see that no one can solve his problems except he himself."

Johanna had often entertained these same thoughts, but hearing them from her father's mouth gave them so much more weight.

Father continued, "That was all fine up until the floods last year, which affected a large part of the royal farms, and the royal family's income from those farms. King Nicholaos did not want to know about it. He sacked the adviser who suggested that they cut spending. Then he neglected to deal with the succession problem."

"Does anyone know why Roald's younger sister was made heir?"

"Roald was sickly. He was not expected to live."

But he did live, and Celine had not. Now he was back, but why was there so much secrecy still? "And now the king wants protection with extra troops? Against priests?"

"Yes, I know, I thought he was crazy, but the envoy said that it was necessary to protect our borders, which is fair enough, and something that should have been done long ago. I just didn't think that it was worth the level of investment that he wanted. I knew there was something that he wasn't telling me. But something else happened that helps me understand it. I got this today." He reached into his pocket and gave her a crumpled piece of paper that looked like a page torn from an account book. Which, when Johanna unfolded it, was exactly what it turned out to be.

In the neat writing she recognised as belonging to Master Willems, it said,

I have it from sources I can't disclose that there are hostile actions at the border. There are marauding groups of bandits, affiliation unknown, accompanied by creatures that may or may not be demons. They have

reportedly invaded farms at the Bend. Their origin is unknown. They are coming in our direction.

Johanna met her father's eyes. They both knew what Master Willems meant—he had seen this on the wind—but his insistence at denying his ability amazed her. At least he had done as she told him.

In a few sentences, Johanna told Father of Loesie and her baskets.

Father knew of Loesie, had met her even, and had never told Johanna to stop seeing her, although he no doubt wished she would. Loesie did not meet the "appropriate lady's companion" standards. The world of willow magic and wind magic was strange to him, but he seemed to understand the need for her to talk to other people with magic, even if those people were a little odd.

Probably Johanna's mother also had the gift of magic, although her father had never explicitly said so. He would have been used to magic. He might even have married her because of that; many river and ocean traders did.

"This is the thing that worries me. There are lots of rumours about impending attack that seem to have no basis, but when you add up all the stories, the picture becomes quite disturbing. You have seen these demons, and Master Willems has seen them. Your friend has been attacked by them, and had her family killed by them. People like to say that demons don't exist, but things live in those eastern forests that no one has any knowledge of. I've only been into the edges of the forest, but I've heard the murmurings and whisperings in the leaves."

Johanna nodded. She had been with him in that Burovian forest. The thought of that forest still made her shiver, with its gnarled tree trunks and whispering leaves. She still heard the voices, and still felt the fear that they might call her deeper in until she had lost her way.

Father continued, "People from the court say that the king genuinely believed that Celine would rise from the dead. One night, soon after her death, he claimed to have seen her ghost wander the corridors of the palace. He got the Shepherd to do prayer sessions at the spot where he saw her. When that didn't work, he started giving money to the Church. He built a new church. He bought the statue. He encouraged everyone in Saardam to go to church. More prayer would mean more chance that Celine came back."

"But that obviously didn't work either."

Father shook his head and sighed. "It gets very strange after that. The court envoy told me that the king employed an ever-stranger string of people. He said they danced on her grave and performed rituals."

"Was that why a Burovian religious order got involved?"

"I honestly don't know." But it worried him, she could see that.

A chill crept over her back. In her mind, she heard the words of Shepherd Romulus. *You're asking for someone who can perform an exorcism. The Church does not provide these people. Exorcisms are quackery that most likely make matters worse than they are. Demons are manifestations of the Triune. They are repelled by prayer, not by fake magicians with horseshoes, goat's blood and other items that wouldn't look out of place in the Lord of Fire's dungeons.*

Exorcism, necromancy, both aspects of the darkest corners of magic.

She looked out the window, where the roof of the palace protruded from above the houses.

Would King Nicholaos have been so stupid to have engaged the services of a necromancer? Why, if he was as devout a churchgoer as his behaviour suggested? Why, if his Church forbade any of those dark arts performed by people who were said to have sold their souls to the Lord of Fire? Why, if the king had another child? "If I understand correctly, the king wants to quickly put together a bigger army because he fears trouble with Burovian magicians?"

"That pretty much sums up my conclusions. Another reason why you could be a good choice: your unusual abilities."

Father grabbed her hand and squeezed it, and that was as much a sign of affection as he would ever give her.

CHAPTER 8

A QUEUE of coaches lined up to get into the forecourt of the palace, a fenced compound surrounded by gild-topped metal latticework. The driver whistled for the horse to slow down. The horse seemed to dislike one of the other horses in the queue. It made snorting noises and shied sideways. The driver yelled at it, but that had little effect.

Other horses in the queue also snorted. One of them gave a soft neigh. From a bit further off came another shout. "Whoa! Easy, girl, easy."

Father peered out the window. "What's spooking the horses?"

From her position in the coach, Johanna could see over the wall to the right of the palace into the garden, an oasis of tranquillity compared to the forecourt. It was where the king grew his roses and where water tinkled in mysterious ponds surrounded by weeping willows. Johanna had been there once, back in the time when Queen Cygna held *Children's Day*. Both the prince and his younger sister would have been there, but she only remembered Celine. She had been wearing a yellow dress and her mother had to keep telling her not to crawl on the grass. The princess chattered a lot and spoke like Johanna's grandmother, very formal and stiff. Johanna remembered finding it funny, and she remembered not wanting to curtsy for a girl younger than her. It all seemed so painful and awkward now that Celine had been dead two years.

The rose garden now held a gazebo in her memory.

The coach reached the bottom of the steps. With a wobble of the floor and a creak of his leather boots, the driver left his position to open the door.

Father went out first and then helped Johanna, because the awkward dress with its hoops made it impossible for her to see the narrow coach steps.

A huge crowd had assembled near the palace entrance, held back by two lines of stiff-faced guards in Carmine livery. The onlookers were common people who came to watch the latest in fashion and catch up on the juiciest gossip: who went with whom, what who was wearing, that sort of thing.

The sun had just set and a soft glow of candlelight flooded from the porch and main foyer, where Johanna caught glimpses of the genteel folk in colourful garb. She'd been worried that her dress was too exuberantly blue but, judging by the line of noble ladies lined up for the entrance, it looked like bright colours were in fashion this year.

A ripple of surprise went through the crowd when Father took her by the arm and guided her up the steps.

Johanna didn't miss the comments.

"Look, it's Dirk Brouwer and Johanna."

"Isn't that a gorgeous dress that she's wearing?"

Johanna averted her eyes. At least they didn't say *She looks like a dressed-up cow*. But some of them were sure to be thinking that, or worse things like *Did she buy her way into the ball?*

Johanna felt uneasy. Those people on the other side of the line of guards were the ones she'd have to talk to tomorrow about accounts and deliveries of spices and cheese. She wasn't any better than any of them and didn't want to look like she thought she was.

She remembered another visit to the palace, when she was sixteen, the age at which all young women were presented to the King. That had been a most miserable and wet day, in which Carlotta Franzen had slipped and fallen flat on her backside. She now remembered that Prince Roald had been there, and he had rushed forward to help her up. He'd been a gangly youth, and his startling blue eyes had the expression of a frightened rabbit. Blond-haired and still soft-cheeked, the prince had not been unpleasant to look at. Carlotta had been insufferable all afternoon.

On top of the steps a throng of beautifully-primped nobles waited to be allowed into the foyer and hall, the men in rich-coloured suits, the women in frilly dresses, with extravagant hair —some wearing high-heeled shoes on which they could barely walk. Johanna knew most of them. She noticed some daintily raised eyebrows at her and Father's presence.

The palace stood on a low rise and from the top of the steps, you could see over the entire city. To the left were the royal gardens which sloped to the Saar River. Then the harbour and the merchant district with its gabled houses and red roofs. In the distance were the windmills which kept the island on which the city was built above water, and all around, flat land, intersected by silver ribbons of canals. At the horizon there was a lighter-coloured ribbon of sand dunes, but the ocean on the other side remained out of view.

Johanna met the eyes of a young woman who had been looking at her, Carlise d'Agincourt. She had beautiful golden hair held in place with jewelled pins. Her dress was golden with white lace and fitted her narrow waist perfectly. She stood next to an older woman, her mother, who was from the de Weert family but had attained her noble status through her marriage to a Burovian minor royal.

Of course these women were all there for the same reason. Many of them were like her, from families who would not have been the first choice for the prince's bride.

She felt very small. Father seemed so certain that King Nicholaos liked her, but seeing all these beautiful people, she doubted that he would even remember who she was.

A dog started growling and barking. It strained at the leash held by one of the palace guards. A woman lower on the steps squealed. In the forecourt, a coach horse neighed, and then another one. More dogs started barking. Men shouted orders.

Someone behind Johanna said, "He shouldn't have brought the stupid animal. It spooks the horses."

The woman who had squealed was Gertrude Hendricksen, one of the guests. She was here with her father, and he, of course, had the monkey on his shoulder.

Guess that explained why the horses were so nervous. Johanna shivered, although the evening was quite warm.

Finally they entered the foyer with its chandeliers and stained glass windows and smooth mosaic floor with the Carmine House's crest—the rooster—in stone of various shades of brown. It was noisy in here, with talk echoing back from the ceiling. Chamber music floated in through the open doors which led into what was called the garden room, a big and luscious hall, where all official functions were held.

A courtier came to take Johanna's overcoat and Father led her into the hall. The dais with the king's, queen's and prince's chairs was at the far end. A long table had been set up here, with a pristine white tablecloth and precious gold-rimmed plates and crystal glasses. A chamber orchestra played at the bottom of the steps to the dais. More groups of dressed-up noble guests stood here and there on the floor.

If the royal family was in some kind of trouble, this hall definitely showed no sign of it.

Long tables with glittering silverware were set around the perimeter of the room, tables groaning with delicate porcelain, crystal glasses, carafes of wine, gold tableware and dainty candle holders with slender white candles. Servants were carrying in trays of exquisite canapés, fancy cheeses and unfamiliar fruit, and covered dishes with huge silver lids that left wonderful smells in their wake.

No one was dancing yet. People stood talking in knots of garishly-coloured costumes, ruffled collars and fluffed-up hair, in a display of the latest Lurezian fashion. Johanna hated to think of how much money in clothing, footwear, hats and jewellery was walking around on the dance floor. That was probably her merchant upbringing talking.

All these women must have spent the entire day in front of the mirror. The scents of heavy perfume and powder threatened to overwhelm her. What was she doing here? This was not how Father had brought her up. This was not the type of life she wanted.

A couple of nobles deep in discussion burst out in laughter as Johanna and her father passed. Amongst them stood Octavio Nieland, a tall imposing figure. He wore his dark hair in a pony-tail, sleek and simple. His shirt was quality silk, cream-coloured, with simple ruffles, and his overcoat was dark blue. He held a long-stemmed glass with a be-ringed hand. He met Johanna's eyes over the rim of his glass. His eyebrows rose.

"Johanna, how nice of you to join us." It sounded like *what on Earth are you doing here?*

He gave a little bow. "We must have a dance later tonight."

Johanna shivered. This man was beating down Father's door to ask her hand in marriage?

The people in his group had stopped taking and all looked at her. His sister Julianna was there, in a dress very similar to the pink dress Mistress Daphne had shown Johanna. Except it looked stunning on her. Julianna Nieland, of course, had the figure of a lady, the wide hips and the narrow waist.

Her skin was also naturally pale, not ugly and freckled like Johanna's, and the red paint on her lips and the blushes on her cheeks had been applied with a subtle and delicate hand, and probably not by the maid. The others in the group were their cousins, the young men in colourful trousers and jackets with high-heeled boots and frilled shirts, the young women all dressed up like sugar cakes and acting as if it came natural to them.

Father led Johanna away from the group, giving a polite bow to Lady Suzanna Nieland, who must be well into her seventies by now. The lady regarded the newcomers over her monocle with an expression of curiosity.

"What a bunch of empty-headed peacocks," Father muttered, and he didn't seem to be overly concerned about whether or not the Nielands were within earshot.

Whether they were or not, or whether the surreal sweet strains of music drowned out Father's words, Johanna could still feel their gazes prick in her back when she and Father reached the other side of the hall. One thing she knew for certain:

Octavio Nieland didn't want to marry her. He wanted to own the Brouwer Company. She would be an unfortunate part of the bargain and would probably be treated as such.

On the other side of the hall, Father found a group of his colleagues, older, grizzled company owners, captains and other men of boats. The men, merchants or minor nobles, were from mixed heritage, as was common amongst merchanting families. Many of the well-off citizens from all the surrounding countries sent their sons to Saardam to work. Johanna had seen most of them before, and knew all their names. The way they stood slightly apart from the nobles and other guests made it clear that they were also not regular guests at occasions like this. The king had really cast his invitations wide this year.

There was the half-Lurezian Captain Murain who traded fabrics up and down the rivers. With him was his Estlander wife, Lora, a short rotund woman who was the opposite of what Johanna imagined her mother to have been like. She laughed a lot but spoke with such a terrible accent that Johanna had trouble understanding her.

There was the Estlander merchant, Master Deim, whose brother lived in Saardam and who owned seagoing ships and was in partnership with a Saarlander noble family to crew and kit out the ships. He was a man of tall tales, and only interrupted his current story, about foreign ships shadowing his brother's, to greet Johanna and her father exuberantly.

With his soft face and friendly eyes, Master Deim was one of these people hard to dislike, but oh, he was such a chatterbox.

The other men greeted her father with claps on the shoulder, and bows to Johanna, calling her sincere but laugh-worthy names, like fair lady and golden maiden. She guessed it came with their eastern and southern heritage, because those people were always more pompous. But they were also more open and generous with compliments.

Not used to this kind of male attention, Johanna found it a bit embarrassing.

She remained next to her father, listening to their laughter and familiar tales, normally spun in the comfort of her father's study. Master Deim, already red-faced from the wine, leaned closer to her than necessary. "You know, if your father is going to invest in seafaring ships, he'll need to buy protection. There are many lands beyond the Horn, but not all of them are friendly."

She nodded politely. Each year several ships went missing in seas past the Horn. The land route to the silk-country was much more reliable, and shorter. Yet there was much more glamour associated with the high seas. Sailors who left and returned safely were celebrated as heroes. Something lived on the other side of the Horn that did not like other people coming there. There were tales of monstrous creatures, sea serpents and dragons. Ships went missing each year.

A servant came past with a tray of glasses and Master Deim was the first to take one. Johanna took a glass, too.

He lifted his to her and took a good swig. "Might as well enjoy the good life while it lasts."

"While it lasts?" His words sent her heart into a rapid beat. Had he seen ill omens on the wind? Johanna could usually sense if a person had magic. Master Deim had not struck her as such a person, but then again, sometimes people surprised her.

He laughed. "Last time I went drinking, the wife locked all the doors on me and I sat all night in the street. Cold, it was, too. So this time, I've been smart and I'll sleep in the barn. At least all those cow ladies do is fart in the water." He laughed again, a rolling belly laugh that, no matter the sad rumours surrounding his marriage, made Johanna laugh as well.

Sea cows farted. A lot. Bubbles in the water. The image of Master Deim sleeping in his finery amongst the harnesses and bags of potatoes next to the bubbly water was priceless.

She should calm down about Loesie's warning. So far, there was no proof that any of it was true. The willow wood did not usually lie, but Loesie was clearly possessed by something evil, and anything she had touched should be treated with suspicion.

Master Deim's face turned serious. "You know, between you and me, I worry about my wife's churchgoing. I think I've been a good person all my life. Paid all my dues and never harmed anyone. Gave a whole lot of poor buggers jobs who would've starved otherwise. What right does this Shepherd have to say that we are bad people? We are not, and this country has prospered because of us."

"I understand," Johanna said, but she felt uneasy. Did *us* mean merchants or people who had magic? Magic that was more common in people from the east, like him, and like her mother?

Many of the Brouwer company deck hands, too, were refugees or ex-mercenaries from eternal petty conflicts on the eastern Estland border. People there starved to death, so the lucky ones came to prosperous Saardam where they hauled sacks of potatoes or cheeses all day, and could afford to feed their families.

She looked away, and noticed Octavio Nieland observing her from the other side of the hall. His intense expression sent a chill down her back. Dark and brooding, Nellie called it. Others called him handsome, but all those descriptions were just different words for *bully* to her. There was no way she would ever agree to marry him.

She turned away from him, back to Master Deim and his uncomfortable conversation, but could still fell Octavio's gaze pricking at the back of her head.

Father was talking to another merchant on Johanna's other side. He gave the appearance of being relaxed but she could see that he was nervous, with his thumbs jammed in his belt. He wasn't drinking. "Gerald, have you met my daughter, Johanna?"

"No, I have not." The fellow was grey-haired, with a short, neatly-clipped beard. He wore a long, elegant coat and a simple white shirt. No lace. He took Johanna's hand. "My pleasure, madame."

"You're Burovian?" She recognised his accent.

"Yes, indeed, I am. How did you guess?" He laughed.

"He's the captain of the ship that brought Roald back," Father said, his voice full of meaning.

Whoa, did he belong to the religious order that the king was said to have offended?

The man laughed. "Not sure if you'll thank me for it, but it's true, lady."

"And how are things in Burovia?" Johanna studied his clothes, but could see no sign that this man was a monk.

"As good as can be." There was meaning in those words, too, but Johanna had no idea what he was trying to say.

He smiled as if she knew what he was talking about.

Johanna turned to her father, but he was talking to the merchant next to him. So she chatted to the Burovian merchant, but became none the wiser about his mysterious remarks.

Looking around the circle of her father's acquaintances, all well-to-do merchants and boat people in their fineries, it struck her that there was a reason Father had joined these men: they were all from outside the city and they would either have magic or employ someone who did. None of them belonged to the Church of the Triune.

As potential bride to the prince, she was their spearhead: religious enough on the surface to be attractive to the royal family, but ultimately loyal to them. If the choice was Church or magic, Johanna would have no choice but to choose magic. Magic went with merchants and people who owned boats. She was their pawn, their puppet, their spearhead into destroying the influence of the Church in Saardam so that they could conduct their business freely along the rivers regardless of borders. Why hadn't she seen this coming earlier?

Her head reeled.

At that moment, a fanfare of trumpets blasted into the crowd. Conversations dissolved, groups split up and people lined up on both sides of the hall.

CHAPTER 9

D AZED AS SHE WAS, Johanna ended up a couple of
rows back in the crowd.

Two rows of King's Heralds lined up on both sides
of the aisle.

First to come into the hall was the king's speaker, carrying
the staff. Then followed King Nicholaos, wearing his Carmine
cloak. The circlet on his head crowned his severe, bearded face.
She hadn't seen him close up for a while, and thought that grief
over his daughter's death had aged him terribly. His hair used to
be ashen blond, but it had gone grey. His skin had never been
good, but now it resembled the colour of dirty linen. His cheeks
looked hollow.

Queen Cygna walked behind him. Not even the occasion of
the ball had convinced her to change out of the black dress and
veil she had worn since Celine's death. She looked down as a
prisoner being led to the gallows, with her face mostly hidden in
the shadow of the black lace.

Behind them followed a tall and thin young man with short-
cropped blond hair and a short blond beard. The way Prince
Roald walked—stiff and staring at his father's back—made him
look ill at ease and awkward. Since Johanna had last seen him, he
had changed so much that she didn't think she would have

recognised him if she'd met him in the street dressed in civilian clothes.

Two ladies in the crowd behind Johanna whispered that he looked well, and he did, but he did not wave, raise his head or talk to anyone the entire way through the hall. He looked petrified of all this attention he was getting.

What if he was painfully shy and was looking forward to dancing with primped-up, hopeful girls just as little as some girls were?

Behind the royal family followed a procession of minor royals and guests. Of course there was Princess Josafina of Estland, in the dark red of the Aroden house. She wore her hair piled on top of her head like a giant dome, and Johanna wondered how much of it was real. She was a cousin to the king who, failing a husband or a country to rule, had made Saardam her permanent home.

The couple of boys trailing her were presumably some of the Estlander baron's six sons who had been sent to their aunt for education.

Behind them walked a bearded man dressed in black leather. He was at least a head taller than Princess Josafina, and his beard, huge and bushy, covered the top of his chest above his considerable belly. He wore his hair, brown and curly and greying at the temples, in a loose ponytail. His arms, mostly bare save for the jerkin's very short sleeves, rippled with muscles and bore more scars than those of the average sea cow handler.

Johanna had never seen Baron Uti of Gelre before, but this man fitted the descriptions that went around of him. He was said to have been a fierce warrior in his younger days and still looked the part. His expression was curious rather than angry, but he would no doubt be a force to be reckoned with if he was upset. With him were Master Lanston, ambassador from Estland, and two men in long Burovian capes she had never seen before. People from this religious order?

The Rede River separated Gelre and Burovia. Both were thickly-forested countries and one of Gelre's main towns, Florisheim, lay opposite the Burovian town of Velsdam. Apparently, the river was small enough to cross by barge at that point so there was a lot of contact between the two towns.

On the other side of the Estlander ambassador walked a man with rust-red curls down to his shoulders. He wore brown woollen trousers and a white, long-sleeved shirt and a leather jerkin embossed with some kind of sigil. He looked exotic and foreign, not proper at all, with that long hair and his strange clothing.

He was talking to the ambassador, and as he walked past, his eyes met Johanna's in the crowd. His eyes were brown, his chin strong and smoothly shaven. The corner of his mouth went up a fraction.

A shiver crawled over Johanna's back. Magic, as strong as she'd ever felt it. It radiated from him.

The procession went up to the dais, where Queen Cygna and Prince Roald took their positions on either side of the King's chair and all the other royals and guests found their places on the table behind and to the sides of the royal family. The red-haired man ended up at the back where Johanna couldn't see him anymore, although the touch of magic still made her skin prick.

She clamped her arms around herself. If people from the east had magic as strong as that, what hope would there be for Saarland to defend itself in case of a conflict? Especially if the Church started banishing people with magic?

A serious-looking man in a Carmine coat had taken up a position behind the prince's chair. Johanna wondered who he was—apart from a member of the royal family's courtiers—and what he was doing there, because no one else had a personal minder.

Another trumpet fanfare signalled that the royal family was seated.

All the guests now filed past the dais, where each one bowed or curtsied to the king. Johanna and her father lined up with Master Deim and the other merchants.

Slowly the line shuffled forwards.

When Johanna and her father's turn came, the king looked at Father and gave a barely perceptible nod that made Johanna's heart race. What had these men been negotiating behind her back? Prince Roald sat in a stiff position, staring into the back of the hall. He didn't look at anyone or talk to anyone. His foot jiggled.

On the other side of the dais, the queue dissolved and guests broke off into pairs or little groups which scattered across the floor. Johanna and her father stopped to look back at the dais, where guests still filed past.

"What do you think?" Father said in a low voice.

She glanced at Prince Roald, who was still jiggling his foot. "He seems frightened."

"Frightened? I would have thought he was bored."

"Wouldn't you be frightened if you were told to pick a girl out of all these dressed-up dolls, and you knew none of them?"

"He should be used to being the centre of attention."

Should was an easy word, but nothing was as it should. Roald looked healthy enough. Why had the king shielded him so? "Did the king tell you what's wrong with him and why he had to be sent away?"

"He has a very fragile personality."

Did that justify the special treatment? Then something else occurred to her. "Does he have magic?"

Father's eyes met hers squarely. "They say magic might have had something to do with it."

"But magic would make him more suited to the job. Think of all the things I know because of the magic in the wood." And magic didn't give a person a *fragile personality*, whatever that might mean. When it came to the prince, people spoke in impenetrable metaphors.

"What would the Shepherd have to say about a prince with magic?"

True. And religious as King Nicholaos was, that could be a problem. She glanced at the prince again. When meeting someone for the first time, she usually had at least a suspicion if someone had magic. Like Master Diem. She felt that with Master Willems, too, and Loesie. She had felt nothing when Roald passed her, but he might have been overshadowed by the red-haired man behind him, and Johanna tried very hard not to think of that chilling look in those brown eyes.

It was a mystery.

By now, the line to greet the king had dissolved.

A bell rang. The king rose from his seat and motioned for silence. The music stopped, and chatter and laughter died.

Roald remained in his chair, looking at the ground. His mother leaned across the empty chair between them and said something. He jerked his head up.

"Thank you all for being here with us today," the king said. "Today, our annual ball, is a great occasion. As you will have seen, Prince Roald has joined us in this occasion. He has recently returned to Saardam and will be taking up his duties as crown prince shortly. No doubt that's why we see such a wonderful presence from all the young ladies today. There will be a few words from my son later on, but for now I trust that you will amuse yourselves without my interfering. Enjoy the sounds of the orchestra and the wonderful dishes from our trusted cook. Feast and be merry."

The orchestra struck up a waltz that went with a dance called the dandelion. It was a light and frivolous tune, designed for a circle of friends, but Johanna danced it with Father. He wasn't a bad dancer, but he trod on her toes several times. It was crowded, and he was no doubt thinking about other matters. Then the herald called out for a change of partner, and she lost him in the crowd. She danced with a merchant's son, then a nobleman with bad breath and then decided to get something to eat at the tables around the perimeter of the room, where she found Master Deim in a heated discussion with a group of merchants.

"He's asked Dirk Brouwer," one of the men was saying.

"He came to me, too," another man said. "Asked me to contribute for the good of the country. He was not at all clear about what had happened that warrants such an expansion of the army. King's orders, he said, but you know what? I think the King is seeing things that aren't there."

"Don't know about that," Master Deim said. Oh yes, Johanna was right about him feeling magic. She didn't know if it was wind or wood, but it was definitely there.

"Who is about to invade us, then? Where will these people

come from? I've been up and down the Saar and Rede Rivers as far as one can go, and I've seen no proof of any hostilities."

"It's not something you can see," Master Deim said.

The other merchant's eyes went wide. "It's a magical thing?"

"Shhh!" another said.

Then they whispered to each other, and Johanna could no longer hear them.

She went to stand closer, but at that moment, the music stopped and King Nicholaos took to the podium once more, and everyone fell silent.

"As you have seen, tonight is the joyous event that our dear son has again joined us, ready to begin his duties as crown prince. I present to you, my son Roald."

The young man rose and the crowd cheered, rather half-heartedly, Johanna thought. His father placed his hand on his shoulder and guided him to face the people. The king whispered in his ear. Roald nodded and King Nicholaos retreated.

Roald stared into the crowd, his eyes unfocused.

And stared. His lips moved, but no sound came out.

He scrunched up the hem of his tunic with white-knuckled hands.

Some whispers rose in the gathered audience and someone behind Johanna let out a nervous chuckle.

"Um—welcome to the palace," Roald finally managed to say. His voice was pleasant, but didn't undo the unsettling effect of that too-long silence.

"Welcome," he said again. "Um . . . thank you all for coming. I think it's time for dancing now . . ." He looked over his shoulder.

King Nicholaos went to his rescue. "You will be aware that Roald is interested in the young ladies of our fair city, and we have invited some of them here. Ladies, you may all come forward and line up."

He guided his son down the stairs to the dais. The man who had been standing behind Roald's chair followed the pair. "Ladies, ladies," he called out. "Please line up here so that I can tick off your name from the list."

"Here you go, daughter." Father gave Johanna a tiny push in the back.

About twenty young women had already formed a line. Julianna Nieland, in her pink dress, was one of them. She gave Johanna another one of her "what are you doing here?" raised-eyebrow looks that seemed to be permanently plastered on her face when Johanna was around.

Johanna turned away from her. She wanted no prince, but to have Julianna Nieland snatch the prince's favour instead would be insufferable. That would be like being sixteen all over again and watching Carlotta Franzen strut around like a peacock because the prince helped her up when she fell.

Roald faced the group. He held his back unnaturally straight, and kept looking to the side, but his father was talking to the courtier with the list. The man proceeded to call out each girl's name and marked her off as if she was an item in a delivery.

While the orchestra played softly, Roald and his father inspected the line. King Nicholaos made small talk with the girls, and each curtsied. Johanna was sweating under her gown. Why on earth was she doing this? It was like being a cow for sale at the markets.

In the middle of the soft musical tones, there was a loud discordant twang.

Conversations stopped. People turned their heads to the orchestra.

From in the middle of the seated musicians, the lutist rose, his face red. One of the strings on his instrument dangled loose.

He stammered, "Um, I'm sorry, my string . . ."

In that moment of silence, Roald let out a giggle. He arched his back and clapped his hands. "Hehehehheeee! That's so funny!"

His voice echoed through the hall and made the hair on Johanna's neck stand up.

Master Hendricksen sometimes brought his monkey when he came to talk to Father. It sat on his shoulder, as it did tonight; and when it got excited it made a sound like that.

The King tried to get his son to shut up, but Prince Roald laughed and laughed. No one else was laughing. The faces of the noble ladies showed expressions of horror. One woman at the front of the crowd gestured for her daughter in the queue to come back to her.

On the dais, Queen Cygna sat as stone, staring at the other side of the hall. Johanna could see her dead-faced expression through her veil.

In the eerie silence, the King said, his face unemotional. "After that—um—interlude, I think the orchestra needs some time to fix up the—um—problems, but we can proceed without music."

But no one could dance without music, and the lack of music made uncomfortable moments so much more awkward.

Murmurs broke out throughout the hall. A lady behind Johanna whispered to her neighbour, "He's not good in the head. No wonder they've kept him hidden for so long."

Another said, "Pity the girl who gets to marry him."

"Oh, you're only saying that because you have no daughters. A prince is a prince. All young women want to marry a prince."

"Look then. Magda has already withdrawn her daughter."

It was true. The girl in question stood with her mother. She was talking and gesturing angrily and wiping her eyes. Black kohl had smudged over her cheek.

The lute player ran across the hall with his instrument and a new string and re-settled in the orchestra.

Soon, the music started again. A servant with a tray of drinks went up the dais and offered the first one to Queen Cygna, but she refused. When the servant had gone to the guests, she lifted her veil and dabbed at her eyes.

Johanna didn't know where to look. This was all so embarrassing and deeply horrible. Johanna could imagine the pain. The young Princess Cygna, youngest daughter of the king of the northern land of Scandia, married off at her sixteenth birthday to a crown prince she had never met of a country where she had never been, pregnant the same night. By all accounts, Roald's birth had been long and difficult, not in the least because of Cygna's young age, and all for nothing. The prince would never be suitable to rule a country. Many diseases could be cured, but those in the head were forever.

There was some action in the line. Out of all the girls, the prince managed to pick out Julianna Nieland. The king took her hand and put it in his son's. She looked terrified.

Roald led her into the middle of the dance floor. He walked stiffly, but Julianna appeared to waver, and her face was so white that it looked like she might faint.

The music began. Roald was a stiff, clumsy dancer, and trod on Julianna's feet several times. He spoke to her a few times, and Julianna arched her back further and further from him.

Normally, Johanna would have felt vindicated if Julianna embarrassed herself, but this was beyond embarrassment.

Then all of a sudden, she screamed, wrenched herself from Roald's grip and ran across the dance floor where she threw herself in her mother's arms, crying. Lady Suzanna Nieland stood too far from Johanna to hear any of what they said.

The girls around Johanna craned their necks.

"What happened?"

"What did he say to her?"

Julianna was still crying on her mother's shoulder. Her brother patted her back. Lady Nieland cast the king a disapproving look.

"Johanna Brouwer," King Nicholaos announced.

Johanna had been looking at the Nieland family, and returned her attention to the king, heart thudding.

"My son wishes to have a dance with you."

Too late to back out. Roald met her eyes with a small frown.

Johanna took his hand and curtsied, first to the king and then the prince, but her mind felt blank, as if she was in a very bad dream. Had Father known what state Roald was in? *Magic might have something to do with it*. What nonsense.

Roald was a halfwit, and Father would have known that. That showed what he thought of her: a chess piece that he could use to advance the business. The anger made her even hotter under the stifling dress.

But she would rather die than make a scene like Julianna Nieland. She would dance with him in a dignified way. Whatever he said to Julianna was nothing that Johanna wouldn't have heard before. She spoke to the ships' boys and deck hands. She heard their swearing. She knew where they went after work, and because those ladies, if they deserved that term, always knew who of their regular clients was out of work, Johanna spoke to them as well. Helena from the harbour-side bar was not a bad person. She and her friends were useful and, like Mistress Daphne, full of gossip. Nothing the prince could say to her would make her scream and run off.

Sure enough when she raised her head, it was to find Roald looking at her. At her chest, to be more precise. At the point where the small groove between her breasts vanished under the dress.

"Roald, now behave yourself," the king said.

Roald giggled. "Oooh, I like this one. I get all the good girls today, don't I?"

"Yes, but don't say anything rude." King Nicholaos gave a forced smile. "Go on, then, show her your dancing skills."

"I think I like this ball after all."

Roald took Johanna's hand. His hand was sweaty and when he faced her in the middle of the dance floor, his breath stank of liquor. From close up, his face had a ruddy complexion and his skin was flaky. Probably from spending too much time inside.

The orchestra started to play a dance that was called the prince's waltz, a slow dance with quite complicated steps.

"You are very pretty." His eyes were still uncomfortably focused on her breasts.

"Um, thank you, Your Highness."

He laughed, loudly. "Hehehehee! You hear that? She got it right, Mother!"

On the dais, Queen Cygna did her best to pretend she wasn't there.

"Shall we start dancing. . . ?" She almost said *Your Highness* again to set him off a second time. Instead she pulled him into a move she hoped was a waltz, but she seemed to have totally forgotten the steps.

Roald was clumsy. He stepped on her feet several times, and kneed her in the thigh once. He couldn't do turns. Everyone was watching and Johanna didn't know where to look.

Roald was oblivious to the attention. "My mother says I have to ask you questions. Do you like questions?"

What to reply to that? "Um . . ."

He was still staring at her breasts, leaning over and peeking into her dress, as far as he could go without touching. Johanna was overcome by a desire to run out of the room, but she reminded herself that she wasn't going to make a scene like Julianna Nieland.

"I don't like the questions Mother wants me to ask."

"Shhh. You can ask questions, but you don't want everyone to hear them, Your—um—what would you like to know?"

"Oooh, secret questions. I like that."

All around the hall, the nobles were looking on, their faces stiff in horror and secret fascination, pretending this wasn't happening. Pretending that they didn't see the prince staring at her breasts. She could already hear the comments *She shouldn't have worn that scandalous thing, cheap try-hard that she is.*

"Do you like gingerbread biscuits?" Roald asked.

"Yes, I like gingerbread biscuits." For some reason, she thought about Loesie, who would be wondering where she was. "Our cook makes very good ones."

"I don't like gingerbread biscuits."

"Oh, I'm sorry to hear that."

He laughed his high-pitched laugh again, oblivious that everyone was staring at him.

And then he said, giving a look at his father, "My father wants me to ask you why you want to marry me." He bent close to her ear and she could smell the liquor again.

He waited for effect, and then said, "But I'm not going to ask that."

"You aren't?" At this point, she was reacting with the sole purpose to survive this dance without upsets.

"Oh, you want to tell me anyway?" He bent closer again. His alcohol-laced breath tickled the bare skin on her chest.

She almost gagged and had to restrain herself not to rip herself out of his grip, which was surprisingly strong.

"I'd like to know."

She was dizzy; she panicked. She didn't know what she was

doing, thinking nothing but that she *had* to get out of his grip or he'd do something embarrassing to her under the eyes of all these people.

"I don't really want to marry you." What else could she say? She couldn't do this. She couldn't. Her father couldn't honestly expect her to shackle herself to a crazy man.

He retreated and nodded. "Good. Because I don't want to marry you either. Your tits are too small."

And with that, he stepped back, gave a mock bow and turned away. Johanna walked away as fast as she could without running. The king gestured his son that he needed to go back to the waiting line of girls. Roald crossed his arms over his chest and said something, to which his father grabbed his shoulder and spoke to him sternly.

Roald squealed, "I don't want to!"

And King Nicholaos spoke to him more sternly.

The people around the dance floor watched this exchange with morbid curiosity displayed on their faces.

Only three girls remained of the original twenty. All three were nobles, with white faces and wide eyes. Johanna would have grinned at them if she hadn't felt so awful.

To her horror, Father was right behind her. She met his eyes squarely.

"I can't—"

He took her by the arm and dragged her off to the side of the room, under the arched gallery, where the light was dim and only a lone palace guard watched.

At the same time as Johanna began with, "I'm sorry, but—" he said, "Johanna . . ." There was a tone of warning in his voice.

And then they were both silent.

"I can't do this," she said, eventually. "I'm sure you understand."

"Shhh. Johanna, this is a great opportunity."

"Marrying an idiot?" She fought to keep tears out of her voice. What did he think she was? "Did you know about this?"

"Think about it, Johanna. In a number of years' time, I will be dead. King Nicholaos and Queen Cygna will be dead. If he survives that long, Roald is too simple to govern our country. Who does that leave in power other than the prince's wife?"

"I don't care. You didn't answer my question. Did you know about this?"

"It is a wonderful opportunity for us."

Johanna stared at him, the horror of what he said coming over her. He wasn't going to answer the question, because he had known. He was simply using her as a piece in a game. "I thought you loved me."

"I do, and I don't know what else to do for you. You want freedom and power, I give you freedom and power."

"Not like this."

"Then there will be no option but for me to agree to give you to Octavio Nieland." His face was hard.

"No. You don't understand anything. I will not be given to anyone. I'm happy to remain a spinster for the rest of my life. Listen to what I say for once: I don't want to get married to anyone."

She turned on her heel and ran away from him.

CHAPTER 10

ALL OF A SUDDEN, Johanna found the hall too hot and too noisy. The smell of sweat mingled with perfume and food made her feel dizzy. The tight bodice of the dress constricted her breathing. Everyone seemed to be looking at her, and those haughty noble faces carried expressions of pity. She could hear their mocking voices. *Poor simple girl. She really didn't know what she let herself in for, didn't she?*

She pushed herself through the crowd until she came to the side of the hall.

Through a set of double doors, she ended up in the gallery that ran between the hall and the garden, a long corridor, with on the right-hand side doors that led into the hall. Muffled sounds of talk and laughter and music filtered through the closed doors. Moonlight slanted in through the arched windows on the left.

She stopped in front of one of those windows, seeing the beautifully sculpted garden and the golden statue of the Triune through a haze of tears.

She'd gone and undone all of Father's hard negotiating work. He had every right to be furious with her.

And of course he was right. She was his only heir. If she didn't marry, the company would stop with her. If she could put up with Roald, it was the best position for her to be in. The king seemed to like her. Roald probably didn't have much of a say in it. Pretty much like herself. All she needed to do was . . . She shuddered at the thought of letting him touch her.

What was Father thinking?

She stood in front of the window bathed in pale moonlight, clamping her arms around herself and calming herself by leaning her forehead against the window. The glass fogged up where she breathed on it. She didn't know what to do, and what she'd say to Father. She would have to apologise, but she wanted an apology from him, too. She might even have agreed to a meeting with the prince had he told her what was going on.

The sense of betrayal stung worse than anything else. That her father would *sell* her without telling her.

That's what you get for failing to grow up, said the little voice that sounded like Nellie. Grown-up girls got married, plain and simple.

If she *had* to marry right now, she would choose . . . Master Willems. At least he knew how the business worked and wouldn't want anything out of the deal other than to keep his job.

Yes.

It was silly. And impossible. He was just a shopkeeper's son. And he was heavily involved in the Church. He probably didn't even like her. She trusted him, and that was more than could be said for any other candidates.

She didn't want to get married.

The way Roald stared at her breasts made her shudder.

This was a dreadful place and not one where she belonged. Loesie would be wondering where she was. She'd be hungry. Maybe she'd go wandering around the docks, with all the problems that would bring.

In the middle of the floor of the gallery was a large plain slab of marble with a carved inscription. Four pillars marked the corners, each with a candle on a sconce. A faint breeze made the flames flap, casting moving shadows over the stone.

Johanna pushed herself away from the window and walked over. The inscription on the marble slab said,

Born from dust, return to dust,

with underneath a name.

At the tender age of nineteen. Our beloved princess Celine Maraina Hestia Carmine de Lacoeur van Leeuwen.

No one ever listed all the royal family's names and titles. You needed a whole page for that.

Celine, felled suddenly by a deadly infection. Celine, younger sister to Roald. Celine, first heir to the Carmine Throne.

Johanna remembered hearing the news of her death. She remembered the day of her funeral, how queen Cygna had broken down and collapsed on the dais. She remembered the king's silent and emotionless appearance.

She remembered the talk about Roald and the speculation about his absence.

There had been whispers that he'd been glad she was dead. Some even said that he might have killed his sister. No one understood why he had been passed over for the throne anyway, although the reason for choosing Celine was widely rumoured to be to attract local princes in marriage, influential princes from large kingdoms. But the royal family had never confirmed this rumour. They hadn't married Celine off as soon as she turned sixteen either. Knowing what Johanna knew now, it all made sense. The Carmines were a dangerously small family and they carried a curse that was worse than that of magic: that of madness. Potential suitors would find out about Roald, and would worry about any children Celine might have. That would have repelled a lot of potential candidates, especially those from other royal families. They'd been marrying each other's cousins for so many generations that no royal family was unrelated to the other royal families.

Add to that the fact that King Nicholaos had made himself unpopular with the nobility of the surrounding lands by giving the Church of the Triune legal status, and you had a problem. A big problem.

And because of Celine, Johanna stood here. Because of Celine, she had failed her father.

She buried her face in her hands.

A voice behind her said, "Lady."

Johanna gasped and turned around. "Who's there?"

"It's only me." From the shadows of the porch came the red-haired man she had seen with the king's guests. He bowed. "Excuse me very much, my lady. I seem to have startled you. That was not my intention. I merely sought the way to the garden. I'm quite hot." He spoke with a curious accent.

"Oh . . . Down that way, I think." She pointed half-heartedly to the end of the passage.

From close up, the prick of magic was so strong that it made the hairs on her arms stand on end. What kind of magic was it? Not willow magic because that was much more subtle. Not wind magic or he would follow the way to the garden by the guidance of the breeze. If she was to have any chance of finding out, she needed to touch his bare skin. His arms were mostly covered by long flowing sleeves. His hands were long-fingered, but hands were really not much good for magic transmission. Hands touched too many other things that they easily became contaminated.

His neck . . . She stared at the way the light danced in his hair. Felt that most horrible of feelings creep up on her: a blush. Fortunately, it would be too dark for him to notice.

"I don't think we've been introduced, my lady, my name is Kylian, prince of Gelre."

"Baron Uti's son?" Her voice sounded small and immature to her ears.

"The very one." He bowed.

"I'm afraid I can't compete with that. My name is Johanna Brouwer."

"Oh, the famous merchant's daughter."

"You know me?" Surely he said that to humour her.

"Who hasn't heard of the famous Brouwer river barges? They bring spices and tobacco all up and down the inland towns. And you were dancing with the prince just now. Your name was whispered all over the hall."

"Um . . ." Johanna was going to say *not in a good way, probably*, but that would lead to all sorts of conversations she didn't want to have. Also, it made sense that he'd know Father's ships, important as the river trade was to the inland towns, but she had no idea why he would know her. She wasn't famous at all. She had been to Lurezia once with her father, but no one knew the Brouwer Company there, except other merchants, whom Father had spent ages talking to. To the fourteen-year-old Johanna, it was nothing but a big, strange city that stank, where no one spoke her language.

In the hall, the orchestra struck up a tune called The Swan that involved a dance where the man held the woman by the elbows from behind and the pair moved across the dance floor in an elegant glide.

He bowed again. "Lady Johanna, I would be most pleased to have this dance." He held his arms ready.

"Um . . . Isn't the dance floor in the hall?" Except she didn't really want to go back there, not to watch the embarrassing spectacle of petrified girls dancing with Roald if there were still any girls left who wanted to try, or to see Roald throw more tantrums, or see Father's pained face.

Johanna felt like an idiot. She was turning into another version of Nellie, always worrying about this or that and what people thought of it. Nellie never had any *fun*. And Johanna's life was not much fun at the moment. What happened to the girl who two days ago danced down the church steps wearing clogs?

Kylian was handsome, and smiled at her with quiet intelligence. Not the predatory look of Octavio Nieland. Not the dumb look of Prince Roald. Not the expectant looks of all the nobles. Or the suspicious looks of anyone who knew about magic.

What was the harm of one dance? She had danced with plenty of young men at other occasions, albeit none as formal as this one. After tonight, he would go back to the baron's castle. She would go back to being plain Johanna and she would never see him again.

But there is no one else here, the annoying little voice in her head said.

She forced that little voice to shut up and put her hands in his. His palms felt warm and dry. Pleasant, not at all like Roald's sweaty hands.

And his magic—whoa! It swept her up in a maelstrom of visions, of his home, the town of Florisheim by the Rede River.

She saw the castle high above the roofs of the town, with a forbidding entrance, a fat round tower on which flew the flag of the barony.

He turned her around and took her lightly by the outstretched elbows from behind. They danced, like a pair of silent and ghostly swans, across the vast empty floor of the gallery.

He whirled and whirled, remembering steps and patterns effortlessly, and she felt like she was flying. His magic made her steps light and her mind unburdened. He guided her with confidence, avoiding marble pillars and potted plants without breaking his step or any of the dance patterns. His touch on her elbows was light but sure. His body behind her radiated warmth, but never touched her.

It was all so proper and boring. Deep inside her, she yearned for the warmth of another person's touch and for something *not proper*. That's why she'd come out here, right? That was why she'd agreed to dance with him in the first place. If her stunt with Roald meant that she would remain a spinster for the rest of her life, would it be wrong to have a little taste of what she would miss?

Very wrong, the little voice in her mind said. It sounded like Nellie.

The music was finished, and half-hearted applause rang from the hall. Kylian let go of Johanna's elbows and warmth lingered in those small spots where he had touched her. She turned around, meeting his brown eyes.

Silence lingered between them as the magic of his touch fled her body.

"Did you like that?" he asked.

"You're a very good dancer." She felt her cheeks glowing.

He smiled.

Her heart thudded against her ribs. What was she doing? She should be sensible and go back into the garden room. Father would be looking for her in the crowd. Or King Nicholaos. And all the nobles would be wondering where she was. *Run home crying* the rumours would go.

She hesitated, but the moment to end this encounter was lost. The orchestra started the next dance, a faster piece.

"Do you want another dance?" Kylian asked.

"Not really, I'm quite hot. I should probably—" Why was she still fighting?

"Come." He took her arm.

"Where are we going?" Panic clamped around her heart. This wasn't right. Young women got into trouble this way, and everything about him smelled trouble.

That's what you wanted, right? It's your own fault, the little voice that sounded like Nellie said.

"I was on my way to the gardens. Let's get some fresh air. I'm quite keen to see this fabled gold statue that's rumoured to be here."

Johanna still protested. "I don't really know how to get there. I'm not so familiar with this part of the building. I should go back to the ball—"

If only she could think clearly, but she was hot and cold at the same time and her cheeks glowed like they were on fire.

Kylian laughed. "Oh, those people in there are boring. Were you forced to dance with the prince? Did you know he was an idiot? The king did hide his son well enough, didn't he?"

He had no right to call any member of *her* royal family an idiot, but at his words, her anger at her father re-surfaced. For all she knew, she *should* do something stupid, because . . . because she could. And she would probably be talking about this night for the rest of her life, so she might as well make sure that something good happened. Or at least something daring and not-boring.

CHAPTER 11

A SET OF DOORS at the end of the hallway led to the garden side of the palace. Bathed in moonlight, the paving looked grey save where potted plants cast ink-black shadows.

Kylian tested the doors. They opened, letting a chill breeze into the somewhat stuffy gallery. The curtains billowed inward.

She clamped her arms around herself. "Brrr."

He slipped his jerkin off his shoulders and draped it over hers. It was leather: heavy and rough and imbued with smells of forest, wood fires and something unmistakably *male* that made her shiver.

They walked onto the forecourt, where the moonlight cast deep shadows of the walls and clipped bushes. Water burbled in a crystal-clear pond. Three young willow trees lined the water, the type from the south that trailed their branches in the water.

"It's pretty," he said, pushing away the curtain of willow branches.

"Yes. I guess it's very different where you come from." She was babbling and she knew it.

"Very different," he said. "We don't have large cities, only small towns by the river, surrounded by wooded hills. This land around here is so flat. Do you know what hills look like?"

"I've seen them when going up the river with Father."

Although she hadn't gone east into the Rede River, but continued to follow the Saar River to Lurezia. She'd seen *forest*, too, dense stands of trees much larger than any tree that grew in Saarland. The ground underneath was covered in leaves and moss and her footsteps had made not a sound. It was kind of scary not being able to see far or being in such a dim and dark place where evil could jump on her from behind every tree trunk.

He continued, "The forest is magic. It speaks to me of the things it has seen. It breathes life. Do you ever feel like that?"

She nodded, still hearing the whisperings in the forest when the wind raked its fingers through the boughs. There was a smell of mushrooms and rich soil and magic.

"Did you find the forest scary?" His eyes were dark in the low light, and his red hair looked black. When had he come close enough for the male scent of his body to become so over-whelming?

"I did." A bit later, she added, in a whisper, "Are there wolves where you live? Bears? Demons?"

"All of those, and more. Ghosts, wraiths, spirits. Magical creatures. Some good, some evil. People don't belong in the forest. We're mere guests and live by the rules of the forest." He sounded almost reverent. His magic was sure to involve forest and trees.

"Sounds scary."

"It's not, when you know how to listen, which I'm sure you can."

There was no point in denying her magic. "I speak to willows. The wood tells me stories."

His face split into a smile that made his eyes twinkle. "I know. Why else would I single out you, of all girls?"

Had he done that? With just a single exchanged look across a crowded hall?

"It must be quite hard, feeling magic and listening to the Shepherd denouncing all magic as evil."

"It is hard. But I want to convince the Church that magic can be used for good as well as evil."

"Bah, good luck with that. You might as well talk to a rock. They will not listen."

Normally, Johanna would have argued, but after having talked to the Shepherd about Loesie, she resigned herself to the fact that he was right.

The Church wouldn't listen. The Church had its own agenda, and that involved banishing everything they didn't understand or couldn't control. It involved getting money from the royal family that they should be spending elsewhere, or worse, didn't have.

Worse than that even, King Nicholaos was blind to what was happening.

They walked in silence, side by side. He was close enough that she could feel the warmth radiating from his body, a comforting cocoon in the chill of the night.

Via the beautifully paved and maintained path, they came to the far end of the gardens. The king had ordered a grassy mound to be built here, from where you could see over the city. Stone steps led to the top, where there was a circular paved area surrounded by a knee-high wall. The stars were out and light from the moon cast a silvery sheen over the roofs of Saardam.

"Do you know why the Moon has a ring around it?" he asked.

"Because there is mist up there where the Moon is."

He laughed. "Not quite. The Moon is so far from us that you could put the Saar and Rede rivers end to end and straight up in the sky and it wouldn't reach the Moon."

"How do you know that?"

"I study the skies."

"Do you have a looking glass? I've got one, too."

"We have the best looking glasses available in all of the western lands. My father has also hired a man called Rinius who studies the skies."

"The one who wrote the book?"

"You are familiar with it?"

"I have a copy." Father had bought it for her on his travels, knowing her interest in such things. It showed the diagrams of the stars and where planets would be at certain times of the year.

"You better hide that from your priests. Rinius is a wanted

man for spreading heresy throughout all the southern lands where the Church has a hold on ruling families."

"The Church of the Triune is not the same as those southern churches."

"Tell me honestly that your priests won't declare the natural sciences heresy and I'll believe you."

Johanna said nothing. She couldn't say anything of the sort. What was more, she believed him. The sciences said many things that were against belief. To some, magic was just another science.

They continued down the mound and came to the end of the laneway, where the longitudinal flower beds gave way to features set in a circular pattern, depicting a rose.

In the middle was a pond in which stood a pedestal and on it the gilded statue of the Triune, silhouetted against the night sky.

"Urgh," Kylian said, looking up at it. "What a hideous thing."

"Are you always this rude when visiting strangers?" Not just rude, blasphemous. She had never heard anyone talk like this, not even Father's merchant friends, none of whom had any love for the Church.

"It *is* a hideous thing. Look at the slobbering mouth of the dog, and look at the hollow face. The bearded man looks like a sanctimonious piece of shit. He doesn't care about the world at all. He just cares about being *seen* to do good."

"The statue embodies the fragmented nature of the human spirit. There are three parts. Some of human nature is good, some is indifferent and shackled in tradition, and some is just plain bad."

He chuckled. "Like magic, huh?"

Unease creeping up in her, Johanna looked out over the harbour, where the boats bobbed on their moorings.

A breeze stroked her skin and brought the sound of barking dogs. Seriously, they weren't still carrying on about Master Hendricksen's monkey, were they?

"Your Church says there is no magic and any who say otherwise are evil. Your king does not believe in it."

Not just the Church—the majority of people in Saardam who didn't have magic didn't believe in the few who did. In the past, they had called people with magic witches and drowned them to test it. If a woman floated, she was a witch and would be killed. If she sank, she was not a witch, but she was dead anyway. But that had been in the time of Johanna's grandmother, and no one in the family had magic then. And there had been no Church.

Kylian continued, "Why let yourself be ruled by this Church? They are nothing but tyrants in disguise. Even the name says it all: shepherds. They expect their followers to be sheep, incapable of thinking for themselves. The Church is run by old men who are scared of magic, or maybe jealous of the ones who have it."

"They are still our people, our citizens. I do not want to be an enemy of the Church. The Church does a lot of good."

He snorted. "Some good."

"It does! It helps poor people. It gives them food and clothes."

"In exchange for their vows and adoption of their ludicrous beliefs."

Johanna glared at him. "Are you determined to offend everyone? Or are you so absorbed in your own wealth that you have no idea what it's like to be poor?"

"And you, of course, would have an excellent idea what it's like to be poor." His voice sounded sarcastic.

"I've never been poor, but I talk to people who are. If it wasn't for the Church many of them would die in winter."

"That has nothing to do with the way they treat people with magic. Poverty is a solvable, petty issue. Magic is mysterious, dangerous and it won't let itself be denied. If you ignore it, it grows stronger. You cannot banish magic, you must use it." He trailed a finger through the air, describing a path that traced the profile of her face, but his finger never touched her.

Johanna shivered. He put in words what she had thought many times.

"In Gelre, we use magic in government, and at court. We could use you. All of you with magic. If those men of the Church become too much of a problem, you will be welcome with us."

"Is this why you're here? To 'rescue' people like me from the Church?"

He chuckled. "We're here because we do not want our allies to fall to an institution that goes back to burning and drowning witches."

Which didn't answer her question. She wanted to ask him if he thought that persecution of shepherds, as happened in many eastern countries, was any better than persecution of witches, but it didn't seem so important now. Persecuted in many lands, the Church of the Triune had found fertile ground in Saardam because Shepherd Romulus offered the king solace after the tragedy of Princess Celine's death. A melting pot of people and cultures of the Western Lands, Saardam lacked a clear moral direction. The Church of the Triune fitted in that gap. That was all there was to it.

She walked around the pond so that she faced the head of the Holy God. What had he said again? *A sanctimonious piece of shit?* How dare he talk like that about people's deep beliefs?

The subtle sounds of the night drifted on the air: the soft slap of water against the quay wall on the other side of the wall around the garden, the faint sound of music, talk and laughter that came from the palace at their back. The neighing of a horse in the palace forecourt where all the noblemen's horses waited until the party had finished and they could take their masters back home again.

Kylian said softly, "You know you're not like any woman I've ever met?"

Johanna turned her head sharply to him. "Then you haven't met any real women, only dishrags."

He laughed, and it served to make her even more annoyed. "I travel all over the western lands and have not met a woman who is both pretty and in possession of magic skills. You're so wild and untamed, I can feel the magic flow. I could teach you to use your magic properly. Then nothing you ever wanted would be out of your reach."

"No, I don't want that. That's manipulating people. That's how magic gets a bad name."

"You're such a fierce one"

"When people annoy me enough."

"I annoy you?"

"Yes. When you say things like that, and when you're rude about our beliefs. What do you even know about—"

She started to walk away. This man was an insufferable arrogant prick. But she didn't get far.

"Wait." He grabbed her wrist.

"What? You want to apologise?" She tried to yank her arm out of his grip but he was very strong. "Go ahead. I'm waiting."

He paused, facing her. Dark, brooding, his gaze intense. An envelope of air around him breathed his male scent. For a while, the only sound was that of his breathing. A breeze picked up and blew a strand of his hair forward over his shoulder. The tips of it tickled on the bare skin of her upper chest.

She pulled at her arm again. "If you're so honourable, you would let me go. My father will come looking for me any time now."

His face showed mock surprise. "Oh? I thought you would be too mature for these sorts of tricks. But you can always become like one of those dumb ladies inside." He put on a high voice. "Let me go or I'm going to scream."

"I can scream if you want me to."

"Be my guest. Scream."

He took a step back, while still holding on to her arm.

There was no way she was going to give him that satisfaction. She tried to twist out of his grip. Her voice came out as a grunt. "Let me go."

She twisted her arm further, sure she'd have bruises tomorrow. But the only effect of her struggle was that she came closer to him and his grip tightened. He laughed.

"You're doing that all wrong. You have to hold my wrist, like so."

His other hand took hold of her free hand and placed it on the arm that held hers.

"Grab it tight so that I can't move."

She did, although she had no illusion that he could still move as much as he wanted.

"Now twist sharply."

She did as he said and her arm came free.

"See, that was easy."

"You let me go."

"If you do this quickly, it will take most people by surprise. Remember it for when an unwanted suitor tries to grab you. Want to try again?"

Johanna hesitated. This was one strange man. Dangerous, challenging, mysterious, crackling with magic.

She faced him, her chest heaving with deep breaths from the struggle. He returned her stare, unwavering and not in the least flustered.

Johanna's cheeks felt like they were on fire.

He said, his voice low, "Has a man ever kissed those ruby lips of yours?"

"What business is that of yours?"

"It's more interesting for me if it's the first time for you."

"Who said you could kiss me?"

He laughed, trailing his finger over her cheek. His touch made her shiver. "Twenty-three and never been kissed?"

"Twenty-four." She looked defiantly into his eyes. He was talking to her as if she were a little girl, thinking she was afraid of men, huh?

"See, I'm not holding you against your will." He spread his hands. "You can run to your father if you want. Run, little girl, run!"

Johanna didn't move.

Kylian leaned closer, enveloping her in his warmth. His lips brushed hers fleetingly. He smelled of leather, smoke and fire.

"Like that?" He was teasing her.

"That's fine by me," she whispered. "I'm not afraid of you."

"Well, there's plenty of time to establish the truth of that."

He took her in a rough grip and pressed his mouths on hers. His lips forced hers apart and his tongue came into her mouth. She hadn't expected that, and let out involuntary moan. She struggled to breathe. His hands slid up her sides, over the tight bodice of the dress.

He let go and stared at her in the moonlight. He chuckled. "Still not afraid?"

Johanna gasped for breath but shook her head, her heart still thudding. Was that what kissing was like? It was disgusting.

But it was naughty. It was like what men said about smoking. You hated it the first time, thought it was all right the second and after that you couldn't stop doing it.

He was still holding her waist, looking down into her face, his lips slightly parted.

That second kiss was coming up right now. He covered her mouth with his and now she knew what was coming, didn't flinch or try to pull back. She relaxed in his arms.

Yes, that was much better.

He chuckled. "My, you're learning fast." His lips brushed the tip of her nose. "You're so pretty, wasting your life in this silly provincial town. Since you're not going to marry the prince, would you like to come back with me? I could teach you magic. You could talk to Rinius, be his assistant, even. We could . . . continue this activity undisturbed." He ran his tongue along the line of her jaw.

Johanna shivered.

Get out of here, start anew, what an opportunity. She'd disappointed her father by refusing to marry Roald. She didn't want Octavio Nieland. She didn't want to marry at all, but if she had to, why not someone from outside the stifling Saardam society?

He kissed her again, this time longer. She tried replying to him, tickling his tongue with hers. He chuckled without breaking the kiss. His hands raked through her hair.

Then, suddenly, there was a sound she recognised: the ringing of church bells, the clanging distorted by the breeze.

At this time of day?

Johanna stiffened. Kylian let her go.

"What's going on?" she whispered.

He said nothing, but turned his face into the wind. His eyes were alert, his face tense.

"Can you feel anything?" She still didn't know what type of magic he had. Something to do with the forest. Maybe he had wind magic, too. Was it possible for one person to have more than one kind of magic?

She repeated, "What's going on?" Her heart was thudding.

He looked sideways, and then without a word, bolted down the path.

She called after him, "Hey!"

But he didn't listen or stop. He jumped into the hedge that shielded the garden's outer wall from view, pulled himself up over the wall and down the other side, leaving Johanna standing stunned and alone in the garden.

She clamped her hands around herself. When had the air become so cold?

Distant sounds drifted from the city: the barking and howling of dogs. The neighing of horses. People shouting.

A cat raced through the garden, yowling, with all its hair standing on end. Goodness, what possessed that animal?

Feeling shaken, Johanna climbed onto the mound where they had looked at the stars so that she could see over the wall. There was an orange glow in the city, a street or so back from the harbour. Vicious flames rose from the roof of one of the canal houses. That was nowhere near *her* house, was it? She traced the outlay of the streets in her mind. She didn't *think* it was in her street.

There was a soft sound of footsteps behind her. Johanna turned around.

Someone had come into the garden from the gallery and now walked up the steps to where she stood. A woman, thin and shrouded in black. Her tread was light, as if she floated.

Johanna curtsied before the queen. "My excuses for being in your garden, Your Highness. I was hot and—"

"What is going on in town?" Queen Cygna's voice was sharp, almost nervous, and with the distinct accent of the northern lands. She gasped and raised a dainty hand to her mouth. "Fire."

Johanna turned around. The fire had spread. Flames licked the roof of one of the harbour-side warehouses. "Is that Master Deim's warehouse?"

The Queen couldn't answer that. She probably didn't know who Master Deim was.

"Listen to the poor horses," the queen said.

The breeze brought sounds of neighing and men shouting and dogs barking. In fact, the horses had been nervous all afternoon. There was magic in the air and she couldn't feel it.

"With your permission, Your Highness, I think we should go

inside," she said, and Queen Cygna did not object. She walked silent next to Johanna on the path towards the palace. There were things Johanna wanted to say, but didn't know how to broach them. About Roald, about Father, about herself. But she couldn't find the right words. The queen had seemed so very fragile and upset at Roald's misbehaviour. She didn't want to risk saying something inappropriate.

Just outside the door, the queen held Johanna back.

"Thank you." Her voice was soft.

"Your Highness?" *Thank you*, what for?

The queen hesitated. Seen through the black veil, her face was exquisite, her skin soft and pale, as yet marred by few lines, her eyes the clearest blue. A few wisps of flaxen hair peeped out from underneath the black lace.

"Roald is a good boy. He gets confused easily and takes instructions literally. He doesn't know when it is appropriate to say certain . . . things. He gets these ideas into his head and wants to talk about them with everyone. I'm afraid his father did some explaining about what's involved in getting married, and he took an unexpected interest to certain private parts of it. I'm truly sorry for anything upsetting that he might have said to you. But I say again, even if he is unusual, he is a good man and would never harm anyone."

"I understand, Your Highness."

"No. You do not." She patted Johanna on the arm and then froze, looking over Johanna's shoulder. "Look."

As they both watched, a creature sleek and agile like a cat, but made entirely out of fire, jumped from the flames onto another roof, setting it alight with a touch of its tail.

Queen Cygna gasped. "Fire demons." The firelight made her face look pale. Her eyes were wide.

"I need to go to my father. His warehouse is somewhere over there."

"Yes, you should do that." The queen's eyes were wide. "But after you have done that, you should get out of here, and you should warn everyone to do the same. You cannot fight these creatures and their masters."

Johanna's heart jumped. "Your Highness, do you know what

those creatures are and where they come from?" She saw snarling demons shown to her by Loesie's basket. A chill went over her. The prick of magic made the air crackle. *Loesie*. She was in the barn. She was either possessed and part of the evil, or she was in danger down there near the fire.

The queen said in a low voice, "My husband and his advisors played with things they didn't understand. The Burovian priests were blind for money, and promised things that were not theirs to promise. My husband gave them money, even though I told him it was a bad idea, but like so many times, the voice of a woman doesn't count. He didn't listen. He was too keen to have Celine back, and he believed that they could resurrect her."

"He was talking to a necromancer?"

The queen nodded, her face sad. "Whether or not he could do as his disciples said remains to be seen. I don't think so, but he's a powerful magician."

"Who is this man?"

"I never saw him, and I don't think my husband did either. We dealt with his followers. They call themselves the dawn order, but they're nothing more than practitioners of dark magic. I told him not to get involved, but he was too impatient."

"Are these priests from the sanatorium where Roald was?"

"No, no, not at all. Those good men have also come into danger because of this ill-considered deal. They're also angry with us, with good reason. The order of the dawn has performed evil rituals in the forest that have disturbed the demons. It was my hope that our withdrawal of Roald could stop their anger, but it's already too late. Humans and magical creatures both come under the influence of anger. Only humans are capable of forgiveness. You must run and save yourself while you still can. All of us are lost already. Wherever we go, they will find us. Don't trust any easterners."

And then, silently and much more quickly than Johanna would have expected for a royal, she was gone.

CHAPTER 12

J OHANNA'S HEART still beat high in her throat when she came back into the main hall, where the festivities continued as if nothing had happened. The air was heavy with the smell of sweat and alcohol. Waltzing couples filled the dance floor. The music, talk and laughter drowned out the shouts and neighs from outside. The doors on the far side of the hall were closed, so none of the stewards had yet come in to warn their masters and no one had seen the fire.

Don't trust any easterners. There were easterners everywhere in the crowd, amongst the guests and the servants, and in the distinguished party at the dais. There was no way that they were all bad, and there was no way to determine if any of them had knowledge of what was happening outside.

The king sat alone at the dais, flanked by two empty chairs. Why didn't Queen Cygna warn her husband about the fire?

Father sat on the other side of the hall, talking to Master Deim. He didn't look like he'd missed her, but she was sure he had. She felt guilty and horrible all in one. It was not good for business to let feelings rule your actions, Father would often say, and she had well and truly done that. However, there were more urgent issues to deal with now.

Johanna pushed herself across the dance floor. "Excuse me, excuse me. Please let me through."

That earned her a few turned heads and surprised expressions. One nobleman said something lewd about the prince, but fortunately he was too drunk for his words to make sense.

Johanna was about halfway when the doors to the hall burst open and a couple of palace guards ran in. The panicked neighs of horses drifted into the hall through the doors which the guards had left open. People stopped dancing. The orchestra played on, but several of the musicians were looking at the open door instead of the conductor. A couple of noblemen ran into the foyer.

One of the guards was talking to the king, who nodded. His face looked pale and old. He dismissed the guard with a wave of his hand and rose.

The music stopped. Now even the last couples stopped dancing. Some people made complaining noises, others wondered aloud about the time.

"Friends, family," the king said. Even his voice sounded tired. "It seems like it is time to end the festivities. Please go home and be safe."

Two guards accompanied him down the steps.

People around Johanna protested.

"What? It's too early."

"What's going on?"

The king said no more. He made his way through the hall surrounded by the royal guards to fend off the questions.

Johanna felt revolted. How had the country ended up with such a weak man for a king?

He was not going to tell the people of the predicament he was in? He was not going to warn them about what he'd done or apologise? Pray for their safety? Even tell them that the city was on fire?

The orchestra members were packing their instruments and the first people were already leaving the hall.

She'd better go and find Father.

But now that everyone was agitated and looking around for their friends and family, she couldn't see him anywhere. Not in the hall and not in the entrance foyer, where courtiers were playing business as usual, handing the noble lords and ladies back their coats and cloaks. A line of people filed out of the entrance. A concerned murmur filled the space where previously there had been music and merrymaking.

Johanna pushed through the crowd, looking for Father's blue coat. She called him and asked people if they'd seen him. No one had.

Then a man on the front porch yelled, "There!"

A woman shouted, "Oh, look! Is that near our house?"

Another woman shrieked.

Several people started yelling at once.

"What is that thing?"

"It's a work of evil magic."

Johanna was in the back of the crowd and could only see the orange glow of the fire against the pillars of the entrance porch, but she'd seen the fire devil.

There was a commotion outside, voices shouting, horses neighing, the crack of whips.

A gust of wind brought a wave of heat from across from the city. It filled the foyer and blew open all doors in the entrance hall. Curtains billowed; the candles blew out. A scent of fire wafted on the wind. People around Johanna pushed and screamed. The wind pricked with magic.

Several people turned around and ran back towards the palace, but the palace guards were just shutting the doors and wouldn't let anyone in.

One guard called, "Everyone go home, go home now!"

Outside on the steps, groups of nobles were still waiting for their coaches to turn up. A long line of them filed out the gate. The horses were nervous and several grooms had trouble keeping their charges under control.

The animals could smell magic. They had been smelling magic all day.

Johanna walked up and down the stairs, yelling for Father, but she didn't see him and no one knew where he was. She couldn't imagine that Father would have gone home without her. Where was he? Father was the only family she had left. Panic clamped around her heart.

She ran up and down the stairs along the line of people waiting to be picked up by coaches.

All the nobles were agitated, looking around for family, craning their necks to see if their coaches had arrived yet. She spotted Julianna Nieland, crying on the shoulder of her brother. At least they were together. Other nobles, too, were in panic, wondering aloud about the safety of their houses. Older people talked about legendary fires of the past, most of which had resulted in significant damage to large parts of town. That did nothing to ease people's minds.

Some people were too nervous to keep waiting and walked out the gate. The church bells were still ringing. Horses neighed and their handlers shouted. Over the top of all that noise came the occasional pop of flames.

Father had to have been left behind inside the palace. That was the only conclusion Johanna could reach. Maybe if she asked the guards, they would open the door for her.

The moment she decided to go back, there was a tremendous crash, followed by a growl, and splintering of wood. One of the solid palace doors had burst open in a jagged hole of splinters. Metal flashed in the darkness underneath the porch. A guard shouted, his voice suddenly cut off in a snarl.

A woman screamed. Several dark shapes came out of the wrecked door and bounded into the forecourt. They were soft-footed and agile like cats, but much bigger.

People were pushing back up the stairs. Johanna was in the middle of the mad crowd, barely able to see where the steps were. She stumbled several times, each time afraid that she would fall and that the crowd would trample her.

A young woman fell and couldn't get up because other people were stepping on her dress. Nobody seemed to care. Johanna tried to reach out to the woman, but her arm wasn't long enough and the crowd swept her away.

A horse in the forecourt reared, kicking its front legs. The coach behind it tipped on its side. The cabin splintered. Several of the dark creatures ran to it. One grabbed the horse by the throat. There was a woman's high-pitched scream—cut off. A snarl.

"Oh, by the Holy Triune," a man called out.

It was surely a sign of despair that *nobles* were invoking the Triune.

Johanna gathered the folds of her dress around her, but the awkward hoops made it hard to move. She couldn't see her feet. Couldn't see where the steps were. People pushed her in all directions. Some were trying to get down, others, like her, wanted to get up. There was screaming. There were snarls. Harsh voices of men in a foreign language in the forecourt.

Johanna reached the porch, ran between the marble columns and stepped through the wrecked door. The bottom of her dress caught. The wind had blown out all the lights in the foyer. Snarls and growls and screams continued behind her.

She ran across the foyer with its floor covered with glass and splintered wood, into the big hall where it was dark but where mere moments before everyone had been dancing and laughing. She went out the side door into the garden room, dark, too, with a lingering scent of perfume where Queen Cygna had been. A sharp breeze cut in through the open doors on the far side of the hall. The glass lay in shards on the ground. Someone ran in, carrying a sword. He stopped.

"No! Go back!" His voice was rough with fear.

Johanna pressed herself against the wall in an alcove. She didn't *think* his shout was directed at her.

Several figures ran into the gallery from behind her, over Princess Celine's gravestone. Three—four men with long spears. With them was a dark, round-backed and long-haired creature that broke into a flat-footed run. It spotted the guard and grabbed him around the throat before he could run. He screamed as he fell, and the animal snarled, shaking its head vigorously so that the dead man's legs flopped from one side to the other like a rag doll.

One of the bandits whistled hard. The creature lifted its head and loped back to its owners. It halted in a rectangle of moonlight that fell into the gallery through a window. It had small, furry ears, little beady eyes, and a long nose that wriggled as the animal turned its head and looked from side to side. A bear.

It passed not a few steps from where she hid. She pressed

herself into the alcove as much as she could. The door to the main hall was at her back and it could open at any time. Worse, the wood showed her what was happening on the other side of the door.

A couple of citizens had entered the hall. Silhouetted against the glare from the fires outside, she counted two men in uniform and a group of five or six nobles, judging by the clothing. A woman in the group was crying, holding her companion, a man in a ruffled shirt. Another group followed them, these ones running from whatever pursued them outside.

A second bear bounded into the entrance, followed by two tall men in furs with long hair.

"It's following us!" one of the women screamed.

A men yelled, "Be gone with you, demon!"

But the bear jumped for his throat with a snarl. The man's shout turned into a scream. While the two bears rounded up the nobles in the far corner, the bandits who had walked past Johanna had entered the hall where they met up with their comrades with claps on shoulders. One of the men whistled.

As one, the two bears leapt into the group of nobles.

Johanna hardly dared breathe.

People tried to run, but the women wore stupid dresses that were not suited to running. The men were unarmed, had never held a weapon and had no idea how to defend themselves. None had any magic, except Johanna, and she had no idea how to use it to help them. She couldn't stand it any longer; she had to step away from the door.

In the chaos of the garden room, the panicked shouts became screams of terror, mixed with unearthly snarls. Something fell with a thud across the open doors into the hall, a few steps away from her. It was one of the nobles, dressed in court finery. The side of his head hit the ground hard. He twitched and didn't move. A dark stain spread out from under him.

Johanna pressed herself against the wall, careful not to touch the wood. She didn't dare run towards the garden. Once she was there, she was trapped because with this dress she couldn't even begin to try climbing the walls as Kylian had done. But the bandits would discover her soon.

The screams became less and trailed off altogether. The only sounds now were the foreign voices, and the snorts and sniffles of the bears.

Those voices became, too, became softer, as if the bandits were walking out of the other side of the hall. Johanna pressed her hand to the wood once more, just in time to see the silhouettes of bandits and the bears in the doorway as they walked into the foyer.

What now?

Johanna sneaked to the door and looked around the corner.

A single torch still burned in the hall close to the door. She stepped carefully around the body of the nobleman and slipped the light out of its bracket.

Holding it aloft, she slowly turned around. The floor of the hall was covered in bodies, noblemen in their finery with bloodstains spreading on their white shirts, noble ladies with their dresses ripped.

A wave of dizziness overcame her.

Father. She desperately didn't want to look at the dead, but took her torch to each body on the floor. All those fine clothes covered in blood. Several victims had their faces ripped off.

Father was not there.

Dazed as if in a bad dream, she went into the entrance hall, where she found the bodies of five guards in puddles of blood. No one left alive there either.

The palace steps were empty, orange in the glow of the fire.

In a corridor off the hall, she found another body in brown robes. One of the Shepherd's helpers. Her head reeled with the idiocy of it all. Who in their right minds would kill a harmless priest?

But a chill took hold of her. Priests were probably what the attackers had been after.

The door to a room on the right stood open. Johanna went inside. Her footfalls were soft on luxurious carpet. This appeared to be an audience room of some sort, with a number of chairs around a low table.

Even before she saw them, Johanna knew by the tang of blood that there were dead people in this room. Part of her wanted to run away. She had seen enough blood to last her a lifetime, but part of her had to know who the victims were.

On the couch, a red stain spread out from the body of a woman in a long black gown with lace. Queen Cygna's veil had fallen off, and her open-eyed face looked surprised. There was a second body on the carpet. Johanna didn't need to see the Carmine cloak to recognise the king.

She brought her hand to her mouth to stop herself crying out. Her head was reeling. What had King Nicholaos done to justify this carnage?

Worse, somewhere in the palace, the men were still on their rampage. They would find Roald. He would not be able to defend himself.

Saarland was finished. Everything was lost.

CHAPTER 13

SURPRISINGLY, Johanna's head remained clear enough to think.

First, the crown and staff were symbols of the Carmine House, and no bandits should get their hands on them. She dropped to her knees to fish the crown out from under the table. The staff, though, was under the king's body. Carefully, she rolled the king over. She had to do her best not to focus on the gaping wound in his stomach or she would surely faint, or throw up, or both. His face was undamaged, with his eyes half open. Carefully, she unfolded his fingers, still warm, and removed the staff. She took it and the crown into the corridor. A few doors down was a broom cupboard. Johanna stumbled in, upsetting a bucket with the bottom of her dress, and placed the precious items on the top shelf. She pushed the door shut. There. At least the bandits would have to look for the symbols of Carmine power.

Next, she had to get out and save herself and Father and the house. Then they would take the *Lady Sara* upriver and go to Mother's family.

It felt improper to walk away from the King and Queen, who could have been her parents-in-law, but she could do nothing except whisper a few lines of prayer. King Nicholaos would have liked that.

The hallway was still empty. As fast as she dared without making too much noise, Johanna ran out the door. The steps were awkward because she couldn't see her feet in that stupid dress. Then through to the forecourt, now a mess of ruined coaches, dead horses, bodies and fine clothes covered in blood. Already, flames licked the top of the palace roof.

She stopped briefly at each body, but saw none that looked like Father.

A man with a bear stood at the gate. It gave a low grunt, probably because it smelled Johanna. The man said something and the animal settled.

Johanna slipped out of a side gate.

First she had to go home to get changed out of this ridiculous dress.

She ran through the streets of the merchant district. Many people ran through the streets, some carrying packs and children. A coach driver was trying to control his panicked horse while a noble family got into the cab. Where would they be going? These bandits were destroying everything in sight. The sky was orange with the glow of the fire that would lay all of the inner city to ashes. This was worse than the big fires of the past.

Johanna ran. The hoops of the dress flopped awkwardly around her legs. Her shoes hurt. She wished she had her clogs.

Once she spotted a group of men with two hairy and flat-footed bears.

One pushed in a shop door with ease, before a man threw a burning torch inside the shop. Within moments, flames burst out the windows and the glass broke. The men laughed in their guttural, foreign voices.

Johanna ran.

Her house. Father, Nellie.

The houses at the far end of her street were already on fire. Against the glow, a group of people were fighting in the street. Women screamed. A dark shape lay motionless on the cobbles.

Fire reflected in the upstairs windows of Johanna's house, still untouched but probably not for long. She ran up the front steps, pushed the front door open. Her heart jumped. Would Father have made it back here?

"Nellie, Father?"

There was no reply, except the sound of breaking glass from further down the street.

"Nellie, where are you?"

Johanna walked into the kitchen—empty—the living room—empty, too. Koby would have gone home. Nellie's sewing work lay on the table in the living room, but obviously, she wasn't here either.

It was useless. There was no one here, and too little time to look for them. Johanna ran upstairs, pulling at the laces that held her bodice together. The bodice loosened, but she couldn't reach all the buttons. She pulled the bodice down, and then tried to lift it over her head, but it was no use. She pulled at the skirt with the hoops. The dress was stuck. "Nellie!"

There was no reply. She pulled again, but the fabric was too tough. She stumbled down the stairs into the kitchen. Now where did Koby keep the knives? She rummaged through the drawers, eventually finding a pair of scissors. They were old and blunt, and cutting through the fabric was hard, but she freed herself from the skirt with the hoops and then managed to wrench the buttons loose. *Sorry, Mistress Daphne.*

Then she went back up the stairs in her underclothes.

People were shouting in the street. The smell of smoke drifted under the door. She took her comfortable everyday dress from the cupboard and slipped it on. Then her vest over the top. Then she collected a handful of other clothes in a soft travel bag that she had used to go to Lurezia.

Then back to the kitchen, grabbed a tea towel, and yanked the handle of the pump until water came out, wet the towel and tied it over her nose and mouth. Then she grabbed Father's long coat from the stand, wet it as well, and put it on. It was freezing. Then her clogs. And her second-best shoes just to be certain. She buttoned up the bag.

She opened the front door. A cloud of acrid smoke billowed through the street. Several people ran past at high speed.

She pulled the front door shut behind her and ran down the steps, down the street the way she'd come. Fire was already eating at the neighbour's house.

Down the street, into the marketplace, past burning shops. A woman called her name. "Johanna, stop, Johanna!"

She stopped, seeing a thin figure run towards her.

"Nellie!" She swept Nellie up in her arms. She smelled clean and warm

"Oh, thank the holy spirit, Mistress Johanna, you're alive."

"Where is Father?"

"Didn't he come back with you?"

"No, I ran from the palace. I couldn't find him anywhere." A deep sense of guilt took hold of her. She should have looked better. Father would be around there somewhere looking for her. What if he was injured and needed her help?

"I was looking for you and Koby," Nellie said. Firelight reflected in her eyes. "And then I saw the fires and saw those creatures. I didn't know what to do. Those are the demons, right?"

"They're bears. They came into the palace," Johanna said. "The king is dead. The queen is dead."

Nellie clamped her hands over her mouth. "What about Prince Roald?"

"I don't know, Nellie." How many people had been killed there?

"Let's go home and wait for the master."

"We can't. There's fighting in the street. The house will burn soon. No one is even trying to put out the fire." All the houses were built mostly of wood. There would be nothing left of the city.

"No. Then where can we go?" Nellie's voice sounded small.

"I was going to the *Lady Sara*." But a sense of dread took hold of her. She had wanted to take the sloop upriver and wait out the trouble, but without anyone to handle the cows, could she even get it out of the harbour?

They ran through the streets. Every time Johanna saw the silhouette of a man, she hoped it was Father. Maybe he would have gone to the harbour as well. Several times, they had to hide away from bands of men with bears.

There was fighting at the quayside as well, and men were

breaking windows of merchant offices. A fire burned in a warehouse, and its reflection of the flames in the water was gold.

Father's office was still safe, but a fight blocked Johanna and Nellie's way to it.

The fire in the Deim warehouse had spread to neighbouring warehouses.

"Look at that, Nellie. It's getting so close to the armoury." If that caught fire, there would be disaster.

The ships' boys had moved the *Lady Sara* to the dock at Father's barn, which was still free of fire, but she and Nellie couldn't get there because the warehouses along the wharf were on fire.

Nellie froze. The firelight reflected in her eyes. She raised her hands to her mouth. "It's terrible. What can we do? Where can we go?"

"Come with me."

Johanna ran to the quay. The low tide had uncovered a set of barnacle-covered slippery steps that ran down to the water. Between the larger boats lay a dingy with a pair of oars. Johanna jumped in, starting to untie the knot.

"Come, quickly. Be careful, though, it's—"

Nellie gave a little yell and slipped, falling in a heap on the steps.

Johanna jumped out, almost slipped herself on the algae on the steps.

"Are you all right?"

Several men yelled on the quay above them. There was the sound of running footsteps. Johanna threw Father's dark cloak over herself and Nellie and crouched on the steps. The men ran past.

The roof of the armoury was now on fire. "Quick, Nellie." She more or less dragged Nellie into the boat.

Then she untied the rope and grabbed the oars. Her first stroke missed the water and the right oar clanged into the hull of the large boat.

She pushed the oars deeper. They now found resistance and slowly, the dinghy moved into open water. Oof, it was a long time since she'd done this.

As they pulled away from the quay, the glow of fire became stronger. The entire row of offices on the quay were on fire. A couple of men ran across with buckets. Johanna wasn't sure where they were going or what they hoped to do.

Nellie was crying. "Oh, what can we do, what can we do?"

"Be quiet, that's what. We don't want to draw attention to ourselves."

They reached the sea cow barn and went in under the ship doors. The animals were restless, sloshing in the water, blowing and snorting. They weren't crazy—they could feel that something was up.

Several bumped the dinghy, increasing Nellie's panic even further.

There was a rustle in the corner of the barn, amongst the stack of crates.

Johanna called, "Loesie? Loesie, are you there?"

A couple of crates moved aside, and Loesie rose, her eyes wide in the glow of the fires. "Ghghghgh!" Her eyes were wide. She pointed to the door, where fire was reflected in the water.

"Yes, the whole city is on fire. They were demons, as you said. The royal family has meddled with evil magic and now the demons are angry." Oh, why had Master Willems said nothing about it earlier? Most of the merchants knew of his hidden talent. They would have believed him, even if they'd never say so in public. They would have started rumours and people would have been warned.

And now . . . the entire sky glowed orange with fire in the direction of the palace. There was shouting and screaming. Glass shattered. Things exploded in the warehouses.

"We have to get out, before they discover us," Johanna said. *Before the armoury goes up.*

"But how?" Nellie sounded close to tears.

"We'll take the *Lady Sara*."

"But you don't know anything about sloops."

"I know a bit." Not much, and she'd only seen the deckhands do things. She had no doubt that getting the cows harnessed and going in the same direction seemed easier than it was.

"Ghghghghgh," Loesie said, pointing at her chest.

"Loesie knows about sloops," Johanna said. "She's come here by herself." Although the barge owned by Loesie's family was much smaller than the *Lady Sara*.

Nellie edged further away from Loesie.

Loesie was already wriggling the harness rigging off the hooks, and filling the feed pouches with carrots, like Johanna had seen her father's boatsmen do many times. The cows splashed and snorted in the water, raising their rounded and whiskered snouts; they wanted the carrots. More than anything else, they wanted to get out of here. But even over the noise they made, there was the sound of shouting at the quay.

Johanna opened the barn door a fraction.

Down the wharf, a group of bandits attacked a group of men. There was shouting, swords were drawn. Several of the men looked like palace guards. The others were rogues with long hair and leather jerkins. They had dogs, and a shaggy bear that ran across the quay. It disturbed her how well those large creatures obeyed people. She'd heard about bear magic, but what was the power of bear magic? Why couldn't she feel it?

One, then two people fell onto the cobbles and didn't get up.

Johanna felt chilled watching. These bandits just mowed innocent people down as if they were animals. Whatever the royal family had done, this didn't justify it.

Loesie had walked down the platform to the water and had hooked the rigging onto the sea cows' harnesses. Six animals were already chomping on carrots; a couple of big hairy bodies were jostling for the remaining two spots.

"Come, Nellie, help me." Johanna grabbed the corner of a bag of carrots. It was much too heavy for her alone to lift. Nellie grabbed the other corner. Together, they heaved it out of the barn, onto the jetty and the gangplank, onto the flatly sloping cargo hatch of the *Lady Sara*.

They carried a number of other sacks to the deck. There were potatoes, firewood, oiled cloth, and crates of which Johanna had no idea what they contained, but it would be something useful, because things needed for the boats were stored in here. Freight went into the warehouse.

"Take as much as you can," she said to Nellie when passing her on the way out.

Nellie was crying; the front of her apron was filthy. "Oh, Mistress Johanna, I don't think I can lift any more. My arms are so sore. What are we going to do?"

"We'll stay alive, that's what we'll do. We have to get out of here before they discover us. We can come back later, when the fires are out and the demons have had enough of setting fire to things." *Or until there is nothing left to burn.* Johanna's arms were sore, too, but she wasn't going to say anything about that.

"But where can we go?" Nellie's eyes were wide.

Fire lit up the sky in a terrible display of orange. The palace guards were still fighting on the quay in front of Father's office. The building itself was on fire. More and more bandits ran onto the quay, and the poor guards were heavily outnumbered. Any moment and the bandits would start setting fire to the boats.

Loesie walked along the side of the *Lady Sara*, holding the reins. A tricky operation. If the cows panicked and bolted, she would go over the edge or let go of the reins. Many an inexperienced boatsman had spent hours waiting for escaped clutches of cows to return after such a mishap.

Johanna heaved a couple more bags on board. She helped Nellie with a stack of oiled cloth.

The roof of the armoury was on fire and it would be a matter of time before something exploded. The cows would panic. This was their only chance to get out.

Then there was a heavy splash: someone had fallen into the water.

Johanna gasped and turned around, but Loesie still stood on the deck.

"Look, there!" Nellie sat on the cover to the cargo hold, pointing.

On the other side of the harbour, a bandit peered into the darkness of the water, bow drawn. He didn't fire. Possibly he couldn't see the head of the man swimming. But backlit against the fires at the quay, Johanna could.

"Who is it?" Nellie asked.

"I don't know. One of the ships' boys or fishermen, probably. Let's go."

"But he'll drown."

"Looks like he swims very well." Surprisingly well, actually. "He'll save himself. Is everyone ready?"

Loesie had the rigging tied up securely. The sea cows were pulling at their harness. Johanna jumped onto the jetty and loosened the ropes. The *Lady Sara* slowly receded from the quay.

"Ghghghgh!" Loesie stood at the stern. She had tied up the reins to the bar across the deck for that purpose. She pointed at the water.

The swimmer was coming in their direction. A weak man's voice sounded over the water. "Stop . . . stop . . . don't leave without me."

What to do? What if he was one of the rogues? No, that couldn't be.

"Loesie, wait. We'll pick him up. Nellie, come on. Stop crying. Help me with this rope." The trailing end of the rope had fallen into the water. Johanna pulled it to the harbour-side of the boat, and tried to throw it at the man. But the rope was heavy with salty water. The rough fibre scratched her hands. When she threw it, she almost toppled into the water after it.

The rope made a splash in the water. It fell far short of the swimmer.

In her mind, she heard Adrian's laughter. *It will be a long time before you make a decent deckhand, mistress*. He'd said that so many times after she'd fumbled trying to "help" him. Then again, she had never considered that one day she would have to be a real deckhand.

To her surprise, the end of the rope hadn't disappeared under water: there was a wooden float on the end.

The swimmer had come closer. She whispered as loudly as she dared, "Here, hang onto the end of the rope!"

Moments later he grabbed the float. Johanna hauled at the rope, but couldn't lift him out of the water.

"Use the handholds!" she yelled down, but either he didn't hear it or he couldn't see them. "Nellie, Loesie, help me!"

It took all three of them, or mostly Loesie and Johanna, to

pull the man up on the deck. He fell to his hands and knees, coughing. He wore a dark jacket of velvet that would have been very heavy in the water judging by the size of the puddle that formed around him. His trousers had ripped and were covered in mud.

"C . . . cold." His teeth chattered.

Despite the state of his clothes, he didn't look like a common citizen. In fact, he looked like he had been a guest at the ball.

There were shouts from the quay. A group of huge men with long hair and leather jerkins ran across, pursuing a couple of palace guards who ran onto the wharf where the *Lady Sara* had been moored.

"Let's go!" Johanna yelled at Loesie. "Go, go, go! Come on, help me get him into the cabin." This to Nellie.

Nellie came and grabbed the man's other arm. He went into another coughing spasm.

"Killed, they're all killed," he whispered. He was shivering.

Johanna pulled him to his feet and together with Nellie, moved across the narrow walkway between the sloping lids on the cargo hold and the railing. Meanwhile Loesie yanked at the reins. The sea cows threshed in the harness; they wanted to be out of here. Slowly, the boat started moving again.

A group of men with two bears ran onto the quay. One threw a burning torch which trailed sparks as it flew through the air. It landed on the deck, but Johanna could kick it off the other side before it had ignited anything. The flames hissed out into the water and probably spooked the sea cows, but fortunately, that made them move more quickly.

Soon, the *Lady Sara* was too far away from the wharf to be within their reach. Shouts drifted over the water and echoed in the stillness. They sounded like curses, but in what language she didn't know.

Then—a brief moment of eerie calm, followed by a huge roar of fire. The very air was alive with vibration. Next, the roof of the armoury blew sky high. The sound wave followed moments later, and a blast of hot air. Burning debris rained over the surrounding quay. A ball of fire billowed out, devouring every-thing in its path. Every boat within reach of the fireball was set alight, right down to the steps where Johanna and Nellie had taken the dinghy.

Nellie and Johanna finally reached the cabin with their charge. The door was narrow and it took some manoeuvring to get the man inside, unsteady on his feet as he was.

Once inside, Johanna sat him on the chair at Father's writing desk while she searched for blankets or any spare men's clothes that Father or the deckhands might have stored here.

The cabin's main windows faced away from the glow of the inferno. While moonlight shone into the side window, it was pitch dark in the far corners of the cabin. There was a storm light against the back wall, but while there was probably a candle in it, she had no way to light it. Tomorrow, she would have to get out the flint and steel and get the galley fire going, but for now, they would have to survive in the dark. She hoped there would be wood or peat on board. Stupid that she hadn't checked. It would be miserable on board without a fire.

Their refugee's teeth chattered.

Johanna found a blanket on a shelf and handed it to him. "Here, take off your wet clothes and use this blanket."

He rose from the chair and held his arms wide. "Can you . . . can you help me?" He shivered so much that he could barely speak.

For one moment Johanna considered that undressing a man would be seen as highly inappropriate, but then she decided to hell with it. He was wet, cold, exhausted. They were all tired and should help each other.

With hands numb through fatigue and cold, she tackled his sodden jacket—oh boy, that thing was heavy. She gave it to Nellie to find a place to hang it to dry. Nellie disappeared into the door at the back that led to the galley.

Then the shirt. She peeled it off his thin arms.

Through the window at the front of the cabin, she could see Loesie in the moonlight, standing at the stern watching the cows.

The *Lady Sara* made a slight turn. Moonlight came into the window and showed her the man's face.

It was Prince Roald.

CHAPTER 14

JOHANNA STARED at Prince Roald, not knowing what to say. All she could think of was the way he had stared at her chest during the ball, which now seemed ages ago.

Behind her Nellie gasped. "Mistress Johanna, what are you doing?"

A soft glow spread through the cabin. Nellie stood the door opening carrying a storm light. Bless the *Lady Sara*'s crew. Someone had left coals burning in a firebox.

Johanna would have laughed had this been a normal day. With her taking off Roald's shirt, this could be seen in an entirely different way. But it was not a normal day, and he was shivering and his clothes soaking wet. Did Nellie ever stop worrying about what was appropriate?

Also, she obviously didn't recognise him. With the way in which his parents had kept him hidden, how many people would know what the prince looked like?

Johanna handed Nellie the wet shirt. "Here, hang that out, too." She was starting to shiver as well, and hoped that there would be more blankets.

Roald gave a sob. His face twisted into a pained mask. "They're all gone," he cried. "All gone, all gone!" He spread his hands. His palms were scratched from where he had cut himself clambering up the rope.

"I know." Johanna draped the blanket over his shoulders. If he was a normal person, she might have hugged him, but now she didn't know if it would make him angry. Or, heaven forbid, if it would make him stare at her breasts again. He was much stronger than she was and if he got something in his mind, she didn't think she could stop him.

That thought disturbed her deeply.

What were they supposed to do? She looked out the window.

The sloop had turned upstream into the mouth of the Saar River. Houses made way for farms and barns. The glow of fire lit up the fields and the willows. A herd of black-and-white cows stood at the riverbank with the glow of fire turning them pale orange. Their distraught moos echoed over the landscape.

The entire inner city was on fire. The palace was destroyed. Father's office, destroyed. Their house, destroyed.

Anger burned in her.

"We will get whoever did this. We will avenge whoever died here. We will avenge our king and queen."

"How do you know they're dead?" Nellie asked, her voice timid. "They might have fled like us."

"I saw the bodies," Johanna said. "They're all dead, most of the people who were in that hall."

"What about your father?"

Johanna shrugged. "I don't know." Her eyes clouded over.

"They're dead!" Roald cried. He sank to his knees, leaned his head against cabin wall, pushed himself off the wall and let himself fall back against the wood. His forehead hit the wall with a clunk.

Johanna gasped.

He did it again, and again.

"Your Highness, stop. Please stop!" She pulled at his shoulders, but he slipped from her grip and continued to bash his head.

Nellie looked as if she had seen a ghost. Her lips moved. *That is Prince Roald?*

He squealed, "All gone, all gone! Like my sister. Dead."

With every word, he bashed his forehead into the wall.

Johanna yelled, "Stop it!"

He'd hurt himself. She threw herself between the wall and his head. His forehead hit her hard in her right breast. She had to clamp her jaws to stop herself from yelping. He wailed and let himself slide to the floor. She fell, too, unbalanced by the movement, and collapsed on top of him. He was screaming and threshing about, hitting his hands on the legs of the chair.

Nellie started screaming, too.

"Be quiet, both of you!" Johanna screamed as loud as she could, while she struggled to pin Roald's arms down.

Nellie fell quiet and a moment later, Roald did the same. His eyes stared into nothingness. He was panting, his pale-skinned and hairless chest heaving rapidly. His lips moved but no sound came out. Chilling. Johanna had no idea what to do or what to say that would not set him off again. She knew nothing about people who weren't right in the head.

"Mistress Johanna?" Nellie said, timid.

Johanna glanced up at her, still keeping Roald down.

"Are you all right?"

"As soon as he calms down, I will be."

Nellie blinked, her eyes wide. "Mistress Johanna, do you know that you're wrestling the crown prince?"

"I guess I've noticed."

"But . . . but . . . you can't do that."

"I should have let him hurt himself?"

Nellie swallowed visibly. She was still staring at Roald as if he was something horrendously evil, like her brain was trying to process what Johanna already knew. "He isn't . . . he wouldn't . . ."

"I don't know what he would or wouldn't do. I don't know anything about his . . . condition."

Nellie backed further into the door. The words *I don't want to deal with an idiot* on her face. "But you can't . . ." Her chest moved in quick breaths. "He is . . ."

"All right, all right." Johanna released him, since he appeared to have calmed down.

Roald sat up straight and stared at Nellie, or rather, at her dress. A button had come undone. She looked down, noticed it. "Oh." She did it up, her cheeks going red, and then she curtsied. "Your Highness." But her face showed her fear.

"You have big tits."

"What?" Nellie's voice rose into a squeak.

"Tits. Boobs. That's what you call them, isn't it?"

"Your Highness—I . . ." She gasped and clamped her hands over her chest. Her eyes were so wide that the whites showed on all sides. Poor Nellie, she looked like she was going to faint. Johanna put her hand on her shoulder and guided her out of the cabin into the cramped galley. Between the furnace and the wall there was barely room for both of them.

Johanna whispered, "Calm down, Nellie. He's not aware of the effect of his words." Or maybe he *liked* the effect of his words. Her voice sounded muffled in the constricted space.

"But he's an . . ." She lowered her voice and whispered, ". . . idiot."

"He's the only member of the royal family left alive."

Nellie gulped. "But did you hear what he said. It's simply scandalous."

"Do you want to know what he said to me while we were dancing?"

Nellie brought her hands to her mouth. "So that is why Celine became crown princess."

Johanna nodded. "But he's all we have now. Nellie, please listen. I don't know what's happened in Saardam, who is still alive and who isn't, except I know the king and queen aren't. I don't know who the bandits are except that they came in revenge because the king did something. I think he hired a necromancer to bring back Celine."

"He couldn't have done that! That would be the worst of evil magic. He supports the Church."

"Unfortunately, that's what he did. The king gave his fortune to the Church because he believed that Celine would be resurrected, or that they would cure Roald. But the Shepherd couldn't do that, of course. When he says during mass that the dead will live on, he means that their spirits live on in us. The king believed that Celine would come back to life."

"Why didn't he ask one of Roald's cousins to step in as crown prince? I'm sure Prince Jona from Burovia would have been more than happy to come here."

"Because all of that part of the royal family don't agree with the Church and have disowned the king. I think it was the King's plan to make the Reverend Romulus regent on behalf of Roald, but leave Roald on the throne. In any case, I don't know what will happen, but chances are we three—four, with Loesie—will have to get along with each other. Let's try to behave nicely."

Nellie swallowed, opened her mouth and swallowed again. Her expression said, *But she's bewitched* and *He's an idiot* and *He said a scandalous thing to me*. But, small-minded as Nellie might be, she wasn't stupid, so she said only, "Where can we go?"

"First, we need to find somewhere Roald can be safe. If you go down the ladder just outside the door, you'll get into the hold. It's big, but it's dry and empty. You'll find some blankets and oiled cloth down there. See if you can make a bed for us. I'll tell Loesie to tie up at fisherman's corner. Then we'll see what we can do in the morning. The fires may have calmed down enough for us to go back." She didn't really think so, nor did she believe that the bandits would just walk away from their prize after conquering it, but she didn't want to frighten Nellie more than necessary.

Nellie nodded, her face pale, and left.

Johanna went back into the cabin, where Roald lay on his back on the narrow bed. How had she not noticed the stench of male sweat before?

"Your Highness . . . You can get up."

He pushed himself into a sitting position, his face sweat-slicked and haggard. He passed a hand through his rumpled hair. "I'm so tired." And then a bit later, "Everyone always says bad things about me."

"Who does?"

"That girl doesn't like me."

Like that was a surprise. Poor Nellie.

She sighed. She didn't have the time or energy to argue or try to explain what he probably wouldn't understand. For some reason, Queen Cygna's words about her son came to her *Roald is a good man. He doesn't always understand, but he would never harm anyone.*

137

That might be true, but he was completely obsessed with the other sex and the different parts of their anatomy.

"You can sleep here," she told him. The captain's bunk wasn't much—very narrow—and the cabin was tiny and definitely not fit for a prince.

Johanna backed to the door. "Well, goodnight, Your Highness."

"No!" His eyes were wide.

"What's the matter? You can go to sleep. I have to help Loesie and Nellie. We have to get to a safe spot to tie up for the night."

"No, don't go. I need help."

Oh, she wanted to get out, because there was no way she was going to help him take off his trousers.

She backed to the door, stepped out and shut it. The last she saw was Roald sitting on the bed in his wet trousers.

The night air was cool and fresh. Loesie stood at the stern with the reins. Scuffling noises in the hold suggested that Nellie had found something to make a bed. Johanna joined Loesie at the bow, but everything seemed under control here. The entire horizon behind the boat lit up with orange light.

She had best check on Nellie.

When Johanna walked past the cabin, she glanced inside.

Roald still sat on the bed, his hands jammed between his knees, staring at the door. The only things that moved were his blinking eyelids. His face was utterly blank. He had not started to remove his clothes. Maybe he was used to people doing this for him. Maybe, with his simple mind, he didn't know how to do it.

A feeling of shame came over her.

Here was a young man confused and scared, who had lived hidden away from the world for most of his life. People might have told him that he was shameful and not worth anything. He'd lost his parents and was all alone, and this was how they treated him?

He frightened her, but that was not how she would want to be treated.

She braced herself and opened the door to the cabin.

"Your Highness, do you want me to help you?"

His expression remained blank.

A smile or some sort of reaction would have made her feel more comfortable, but she guessed the absence of a reaction was as good as an approval.

She knelt at his feet and undid shoelaces. They were wet, and she had to pull hard to get the knot out and even harder to get the shoes off his feet. His socks had lost shape with their soddenness. His feet were pale and slender, with long toes and clean nails, but the pads of his soles bore a few spots of callus. She wondered what he'd done to earn those.

Then she asked him to stand up, which he did without comment. Then she had to figure out how to undo his belt. The trousers were quite loose and fell down by themselves. Underneath he wore silken shorts with the Carmine Crest embroidered. Johanna had already decided enough was enough and there was no way she was going to bother with those. That would be asking for trouble. She never even saw Father in any state except fully clothed. Roald's legs were as thin as the rest of him. The skin had little pimples and a coating of blond hair. He had a rash on his upper legs. Was she meant to do anything about it?

His skin puckered in goose bumps. He had a few sparse chest hairs, but nowhere near the carpet she'd seen on the men who unloaded the ships.

She draped the blanket over him. "Come, Your Highness, get in the bed. You'll be warm."

He climbed awkwardly onto the narrow bed. Johanna draped the blankets over him and retreated to the door. "Well, goodnight. Sleep well."

He said, "I'm hungry. Can you get the cook to bring us some food?"

"We don't have a cook."

"What about the other girl? The one with dark hair and no tits."

"That girl is Loesie and she's steering the boat." It was going to be a very long trip if he kept talking about women like that.

"I'm hungry."

"We'll eat tomorrow." Once they got the furnace in the galley going and they were in a safe enough spot to stop.

"I want to go home."

"Me, too, but we can't."

"I want to go home. Why don't you take me home? That's what servants are for. That's what my father says: if you don't know what to do, ask the servants. They will help you. Is that right?"

"Yes, that's right, but I'm not a servant."

"Aren't you? But I thought . . ." He frowned at her, and then a spark of emotion lit his eyes. "I know. I remember you. You are going to be my wife."

"Your Highness?" Last he'd said was that he didn't want to marry her.

"I . . . I was only joking."

"Joking, Your Highness?" Her heart was thudding in her throat.

"I said you were ugly, but you aren't ugly. You're much prettier than the other girls."

"Um—thank you, Your Highness."

"But that doesn't matter now, does it? The other girls are dead. Everyone is dead." He rubbed his hands into his face and started sobbing. She positioned herself so that she could grab him if he started banging his head into the wall again.

"They're all dead. All dead!"

"Please, Your Highness . . ."

He didn't react. Johanna stood motionless in the cabin. Had he been a normal person, she might have sat on the bed and tried to comfort him, but he wasn't and he scared her.

"Come . . . Your Highness. Please go to sleep now." She felt so incredibly awkward. Mortified. She didn't want to touch him anymore. Not while he thought that she was going to marry him.

He looked up at the timber ceiling. There was a portrait of Mother in the cabin.

"This sloop is moving." It wasn't a question. He would know river travel from his trip to the sanatorium.

"It is."

"Where . . . where are we going?"

"For now, to find a safe spot. Then, to get help. To save Saar-land from the barbarians."

"Yes." He nodded. "That's good."

"Well then, I should check on the others." She grabbed the door handle.

"No, don't go."

"Your Highness?" She stopped, wondering if she would ever be allowed to escape to freedom.

He patted the edge of the bed. "Sit here. My mother does that."

How embarrassing. Queen Cygna sat with her son until he fell asleep?

"Tell me a story."

"I . . . I don't know any stories."

"But I have to have a story. I can't sleep without a story."

Johanna forced herself to come up with some silly story about a cat which jumped aboard a ship in the orient and trav-elled the world. Letting her mind wonder through Father's tales was strangely relaxing. She felt certain that he was alive, and that many other people were still alive, and that they'd rebuild the city from the ashes and that they'd drive out the bandits. After all, what nation that could send ships across the high seas would not be able to defend itself and rebuild?

While she spoke, he stared at the ceiling, and gradually, his eyelids fell shut and his breathing became heavy and regular.

When Johanna was certain that he was asleep, she rose and tiptoed to the door.

Outside, it was pitch dark, with the glow of the burning city reduced to a thin stripe on the horizon.

The cool fingers of the night reached through her clothes. The water rippled against the sides of the boat and occasionally there would be a snort or a splash from one of the cows.

Johanna could only just make out Nellie's silhouette, holding onto the railing watching the fires. Loesie was a ghostly white spot at the bow.

"Did you find what you needed in the hold?" Johanna asked.

"I tried my best, but it's very dusty down there, mistress. I found a straw sack and some blankets. We won't get wet, and we may not get cold, but that's all there is to be said."

"Thank you, Nellie."

Johanna joined her at the railing. Neither of them said anything for a while.

"Mistress Johanna?" Nellie's voice sounded timid.

"Yes."

"I didn't know the rumours were true."

"What rumours?"

"That the prince . . . is a halfwit." She let a silence lapse. "I know it's a horrible word, but what else do I say?"

"I guess it's true enough."

"So that is why Celine was crown princess even though she was younger."

"Highly likely." It didn't really matter anymore, since everyone was gone. Roald needed a wife. He needed children. Without the Carmine House, Saarland would be reabsorbed into Estland or annexed by Burovia, and that would not be good for anyone.

"Poor Queen Cygna."

Johanna didn't reply. A chill crept over her as she remembered the Queen's open eyes.

"What are we going to do, Mistress Johanna? You know that friend of yours scares me."

"I know, Nellie, but Loesie is a good person."

"She's touched by the Lord of Fire."

"Magic, Nellie. Magic."

"Oh, Mistress Johanna, don't say that!" She made a unity with her hand and glanced skyward.

Johanna shrugged, but Nellie couldn't see that in the dark. What would they do? Johanna and Nellie, a witch struck mute by magic and the only surviving member of the royal family, who, it occurred to her, would be the official king in exile.

"I think we need to get Roald to safety. We need to find advisors for him. We need to have an official ceremony to make him the king. Important people have to witness it."

And then? With the demons in possession of Saardam, there would be war. If Roald was too simple to want to reclaim the city, someone else would. Surely someone was still alive in the city? Father? And what would they do?

And then a chill. What about the Church? Would everyone who supported the Church be killed by these bandits?

In the pale moonlight, the river showed up as a bright ribbon of silver. They were coming up to the loop called Fisherman's Bend, where a couple of other sloops lay moored. Fortunately no one was on deck.

Johanna helped Loesie guide the cows to a free pylon. Lifting the heavy rope over the top of the pylon was hard, with her arms as cold and sore as they were, but Johanna and Loesie managed it without bumping into any of the other boats.

Loesie worked silently next to her, and Johanna almost forgot her friend's condition.

"Let's go to sleep," she said, when the sloop was tied up, and the cows untangled from the harness and left to graze. Her arms ached, her eyes felt gritty with tiredness.

Nellie sat on the sloping cover to the hold. She eyed Loesie warily when they passed.

Loesie gave a sniff that made Nellie flinch. Irritated that she didn't help, Johanna guessed.

"You can look after breakfast tomorrow," Johanna said to Nellie.

She expected protests about not knowing how to light the fire and where things were, but Nellie said nothing.

Johanna was first to descend in the ink-black hold where the glow from the storm light barely made any impact. She found the bed that Nellie had improvised: a rough sack filled with straw that was normally spread in the bottom of the hold to absorb any cheese juices and was still relatively clean. Nellie had spread blankets over it.

No one undressed. Nellie was too scared of Loesie to want to sleep next to her, so Johanna went in the middle. She pulled the blankets and then the oiled cloth over her. Nellie took off her shoes and went on one side, Loesie on the other.

Getting to sleep, though, was another thing altogether.

The blanket was itchy and straw kept poking through the material of the sack. The *Lady Sara*, being empty, rode high in the water, and was tugged by the current of the river. The hull softly bumped against the pylons.

Several times, Johanna got up, climbed up the stairs to check if the sloop was still tied up, which it was, or if other people had come, which they hadn't.

And she didn't know whether to be happy or sad about it.

CHAPTER 15

JOHANNA AWOKE to a ray of light on her face, feeling cold and sore all over. She stared at the bottom of the doors of the empty hold, where normally grain was stored.

She sat up, pushing the oiled cloth aside, letting biting cold air touch her skin. A thin shard of light came into the hold from where the cover had been left ajar. There was no sound except the slapping of water.

Nellie was still asleep next to her, wearing her clothes and resting her head on a pile of empty grain sacks. Loesie was gone.

Johanna rose. Her clothes were damp from the cloying humidity. She draped the cloth—normally used to cover the cargo in the hold—back over Nellie, who stirred. Her face, pale and smudged, scrunched briefly, but relaxed again as she rolled onto her back.

Poor Nellie.

Johanna clambered up the rickety ladder to the deck. The countryside around the boat was delicate green under a thick layer of mist. The mooring ropes were tied to a couple of mooring posts that were normally used by barges to wait until they could come into harbour. Last night there had been two other boats, but they had gone.

There was a small beach and reeds to the sides. A couple of ducks paddled along the edge of the reed bed.

The most eerie thing was the complete silence. The church bells had stopped ringing. If anyone was still shouting, their voices were inaudible from here. That raised the question: was there anyone left to shout at all?

Over the misty paddocks, she could see palls of smoke still rising from the city, although the flames would not be visible in daylight. From a distance the devastation looked oddly peaceful.

She could see no signs of life.

Loesie sat hunched at the captain's bench, with an oiled cloth over her shoulders, staring motionless over the riverbank. When Johanna came up to her, she started to sag sideways, then gasped and pulled herself upright. She looked around in a confused way.

Johanna sat down next to her. She had done a good job in detaching the sea cow harness from the stern and loosening their individual harnesses. The cows were grazing on the bottom, stirring up clouds of murky water punctuated with bubbles. Wherever there were sea cows, there were always bubbles.

"Have you seen anyone?"

Loesie shook her head.

"Any other ships?"

She shook her head again. Her face was pale and smudged.

"You go and have a sleep. I'll take over."

She rose and only then Johanna noticed a rusted knife in her hands.

"What are you doing with that thing? You said there was no one here."

Loesie clutched the weapon to her chest. "Ghghghghghghgh!" There was a wild look in her eyes.

"Whoa, calm down. I'm not going to do anything to you." Johanna held her hands up, heart thudding. For a moment, it was as if Loesie hadn't recognised her.

"Ghghghghghgh!" Loesie's voice sounded distressed. There were tears in her eyes.

She backed away slowly until she was a few paces away from Johanna, then turned on her heel and ran.

Nellie was just climbing out of the hold, and Loesie almost crashed into her. Nellie gave a startled shout when Loesie pushed past and disappeared into the hold.

Nellie strode to Johanna's side, her cheeks red. "That's what I mean, Mistress Johanna. She doesn't act like a normal person."

"There's nothing I can do about it," Johanna said. She both agreed with Nellie that there was something disturbingly wrong with Loesie, and wished she'd stop complaining. "Loesie is my friend. I'm not going to abandon her."

Nellie gave her the *I-never-approved-of-this-friend* look.

Good grief! If it wasn't for Loesie, they might all be dead along with a lot of other people in town.

Johanna let herself drop on the wooden shutters that covered the hold. The willow wood sang to her. It showed her smoke drifting through an orange sky. The glow from the fires reflected in the slow-flowing water of the river. There had been a shower overnight and now the banks of the river were cloaked in mist. The road along the river glistened with puddles.

The planks moved when Nellie sat down next to her.

"I'm sorry. I don't really want to abandon anyone either. I shouldn't have said that." She folded her hands in her lap. "But she does scare me. What is wrong with her?"

Johanna sighed. "I wish I knew."

Whatever had been done to Loesie scared her, too. Whoever had done it, and why. The images from the wood had shown her bears, and the body of a woman. She now wished that she had the basket Loesie had given her, since the magic faded from them after a few weeks, and, knowing what she knew now, she would like to see the images again.

"Have you seen anyone this morning?" Nellie asked. She scanned the horizon where mist cloaked the burning city. "Is anyone still alive?" Her voice sounded small.

"I don't know."

But at that moment, there was a faint sound of a whistle behind them. Johanna turned into the light of the early sun. Something moved on the road that led into town. She went into the galley to get the spyglass.

"What is it, Mistress Johanna? Can you see something?"

Johanna put the spyglass to her eye. The eyepiece fogged up but she wiped it with her dress.

"There." She pointed at the riverbank, where the group of

men was coming over a ridge, towards the city. There were at least fifty of them. Many of them rode horses. She could see no bears.

"I see them too. Can you see who they are?"

Johanna studied the people, still too far away to recognise faces. The view field of the spyglass was not very big and it was hard to hold it still for long enough to study individual people. They were also silhouetted against the sun. But several people wore furs or dark clothing. They also had dogs, hence the whistling.

"I don't know. It doesn't look good. Let's hide in the cabin. I don't want to be seen when they get here." Especially not with Prince Roald aboard.

They went into the galley, which had a small window to the side. Pressed against each other so that they could both see, Johanna and Nellie watched the group ride past: rugged men in leather jerkins with long and untidy hair, laughing and talking as if they owned the world. They were bandits.

Johanna only dared speak once they had passed. "They've occupied the town."

"Where are they from?"

"My guess: Burovia." But gangs of Burovian forest bandits would never come this far out of their usual home. Someone had to have ordered them here. Someone who was holding these bands of rogues together in a way they had never been before. And for some reason—was it just something that King Nicholaos had done?—they decided to invade.

"Do you still think we can go back home?"

Johanna shook her head. "Not now. Not with the prince. If they killed his parents, they'd have no trouble killing him. We need to make sure he's safe first."

Nellies eyes grew wide. "Then what are we going to do?"

"We should go the Aroden castle. The duke will help us. The castle will be a safe place for the prince while we find out what is going on in the city." Not to mention that her uncle lived there. He would surely help her find Father. "Come on, let's get going."

She rose and went to the bow where Loesie had tied up the harness and the individual ropes that held each of the cows. A standard team consisted of eight animals. The pull beam that stuck out the front of the boat had a central bar and eight cross-bars, each with a set of slots for the ropes that went from the cow's harness to the bow.

She untied the ropes and slowly reeled the animals in, one at a time. She asked Nellie to guide the ropes into the slots, and tie them off at the bar on the deck, but her knots were awkward and it was clear she had never done anything like this.

Neither, for that matter, had Johanna. She spent a long time getting cows into their right positions in the team. All she knew was that you started from the front, but the animals must have known that she was inexperienced, because they twisted the ropes and went into the wrong places, tangling up their harnesses. There was, she remembered too late, some sort of hierarchy in the team. The dominant animals were supposed to be at the front, but how could she workout which ones they were? One sea cow looked pretty much like the other.

Nellie stood helplessly to the side. The one time that she tried to help, she almost fell off the boat. Since Johanna didn't think Nellie could swim, she told Nellie to keep out of the way.

Meanwhile, the sun rose and rose. A couple of horses and carts came past, but most of those Johanna judged to be local farm traffic. They had to get moving.

"Look, can you go and get Loesie to help us?" she asked Nellie.

Nellie left and Johanna continued struggling with the tangling ropes and the cheeky cows.

There was a scream.

Johanna jerked around, letting the rope slip from her fingers. "Nellie!"

She came running towards Johanna. Her cheeks were red. "Oh, Mistress Johanna, it's awful. The prince . . ."

Roald. Her heart thumped. Something had happened to Roald. They'd forgotten to give him pills or some other medicine. "Is he all right?"

She made for the cabin, but Nellie held her back. "Yes, he's fine but you can't see him like this."

"What is wrong, Nellie?"

She burst into tears. "The prince . . . the prince . . ."

What?

"Calm down, Nellie. Tell me. Sit down." Johanna sat her on the edge of the cover of the cargo hold. She was shaking and shivering. Tears were running over her cheeks.

"The prince," Johanna prompted. She glanced at the horizon. They should really get out of here soon.

"I went to get the witch, as you said—"

"Loesie. Use her name."

"Loesie. I walked past the cabin, and the door opened. The prince came out, and he . . ." Her eyes widened. "He was in his underclothes. Scandalous!"

Johanna breathed out a heavy sigh and had to restrain herself from rolling her eyes. *He was in his underclothes!* Good grief. "Come on, Nellie. There's no time to worry about indecency. We need to hurry."

"But Mistress Johanna, I can't. I don't know how to say this: he tried to touch me. Indecently." She hid her face in her hands. "He grabbed me from behind, and he . . ." Her voice dissolved into sobs.

Oh, no. "Did he . . . hurt you?"

"No. I . . . hit him and I pushed him away. Oh, Johanna, I hit the crown prince."

"Did he seem upset when you hit him?"

"No. He laughed at me. But I hit the crown prince!"

"Calm down, Nellie. Sit here. I'll talk to him. But first, we have to get going. Here, hold onto these ropes, then I will get Loesie."

Johanna wobbled along the narrow walkway, her legs uncertain. It was one thing talking to Nellie like she knew what to do, but another having to deal with the problem. Roald was a man and he was strong even though he didn't look it. What would she do when he tried to grab her?

The door to the cabin was closed again. Fortunately. She'd deal with this later. There was no time now.

Johanna found Loesie under the oiled cloth in the hold. She lay down, but turned her head when Johanna came down the ladder. Her grey eyes blinked at the light.

"I'm sorry to keep you from your sleep, but I need your help. We need to get going, but I can't handle the sea cows by myself."

Loesie pushed herself up, attempting to straighten her dishevelled clothes. Johanna didn't like the look in her eyes. Far-off, not really there. Not herself at all. What was going on in that mind of hers?

"I want to go to Aroden castle. We'll be safe there. But I can't get the cows in the harnesses by myself." She almost said something about Nellie being useless, but that felt unkind. Nellie had never any experience in things like this, and Johanna couldn't blame her. But she was a nuisance. Once they got going, Nellie would be able to make herself useful by cooking, but even that meant Johanna had to get the furnace going, because Nellie wouldn't know how to do that.

There was so much to do. Normally, the *Lady Sara* had a captain and a minimum of four competent deck hands who knew what they were doing.

Loesie threw off the covers and accompanied Johanna up the ladder, past the door to the cabin—still closed—and to the front of the boat. She hissed and hmmmed and pointed at the rope harnesses. Yes, Johanna had probably gotten it all wrong.

Under Loesie's direction, they managed to get each animal tied up to their individual bars in the beam. Loesie untied the mooring ropes and hauled them in. Feeling the pressure against their backs, the cows started swimming. Johanna flung the bait into the water to keep them going and the boat slowly started moving. Johanna scanned the riverbanks, but could no longer see any people.

Next, the furnace.

She went into the galley. Next to the furnace lay a stack of peat bricks and a basket of kindling. She put kindling and one fire brick inside the stove, then stuck a stick from the kindling basket into the glowing coals of the firebox. When it burned, she used it to light the kindling. Soon, the fire was going.

Meanwhile, she'd gone through the cupboards in the galley and found a pan, a couple of battered plates and an assortment of cutlery. There was also a bag of oats, so they could make porridge. She was beginning to get very hungry. She left Nellie to this task, because it was high time to look after Roald.

She knocked on the door that connected the galley and the cabin. "Your Highness? Do you need any help?"

A muffled voice came through the wood. "If you're that crazy woman, then don't come in."

Nellie said, "That's what he's been saying all along, Mistress Johanna, and he's talking about me. He—"

Johanna shushed her and opened the door. Roald sat at the edge of his bed, wearing nothing but his underpants.

Nellie shrieked.

Roald laughed.

"Calm down, calm down, Nellie." But she noticed the skin on his chest, mostly hairless, but with a distinct tan. His arms were thin but with corded muscles. This probably accounted for the strength he had shown climbing up the side of the sloop last night. There was no way any of the women could win a physical argument with him, if he decided to do something stupid and if they needed to stop him.

His eyes, startlingly blue, met hers. He gave a dumb grin.

Johanna's cheeks grew warm. Had he no shame? "Are you all right, Your Highness?"

"I'm hungry. Where is breakfast?"

"We're working on it."

"I want breakfast. They always bring me breakfast at this time. Where are the servants in this place?"

"There are none. We're on a boat on the river. We should be lucky that we're still alive, but you're going to have to be a little bit more patient for breakfast."

"I'm hungry." His voice was angrier.

"Yes. We're hungry, too. Breakfast is coming." *It just might not be what you expect.* "But first, you must get dressed. You can't have breakfast like this. Wait, I'll get your clothes."

She went back into the galley, where Nellie was scrubbing the inside of the pan with a piece of cloth. Her cheeks were red with the effort.

"What are you doing?"

"This pan is disgusting."

"I'm sure that doesn't matter for once." It was only stained anyway.

"I'm not going to eat breakfast out of anything this dirty."

"The porridge will be cooked! Come on, Nellie, everyone is hungry! It doesn't matter."

"It matters to me. Everyone stop screaming at me! I can't do this. I'm useless." She let go of the pan, which fell to the floor with a clang. She hid her face in her hands and started sobbing.

Great. She was stuck on this boat with a prince who wanted to be served, a witch who couldn't speak and a maid who had fallen to pieces.

Johanna picked up the pan, filled it with water and set it on the stove. Then she turned to Nellie.

"Listen to me, Nellie. You're going to do this. This is not what I would have chosen to do today either, but this is what we've got. I, for one, would love to know where Father is." She had to pause because her voice threatened to crack. "But we've got other responsibilities. You and I are the only sane people on this ship and we're going to have to keep it together. So you're going to do your share of work, and stop complaining about things we can't do anything about, and just stop being prissy or I'll push you overboard. And I mean it!" Her voice had become louder while she was speaking, and the last sentence rang in the silence.

Nellie started at her. She opened her mouth, licked her lips and closed it again. "You wouldn't really do that, Mistress Johanna?"

Johanna shrugged. She felt ashamed. It was the first time ever she'd screamed at Nellie. She was losing it as well.

"Look, we're all tired and hungry. Make the porridge. We'll stop at a farm to see if we can barter something in return for some eggs or milk. I need Roald's clothes. Where did you hang them?"

"They were in front of the stove but I had to move them. They're not dry."

She handed Johanna a heavy bundle. The heavy velvet jacket was as wet as it had been last night. The shirt had some dry patches, but it was badly stained. The trousers were also still soaked.

"He can't wear this. He'll get sick."

"We don't have anything else."

"Can you hang it closer to the fire so it can dry?"

Nellie looked like she wanted to protest again, but she thought the better of it and took the coat and trousers from Johanna.

She took the shirt into the cabin. They really needed to get different clothes because, for his safety, Roald couldn't be seen in the Carmine jacket, but she didn't know that any of them had money, and the nearest river towns were not until they reached Estland. If they got that far.

"I'm sorry, Your Highness, the rest of your clothes are still very wet."

He took the shirt from her without a word. Made no attempt to put it on. His naked skin was covered in goose bumps, but it didn't seem to bother him.

"If you want breakfast, you're going to have to put the shirt on."

He simply spread his arms.

So, she had to do that for him as well, huh? She shook out the shirt in order to hide that it wasn't completely dry. In fact, damp was probably a better word for it. Yet he didn't flinch or shiver when she put his arms in and pulled the shirt over his shoulders.

While she did up the buttons, he glanced at the door. "Where is the crazy woman?"

"You mean Nellie?" Seriously, he was getting under her skin. Didn't anyone teach him manners? "She's not crazy. She's very upset that you touched her. You shouldn't do that anymore."

A small frown crossed his face. "I can't touch a girl? My father said that the whole country would be mine, with all the girls in it."

Well, your father was wrong, then. Good grief. "It is not appropriate to go around touching women, even if they are the women of your country. The women may be married to someone else, and the other person won't be happy."

"Oh." His frown deepened. "My father says I should get married. Are you married?"

"No, I am not, but—" Had he already forgotten that his father was dead? Did he understand what *dead* meant?

"If I marry you I can touch you, right?"

"Yes, but—"

"Then we should get married. I want to touch a woman."

"Maybe you should discuss that with your court advisors. A crown prince doesn't just marry the first girl he comes across."

"Oh, you mean the Reverend Romulus?"

Since when was he a court advisor? "Yes, if you want."

"Is he married?"

"No. He's a priest."

"Then how can he tell me what I should do?"

Johanna couldn't restrain a snort of laughter. "You best never let him hear that."

He giggled. "You think it's funny I said that?"

"It's not appropriate."

"When something is funny, it's never appropriate."

Johanna laughed aloud; she couldn't help it.

He gave a squeal. "You think I'm funny!" He slapped his thigh. "A woman thinks I'm funny. The other ones just sneak into my room and bow." He put on a high voice. "Your majesty, do you want tea? Do you want me to do up your shoelaces? Ha ha ha ha!"

He did such a convincing imitation of a courtier that Johanna laughed again.

"Shh, Your Highness, sit still so I can do up the buttons."

Laughing felt good. How nice it would be to be able to forget the horrific scenes from last night and the hopeless situation they found themselves in. Roald didn't really care. He was incapable of caring or had a short memory. Who knew what went on in his head? Because clearly, something went on in there and while he was certainly odd and childish, *stupid* was not how she'd describe him.

She did up the buttons on his shirt.

"I'm sorry, but your trousers are still really wet. I've asked Nellie to hang them close to the furnace."

He rose. "That doesn't matter. I don't like wearing them anyway."

"But you can't go outside like this. And you'll be cold." She looked around the cabin and her gaze rested on an empty grain sack that was tucked under the desk. "I can make you a skirt out of this, so at least you can go into the fresh air." Some of the Burovian warriors wore short skirts.

She crawled under the desk to retrieve the sack, aware of his keen gaze on her backside.

Did people in the palace really dress him every day? Did his mother do that for him? Surely he didn't treat all female courtiers like this. Did he? And they put up with that behaviour?

His waist was very slender and the sack fitted around him like a skirt. With great embarrassment, she noticed how his underwear strained in his crotch. Heavens.

She took his belt and looped it around his waist. "There." She stepped back looking at her handiwork.

"See? I didn't touch you."

Thank heavens.

"But I want to touch you."

"No, you can't."

"Why not?"

"Because I'm not a cheap woman."

"I have money. Lots of it. That's what sailors do, right?"

She cringed. "No, Your Highness, because you are not a sailor. You are a prince."

He let himself fall back on the bed in a theatrical gesture. "Being a prince is boring." He sighed. "If I'm nice, will you let me touch you?"

"Your Highness, you shouldn't speak of touching women all the time. That's not—" She'd almost said *appropriate* again, but she realised he probably had no idea of what it meant. That was his problem. He did not understand *appropriate*. "Touching women is very special. You don't talk about it with other people."

"Oh, like a secret?"

"Yes." Fine, if that got him to shut up.

"Oh, I like secrets. Can it be our secret? You and me?"

"Um—I suppose." She was desperate to get out of here.

At that moment, there was a squeal from the galley.

What now?

Johanna opened the door. Nellie stood at the stove staring at smoke rising from the pan. "Oh look, Mistress Johanna. This is much too hot!"

Johanna bent over the pan. Blackened porridge coated the bottom of it. This was probably why the pan had been dirty in the first place: it was too thin for cooking on hot fires.

Nellie cried, "What can I do now? What are we going to eat? I have to start all over again!" She wiped her cheeks.

"Calm down, Nellie."

"But you all think I'm stupid. I don't know what I'm doing today. I'm not a cook, but—"

Roald came into the galley. He picked up the smoking pan and poked at the bottom with a spatula that hung above the stove. He scraped some of the blackened porridge away.

Johanna retreated, pushing Nellie out the side door onto the deck, still sniffing.

Roald scraped all the burnt bits into a heap and tossed them on the sideboard of the stove. Then he took a chipped cup from the back shelf and filled it with water. He tipped this into the pan. He measured out oats from the sack and tipped this into the water.

"You can't put too much oats in," he said, and his voice sounded definitive.

Nellie turned to Johanna, frowning. "He knows how to cook?"

Johanna put her finger to her lips.

That the prince wasn't entirely normal also didn't mean that he couldn't listen. In fact, she suspected that he could do just that very well.

Somewhere in that Burovian sanatorium, he had clearly learned to cook camp meals. Johanna suspected that sanatorium was probably not the right word for where he had been. He seemed to have spent a lot of time outdoors.

Not much later, all four of them sat on the covers of the hold, eating bland and watery but steaming hot porridge. Until then, Johanna had not realised how hungry she was and how much it affected her mood. They ate until there was nothing left in the pan. When she finished, Johanna lay back on the sloping surface of the cover, watching the clouds track through the sky.

Nellie sat with her knees pulled up against her chest, looking miserable. Loesie had stayed a bit away from the group, while Roald was using his fingers to scrape every last bit of porridge from the plate.

"It was good. Thank you," she said, but he continued licking the bowl and didn't react.

"It wasn't good. It needs honey." He still didn't look at anyone.

"We don't have honey."

"I want honey. Tell the kitchen staff to order honey."

CHAPTER 16

THE SLOOP MOVED upriver at a steady pace. The mist rose mid-morning and the sun came out.

It was spring, the time when the river swelled and spread into the surrounding paddocks. The sea cows found it hard going and their movement was slow. Fortunately, also because of the water, no one on the riverbanks could get close enough to the *Lady Sara* to see who was on board.

A few boats met them coming down the river. Some of them Johanna even recognised, but they couldn't stop and after a few attempts, she had to give up trying to warn them of the events in Saardam, judging that it was probably better not to draw attention to themselves for Roald's safety. Women didn't crew river sloops, and they would be very visible even if only because of that.

Between themselves, they gathered up anything that they could barter with farmers along the river in return for food, more comfortable clothes, sheets, blankets and, at Roald's insistence, honey.

It was depressing to see how little they had.

They could not possibly give away Roald's Carmine jacket, although it was more brown than red after its encounter with the brackish harbour water. He did have his pretty ruffled shirt and belt with an elaborate buckle. Johanna had no idea if it had any significance. But the jacket definitely did, and if anything, he needed something less conspicuous.

Johanna had a necklace and a brooch that was her mother's, but she would rather work hard labour than trade either one.

Nellie had a few coins from their visit to the markets. She also had a small prayer book. "But please, Mistress Johanna, only show it when we couldn't possibly survive without selling it." She had tears in her eyes.

"We may need it badly," Johanna said, although she had no idea how much of a market they would find in Estland for a book of Triune prayers.

Even if Estland hadn't been hostile to the Church, people in the country usually lived by the rising and setting of the sun, and the seasons, and the cycles of growth and death, helped by magic or not. They didn't need the Church. And more likely than not, they couldn't read. A book of prayers wouldn't be worth much to those people.

Roald had his seal ring and a heavy gold chain, but nothing of value that wouldn't immediately give away his identity, or raise the suspicion of people likely to think that they had stolen those things.

Tendrils of mist still drifted over the river, restricting their view to the willows on both banks, the reedy riverbanks, and brown churning water disappearing out of view. There were no other people, no houses. Small islands went by, green with buttercups, grazing cows and the occasional rabbit.

There were no villages along the river, but in the afternoon, they found a mooring post in a river bend. There was a little beach surrounded by waving reeds and a path that led up the riverbank. The truncated stems of a couple of willows showed that people lived nearby who cut the trees regularly to make baskets. The mooring post, too, meant that there was a farmhouse or small settlement, probably just on the other side, from which farmers loaded cheeses onto the passing sloops.

"Let's stay here for the night," she said. They wouldn't get to Aroden castle or even Estland today. Johanna wasn't even sure how to tell that they were in Estland, or how far it was. She wished she'd paid more attention when she came this way with Father.

Loesie steered the sea cow team into the still water. She handed Johanna the rope and Johanna managed to catch the post with the loop on the end, but when the line snapped taut, it almost pushed her into the water. She just managed to hang onto the rope. That was silly, standing where she did, in the way of the rope.

Loesie laughed, an eerie panting sound that made a chill run down Johanna's back. She stared at her friend. It was almost as if Loesie had done that on purpose.

Johanna ran a second rope to the jetty so the sloop wouldn't swing too much. They loosened the ropes on the sea cows' harnesses so they could graze. Most of them swam off towards the reeds.

All this was done without exchanging a single word. Loesie couldn't speak, of course, but Nellie also said nothing, seated on top of the shutters that covered the hold. She met Johanna's eyes, looking utterly miserable. Roald was in the cabin, probably asleep.

Then Loesie said, "Ghghghghgh!" She pointed at the riverbank.

Johanna peered. "What's the matter?" She couldn't see anything on the bank except grass. No, there was a young willow tree in amongst the reeds.

"Do you want me to look at the wood?"

Loesie nodded, and her expression was anxious. The chill that Johanna had felt earlier came back. Maybe it wasn't to do with Loesie. Maybe something bad had happened here.

Johanna stepped from the deck onto the jetty. She knelt and placed her palm flat on the planks, but if they had ever told a story, it had dissipated long ago.

She walked towards the shore, where the jetty went through the reeds into the grassy bank. Her footsteps sounded loud on the wood.

A path led from the jetty up the river bank and the flattened grass on both sides showed that someone had come this way perhaps as recently as this morning, but no longer ago than yesterday.

Johanna turned off the path. Wading through the knee-length grass, the bottom of her dress became wet. The willow tree stood in a soggy patch of land. Johanna disturbed a coot, which flew up with a loud shriek that made her heart beat like crazy.

Phew. Stupid to get so excited over a simple bird. She was so tense.

The trunk of the tree, a mere sapling, was wet from the mist. Johanna closed her eyes, but all it showed her was greyness. Did that mean no one had come here recently, or that there had been too much mist to see it?

Then she waded back through the grass to the jetty. She wanted to follow the path to see if they could find some people, but she couldn't go alone.

Who would she take?

Loesie could handle the boat, and could stay here, but Johanna didn't trust her. She might take off with the boat and then they would be lost. Nellie wouldn't do anything stupid, but Roald might do something stupid to her. Loesie didn't care that he was the crown prince and he was oblivious to her, so she and Roald seemed better matched in an odd sort of way. That made Nellie the best to stay on board, not that it sat well with her, either. Nellie could do nothing if someone came.

She heaved the bag with the few things they had to trade onto her shoulder.

"But what if there are bandits?" Nellie looked uncertain, standing at the deck.

"Just don't show yourself," Johanna said. "We'll be back as soon as we can."

While Johanna led Loesie and Roald up the path, Nellie walked to the back deck, and climbed down the ladder into the hold.

The sun came out, and instantly, the grass turned brighter green. Johanna noticed dandelions and daisies she hadn't noticed before. A lark did its singing dance high into the sky.

But then Johanna cleared the top of the riverbank.

A blackened, burnt-out shell stood where there had once been a farmhouse. The roof had fallen in and blackened beams pointed at the sky like ribs in a rotting corpse. A smell of fire gone out days ago drifted over the meadow, full of green grass and buttercups. There was a barn, also burnt out, in the middle of a vegetable garden with neat rows of seedlings. Daisies, poppies and cornflowers bloomed in the edges around the garden like a parody on the scene of death.

Loesie made a soft hissing sound, and Roald stared, his expression so empty that it chilled her.

"By the heavens . . ." Johanna raised her hand over her mouth.

A rutted track led past the farmhouse past marshy ground. On the other side stood the burnt-out remains of a mill, with a few more burnt-out houses. A wisp of smoke still trailed from one of them.

A few cows lay peacefully under a tree and a couple of sheep grazed in a paddock, but she could see no other sign of people.

"Come," she said to Roald and Loesie. "We need to help survivors."

A little voice inside her said, *What if there are no survivors?*

An entire village murdered.

What would they find further upstream? Where did the destruction end?

They walked down the field. At the back of what was left of the farmhouse, sheets and clothes were flapping on the clothesline.

"See if there is anything that fits us," Johanna said. "Get all of it, including the sheets."

Loesie went into the garden and Johanna continued past the burnt-out shell of the house, with Roald following her like a little duckling.

She looked in through the opening where the door had been, which now lay in burnt pieces on the ground. The room was a kitchen, with the remains of a table and chairs in the middle. Shelves and a simple cupboard had been reduced to a pile of burnt planks.

Amongst the blackened ruins were some items that had strangely remained untouched. A bowl, half of a broom.

The air smelled strongly of stale wood smoke.

There was a charred lump on the floor, with bits of fabric adhering. Next to it was a smaller lump, with bits of a pink blanket.

Bile rose in her mouth when she realised what she was seeing. A mother and a child, burnt to coal.

With a trembling hand, she reached for a beam of wood. It must have been a roof beam, because she could see the surrounding of the house.

The attackers had come in the morning along the road that led past the mill, a group of men in leather jerkins and furs riding horseback, in the company of three bears. They carried flaming torches. At the mill, they stopped. One went in and threw the flaming torch in to the barn. A man ran out, and was attacked by a bear. His screams rang in her ears.

Johanna jerked her hand back from the wood, breaking the vision. The wood was crying for these people, mindlessly slaughtered by barbarians. They were innocent peasants. Whatever the king had done, nothing justified this mindless slaughter.

She leaned against the wall, her head reeling.

"Do you think they have honey?" Roald stepped over the remains of the door and went into the kitchen. He paid no heed to the bodies on the floor.

On the other side of the kitchen was another door that led into the pantry. Roald went in, ducking his head under a ceiling beam that had fallen cross the door.

There were clanging noises inside, and a moment later he came out carrying a pan filled with a few jars.

He showed the contents to her. "Look, there are peas. I like peas. And apples."

The contents of the pan consisted of a mix of foodstuffs in jars, most of them looking slightly smoked from the fire. There were dried apples, some potatoes, dried beans, flour and eggs.

"And look, there is honey."

There was, too. Roald's cheerful expression was eerily at odds with the horrible situation.

"Please, Your Highness. People have died here. Did you see the bodies on the floor?"

He frowned and looked over his shoulder. And said nothing for a while. Johanna didn't want to look at the mother and child again. She still felt queasy from the memory.

"Oh," he said eventually, although he didn't sound convinced.

"That's all? People died for you, or for what your father did. It was none of their fault. Can you show some respect?"

He turned to her. He had a smear of soot on his face. "But . . ." He frowned. "You said to get food. Aren't you happy?"

Hadn't he heard what she said? She breathed in to say something angry, but let her breath out again. It would be a waste of time. His mind seemed unable to deal with the feelings of others. Either he didn't understand them, or didn't notice them, or he had to act like this to cope with what had happened to him. Who knew how he had been treated for most of his life?

"Yes, I'm happy that you got food."

He flashed a childish, innocent smile that made her choke up. Imagine the bliss of not being able to comprehend the horror of this invasion.

Loesie had taken all the washing off the line. There were sheets, trousers and shirts.

Next to the burnt-out barn they found a wheelbarrow that was still useable. They piled the sheets and clothes in, together with the pan and its contents, and went to the other houses.

In the forecourt of the village lord's house, they disturbed a group of crows picking at a corpse. Neither of them felt inclined to look closer. The sweet scent of decay told the story louder than anything else could.

The house next to the mill was unaffected by fire, yet still uninhabited. Inside they found sacks of grain and some flour, but also some cheeses and a smoked ham, as well as plates, cups and tableware.

They found a metal bucket and went to milk the cows. There were also a blankets and sheets neatly folded on shelves in the wardrobe.

The miller had to be a newly-married man, for everything in

the house was fresh and there was not enough of it for an entire family.

Johanna felt terrible going through another person's house and stealing their possessions, but the little voice in her head said that the people themselves were unlikely to be able to use it.

But what if anyone has survived?

This happened days ago, they would already have come back if they were alive.

It was true, and the thought that all these people had just been killed was too big to comprehend.

Why would anyone do that?

They piled everything into the wheelbarrow and pushed it back through the waving grass. The sun was at its highest and when they came over the rise, the *Lady Sara* looked peaceful, as if they were simply underway to Lurezia and nothing had happened.

Nellie sat on deck, peering anxiously at the riverbank.

"We have food and clothes," Johanna shouted up to her.

They clambered up the ladder. They fashioned one of the horse blankets into a sack so they could haul the supplies up. The sack was heavy, but Roald took the rope from her and seemed to have little trouble with its weight. He lifted the sack to the deck. When he unwrapped the blanket, his eyes glittered like a child's.

"Look, we have cheese, I like cheese." He held the cheese out to Nellie, who almost dropped it. "You like ham? We have ham, too. And eggs. You have to be careful with them, or they'll break."

Loesie stood a little back, as if she was hesitant. Throughout the expedition she hadn't once tried to communicate. The look in her eyes chilled Johanna. Empty, vacant, as if her mind was being consumed from within.

"Did you see anyone while we were away?" Johanna asked Nellie.

She shook her head.

Johanna told Nellie about the burnt-out farmhouse.

"And what happened to the people who live here?"

"They're all dead. And if they're not, they're somewhere else.

It was horrible, Nellie." Her voice wavered. She was tired, she wanted to know where Father was, and wanted to see at least one town that was unscathed.

They cut the cheese with one of the knives they had brought from the farmhouse, and ate from the plates that they'd found in the miller's house. Nellie put a sheet on the bed in the cabin and kept one for the two of them. They climbed down and got some hay to fashion into a bed in the hold.

When it grew dark, they snuggled under the new blankets.

"They're much warmer," Nellie said.

Johanna lay down, staring at the small gap of moonlight that peeped in between the covers.

She could still see the burnt corpses. A woman with a baby on the floor, white skulls in black ash, a piece of pink blanket. "What sort of monsters would do a thing like this? What sort of monsters would burn an entire city? Why?"

"I don't know, Mistress Johanna, but I'm scared." She breathed out heavily. "Your friend scares me. I think the prince is also possessed by evil."

"The prince is ill. He has always been like this." As for Loesie, yes Johanna could agree with her.

"You know how the Church says . . . the Shepherd says there isn't any magic? You have never believed that, haven't you?"

"You cannot deny what you know to exist. The Church may not like it, but magic exists."

She wondered what had brought this change in Nellie. "People who work on the land know it. Many have the magic. Many see the magic. It helps them grow their crops and look after their animals. If the Shepherds left their churches and got their noses out of their holy books, they would see that magic is all around."

"I never saw it."

"Then you also never looked, or didn't want to see it. This terrible disaster started with magic, it's wrought by magic and it's about magic. Turning away from magic does no one any good."

CHAPTER 17

THEY SAW NO ONE on the river the next day. No merchant sloops, no farmers' barges. Once they came past a punt moored on a jetty, but there were no people. When Johanna had come with Father to Lurezia, the river had been quite busy with merchants and other vessels. On that trip, there had been people crossing the river in small boats, people riding horses on the banks, people fishing. This time, it was as if the country had died.

Towards the end of the day, they arrived at the fork where the Rede River joined the Saar River. Both rivers were wide, softly churning expanses of water, and the Rede River especially was brown with the extra water from molten snow. The country on the left-hand bank would now be Estland, that on the right still Saarland. Past the Rede River, the left-hand bank would be Burovia. The tongue of land at the point between the two rivers was a kind of no-man's land that was claimed by Estland, Saarland, Burovia or even Gelre depending on who was speaking. It was marshy ground, not worth much except for its strategic position.

Upriver from the fork, the Saar River curved around in a big loop. Loesie's farm was there, in an area people called The Bend.

Johanna stood at the bow looking over the vast expanse of

water while the sea cows made slow progress through the churning water.

Aroden castle was on the Rede River, so they kept to the left.

Past the fork where the Rede River joined, the country became more hilly and the river faster. Dark swathes of forest spread on both banks.

Johanna had never been here. This had been considered dangerous country until quite recently. She had not attended the Aroden court for that reason, but had heard enough from Father about the bandits who would raid ships and steal all the cargo.

❀

THE *LADY SARA* continued up the river. Progress was slow because the current was strong and they had to make regular stops to rest the cows. Loesie mostly kept to looking after the cows and the ship. Nellie cleaned and tidied, even things that didn't need cleaning and tidying. Roald was happy to do most of the cooking, and turned to be decent at it, albeit very messy, which then annoyed Nellie because she had to clean up after him.

This left Johanna with precisely nothing to do except worry about the lack of people. When she had come with Father, they had stopped at a lot of places along the river to buy and sell. Because the river flooded, no one lived near the banks. At some places houses had been built on artificial mounds so that you could see them from the river. The houses were intact, but they saw no people. Once, they spotted a man on a horse, but he was too far away to talk to.

Three days went by like this. At night they stopped in a safe place, ate from their supplies, and slept. They would leave someone on deck as watch—usually Loesie, because she didn't seem to need any sleep at all. When Johanna came up the deck in the morning, Loesie would shake her head at the question of had she seen anyone.

Then they would harness the sea cows for another day of travel. Johanna was both keen and anxious to get to Aroden castle. Above all, she hoped that her uncle remembered who she was and that they wouldn't turn the group away once they saw Roald.

It was one thing taking Roald to Aroden. It was another expecting the Estlander royals to forget their problems with the Carmine House. The further upriver they went, the bigger and more unsurmountable they became, until she was quite certain that her uncle would order Roald hanged as soon as they entered the castle. The Estlanders hated the Carmine House. It was not for nothing that they allowed minor princesses, like Johanna's mother, to marry rich Saarlander commoners, rather than the royal family. Added to that, Estlanders spoke in a thick dialect and Johanna wasn't sure she could make herself understood.

Why didn't she think about all this before setting out?

Was there any point in going on? Maybe they should go back to see if Saardam was safe—no, that was stupid, too. The bandits wouldn't have destroyed the city and left. Saardam was such a strategic place that no one would give it up without a fight.

IT WAS GETTING towards the end of the third day on the river when a whistle came from the bow of the boat.

Loesie stood at the bar handling the leather straps of the harnesses. The sloop had stopped and drifted into a bed of reeds, where the sea cows were busily tearing up stems by the roots.

"Why have we stopped here?"

"Ghghghghgh." Loesie pointed at the horizon. Her eyes were wide.

Johanna looked.

At first she saw nothing unusual. Just an undulating field surrounded by a hedge, then a path and another field and—smoke. Jagged ruins. Her heart jumped.

"Is that Aroden?"

Loesie nodded.

The castle and the surrounding town, where her mother grew up. "Have you seen any people?"

She shook her head.

Nellie had come up behind them. "Why are we stopping here —oh!" She raised her hand to her mouth. "Is this Aroden?"

Johanna nodded. She couldn't speak. All the hope she'd had to find a safe haven fled with the sight of this destruction.

"Ghghghghghghgh." Loesie pointed up and down the river and then shrugged.

"Keep going," Johanna said.

Loesie flicked the reins to make the cows continue. The sloop slowly gathered pace. Johanna, Loesie and Nellie remained at the bow, looking over the landscape.

Around the next bend they came across more burnt-out ruins, some still smouldering. Not a thing moved, not a bird called. A waft of burnt air drifted on the wind. Oh, if only she could read the wind. Was all of Estland in ruins? Were any of her relatives still alive?

A couple of people, a woman and two young men, ran to the riverbank, shouting. They were filthy, covered in soot. The woman had an ugly sore on her forehead.

Nellie raised her hand over her mouth. "Look at those people. What are we going to do?"

"We can't do much. We must protect Roald." Her voice wavered. She was so tired. The temptation to jump from the deck into the river was great.

"Should we moor here and check the castle?"

"I don't see that there is a point, Nellie. I'm pretty sure that burnt tower there is part of the castle. These bandits have laid the world to waste. There is no town unscathed, and if there are any royals still alive, they will be like Roald, in hiding."

A chill went over her. What if there were none left alive? What kind of chaos would descend upon the western lowlands? Many major royals had been at the ball. What if the Carmine House, the Aroden family and Baron Uti were all dead? Then Roald would be the only royal heir for all of those lands. And he would need to step up soon, so that people could have hope that peace and prosperity would return.

Neither of them said anything for a long time. The sloop moved slowly upriver and the woman and her two teenage sons slid from view. Their voices faded in the distance. Johanna felt horrible about not stopping and helping them, but with Roald on board, they couldn't afford to get involved in trouble.

It started to rain, a soft drizzle that barely made the ground wet at first, but grew more persistent. They went into the tiny cabin where Roald had spent most of his days and where it smelled uncomfortably of male sweat.

Johanna lit a candle and they shared some of their supplies. Roald chatted about cheese and ham and which kinds he liked, but no one else said much. Eventually, he fell silent as well, heaving a sigh.

"Is there anywhere your uncle could have fled to safety?" Nellie asked Johanna, her voice low.

Johanna shrugged. "The duke has a hunting lodge, but I don't know where it is." At any rate, the forests of Estland had never been the safest of places.

"What are we going to do now, Mistress Johanna?" Nellie's voice was timid.

Johanna didn't know, and felt irritated that making the decisions was all up to her.

"Maybe . . ." She stared into the flame of the candle. By its feeble light, Loesie looked wide-eyed and crazy. Johanna was no longer sure if they could trust her. Nellie's face was pale in contrast with her red and raw lips. Her bonnet was in need of a wash, and that made Johanna feel embarrassed. Nellie would normally rather die than wear something dirty.

Roald's beard had grown unruly. He looked the healthiest of all, but his mind was elsewhere.

Johanna let out a deep breath. "Let's find a place to stay for the night away from Aroden. Then tomorrow we'll see if we can turn around and go back. Maybe we can stay at Loesie's farm until we get news."

"Ghghghgh!" Loesie shook her head. She curled her fingers like claws and then made swimming movements with her hands.

Johanna frowned at her. "Do you mean that the men who attacked your farm came from across the river?"

Loesie nodded.

Across the river from Loesie's farm was the marshy no-man's land. They had passed it on the way here, but had not thought anything of it or seen anything unusual. It was a useless piece of land, inundated when it rained and too wet for forests, grazing animals or farming. Some farmers went there to cut peat, and maybe hunt ducks, but it wasn't much good for anything else. That, of course, made it good for hiding. Was that where the bandits lived?

"Do they have a leader?"

"Mmmmm." Loesie nodded. She made some hand gestures.

Johanna guessed what they meant. "He has long hair . . . He rides a horse?"

"Ghghghgh." Loesie shook her head. She pointed at the river.

"He swims?"

"Mmmm." She shook her head again and mimicked riding and pointed at the river.

"A water horse," Roald said.

Johanna frowned at him. "What is a water horse?"

"It's a creature from the fables," Nellie said. "It's a horse that has duck's feet so that it can swim."

Oh. She frowned at Loesie and again at Nellie. Did either of them believe in water horses?

"Well, it's not going to help us much now. We have to decide where to go. We could go to Lurezia for help." Because Burovia wouldn't give it, since they never liked Saarland much in the first place, and Lurezia would probably be indifferent, too far away to care.

She sighed. *Was* there even a place to go?

"We are what's left of free Saarland," Nellie said into the depressed silence.

There was nothing anyone could add to that. The free city of Saardam was dead, and Estland had been gutted. Johanna rose. She needed to be out of this smelly cabin.

It had stopped raining.

Johanna walked along the deck to the sloop's bow and sat down at the driver's bench. The sea cows were unharnessed. Their ropes dangled in the water, moving occasionally. One of the animals was chomping noisily and wetly in the dark somewhere beyond the edge of her vision.

Foggy air blanketed the riverbanks, rendering the greens of

the willows and grass in muted grey. Johanna hugged herself against the cold and humid air.

Someone else came from the cabin. Nellie, judging by the sound of careful footsteps.

"Mistress Johanna? Are you all right?"

"Sit down."

Nellie settled on the bench next to her. "Oh, it's all so awful. Those poor people. I can still hear them calling out for us."

Yes, Johanna could, too. The woman and her two sons begging for help was probably an image that wouldn't leave her for the rest of her life. "Do you know we hold the freedom of Saardam in our hands? We have the only surviving member of our royal family with us. If he dies without an heir, the holding of Saardam will fall into the hands of the nearest relative, who is . . . I don't even know. Not someone who cares about us."

Horror was written on Nellie's face. Everyone knew the story of how the young Nicholaos had settled feuds that went back centuries by opening the port of Saardam for trade. Simply put, Saardam was *too important* to landlocked countries, and it suited the rival nations that a small and insignificant royal family had possession of it.

"We must find a way to take Saardam back from those bandits."

"Yes." Although that wouldn't happen until they had found other survivors.

"And Roald must have an heir as soon as possible."

"Yes." Johanna nodded, grimly. "But everyone who would be a suitable candidate for a wife is dead." The memory of the destruction of the palace made her shudder. Another image she would probably never forget.

A chill went down her back. She clamped her hands between her knees.

Nellie said, "If King Nicholaos agreed to you dancing with the prince, you are a suitable candidate."

Johanna sighed and let her shoulders slump.

Nellie began, "I'm sorry, I would have—"

"No, Nellie. I've thought about it a lot." In fact, ever since

Father had mentioned the trouble of the royal family during that coach ride on their way to the ball.

"In what way did you think about it?"

Johanna thought that she had been stupid and behaved like a spoilt child that day. She didn't want to get married because marriage meant looking after a man who expected to be looked after, who expected a lady of the house who held tea parties and things like that.

Roald expected nothing of the sort. Apart from that one thing that would be unpleasant, she wasn't even sure what he expected. He seemed to be happy for her to tell him what to do. He was happy cooking. He'd been happy chopping wood. Those things he did well and efficiently. It was the talking and relationship stuff he had trouble with.

When Johanna said nothing, Nellie prompted, "Mistress Johanna? In what way?"

Johanna turned to her in the fast-waning light. "I'll protect the prince from people who only want money he doesn't have. I want to make sure that our country and our royal family stay as they are. I'll help Saarland overcome this evil and make it strong again. I will marry Roald."

CHAPTER 18

NELLIE'S FATHER was a celebrant for the Church and Nellie knew the right components of a wedding ceremony. She went into an organising frenzy. She poked Loesie into moving the sloop into a part of the river where weeping willows trailed their branches in the water.

"We'll make a nice feast out of the nicest food we have," Nellie said. Never mind that Roald would have to cook it, while she insisted on turning a farm dress into a simple wedding dress with the aid of a sheet. Nellie might be clumsy, easily flustered and impractical, but her strength was that she knew about clothes and protocol and she loved that kind of thing.

She made a table on the deck from a crate covered with a horse blanket. She went on shore to cut sprays of wild parsley flowers which she fashioned into bouquets. She set out cups and candles on the table. It was all so surreal, and it was hard to comprehend that not far away an entire town had been destroyed and its inhabitants killed or driven away.

Johanna spent most of the day sitting on top of the hold covers watching Nellie, who was in her element and seemed to have found a shred of happiness to lift her from her misery.

THEY PERFORMED the ceremony on the rear deck of the barge in the waning light. Johanna wore the dress, which Nellie had made pretty with ruffles cut from one of the sheets and a necklace of flowers. Roald wore his royal jacket, which Nellie's attempt to wash had only marginally improved. The crown and the staff were hopefully still in the broom cupboard in the palace, but he still had his rings, and his fingers, although quite slender, were thicker than hers. His seal.

Nellie slid the golden ring on Johanna's index finger, the only finger it would fit. It felt heavy and cumbersome on her hand.

Roald stood stiff and wouldn't look at anyone.

Johanna was scared, cold and miserable and shivered through most of it, but inside her, she felt a seed of pride. She held herself straight while Nellie spoke all the words she had heard her father say so many times.

She was nervous, too, and stumbled a few times.

Johanna did this for her country, for the freedom of Saardam. If the four of them were all that was left of the free kingdom, then the four of them would do their best to find other free people and liberate their country.

Johanna didn't know that Roald understood much of Nellie's words. He stared at the riverbank most of the time, and had to be prompted to make his reply.

"I do," sounded like a death sentence coming from those life-less lips.

They went inside the cabin, and ate some of the best sausages Johanna and Roald had collected from the farm, drank the wine from the captain's cabin, but it was not until Nellie said that from now on Johanna and Roald should have the captain's cabin, that it fully hit what she'd agreed to do. And she thought at that moment Roald understood, too. All of a sudden, she was overcome by the desire to scream at Nellie *don't leave me alone with him,* but it was far too late. Nellie announced that she was tired and she and Loesie left.

Johanna stood there in the middle of the cabin, clamping her hands around her as Roald shut the door, and bolted it. No way out.

"We are married, now?" he asked.

"Yes."

He laughed, "Heheheheeee." His eyes twinkled with mischief. "Now I can look."

Johanna cringed, but there was really no way out, and the quicker this part was over and done with, the better.

Slowly she opened the buttons of her dress and pulled the fabric aside. He sat on the edge of the bed as she wrestled herself out of her dress. Watching. She was so nervous he could have knocked her over with a single finger. He just sat and watched, his eyes wide, as she hung up the dress and slid her underclothes off, first the underdress, and then the corset. The hooks came undone; her breasts hung free. His mouth fell open, like a little boy in a sweet store. She didn't think he had seen a naked woman before.

With great effort, she had to force herself to cross to him. She slid the jacket off his shoulders. With a feeling of shame, she noticed that it was still not completely dry.

"Come."

She had to force herself not to shudder. Her fingers trembled as she undid his shirt. His skin underneath was soft and quite tanned, completely without chest hair, and so skinny that his ribs were clearly visible. His nipples, dark brown and erect, lay flat against his chest. No man-boobs here. Apart from his tan, he didn't look very healthy. How often did he forget to eat?

The trousers were harder to get off and not just because she was nervous or unfamiliar with the belt buckle and fastening. He bent over to stroke her naked shoulders very gingerly with the tips of his fingers, making goose bumps run down her back. His hands were cold.

The belt fell off and the trousers came down. He undid the string to his under pants. They fell, too, but remained suspended on a particular part of his anatomy. He grinned.

"I'm a man, see? I know what to do."

She doubted it. She didn't know herself. For all the flirting and the dancing she had done, the kiss from the Baron's son was the closest she'd ever come to the marital bed and that bed loomed ever closer against the back wall of the cabin. The curtains fluttered with a draught.

She sat next to him on the edge of the mattress, the sheets soft under her naked skin.

He sat next to her and cupped her breast in his hand, a skinny, bony hand with large knuckles.

"It's so soft." His chest heaved with deep breaths. His eyes, wide and mad, were on the hair between her legs. "Hee hee heeee. I know what to do," he said.

With one hand, he pushed her down in the mattress. Johanna forced herself to recline willingly. Best not to resist, lest he go into one of his aggressive moods. Blood roared in her ears.

With surprising agility, he jumped on her and pushed her back into the pillows. Naked skin met naked skin. His was clammy, and slick with sweat. He thrust his hips forward, hard, and his member poked painfully into a very sensitive spot. She couldn't restrain a yelp.

"Ow!"

He ignored her and kept pushing, now rocking his hips. She tried spreading her legs, but he was all over the place, smearing slime on her inner thighs.

"Roald, stop. Stop!"

He did, which surprised her, his chest heaving.

"You're hurting me." She was shivering so much that her jaw threatened to seize up. "Maybe it's better if you lie on your back."

"All right." He chuckled.

She clambered off the narrow bunk and waited, trying to get control of her shattered nerves while he settled himself. A wide grin spread across his face.

She stepped closer to the bed. He grabbed her wrist and pulled her. Johanna almost fell on top of him.

"Wait, calm down."

She lifted her leg over him and crouched over him. This bunk sure wasn't made for these types of acrobatics. "Here," she whispered, while holding his member up. The tip glistered with slime. "Hold it like that."

She lowered herself, found the right spot. Breathed in deeply, pushed down. There was a sharp pain and tightness as he slid into her.

He gave a long moan, his head arched back into the pillow.

Well, that was it, she guessed. She was no longer a virgin. But what now? This wasn't "it", was it?

She slowly rocked her hips. He moaned again and gripped her thighs with white-knuckled hands, arched his back so he lifted her right off the mattress.

"Ow, ow. That's hurts!"

But he was bucking and threshing like wild sea cow in a net and Johanna was being bounced about. She managed to get her knees under her, and lifted herself at the same time he arched his back. He slipped out of her.

"Wait, Roald."

But he bucked and emitted a loud "Huuuuhhhh!" and something wet squirted over her right thigh.

He fell back onto the pillow. Johanna sat there, trembling, while she watched a glob of white slime trickle down her leg.

She guessed *that* was it, and it hadn't quite gone where it was intended to go.

"That was good," he said. "I want more."

He stared up at the ceiling. His member had already gone limp. She didn't think there would be 'more' tonight.

She was shivering so much she could barely lift herself from the bed. Her upper legs were a sticky mess and when she felt the sore spot between her legs, her finger came away covered in blood-streaked slime.

There was nothing in the cabin to wipe herself and she didn't want to go outside like this. Nellie would . . .

Oh, Nellie.

The cabin faded in a haze of tears.

Johanna managed to get her underdress back on and lay down in the warm hollow in the mattress next to him. He was asleep in moments. Johanna cried into the pillow all night.

CHAPTER 19

T HE NEXT MORNING she clambered from the bed sore and feeling dirty.

Roald was still asleep and she intended to leave him that way. What if he wanted to do it again? She didn't think she could face that.

She wrestled herself into her other clothes and went on deck.

Nellie stood there, her hands crossed over her chest, while Loesie threw carrots at the sea cows.

Oh holy Triune. Not another fight.

"She wanted to disturb you." Nellie glared at Loesie, who poked out her tongue.

"She could have knocked. I was awake." Johanna found it hard to keep discomfort out of her voice. She couldn't meet Nellie's eyes. There were just too many questions hovering within. She would have heard Roald's grunts last night.

"I wouldn't let her disturb anyone on the morning after their wedding. The union between man and woman is holy—"

Johanna waved her to silence. *Don't talk nonsense, Nellie.*

Tears threatened in her eyes.

Everything hurt, every step she took. In her mind, she still heard Roald give that horrible grunt when he spilled himself. That must have echoed all over the ship.

"Mistress Johanna? Are you all right? Do you want to sit down?"

Johanna glared at Nellie, her wide eyes, her pale face.

What did she think? That the future of the kingdom grew inside her? That she needed mollycoddling because of that? It couldn't even be so, and what was worse, she would have to endure Roald's attentions until it did. What did she know?

She wanted to laugh, and cry and slap her in the face.

"Don't say that to me again."

"Mistress Johanna?"

She whirled at her. "Stop calling me that. Call me Johanna, or call me nothing at all, instead of treating me like a. . . ." Her voice cracked.

Nellie shrank back, her chest heaving, and said nothing for a long time. Johanna stared out over the water, wiping stubborn tears from her cheeks.

"But Mi . . . er . . . Johanna, you *are* the queen now and I will treat you like that." She dipped a curtsey and Johanna had an even greater desire to punch her in the face.

"Please, Nellie."

Roald's ring felt like a millstone on her hand. Like this, it was so visible, and it was too big for her. She took off her necklace, slid the ring off and threaded the necklace through. When she did it back up again, the ring hung between her breasts.

"It's too big. I'm afraid I might lose it."

Nellie nodded.

"Let's just go and see what Loesie wants. If she wanted to disturb me, that means she has something to say."

She went to the bow, but Loesie was no longer there. She stood on the riverbank, her hand on the trunk of a willow tree. People in these parts didn't cut willows, and its branches trailed in the water. Soft green misted the pale wood. Spring came.

"Loesie?" Johanna called.

She looked up and gestured *come*.

The current had brought the boat right into shore. There was an old jetty here and they didn't need the dinghy to clamber out, but the section where it joined up to the shore had collapsed. Johanna took off her shoes and waded through the water to the small sandy beach.

She joined Loesie at the tree trunk. Soft branches brushed over her head, and bees buzzed amongst the little furry balls that were the willow's flowers.

"Anything here?" she asked.

Loesie took her hand and pulled it to the rough wood of the tree trunk.

The green riverbank faded. It was dusk, and a long procession of men on large horses followed the river downstream. Horses and spears and fur jerkins.

"Who are they?" she asked Loesie.

She shook her head. *Ghghghgh.* She pointed up the bank.

They left the shelter of the branches of the tree. Nellie had just come ashore and was wrestling her shoes back onto her feet.

"What's going on?" she asked. Her cheeks were red and flustered. Brilliant sunlight brought out the greens and yellows of the meadow. The top of the riverbank led into an orchard, the trees full of white flowers.

Large daisies bloomed in the grass between the trees, and purple and pink flowers, so different from what Johanna had ever seen.

Nellie was the first one in the meadow. "Isn't this pretty?" She already had a handful of flowers. "We can make you a more cheerful wedding bouquet."

Johanna cringed. "Let's be careful." An orchard usually meant that there was a farmhouse nearby.

"I'm not doing any harm." Nellie continued picking. "If I don't pick flowers, they're going to get eaten by those cows over there."

The cows were grey-brown, very unlike the black and white ones that were common with farmers in Saarland. There was a group of four or five of them in the shade of a tree.

A rutted track led out of the orchard. It disappeared along a bend behind a mass of dark trees.

A pine forest.

A chill crept over Johanna's back. She heard the voices in the wind whistling through the boughs. She felt the tingle of magic that tugged at her senses but showed her nothing because she didn't have wind magic. "Maybe we should return to the *Lady Sara*." Roald was there alone.

"In a moment. When I've got all the flowers I need."

It was the first time that she had seen Nellie being her old self, so Johanna calmed her nerves and sat down in the grass. The scent of crushed herbs rose up to her. The sunlight was warm and comfortable, the meadow a kaleidoscope of cheerful colours. She was just making herself scared by thinking about magic. Likely there was nothing to be afraid of once you got used to the sounds of the forest.

She glanced at Loesie, but she had also sat down and stared into the distance with a dreamy look.

Guess a little rest was all right.

She lay back in the grass.

The next thing she knew, she woke up with the sound of a cow chomping on leaves.

What?

"Nellie, what . . ." She sat up with a jerk. Nellie lay behind her, her head resting on her elbow. Her eyes were closed and her chest moved in regular breaths. A bunch of wilted flowers lay next to her.

"Loesie?"

The field was empty. Loesie was nowhere to be seen.

Nellie opened her eyes. "Oh, pardon me, Mistress Johanna. I think I fell asleep."

"We all fell asleep. The past few days have been tiring for all of us. I guess we earned the rest."

"Look at my poor flowers! I must get some new ones."

"We need to go back. I don't know what Loesie and Roald have been up to, but they must be wondering where we are."

Nellie looked disappointed, but didn't protest.

They walked back over the hill, between the blooming apple trees. Then down the bank to the *Lady Sara* which lay bobbing peacefully, with the roaming lines of the sea cows attached. The animals were grazing on the bottom. Loesie was nowhere to be seen.

Johanna and Nellie waded through the water to the half-rotten and wobbly jetty.

When Johanna was halfway up the ladder to the deck, a dark silhouette appeared at the top. Someone that was not Roald, but a much bigger man with a ponytail.

She gasped but she had nowhere to go. Nellie was behind her and couldn't go down quickly enough. Not only that, two more bandits waded towards them from the shore.

Nellie screamed.

The thug on the deck grabbed Johanna's arm and yanked her up onto the deck. There were not one but three thugs on the deck—all of them bearded and with long-furred jerkins. Two wore ponytails; the third and biggest thug was bald. They laughed when their mate dumped Johanna onto the deck. Behind her, Nellie was struggling against the grip of one of the men who had come up behind them, screaming and kicking.

"Let us go. We're free citizens of Saarland." Johanna straightened herself and tried to sound impressive, as if . . . Roald. Where was Roald?

The men laughed and exchanged comments in a strange and harsh-sounding language. One of the men was tying Nellie's hands up with a dirty rag. Nellie was still kicking at the man, and in response, he grabbed the front of her dress and thrust a hand down.

Nellie screamed.

"Stop it, Nellie. The more you protest, the more they like it. Keep still." *And you might just come out of here alive.* Although maybe not unscathed.

A sixth man now clambered up from the hold, with Loesie over his shoulder. She was pulling his hair, but he set her down as if she didn't exist. Great bundles of hair hung from her hands.

Johanna still couldn't see Roald anywhere. What if they . . . The ring under her shirt felt heavy. If Roald was dead, then . . .

Panic rose in her. If that was true, then the whole future of free Saarland was in her hands.

Then, she heard splashing and growling and yet another thug came up the ladder, pulling Roald with him. Water dripped from his clothes, his hair standing on end on one side of his head.

The men laughed.

Roald's eyes were as wide as Johanna had seen them that day when they fished him out of the harbour. Any moment now and he'd start banging his head on something.

The thug pushed Roald forward to the railing as if he wanted to throw him off the boat. Roald squealed.

"Keep your hands off him," Johanna yelled.

The men laughed again. One pushed Roald harder into the railing. But then the bald one shouted something, and they let Roald go. He fell heavily on his backside. "They'll kill us. They'll kill us!" His squeal chilled Johanna deeply. "They'll kill us. They'll kill us!"

"Shhh, calm down."

Roald met her eyes, and some of the madness seeped out of his face.

The bald-headed bandit leader jerked his head towards the riverbank.

There, on the high bank, approached three more men with a whole team of huge horses black as night. They had long flowing manes and huge hooves. With them were two bears on chains and a pack of dogs.

The bald leader yelled something, and a voice responded from the bank. The group descended to the water, the horses snorting and blowing, tossing their great heads. Some of them waded a bit into the water. The bears appeared nervous, pulling on their chains.

The bandits forced Johanna, Nellie and Roald to clamber down the ladder, and wade through the water.

Johanna sat down to take off her shoes, but a thug pulled her up. Nellie cried when they pushed her down the jetty. "Do you know how much those shoes cost my father?"

The only thing she got in response was more rough handling.

On the riverbank, the bandits hauled each of them in front of another rider on a horse.

Johanna's horse was smelly and the man at her back stank of sweat and chewing tobacco. He snaked an arm around her waist, but she pushed him away. She would not let herself be humiliated.

"I can ride myself. You don't have to hold me."

She glanced at Roald, gave him her best *behave like a king* glare, and said, "Sit up."

He did. His face was so pale that she was afraid that he might faint. Hopefully he would remain quiet about who he was.

The bald leader whistled and the column of horses set off, away from the riverbank, into the forest. Johanna cast a look over her shoulder to where the *Lady Sara* lay. She had to remember this place. One day, she would come back.

WILLOW WITCH

Book 2 of the Ghostspeaker Chronicles

PATTY JANSEN

CHAPTER 1

THE BANDITS had been arguing all day.

From the back of her big black horse, Johanna could make out only disjointed parts of their conversation, which was slow and drawn-out, because often the forest was so thick that the twenty or so horses had to ride in single file.

She thought the argument involved directions or orders given to the group by some boss or landowner. A few of the bandits wanted to go to a town, while the main group said that their orders were to go elsewhere, to a place called Hunter's Rest.

None of it meant anything to her. The only town in this area that she was aware of was Florisheim, but she didn't think they were that far upriver yet. Maybe they were in Gelre, maybe still in Estland, she wasn't sure.

The bandits' strong eastern accent didn't help matters. The only one Johanna could hear clearly enough to mostly understand was her "own" bandit. He was a warm presence behind her on the horse and his beard tickled in her neck. His hands were big, with dirty-nailed, hairy fingers that strayed often or "accidentally" grabbed her in places where a man's hand had no business being. He would pull her against him so that she could feel the greasy touch of his leather jerkin and would be enveloped in its stench of smoke and sweat.

His name was Ludo, or something similar, and he had a rough voice and shaggy long hair like the two bears that bounded tirelessly between the horses and around the main group. She figured that he argued in favour of following orders and getting paid, but there seemed to be some sort of disagreement about whose orders were the most lucrative and who was most likely to pay.

Sometimes there was a lull in the argument, when one or two of the arguing parties got frustrated and urged their horses to the other side of the group or to the front, out of earshot of the main group. When that happened, the main group went sullen and broody. In these quiet moments, Ludo said soft words to her under his breath. Things like *flower of beauty*, and *who gets to taste the fruit of a maiden's sin* and other suggestive things. Johanna kept trying to shift forward on the rough saddle just as much as he continued trying to sneak his hands to her chest. *Because I can't allow you to fall* he'd say, even though the horse moved at walking pace and had a steady and even gait.

Then, fortunately, some of the arguing bandits would come back before anything worse happened. The most important of these was a man called Sylvan, who looked like he was both the fiercest and the youngest in the group. He rode alone on a magnificent horse that was strong and tall with a magnificent glossy black mane and long fetlocks. Sylvan was a scrawny fellow, with an ugly scar across his face from an injury that had just missed his mouth, but had pulled one corner of it permanently upwards. His cheeks, forehead and arms bore tattoos of unfamiliar symbols. His hair was done up in plaits, which swung about his head when he tossed it back as an expression of frustration, which he did a lot. Sometimes he would pull his horse's reins so that it would rear on its hind legs, and speed off into the forest. For a horse that size, this came with a frightening thunder of hooves that made the regular horses skitter.

Then he would wait by the side of the forest path for the rest of the party to catch up. Usually both bears and one or two of the hounds went with him. The dogs would bark, and someone in the party, usually the bald leader, whose name appeared to be

Sigvald, would yell at them to shut up, and he would hurl sharp comments at Sylvan.

Johanna listened and tried to interpret what the men said, and most importantly, where they were going, but she understood only shards of their dialect. The idea of being taken somewhere unfamiliar for money frightened her. Men who did things for money had a reputation of being ruthless. What if they decided to split up the group of prisoners, or kill the most troublesome and worthless of them?

Since starting out, she had been unable to talk to any of the others, not even during the short breaks when the bandits rested their horses.

The bandit who rode before her shared his horse with Roald. Johanna could see only part of the prince's legs, since the bandit was taller and broader than the prince. Roald had screamed a few times when they were first captured, but had been quiet since. Too quiet, Johanna thought. She worried about what the bandit said to him. A single word might upset him enough to do something unexpected and silly, like screaming uncontrollably or banging his head. Even in Saarland, most folk from outside the towns feared halfwits and didn't want anything to do with them. There were stories about people living their lives locked in tiny rooms, or being branded witches and killed. The bandits had to know that he wasn't normal. It wasn't obvious in his looks, but his behaviour would have informed them soon enough.

Nellie and Loesie were somewhere behind her, but since Loesie couldn't speak, and Nellie seemed to have gone paralysed with fear, Johanna had no idea how far behind. With the creep and his questing hands at her back, she didn't want to look over her shoulder and give him the idea that she was curious about him.

So she listened out for Nellie's voice, but heard nothing except the men's drawl in their rough eastern dialects and the *clop clop clop* of horses' hooves on the ground.

The forest was endless. Johanna could make out no clear path. Sometimes they rode between the massive trunks of beech trees, where it was dark underneath and the ground was covered in dead leaves. The only sunlight that made it down to the forest floor came in thin shafts that penetrated the canopy, or patches of brightness in places where a large tree had fallen. The hazy air made the sunlight show up as brilliant rays of light.

Even animals seemed to have fled this place and its pressing silence. Every breath of wind made leaves rustle. Their lilting and whispering voices formed an eerie background to the arguing from the bandits.

Occasionally they would come to a patch of birch trees that, with their black and white mottled trunks, looked like ghosts. At those places there would be short shrubs on the ground with filaments of spider web between them.

The ground also grew hillier. Sometimes they'd come to the top of a hill and there would be a view between trees, always showing more trees and the occasional patch of bracken. No paths, no sign of habitation.

Yet the bandits seemed to know where they were going. The only thing Johanna could say was *southeast,* judging by the direction of the sunlight.

Their day-long argument dragged on, and with each confrontation came a sharp exchange of words, a moment of Sylvan's posturing where he would pull up his horse so that it stood in the way of the others, and Sigvald would shout at him until he moved. Each time Johanna thought that the two would come to a fight.

If that happened, she guessed each of the bandits would take sides. They would watch the fight and it would be a good time to try to escape. She distracted herself from worrying about Ludo's questing hands by making plans for what she would do. Some of the bags tied to the backs of the five packhorses looked like they contained tents and blankets. They would have to take those horses.

She didn't know much about horses herself, but Roald could ride, she thought. Nellie could be prodded to do so, but Loesie . . . She had no idea what was going on with Loesie. Coming from a farm, she *should* be able to ride, but Loesie was not well. Even before they were captured, she had barely tried to communicate for days. Johanna had assumed that was because Loesie's task had been to look after the ship, but there had been no warmth or any kind of emotion in Loesie's expression for a long time. Since the burning of Saardam, Johanna thought.

Loesie seemed to have drawn into herself, and Johanna was no longer sure that she listened to what people around her said. If they had the opportunity to escape and had to make a run for it, would Loesie be able to follow simple instructions? What was going on inside her friend's head?

By the time the light turned golden and Sigvald called the party to a halt, there had been no fight and no opportunity to escape.

The horses stopped, blowing gusts of air out of their nostrils, tossing great black-maned heads. Ears twitched and great eyes roved.

Now that the rear of the group caught up with the front, Johanna could see the others. Roald sat as stiff as he had when Johanna had last seen his face. That was just after they had been captured. The bandits had tied his arms, which caused him a lot of distress. He'd been wailing and Johanna had protested to the bandits that he was little danger to anyone, because he was simple. She wasn't sure how much of it the bandits understood, but they had untied his arms and let him ride. The last time she met his eyes, she had told him to sit up in the saddle and be proud. To her surprise he was still following that order, although the rawness in her own backside had caused her to slump ages ago.

It made her feel guilty.

The bandit riding with Loesie had used a rope to lash her to the saddle so she didn't fall off. She sat slumped, her head forward. Johanna thought for a moment that she was asleep, but then she slowly raised her head. Her mouth hung open. Her chin and front of her dress were wet from drool and eyes were unfocused.

Definitely getting worse.

Johanna tried to catch her attention, but she just stared into nothingness. It was as if Loesie had not only lost her voice, but had now also lost the ability to communicate in other ways. She hadn't been like that when Johanna had met her in the markets. It was as if the spell was still eating away at her.

The bandit behind Loesie on the horse was a grizzled, older man with a long and straggly beard and several missing teeth. Johanna met his eyes over Loesie's shoulder. His irises were cloudy white.

Johanna's heart jumped. She hadn't noticed those eyes before. She knew that sometimes older people's eyes went like that, and then they'd see poorly. It was a coincidence, right? She hadn't really affected him with her magic, right?

Your friend is already dead, said a voice inside her head that sounded like Reverend Romulus.

"Johanna, did you even hear what I said?" Nellie's face was scrunched up as if she was about to burst into tears.

"I didn't. I was . . ." *wondering if Loesie's condition is infectious.* "Sorry, what did you say?"

"I said I don't think I can walk anymore, I'm so sore," Nellie said.

"You can walk just fine."

"But it hurts!" Her lip quivered.

"Come on, Nellie," Johanna said under her breath.

She hurt, too. That was what happened if you weren't used to riding, even if the horses only moved at a slow pace. The shifting of weight, trying to stay in the saddle and trying to move away from Ludo had made her backside raw.

Sigvald gave the reins of his horse to another bandit and made his way out of the group. To the right was a slight rise in the beech forest, a broad mound with trees growing at its sides. Sigvald climbed the mossy flank, where exposed tree roots had made uneven natural steps.

He stopped at the top of the hill and peered in all directions. Obviously liking what he saw or didn't see, he gestured for the others to come. Most of the bandits got off their mounts and led their horses by the reins, but Sylvan rode. Ludo rode, too. The horse made small steps so as not to trip over tree roots that had become exposed on the sloping ground.

The little hill had a flat top. The hounds already stood there, making excited squeaking noises and wagging their tails.

From the top of the hill Johanna could see why Sigvald had stopped here. A creek ran through the valley on the other side of the hill, and on the far bank was a little glade with the first grass and meadow plants she had seen since leaving the orchard where they had been captured.

The bandits all dismounted and took off their horses' saddles and packs. One of the younger bandits took two horses down to the glade to graze.

Ludo let himself drop from the saddle and offered to lift Johanna down.

She glared at him. "Keep your hands to yourself, you creep."

He must have gotten the message, because he went to Nellie. Johanna swung her leg over the side of the horse and peeked at the ground and then wished she hadn't looked. Oh boy, it was a long way down. This horse was a giant, much bigger than the coach horses in Saardam. The younger bandit was already coming back up the hill to take the next two horses to the glade. Not wanting anyone else offer her "assistance" dismounting, Johanna let herself slip feet first from the saddle.

She half-fell and landed hard in the leaves. Ouch.

Ludo had convinced Nellie to let him help her. He first supported her legs and then took her by the waist to set her down on the ground.

Johanna was about to warn Nellie, when she exclaimed, "Hey, keep your hands off me!" She yanked herself out of Ludo's grip and took a swipe at him. "What do you think I am, some cheap woman?" Her hand missed Ludo's face.

Most of the bandits had been rolling out sleeping mats and looked around. One or two laughed. Johanna couldn't see the old guy with the cloudy eyes anymore.

Sylvan glared at his companions, his gaze stopping at Ludo. He sat with his ankles crossed, leaning against a tree trunk. He made a sharp comment. Johanna caught something about making a fire before it got dark. Ludo stomped off after muttering something about slaves, either about being a slave or that they had slaves who should do the work instead.

"Oh, Mistress Johanna, I'm so tired," Nellie cried. "You know I work all day and should be used to it, but this . . ." Her voice wavered.

"You don't need to tell me that. I'm tired, too." It was ages since Johanna had ridden a horse and she certainly hadn't done it for very long back then.

Loesie sat on a tree root, her arms looped around her knees. Her eyes had clouded over again.

"I thought it was a nice ride, wasn't it?" Roald said.

"No, it wasn't! We're prisoners and that smelly man behind me kept rasping his throat and spitting. Disgusting."

"Shh, Nellie." Johanna said.

Nellie raged on, "I don't want to be quiet about it. Where are these filthy bandits taking us?"

"Be quiet. Some of them will be able to understand you."

"I don't care." Nellie's voice cracked. "What now? They expect us to sleep on the ground here? With all these men? We can't even understand any of them. All their words sound like *ghghghghgh*." She made a harsh noise in her throat.

Loesie gave a low hiss, but Johanna wasn't sure if it was directed at Nellie.

Calm down, she mouthed at Loesie, but the reaction chilled her. Whatever lived inside Loesie was taking over her mind.

"Hey, you . . . water!" Sigvald yelled. He threw a bucket in Johanna's direction. It was a battered farm bucket, stolen likely.

Johanna couldn't help thinking about the burnt farm where they had found their supplies. The burnt kitchen, the dead bodies. And the *Lady Sara* still waiting for them at the riverside. She hoped the sea cows had enough to eat, or that someone would release them from their harnesses before the animals starved. Then another scary thought: someone might take off with the *Lady Sara,* and it was all she had left from her comfortable life in Saardam. Her father would need the ship if he was to keep running the company.

"Water!" Sigvald repeated with the sharp wave of a hand.

"Yeah, I'm going." Johanna picked up the bucket. "Keep an eye on Loesie," she whispered to Nellie. "And Roald, too."

Nellie nodded, her mouth set in a grim line.

Slowly Johanna picked her way down the side of the hill, between the gnarled tree roots.

Sigvald yelled behind her to hurry up, and added some words that made the other bandits burst out in laughter.

Last thing she heard was Nellie's voice, saying something about, *Do you call that bread?*

The bread the bandits had given their prisoners at midday was heavy, grainy and almost black. Johanna had seen the type before on her trip to Lurezia, where her father's colleagues had shared this type of bread with wine and rich cheeses. On its own, and stale, it had proven a little less easy to swallow.

Now Nellie was asking about beds, speaking loudly and slowly.

Johanna cringed. She had better get the water before Nellie got into too much trouble. She had never expected a demure maid like Nellie to become so doggedly stubborn about their treatment. It was almost frightening.

A carpet of leaves covered the hillside. They were wet and slippery and once Johanna almost lost her footing. This brought forth another burst of laughter from the young man who was walking down another set of horses, without packs or saddles. He splashed through the stream and led his charges up the other bank and into the glade on the far side, where four horses were already grazing.

Upstream from the place where the horses had crossed, the water collected in a clear pond. Small ripples indicated where water creatures swam underneath. The ground was so soft here that her clogs sank in the mud.

Johanna reached as far as she could and splashed the bucket in, but it was too shallow and all she got was a small amount of water and a lot of mud and leaves. Well, stuff that. The glare from the grassy glade across the creek made it hard to see how deep the water was.

Johanna stared at the horses, wishing that she could join them and lie in the grass. No, she wanted to escape from these bandits and that horrible Ludo with his groping hands. Her legs itched to run, but there was no point. She couldn't leave Nellie with that creep. They'd kill Loesie, or Roald, or maybe both. Why had these men kidnapped such an odd group anyway?

Because some of us look like we have money? Roald's fine hands, for example. And Nellie's lace bonnet.

But if the bandits were really interested in money, they would have killed the four of them and taken off with the *Lady Sara*.

Even if she tried to run off alone, she wouldn't get far with all the bandits watching her and the horse boy bringing another two horses to the glade. They knew this forest; she did not. They trusted the forest; she heard voices in the whispering of the wind.

"Water!" Sigvald yelled.

"Yeah, I'm not your slave," she muttered under her breath.

A bit further, a tree branch had fallen across the creek. Maybe she could reach a deeper spot from there. The creek banks were steeper here, so the fallen tree trunk was harder to reach.

But in one spot on the slope stood a small sapling.

Johanna carefully climbed back up the mossy bank and let herself slide down feet first until she caught the sapling. Then she used the trunk of the sapling to lower herself—

As soon as her hand touched the trunk, the forest changed into a scene of chaos and darkness. Men on horses, rearing and screaming. A couple of peasants huddled together. An older man, and a grey-haired grandmother. Children crying in their mother's skirts.

Men with burning sticks.

Slashing swords. A burning house.

The next morning. Blue-grey light of dawn. Trails of smoke over the grass.

So much blood in the creek.

The cloying scent of it enveloped her, and made her feel sick.

With difficulty, Johanna yanked her hand away from the trunk of the sapling. The golden light of the afternoon returned.

Her heart thudded.

These horrible things had happened in this place not so long ago. She peered at the far end of the glade, in the shade of the trees, and now noticed what she hadn't seen before: the glade was not a natural field at all. The creek looped back around the glade. In the shelter of the trees stood the remains of a house. Next to it, a water mill, its magnificent wheel ruined and useless.

The bandits chose to camp here, in a scene of murder and plunder?

If they considered this a safe place for the night, they would have to know who killed the farmer and his family. Maybe they were even the ones who had done it.

And then: why had she seen these things? This was a beech sapling, not a willow tree.

CHAPTER 2

HER LEGS SHAKING, Johanna filled the bucket. She clambered up the steep incline back to the hilltop, avoiding the touch of any more trees. Loud voices and laughter rang through the forest, and the screams of a woman.

No, please. Nellie.

Johanna hurried as much as she could without spilling the water. At the top of the hill the bandits had a fire going. One of the men came to take the bucket off Johanna, but she ignored him.

That sleazy Ludo had grabbed Nellie from behind. She wormed herself away from his free hand that was trying to find a way under her dress.

Johanna didn't think. She swung the bucket so that the water flew out over both Nellie and Ludo. It wasn't a very good throw and most of the water missed, hitting a couple of packs and someone's sleeping mat.

Ludo looked up at her, water dripping from his hair. His large and hairy hand covered Nellie's mouth. Nellie's eyes were so wide that the whites showed on all sides.

"Let her go," Johanna said in as harsh a voice as she could make it.

Ludo laughed and squeezed Nellie's side. He said something about enjoying sweet fruit.

Nellie gave a squeak. A couple of the men guffawed.

"Let her go," came a clear male voice.

Johanna turned around. It was Roald who had spoken. He stood with his back straight and his thumbs in the simple belt that went around the rough knitted farmer's vest that he wore. The orange light from the setting sun cast his face in strong relief. That and his unshaven chin made him look older and more stern than normal. She had told him to behave like a prince a number of times. She imagined that throughout his life, a lot of other people had told him the same. Somewhere, those words must have stuck, because even in farm clothing, he looked so much like his father it was eerie.

He's the king now. We must have a crowning ceremony when we get to a safe place. She thought of the staff and crown which she had hidden in the broom cupboard.

Roald said, "Let her go, brute. These are my women."

Oh, by the heavens.

"That be so?" Ludo said "Two women for one man, huh?" He continued with a remark of sexual nature that Johanna didn't need to understand word for word to get the gist of it.

The other bandits laughed and jeered at Roald. He took no notice of them, but took Nellie's arm and pulled.

"Watch what I do to *your* women." Ludo's hand found the buttons at the front of Nellie's dress and started to undo them, revealing Nellie's white underdress like a peeled fruit.

Nellie wriggled and kicked.

"Let her go!" Roald took Ludo's arm with both hands and tried to yank him off Nellie, but he was so much smaller and skinnier than the bandit that Ludo dragged both Nellie and Roald around as if neither weighed anything, while Roald struggled to maintain his footing and Nellie desperately tried to do her buttons back up.

Several of the younger bandits were laughing so hard that the tears ran over their cheeks.

Not Sylvan. He still leaned against a tree trunk, his legs crossed at the ankles. The intense look in his brown eyes made Johanna shiver.

A magician?

The two bears lay on the ground next to him, leaning their shaggy heads on their paws. Nothing moved about them except their eyes.

Sigvald wasn't laughing either. He stood on the far side of the fire, watching the struggle with his arms crossed tightly over his chest.

Just as Roald had gotten his feet under him, one of the younger bandits tripped him up from behind.

Then Sylvan pushed himself off the tree trunk. In one fluid motion, he jumped to his feet, rising well over both Ludo and Roald's heads. He wore very dark clothing, and although he was not broad like some of the others, his height made him imposing. The scar on his face even more so.

Ludo stopped dragging Nellie around.

Sylvan brushed Roald aside as if he was a fly. He grabbed the front of Ludo's jerkin, ignoring the presence of Nellie between them.

Everyone fell quiet.

"You are so much interested in selling them, right?" His speech sounded a lot more sophisticated than that of the others.

Ludo retreated ever so slightly.

"Who do you think will pay for damaged goods?"

Ludo made a protest about *just having some fun*.

Sylvan retorted with a harsh remark in dialect that sounded like it meant, "Stop behaving like a child."

Ludo growled, "Oh, fuck off." And added something about bashing his face in and being a soft boy.

"I dare you to try." Sylvan let go of Ludo's jerkin. He yanked Nellie out of Ludo's grip. She squeaked, but he roughly pushed her aside, as if clearing the scene for a fight. Nellie tripped with the force of his push, and fell into the leaf litter.

Johanna rushed to help her up.

"Oh, Mistress Johanna!" Nellie cried. Her face was white, with the imprint of Ludo's hand still over her mouth. She closed Nellie in her arms. Nellie trembled.

Poor Nellie.

Father had appointed Nellie soon after her mother had died, to be a companion to Johanna as a girl. Nellie had been fourteen when she joined the household, and was in many ways, more than Johanna's governess. Nellie might be silly and annoying at times, but she was the closest thing Johanna had to a sister.

Sylvan and Ludo circled one another, under the bandits' cheering.

Over Nellie's shoulder, Johanna scanned the forest for an avenue of escape. She'd planned to use a fight as a time to escape, but now that it happened, it was not a good time to try anything. Most of the horses were now in the glade, and would probably be hard to catch and even harder to ride without reins, and she wasn't that confident that she could put them on quickly. The packs had all been taken down from the horses and there would be no time to sort out what they needed. If they ran now, they could only do so without supplies, and who knew how far the nearest town was?

The two bears had risen and stood behind Sylvan. One of the animals emitted a low growl.

Ludo charged. Sylvan simply stepped out of his way. Ludo swung his fist, but Sylvan ducked. He brought his fist up from underneath. The hand connected with Ludo's jaw with a clearly audible thud. Ludo cried out, and stopped Sylvan punching again by holding him in a strong hug.

They two men pushed against each other. Sylvan tried to free himself but, not being strong enough, only succeeded in pushing the pair of them around in a resemblance of some strange dance.

The other bandits gathered, laughing and shouting. Finally, Sylvan managed to free himself from Ludo's grip. Ludo tried a few punches, but Sylvan was too quick and easily avoided them. Ludo charged and caught Sylvan around the middle. The two toppled onto the leaf-covered ground. At that moment, one of the bears jumped on top of Ludo's back. It grabbed hold of Ludo's jerkin and pulled, ripping a hole in the leather. Then it grabbed Ludo's hair and pulled his head back. Ludo's eyes went wide, showing whites on all sides.

Nellie gave a squeal. "Oh, it's going to kill him!"

But then Sylvan whistled, and the animal let go of Ludo's hair.

Ludo rubbed the back of his head, covered in bear slobber.

He pushed himself up to his knees while glaring at Sylvan and breathing heavily.

Then he started laughing. Sylvan laughed, too, albeit a bit more stiffly, and all the bandits joined in, clapping each other on the shoulders. The two bears dropped back in their sleeping position into the leaf litter.

Johanna joined Roald, Nellie and Loesie at the base of a large tree a little away from the fire.

Nellie whispered to her, "Thank you helping me. I was so afraid that they were going to harm me."

"Shh, Nellie, it's all right. Of course we would help you."

"But they're so big and we're all so small. I'm scared. That man is such a piece of filth."

"Tell me about it. I've sat on the horse with him all day."

"Oh, Mistress Johanna, you shouldn't have to go through that. You're married."

"Not like he cares about that. Listen, we don't need to be big, we need to be smart. The first chance we get, we're going to escape and get back to the *Lady Sara.*" But deep inside she was scared, too. Next time, the outcome of a confrontation like this might not be as good. If Ludo got it in his mind that he wanted to do indecent things to either her, Nellie or Loesie, there would be nothing to stop him.

Nellie asked, "Do you think you could still find your way back to the river?"

"I think so." But in reality? She thought she knew the direction the river would be if it were a straight line. But rivers were rarely straight lines, and they had been riding through this forest for hours. All trees looked the same. If they escaped, how could they get back? With dogs and horses, the bandits would capture them again soon.

She shrugged but avoided Nellie's eyes. To flee successfully, there had to be a place to flee to.

The bandits got serious about producing something to eat. One of the younger bandits had caught two rabbits which Johanna had seen dangling at the back of his saddle earlier in the day. Another man brought a larger animal, with a shorthaired brown coat, a long neck and long graceful legs. Sigvald sent two young men off to skin the animals.

"It's a deer," Roald said.

Johanna had heard of deer, but had never seen any. "Do they all have horns like that?"

"They're called antlers. This one is a young male. Older males have bigger antlers."

Sylvan gave him a suspicious sideways glance as if he wanted to say *What do you know about it?*

"They're good eating," Roald continued.

"Who says you get any?" Sylvan's voice was harsh and strongly accented. Each time he met her eyes, Johanna felt a chill going through her.

Slowly, he rose and strolled to the spot where they sat.

Magic was in everything he did: from the way he sniffed the air to the way he whistled at the bears and the way they obeyed him without the need for chains and cages. It was in the way he argued with the others and the way he rode off on his big horse. Danger swirled about him like a cloak.

He faced the prisoners and sank into a crouch, resting his elbows on his bent knees, studying each of them in turn.

Nellie cowered under his gaze. He simply laughed at her in a way that said *I'm not even interested enough in you to do you any harm.*

Roald stared back at him, and Sylvan held his gaze for such a long time that Johanna felt chilled. There were rumours of people who could read minds, but those rumours were all lies, weren't they?

Sylvan shifted his gaze to her. His brown eyes narrowed, but he remained quiet for a long time. Then he said, "Interesting."

What he found interesting he neglected to mention.

Then he turned to Loesie. He bent closer, looking her in the eyes. "You're magic-touched, eh?"

She kept staring as if he had said nothing.

He pushed her shoulder.

Loesie flew up, making a low hissing sound. Her eyes had gone white again. Johanna shivered with the chill of magic that went through her.

Sylvan laughed. "You're a little cat, eh?" Didn't he feel it?

"Leave her alone," Roald said.

"She belongs to you, too? *Your* women? What do you think you are?"

"I'm—"

"Shhh," Johanna said, before Roald could give away anything.

Sylvan looked from Roald to her and back again, but said nothing.

He poked Loesie again, and she tried to scratch him, but he yanked his hand back quickly.

She growled.

Another bandit got up. "Let me try." He poked her. He wasn't quite so quick in retreating and received a nasty scratch to his arm.

Sylvan laughed. "Now your blood's poisoned and you become a witch, too."

The man's eyes widened. "What? Yer kidding, right?"

The other bandits burst into laughter.

Sigvald didn't laugh. He stood on the other side of the fire and watched, unemotional, with his arms crossed over his chest. The firelight glinted on his bald head.

His eyes met Johanna's. They were cold, calculating. She feared that he knew exactly who she and Roald were. If he came regularly to the towns on the Rede River, he might know the *Lady Sara* or the Brouwer Company flag. He would certainly recognise the marks of the Saarlander royal family, and if not . . . the bandits only needed to search their prisoners, and they would find the ring on the chain around Johanna's neck, and they would find the Carmine crest on Roald's underclothes.

Roald said, "I was only going to protect you from that man. You don't want me to say anything?"

"Don't say anything if it isn't necessary."

"I was only trying to answer the brute's questions."

"They are not our friends. We don't answer questions."

"But Mother says it's polite to—"

"We don't need to be polite. They took us against our will."

Johanna didn't know if Roald understood, or even remembered how they'd been captured, but at least he shut up. Fancy not understanding the concept of being a *prisoner*.

And then another, more chilling, thought: *He's been a prisoner all his life*, like a bird in a gilded cage. People would have been telling him what to do, and most likely he never wanted to do any of those things. Come to a tea party at the palace? Hold a speech? Dance with a string of nervous girls? Get on this boat? Look after these horses? He might not even understand that there had been a difference in his freedom.

Sylvan went back to the fire with a toss of his head.

The young men had returned with the skinned rabbits and the deer and hung them over the fire. One of them sat down at the fire, turning the spit.

Sigvald pulled out a flask which he unstoppered and drank a good swig. He passed it to Ludo, who drank, too, and wiped his mouth.

Soon, the men were all talking and drinking.

Johanna remained with Nellie, Roald and Loesie at the base of the big tree. It was getting cold this far from the fire. Nellie was shivering, but neither Loesie nor Roald seemed to be bothered by the chill.

The bandits talked and laughed. Occasionally the waft of the smoke and the increasingly wonderful smell of the meat drifted in their direction.

"I'm hungry," Roald said.

"We're all hungry." Johanna met Sigvald's eyes again across the orange glow of the fire as he lifted the bottle to his mouth and drank.

"I don't like these monks," Roald said.

"These are not monks." If they were, they'd have some dignity and manners.

"I don't care, I don't like them anyway. They're rude."

Johanna whispered, "Shh, not so loud."

The old grizzled fellow who had shared his horse with Loesie was telling a story. Johanna caught shards of information about a beautiful widow with a young daughter who had rejected his advances. Several of the men made snide remarks about the old fellow's missing teeth and his attractiveness to women.

"What dialect do they speak to each other?" Nellie asked.

"It's Eastern Burovian," Roald said.

Johanna frowned at him. "But we're not in Burovia." As far as she guessed, they were in Gelre. Burovia was on the other side of the Rede River. "Can you understand them?"

"A bit. The monks all speak the same."

Nellie started, "They're not—"

"Leave it, Nellie."

Sylvan got up from the fire and came to them, carrying a leg of meat, dripping fat. He placed it on a wooden plank and proceeded to cut chunks of meat off it with a knife so sharp that he hardly had to make any effort to slice through the meat. One of his bears sat on its haunches behind him, observing his actions with black beady eyes. Waiting to be tossed scraps.

"Eat," he said.

Behind him, at the fire, the bandits broke into loud raucous laughter. Most had red faces from the liquor, but she hadn't spotted Sylvan drink anything.

Johanna took a slice of the meat from the plank he held out to her. "Where are you taking us?"

"You would like to know, huh?"

"Well, yes. I don't understand what you want from us. We're only three innocent women and a harmless man."

"Why were you travelling with a witch with magic so strong that I can feel her presence from miles off?"

Loesie?

Johanna glanced at her friend, who was stuffing pieces of meat in her mouth with both hands. She chewed open-mouthed, letting a trail of fat run down her chin. Johanna remembered the incident with the cheese. A chill went down her spine. She had trusted Loesie with the sea cows, and Loesie had taken the *Lady Sara* upstream as Johanna had told her. She had trusted Loesie not to betray them. "She is not a witch. She has been affected by magic, that is true."

But what if she was wrong, and it was all part of an evil plan and Loesie had been ordered to take the ship upstream by the person who had put the spell on her?

He said, "Witch or bewitched, all the same thing."

No, it wasn't, and if he knew anything about magic, he would know that. More likely, he was lying. "So why do you want her?"

"We protect land from evil magic."

Then why do I feel magic about you? The look on his face was dead-serious. What did people here believe about magic? As far as she knew, the eastern Belaman Church also forbade it. The Church of the Triune was considered a splinter group of the Belaman Church, and had more in common with it than either side acknowledged.

"What are you going to do with us?"

"The Duke will decide. Now eat. We have no use for dead witches." He put the board down and watched while Roald put a piece of meat in his mouth. Then he rose and turned back to the fire.

"He scares me," Nellie said when he had taken his place with the other bandits again.

Johanna nodded. Nellie might not have any magic, but she had a good sense of trust. "I don't know who he is, but he's not one of the regular bandits."

"Do you know what all those tattoos mean?"

"I think they're old runes. I went through Burovia with Father once, and we saw old shrines along the river with marks like that. Can't say if they were exactly the same, though." She looked aside when Sylvan turned his head in her direction, as if he knew they were talking about him. The firelight made the scar across his cheek deeper and uglier than it looked in daylight.

"How dare he call us witches?" Roald said, his mouth full.

"He's talking nonsense," Johanna said.

"Yes, we're not witches. I will teach these monks that they can't say things like this." He made to get up.

"Sit down, please," Johanna said. "We need to plan this."

To her surprise, he listened.

"We need to make a plan to get away," Johanna continued in a low voice. "But we need to be smart about it so that the bears can't smell us." The creatures in question were looking at her with their black beady eyes.

"I think we should wait until we come to a town," Nellie said. "You often say things because you like to believe that they're true, but I don't believe you can find your way back to the *Lady Sara*."

"We'll find our way, once we escape. It might not be the shortest way, but we'll get there."

Nellie pursed her lips.

No one said anything for a while.

"Who is this Duke?" Nellie asked a bit later.

"I have no idea," Johanna said.

"I think we are close to Duke Lothar's land," Roald said.

Johanna frowned at him. She had to keep reminding herself that he'd spent the past few years in this region. "Who is he?"

"Duke Lothar Anselmus Wilhelmus de Marty-Loessinger, duke of Nieheim, prince of Florisheim, commander of—"

"We don't need the entire page of names."

"He considers himself second in line to the Barony of Gelre. He is Baron Uti's half-brother, older than him, but born of the wrong blood. The Baroness Machteld, who is Uti's mother, gave birth to only one son. Lothar is the son of the Baroness' sister Gunhilde, who was much prettier than Machteld and whose four children are said to have had four different fathers, one of which was Uti's father."

Nellie frowned at him. "That's a lot of terrible gossip about a single royal family. It's not very nice."

"It's true. Things that are true don't need to be nice."

"Who told you all this?" Johanna asked.

"Everyone knows this. Especially about Gunhilde. The duke doesn't look like the Baroness Machteld at all."

Everyone in Burovia where he had been maybe, but it was news to Johanna. "But the baron does not consider the duke in line to the throne?"

"No, but the duke thinks he should be. He tried to kill his half-brother twice. Last time was two years ago, when he hosted a dinner for the baron and his family in his castle and planned to poison them. When the baron found out, a lot of the duke's people were cast out of Florisheim."

"I bet they were." They'd probably gone on to become rogues. Maybe these bandits were some of them.

"Why would the duke be interested in us?" Nellie asked.

Roald didn't answer that question. It was probably beyond him. He knew facts and he knew how to do things by routine, but he had trouble doing something with those facts and drawing conclusions from them.

Johanna thought she knew why the duke was interested in them: because of magic. And she wondered how much this had to do with Roald's stay in Burovia and a certain religious order, or with Baron Uti's presence at the ball, and maybe—she shuddered—maybe the burning of Saardam was simply another attack on Baron Uti, dressed up as an invasion by rogues. Had he died in the fire, too?

Some pieces of the puzzle were coming together.

The main figure in the war was Baron Uti, whose son had told Johanna that Gelre used magic at court. And here were a bunch of rogues who wanted to protect the land from magic, or maybe just any magic that was not the right kind, and they worked for the duke.

And the conflict was also about a Burovian religious order, and religious groups forbade magic. And about a king who was said to have been in negotiation with a necromancer, necromancy being a serious form of black magic.

Wasn't this starting to sound like the Church of the Triune had a hand in it? That same church that had been banned from most lands?

Johanna ate her chunks of meat, which were dry, overcooked and hard to chew.

Nellie was having trouble as well. "This meat is very stringy." She wriggled her tongue in her mouth as illustration

"It's because it's a deer," Roald said. "They live in the forest and have to be tough. There's deer, and wild pigs, and badgers, but they're not very good eating. Pheasants and rabbits are, but they live near fields."

"Have you seen all these things?"

"Seen them, caught them, eaten them. Pheasants are best, but you have to pluck all their feathers and that's annoying."

Nellie said, "I don't know how you could stand it, with all these horrible oak trees."

"Beech, not oak. Beech trees are nice and tidy. Oak trees have big knots."

"Well, whatever." Her voice sounded angry, close to breaking.

"No, it's important. With oak trees, you can—"

"I don't care! I hate this forest! It's disgusting! I am disgusting, and there is nowhere to wash anything." She burst into tears.

Johanna put an arm over her shoulder. "Come on, Nellie, I need you to keep it together."

"I'm done with keeping it together. I want clean clothes. Look at this bonnet." She yanked it off. Underneath, her hair was lank and stringy. She lifted up her skirt and showed the underskirt beneath. "Look at my underclothes."

Johanna could smell it before Nellie showed her: the white chemise was streaked through with dark brown stripes of blood. The same dark stripes also ran down the pale skin of the part of Nellie's leg that Johanna could see.

Johanna met Nellie's eyes, pools of embarrassment and horror. "You have your monthly bleeding? Why didn't you say anything?"

"With that disgusting man at my back? He would just have laughed. Ladies' problems are not real problems at all." She buried her face in her hands. "I feel so dirty, Mistress Johanna."

"Cowpats, Nellie. I'm sure we can do something to help you out." She rose and wormed her underskirt from under her dress. She gave Nellie the wad of fabric and noticed that it was pretty dirty, too. "Here. Use this. Wrap it around yourself. Wash it out in the creek tomorrow."

"But it's your best—"

"Use it, Nellie."

Nellie took it without a further word, and went behind the tree.

CHAPTER 3

THE BANDITS talked and drank well into the night. They reduced the deer and rabbits to a pile of bones which they threw to the dogs. The bears got some uncooked chunks of meat, the front legs and the head and neck of the deer, and proceeded to tear strips of meat and sinew off the bones with their teeth. One of the animals then trotted off to the creek and made a mess of the pool where Johanna had tried to collect water. It stood in the shallow water and dug in the sand with its claws. Then it repeatedly stuck its head in the water and nosed around. What it found there to eat, Johanna couldn't see, but it chewed noisily and wetly.

When it got darker, Sigvald made one of the junior bandits get up to pass the prisoners mats and blankets. They were a collection of horse blankets and quilts, probably stolen from farms the group had raided. Johanna noticed that the young man was unsteady on his feet from the liquor. If they escaped now, how many of these men would be too drunk to ride?

The mats were thin. The forest floor was not very comfortable. The beech trees had knotted roots which came right through the thin mats. The blankets were scratchy and not particularly warm. A musty, unwashed smell hung about them.

Johanna wrapped a blanket around her shoulders, and watched the bandits in the glow of the firelight. Nellie sat to the right of her, her knees drawn up to her chest and her skirt wrapped around her ankles. Roald sat to her left. He didn't seem to be bothered by the chilly night air.

Loesie lay on her side on the mat, facing away from the group. Johanna hoped that she was finally asleep.

The bandits talked and laughed, emptying one flask of liquor after another. Their voices increased in raucousness and their slurred speech made it even more impossible to understand the men. She wasn't sure if any of them understood each other anymore. The old grizzled fellow fell flat on his face when he reached for the bottle. A moment later he was snoring, to the great hilarity of the others.

Johanna dozed a bit, leaning her head on her knees, but she kept falling over, and when she lay down, the ground was too hard to be comfortable. It got cold.

An eerie wailing birdcall echoed in the forest.

Slowly, the fire died to a faint orange glow. There were only three bandits left around it, and one disappeared on the other side of the hill and didn't come back. Another fell asleep, and the last one stumbled to his feet. He stood there swaying, silhouetted against the dying fire, before lumbering off to his mat. Not much later, the men were finally all asleep. A couple of them snored loudly.

The bears also snored, a low rumble.

Johanna dozed off, but jerked awake when that bird called again. She had no idea how long she had been asleep—she guessed not more than a few moments—but her heart was thudding. There were no sounds other than the roaring of blood in her ears.

"Nellie?" Johanna whispered as quietly as she could.

Nothing.

Johanna held her breath to listen, but all she could hear was the bandits' continued snoring.

If they wanted to escape, this was the time to do it, now that the men were all blind drunk and asleep. The bandits had even been drunk enough to forget to tie their prisoners up, or to forget to take the dogs back from the meadow. Johanna nudged at Nellie's shoulder. "Let's go."

"What? Now? By ourselves?" Her voice sounded scared.

"This is our best chance. They're all drunk. The bears are asleep."

"I agree. I don't like these monks at all. We should go," Roald said.

"Shhhh. We don't want to wake them up, especially the animals." She didn't *think* Sylvan would set the bears on them, because obviously they had more value alive than dead, but those dogs down near the creek could make a lot of noise if they were spooked, and wake everyone up.

The meadow was invisible from here. Moonlight made light patches on the canopy, but no moonlight pierced through to the forest floor, where it was dark as ink.

All of a sudden Johanna had to think of what happened last night in the cabin of the *Lady Sara* and how scared and unhappy she had been.

She'd been stupid. They had been safe aboard the *Lady Sara*. In fact, she'd been stupid about getting married for most of her life. She'd been a constant worry for her father, her stubbornness a source of irritation for him, and look where it had got her.

I swear when I get out of this alive, I'm going to be a good wife and make my husband happy every night. She didn't care, she would give anything to be back in that cabin and submit to him again. The only part of her that had been hurt was her pride, and in the scheme of things, she was struck by how utterly unimportant that was.

She crawled to her feet. "Let's go. Take these blankets."

Fumbling in the dark, she rolled hers up, and there were noises that indicated that the others were doing the same.

"Do you really think this is a good idea?" Nellie asked.

"Shhh. Loesie?"

"Does she have to come?" Nellie whispered. "We can come back for them later. She'll attract any people looking for magic."

"Loesie is my friend." Why was Nellie always so annoying? *Because she's usually right.* "Come on, Loesie."

"Hmmmm."

"Can you help her, Nellie?"

"Me? But I can't—"

"Please. Nellie, can you just once do as I say?"

"I always do as you say, Mistress Johanna, and it gets me into a lot of trouble. I don't think this is a good idea."

Please, Nellie, this is not the time to have stupid arguments. But Nellie *was* right. Loesie's presence *would* attract attention. From what she gathered, it was what had attracted the bandits to them in the first place.

"Well, tough," Johanna said to herself. She remembered first meeting Loesie in the markets and feeling the magical connection straight away. Loesie had smiled at her in a mischievous way and had handed her a basket that showed a bull doing unspeakable things to a cow in a wide green meadow. Johanna had laughed, and had asked if the calves were good this year, and then Loesie laughed. The secret of magic that they both shared had become a point of friendship straight away.

Like Johanna, Loesie refused to become what people told her to be.

No matter what the Reverend Romulus had said, Johanna believed that the real, happy, mischievous Loesie was still in that ghostly body somewhere and could be cured if they found the right person.

Leaves rustled nearby.

"I'm ready," Roald whispered. He sounded like a young kid going on an exciting trip.

They started down the hill, feeling their way down the uneven ground. Johanna could only hear the rustling of leaves, and had no idea if Loesie was with them. She hoped so, because she was going to have serious words with Nellie if she kept behaving towards Loesie like this.

They stopped when the ground evened out. Johanna listened for sounds indicating that the bandits or any of the animals had woken up, but could hear none.

It was so dark here that it was impossible to see the slightest thing.

"Which way now?" Roald asked.

"We need to get to the horses."

"Which way is that?"

Johanna studied the forest, most of it in ink-darkness. A faint patch of light indicated where the glade probably was. But she could see no horses. More worryingly, she couldn't see the creek.

"I think this is stupid," Nellie said. A sniff indicated that she was crying. "I don't know if you have seen it, Mistress Johanna, but all these people have magic. If we take the witch, these men will know where she is. Maybe she even attracted them to us in the first place. I'm not being unkind to her, but we can't escape like this. You know how magic seeks out magic? It happens with you and Master Willems and the witch."

"Loesie. Use her name."

"I don't care! They will know where we are because of her."

"Ghghghghghgh!"

"Shhh!" Loesie sounded angry now, and Johanna did *not* want to get Loesie angry because who knew what trouble that would cause.

Nellie whispered as loudly as one could whisper, "There is no point escaping! They will catch us. We don't know where to run. We don't know how to get food when we get lost. We can't—"

"Nellie, what's gotten into you? If we stay, it will end up badly, especially for you. Those men haven't seen a woman for a long time. I might have protected you so far, but there is going to be a time that the creep Ludo drags you behind a bush and we will be too late."

Nellie sniffed. Her breath shuddered. "Just so you know, Mistress Johanna, if I had the choice I'd rather unwillingly lose my virtue to a disgusting hairy brute than die by the hand of ghosts or other vile magic. And that's the truth. Call me a coward if you want."

Johanna had nothing to say to that. Coming from Nellie, this statement was so astonishing that words would be inappropriate. Nellie, whose first life rule was "virtue", followed close behind by "appropriateness". She'd actually said that she'd rather—?

"Hang on, Nellie. What are you so afraid of?"

"There's *things* in that forest. Magical things." Her voice cracked. "Ghosts, wraiths, ghouls. Evil things. It makes me feel ill just thinking about them. This is godless country, and no amount of prayer is going to help us. If we go out there, we *will* get lost and those magical beings will find us. We have no defence. Please, Mistress Johanna." She grabbed Johanna's arm in a surprisingly strong grip.

"Then what do you want us to do?"

"Wait until we come to a town."

"They probably won't take us to a town."

"I don't care. Please don't make me go into that forest. Please." She burst into tears.

Well, great. What now?

"Weren't we going somewhere?" Roald asked.

At the same time Nellie said, "No."

Johanna said, "Yes."

Loesie said, "Ghghghghgh!" The tone of distress in her voice made Johanna turn around.

A *horse* had appeared in the forest. Well, it wasn't a regular horse, but one made from luminous mist, floating a forearm's length above the ground. It walked steadily, trailing tendrils of white vapour.

"Mistress Johanna!" Nellie grabbed Johanna's arm and hid behind her.

Roald said, "How does it do that?" In a genuinely interested voice.

Oh, for the inability to feel fear.

"Ghghghghgh!" Loesie charged forward. With both arms, she mowed into the shining apparition. Shards of mist scattered through the night. They swirled, they re-formed, they grew. One horse became six horses.

They were all quite close, a few paces away, in a half-circle surrounding the group.

"Nooo," Nellie groaned.

"Hmmmm!" Loesie made for the closest horse, her arms raised.

"Stop it, Loesie." Johanna grabbed the back of Loesie's dress. Nellie had sounded like she was about to faint, and she didn't want to have to deal with that, too.

The phantom horses paid the group no attention. They stood with their ears pricked and heads in the air. Nostrils and eyes were wide. They bunched together, as if using each other to seek protection against something, real or ghostly.

Johanna noticed what she hadn't seen before: several of the animals had cuts in their coats. Blood—or its white misty substitute—ran from the wounds. Then a ghostly man ran onto the scene, brandishing a sword. The first animal—a stallion—reared and let out a scream.

In the real forest, the horses in the glade responded with whinnies and snorts. A dog started barking and the other dog joined, growling like crazy.

Men shouted in the forest. Someone came running down the hill carrying a flaming torch.

"Come here, everyone, hide." This was Roald's voice.

Johanna stumbled to where he hid, pressed against the trunk of a large tree. When he held a protective arm around her shoulders, her hand touched the tree's bark.

The forest dissolved for a scene of fire and death. Men on horses burst into a farm yard, carrying torches and rampaging through a vegetable garden. The barn door was open and horses ran out, showing the white in their eyes. Billowing smoke rose from the roof. A woman ran away from the burning house, carrying a child. She was mown down from behind by a rider with a huge sword. The child, a toddler, fell in the mud. The rider hacked at it until it was nothing but a chunk of bloody pulp.

Johanna jerked back from the tree, her heart thudding.

Leaves rustled not far from where they stood, followed by the heavy footsteps and hot breaths of a very large animal. One of the bears. Johanna couldn't see it but it sounded like very close.

"Ghghghgh!" Came from somewhere in the dark.

"Shh, Loesie." Who knew what that bear would do if it became interested in them.

The ghost horses pranced between the trees, being light-footed and luminous, while a couple of the bandits tried to round up the real horses on the meadow. Two bandits with torches stood by the side of the creek. Were they looking for the prisoners? The hounds ran through the forest, panicked, whining, barking at everything. One of them would stop near the bandits with the torch, jump around in a little circle as if chasing its own tail, and then continue running.

Johanna could now see, silhouetted against the glow of torch-light, the fuzzy outline of a bear, much too close. It lifted its head, snorting. Its nose wriggled.

Also silhouetted against the light stood Loesie, with her hand outstretched towards the bear. "Ghghghghghgh."

Johanna held her breath. Any moment now and the bear would pounce and they would all be dead. That was why bandits didn't need to tie up their prisoners: because the bears killed any that tried to escape.

Loesie didn't move.

Johanna sat as frozen. She didn't want to see what happened but couldn't tear her eyes away from that silhouette: Loesie with her hand outstretched, the bear lifting its head to her . . . sniffing her palm.

For several long moments, nothing happened. The blood roared in Johanna's ears. Then the animal grunted, lowered its head and trudged back up the hill. A wisp of magic trailed behind it. Loesie said nothing but Johanna could feel the magic in the air. Bear magic, which was said to be evil.

Where did Loesie learn these things? As far as Johanna knew, Loesie only had willow magic, like her.

In her mind, she heard the Shepherd's voice. *Likely, your friend is already dead and demons have possessed her body*.

Way back when all this started, Loesie *did* try to warn her about demons, right? Johanna thought back to that horrible moment when she had seen Loesie at her market stand and realised there was something very wrong with her friend.

Inside her mind, the Shepherd's voice said, *They show us what we like to see*.

What did she like to see? Loesie still in control of her mind, even though she couldn't speak. Loesie recovering. Loesie being the normal, happy Loesie, and speaking again, being healthy again.

A couple of the bandits were now coming back up the hill with one of the dogs. Johanna didn't think the bandits knew the prisoners had gone, but there was no escaping now. There were no places to hide in this forest, and both the hounds and bears would find them quickly, even if they tried to run.

"Let's go back," she said. And hope that the bandits wouldn't notice.

Slowly, they walked back up the hill. The further they progressed, the angrier she became with herself. She had hesitated too much when it mattered. Since when was she afraid of the things she saw in wood? Since when had she been such a coward?

Since seeing that awful forest in Burovia, and hearing its whispering voices.

They found the hilltop abandoned except for a single bear, and resettled at the tree with their blankets. The bear lifted its head, sniffed the air, grunted and put its head back down on its paws.

Johanna pulled the blanket over herself and leaned into Roald, who awkwardly put an arm around her shoulders. His breath tickled her hair.

For a long time, none of them said anything. The bandits were still walking around the forest, coming up the hill to relight their torches in the fire, and shouting to each other. Something about a missing horse and people being out there to steal horses. The latter was Sigvald's concern.

But no thieves were found and after a while, the missing horse turned up as well and all the men came back. They returned to their mats, still talking to each other in the glow of the fire. Their voices were angry. Johanna thought she heard Sylvan's voice most of all. He sat on the other side of the fire and seemed to be angry over someone going somewhere or allowing the horses or dogs to come to a place *where the dead live* whatever that might mean. But after a while the argument faded into brooding periods of silence. Eventually the participants went back to sleep.

"We sleep now?" Roald asked.

"Yes." Then she added, her voice low, "Thank you for standing up for Nellie earlier tonight. I thought that was very brave of you. I'm sorry that they teased you."

"No one can touch my women."

She didn't like being referred to as anyone's possession, but she was glad that he considered Nellie part of the deal. She wondered if the feeling stretched to Loesie, but didn't want to push the point. "Be careful, though. These are dangerous men. Some of them are magicians."

"I'm not afraid of them."

No, she feared as much. She suspected he couldn't lie. Maybe he didn't have the capability for fear either. Right now, she felt jealous of his simplistic way of thinking. He didn't worry much; he just lived. He knew lots of things, but attached little emotional value to them or even to his life. When someone said, "Walk," he walked. He protected what he considered his property.

In the space under the blanket, his body was warm against hers, and in an odd way, comforting. She *needed* that, because she was running out of ideas and no one else seemed to have any.

"I'm sorry," he said.

"What for?"

"I can't look at you tonight. It's not that I don't want to see you, but it's too dark here. I can't see anything."

Johanna almost laughed. "That's all right. You can look some other day." After all the things that had happened, that was what he thought about?

"Yes. I want that. It's good."

If ever they were safe and warm enough, if she could convince him to be gentler, if they were in a comfortable and clean bed, it might be good. Or even in the too-narrow and not so very clean bunk in the *Lady Sara*'s cabin. The thought of the ship left abandoned at a disused jetty on the river made her eyes prick. That was part of her family's wealth, back there. She owed it to her father to try to get back to the ship. And the thought of her father brought more tears.

Roald said, "I just remembered something. My mother said that when I married, I had to tell my wife at least once every day that I loved her. I haven't done that yet. Do you want me to say it three times to make up for it?"

Johanna choked up. For a long time she couldn't speak, trying to swallow away tears which came anyway, leaked out of her eyes and ran over her cheeks. Eventually she managed to control her voice just enough to say, "Just once will be enough. It doesn't become different or better by repeating it."

"It does. Every day, she said, because it's one of the things that people forget to say to each other."

"Oh, you silly." She pressed herself against him, wanting to snuggle in his arms, but likely he didn't even understand the importance of his mother's words; he just repeated them. He didn't react to her touch.

"I love you. I love you. I love you." Spoken in his detached and strangely sincere way.

Johanna wiped tears from her cheek.

In the same sincere way, he asked, "Do you love me?"

She took a moment to think about that, but not for very long. "Yes. I think I do." Or she could come to love him, given some time. Not in the way Father had loved Mother. Not in the way a brother would love a sister. But in a caring way. Roald was honest, simple-minded and immature most of the time, but completely sincere. He hated pomp and ceremony, and he hated being in the spotlight. The more pressure people put on him, the more strange things he did or said. He was odd, and unpredictable especially when provoked, but he was not dumb.

In the darkness, she reached up to him and stroked his cheek. The stubble of his beard scratched under her fingertips. Again, he didn't react, but she tried not to let that hurt her. *He doesn't know any better.*

What sort of upbringing had he received? How much had his mother and father hated him?

"Mistress Johanna? What are we going to do now?"

"Go to sleep, Nellie. We're not going anywhere tonight." And damn, she felt angry about that. She'd have to find another opportunity to escape in a place that was even further from the *Lady Sara*, from where the ship would be even harder to find. What if they arrived at the place where the bandits were taking them tomorrow morning?

The night was full of questions and no one had any answers. The bandits snored by the fire. The bears snored, too, and grunted occasionally, as if they were having a dream about . . . what did bears dream about?

Roald also fell asleep, a warm weight against her. He twitched occasionally. Nellie mumbled in her sleep. Johanna wasn't sure if Loesie was asleep, but every now and then, she spotted a faint glow of magic in the place where she had last seen Loesie. Little wisps that curled into the air. Once, she thought she could make out Loesie's cupped hands by the light of the faint glow. She tried to ignore it, but it scared her. If only she knew what was wrong with Loesie and what she could do about it.

She watched that spot of light, waiting for Loesie to do something that would tell Johanna for sure that she was now possessed by an evil lord, but of course that would be all too convenient a thing to happen. It didn't.

Somehow, Johanna must have fallen asleep, because the dark forest bled into green pastures with cows, and happy farmers bringing cheeses to market. All the usual people were there: the clog-sellers at the markets, the silly nobles with their Lurezian fashion, and even Octavio Nieland, holding his wine glass by the stem with a gloved hand, giving her a look of superiority.

Was Octavio Nieland even still alive?

Nothing would ever be the same, ever again.

CHAPTER 4

THE NEXT MORNING dawned misty and bleak. Johanna woke up in the warmth of the blanket and Roald's body. Leaves and branches of the tree above her glistened with moisture. Occasionally drops fell to the forest floor. Their soft *plocks* were the only sounds in the muffled silence. She lifted her head. Roald was still asleep.

A lone figure stood at the bottom of the hill, looking over the misty glade where the horses grazed peacefully. Not a sign of last night's chaos remained. Johanna could make out some churned leaves at the bottom of the tree where they had sheltered last night, but that was all. That tree was so close to the camp that she was almost glad that the escape attempt hadn't been successful. In the mist the hounds and bears would have a huge advantage. They would never have gotten far.

The man looking over the glade turned around, and it was Sylvan. He proceeded to walk around the bottom of the hill, picking up sticks of wood as he went. He put these in a bag which he carried at his belt. The prick of magic hung in the air.

Something Kylian had said came to her mind. *We use magic at court.*

Clearly lots of people used magic for different things. It looked like Sylvan had set a magical ward to make sure that the prisoners didn't escape. Something that made people feel fear or reluctance to leave.

Nellie's behaviour from last night now made sense. As someone without magic, Nellie was more affected by the spell.

It also chilled Johanna to the core. Since the church forbade magic, no one in Saardam learned anything about it. She had always believed that magic happened by itself and you could read it, but not control it, but she was clearly wrong about that.

It looked like you could imbue the wood with images that made a person scared. What if you could make a person feel anything simply by leaving a piece of wood in a room?

Do you want to sell your business?

Buy my stock?

Marry my daughter?

She shivered. If she was right, people needed to learn about this magic, not run away from it, because entire countries could be controlled by it.

And then a thought: maybe entire countries were *already* controlled by it. Not Burovia, Gelre or Estland, where magic was more common, but Saarland.

Well, that was a very disturbing thought.

Johanna carefully wriggled out from under the blanket. Her muscles screamed protest from having sat in an uncomfortable position all night. Her bladder almost hurt from being too full.

A couple of the other bandits were already up. One of the nameless ones was cooking something in a pot over the fire with another one waving a blanket to fan the fire. The wood was obviously wet, because it produced a lot of smoke.

Johanna ducked behind the large tree. The bear lifted its head, but didn't get up. It was watching her.

Sylvan had disappeared around the corner of the hill, but Johanna held no illusions that he didn't know that she was here. Johanna wavered between seeing what he was doing and relieving herself, and nature won. Wetting herself would be very uncomfortable.

The trunk was wide enough for her to hide behind, but now the horses all stood watching her from the other side of the creek.

"Hey," Johanna whispered, and flapped her hand.

The horses didn't move.

"Scat!"

They just stared at her.

To her annoyance, another bandit had come to the creek to wash his face.

Well, it was not to be helped. Johanna pulled up her skirt but when she squatted to do her business, the man at the creek turned around. It was Ludo. His face split into a leery grin.

And she was to spend another day on a horse with this creep, trying to avoid his groping hands?

Sooner or later, something was going to break.

She remembered what Nellie had said about him last night and shuddered. If doing that thing with Roald hurt her, she could only imagine how much it would hurt for a man twice his size.

Ludo said something. She noticed his exceedingly hairy arms. She wondered if the rest of him—

No, this was definitely not a good thing to be thinking about right now.

"I'm married," she said, making her tone as vicious as she could make it.

Ludo laughed in a "like I care" manner, and went up the hill, hitching up his pants as he went.

By the time Johanna came back to the camp, the others were awake and one of the bandits was handing out dirty bowls containing a lumpy grey substance that did not deserve the word "porridge". He gave her a bowl.

It didn't look appetising, but it smelled of grain and her stomach probably wouldn't mind, as long as it was warm and filling.

As a bonus, too, Ludo sat on the other side of the fire and hadn't made a grab for Nellie.

There were no spoons, but it was so stiff that they could eat it with their fingers. Loesie did it with both hands, as if she hadn't eaten for days. Nellie did this daintily, with a prim expression on her face and not looking at anyone. Her face was very pale. Nellie's bonnet, normally pristine white, was grimy and dirty.

"I want honey," Roald said, poking at the contents of his bowl.

"There is no honey," Johanna said.

"It doesn't taste any good without honey."

"I know, but there is no honey." She knew she shouldn't let his stubbornness get to her, but a sudden wave of irritation made her grumpy.

"I got honey from the farm."

"Yes, but it's at the boat. We're not at the boat. Come, eat up."

Some of the bandits had already eaten and were rolling up their mats. Johanna dug into the sticky substance with her fingers. It was warm, but stuck to the inside of her mouth like glue. She struggled to swallow the stuff.

"I haven't said it yet today," Roald said.

"Said what?" She looked to the side, her mouth full of grainy sticky porridge that she was trying to work into her stomach.

"I love you."

It was the strangest thing someone had said to her while she was trying not to gag. His expression was so sincere that it made her choke up, which didn't help her ability to swallow gluey porridge. She couldn't speak, and brushed his hand with the fingers on her right hand, which weren't sticky.

Roald was so sincere, so innocent, she had to protect him from whatever the bandits had in store for them today. Most of all, she had to protect his identity.

Sigvald stood with his hands at his hips, watching his men. He and Sylvan exchanged meaningful looks, but said nothing. Johanna wondered about Sylvan's status. He seemed to be one of the youngest but was treated as one of the higher-ranking members of the group. She hadn't seen him eat breakfast, or eat last night. He hadn't taken part in sharing the liquor.

With his long plaits, tattoos and scar on his face, he looked creepy. His youth only accentuated the effect. He was too young to have a position of leadership in this group, so it had to have come from his other abilities.

Some of the bandits had already finished with breakfast, and one of those brought the horses back across the creek. The animals were restless, grumbling and nibbling at each other, and probably sensed that they were about to leave. When breakfast was done, the men finished packing and the first ones climbed on their horses. Four remained with saddles and without packs, one each for Johanna, Roald, Nellie and Loesie, with their riders. As she had expected, Johanna was paired with Ludo again. Just her luck.

The column set off through the forest at a plodding pace. They went around the course of the creek, past the ruins of the farm and the water mill. The giant wheel stood idle, with water cascading uselessly over the scoops. Some of them had been destroyed by fire.

From there they went up the next hill. Johanna noticed a sigil cut into the bark of a tree. A sign of ownership or direction? She studied the various tattoos and signs on jerkins or packs, but couldn't see the same sign anywhere. Was that a good thing?

Ludo behaved better than he had the previous day, perhaps because Sigvald stayed close. Maybe he had an interest in delivering the prisoners unharmed.

As the morning wore on, the mist lifted. Sunlight came through, casting brilliant rays of light through gaps in the foliage. Birds broke into unfamiliar songs, nothing like the sound of the larks, lapwings and sea birds that you would hear in the fields of Saarland. These birds sounded musical and melodious. Occasionally, Johanna would see a silhouette of a bird hopping about in the branches. Once she spotted a small bird on the ground, scurrying in the leaves. It was brown with a vivid orange chest. Roald would know what type of bird it was.

Around mid-morning, the lush beech trees made way for scrawny pines. The air had a curious smell here, and the ground underfoot became soft with springy moss, so that the horses' hooves made almost no noise. In places the soil had been churned over. Pigs did that, she remembered.

There were curious signs of previous human habitation: the occasional circle of wooden poles stood on the mossy ground, often surrounding a mossy mound. Mostly, the posts were badly decomposed and some had fallen into heaps, so whatever the posts were for, it had been a long time since people had lived in this area. There were no fields, no farms. The pines looked thin and emaciated. Their sparse foliage let through lots of light. Faint patches of mist still lingered near the ground, giving the forest an ethereal appearance.

The air pricked with magic. Even though these were not willow trees, Johanna had no doubt that they would have stories to tell of death and failure, of ghosts and magic. With the massacre the tree had shown her yesterday, it made her feel cold.

She shivered, despite the nice day.

They stopped for the midday meal in a mossy clearing with another one of those mounds surrounded by tree stumps. The men sat down on the moss.

Johanna's backside was so sore that she remained standing while she ate the dry bread the bandits gave her. Nellie complained, but both Roald and Loesie were quiet, each struggling with their own pain and fears.

Johanna eyed the mound. She took a chance and put her hand on a nearby tree, but all she saw was tranquil forest. Either her magic didn't extend to pine trees, or the images had faded. In most cases, with wood that was part of buildings, images lasted a few weeks, but much longer if no one touched the wood or nothing happened.

She leaned against the tree, studying the mound, noticing that no one, not even de dogs or bears, went inside the circle of posts.

"They're burial mounds," Roald said behind her.

"They must be very old."

"They are. It's been a long time since people lived here. The hunter tribes came here to flee the Westfalian invasion, but the land was too poor to support farming. People moved on to the low country or the river towns. Many people died of the plague while they lived here and they're all buried in the forest."

"I think their ghosts linger in this place."

"Ghosts are not real."

Johanna thought of the white horses she had seen last night. If they weren't ghosts, then what were they? "I think ghosts and magic are real. This place has a lot of magic. You can feel it in the way that it's so quiet here. The moss on the ground takes away all the sounds. Mist hangs between the trees like trails of magic. And then there are these burial mounds. Why did so many people die here while no one lives here now? Did they all just pack up and leave? Don't you think this forest is spooky?"

He frowned at her. Sometimes, when he spoke about all the things he knew, and when he was relaxed, it was easy to forget how awkward he was around people.

"I think it's spooky here," Nellie said. "You can feel it. It's as if the dead whisper in the back of your mind. I'll be glad when we come to civilisation."

Johanna wasn't sure if there *was* much civilisation out here.

"*She* doesn't like it here." She nodded at Loesie, who sat on the ground eating her bread. She didn't look at anyone else, and kept the chunk of bread close to her chest, as if afraid that someone would take it off her.

"Do you feel the magic, Loesie?"

"Ghghghghgh!"

Johanna searched for the other person with magic, Sylvan, but couldn't see him anywhere. Not with the young men, not with Sigvald, not with the horses. Sylvan's big black horse wasn't there either. When had he left?

His absence didn't seem to worry anyone. Sigvald was talking to the older man with the missing teeth and the younger bandits were sharing a joke of some sort.

Guess it had to be all right, then

"You're more familiar with that area than any of us, Roald. Do you have any idea where we are?"

He frowned at her. "I told you yesterday, we're close to Duke Lothar's land."

Not that she knew where that was. "Do you think they're taking us to the duke?"

"Duke Lothar does not let anyone on his land unless they're invited."

"That means yes?" Did that mean they were invited or they were about to run into an ambush?

"Surely the duke will realise his mistake and let us pass?" Nellie said.

"What is he supposed to mistake us for?" Having heard Roald's story about the royal family of Gelre, she hardly thought anyone would mistake the group for innocent travellers. She became increasingly sure that the duke was the boss of these bandits and had sent them with a reason.

A mild commotion behind them signalled Sylvan returning with three dead rabbits tied up by the back legs. His horse's flanks were moving fast and covered in sweat.

Sigvald made a sharp remark, to which Sylvan retorted with a toss of his head. Sigvald replied something about *You can be responsible for the trouble.*

Sylvan said under his breath, "Coward."

Sigvald leapt and pulled him by the leg of his trousers. Sylvan hadn't expected that and fell from the saddle on top of his attacker.

With shouts of protest, a couple of other bandits sprang forward and pulled the pair apart.

There was no time for this, one man said.

Another said that they'd all agreed on something.

A third said he had enough of the nonsense and wanted to go back. Back where, he didn't say or Johanna couldn't make out.

The men were all shouting at each other, filling the quiet forest with angry voices. Roald covered his ears with his hands, rocking from side to side. Johanna knelt next to him—ouch, her backside—and tried to calm him down. He was humming to himself.

Johanna had to do something, or he would start banging his head against a tree trunk, so she started singing the words of a children's nursery rhyme, the only song she could remember.

He lowered his hands and listened to her. His face relaxed.

The argument between the bandits dissolved with the men talking to each other in small groups, with angry glances across the clearing. With Sigvald snapping harsh words at the prisoners that seemed to be about Roald, and sounded like an insult, but Johanna didn't catch the meaning. Perhaps it was better that she didn't.

The men climbed back on their horses and left the clearing split up into two distinct groups: those who agreed with Sigvald and those who wanted to go with Sylvan. Ludo rode with Sigvald, and so did the old bandit who rode with Loesie and the shy young man who shared his horse with Nellie, but Roald's bandit had changed camps.

This worried Johanna a lot. Sylvan and his group rode too far to the side for her to speak to Roald. The horse also moved too much for her to tell if he was rocking from side to side. The bandit would have told him to sit still. Roald was good at following orders, but he was going to be stressed. Not much disturbance was needed for him to throw a screaming fit. He'd been fragile enough at their last stop.

Whenever the two groups came close enough, he didn't make eye contact. Not a good sign, she thought. Maybe he thought the men were angry with him instead of each other. Maybe he didn't understand anger.

Each time Sylvan and his group rode further away, she was afraid that they would split up and go their own way. That fear clamped its cold fingers around her heart. They could not afford to lose Roald.

The vegetation now consisted of mainly pine trees, most of them twisted and knotted, with few healthy branches. Soon, the cover of trees stopped altogether to make way for a field of low shrubbery with the occasional straggly tree.

From the top of the horse, Johanna could see over many hills of it, dark green vegetation dotted with grazing sheep.

Was this the thing they called *heather*? Her mother used to speak of it a lot, because apparently there were big fields of it in northern Estland. Apparently at the end of summer, it bloomed purple. It was the beginning of summer now, still spring, really, so the hills were a dull dark green.

The group followed a track up one hill down the other side. It was more like a sheep track than a proper road, and it was narrow, so the horses walked in single file, Sigvald's group first and then Sylvan's group quite a way behind. Johanna couldn't even see Roald anymore, even though she risked Ludo's attention a few times by looking over her shoulder.

She listened, but heard nothing except the clop, clop, clop of the horses behind them, and the whistle of the wind, especially when they came to the hilltops.

The ground in the valleys was often wet, with scrawny black-and-white-trunked birch trees. Sometimes there was a little creek or pond; sometimes there was only tall grass. If one of the horses wanted a drink, its hooves churned up the soil, leaving deep tracks in the mossy ground.

After they had traversed a few such hills, the forest disappeared from sight.

The ground became increasingly barren, often with exposed patches of white sand on the surface between the shrubs. Sometimes the sand lay in little soft-looking mounds, with animal tracks across its surface; sometimes rainwater had etched deep ruts in the ground, and the jagged walls of earth would show sand of different colours, mostly white, light grey or rust.

Although the travelling party disturbed a few flocks of sheep, they saw no people. Once they passed an abandoned hut, its roof covered in dead heather plants which, apparently, the people had dug, with adhering soil and all, out of the surrounding hillsides. Next to it was a field where the churned soil was still visible, coated in a layer of loose sand. A soft, wind-blown hill of sand lay on the lee side of a timber structure that looked like a well. Sand had also heaped on the lee side of the farmhouse, and threatened to enter the structure's open door.

Johanna shuddered at the thought of what had happened to the inhabitants of the house. All signs of human habitation they had seen since being captured told a story of death and destruction. The burnt-out shell of the water mill, the burial mounds, and now this.

This land was so badly cursed that it sowed dissonance even in those who crossed it. Just look at how the bandits argued all the time.

Not much later, they crested the top of a hill, and the view forward as far as they could see consisted only of white sand.

Sigvald held up his hand. Horses stopped, with much blowing and snorting. Sigvald spoke to the bandit next to him, but they were too far away for Johanna to hear what was said.

They waited. Not a word was exchanged. Horses tossed heads and shook manes. They sniffed the air.

On the horizon to the left and behind, a bank of sharp-edged clouds towered into the sky, topped by a great wedge-shaped protrusion. The sky above was still blue, but the air had taken on that oppressive quality that preceded bad weather.

Sylvan and his group came up from behind. Johanna was glad to see Roald, and glad that he didn't seem to have thrown a screaming fit, although he kept moving his head from side to side.

The bandits went into a discussion which Johanna thought was about which direction to travel. Several men didn't like the sand. Sylvan said to keep going. Sigvald didn't like that either. Johanna suspected that Sigvald didn't like *anything* that Sylvan suggested, but they seemed to reach some sort of agreement.

Sylvan slid from his horse and took it by the reins. He led the animal onto the sand, straight past Sigvald, who said nothing and stood with his hands crossed over his chest.

Sylvan stopped at the crest of the nearest dune, looked at the sky and waved his free hand. A gust of wind whipped up sand around him. He stood with his eyes closed and his hands spread, palms out.

Wind magic.

The men in his group were also getting off their horses. The old bandit had already lifted Loesie down. She stood with her arms clamped around herself as if she were cold. *She also feels the magic.*

Johanna refused Ludo's help in getting down, and so did Nellie. Johanna managed to get down from the horse safely, but Nellie half-fell and landed clumsily. Fortunately the sand was soft and nothing was hurt except Nellie's pride.

Still brushing the sand off her clothes, Nellie joined Johanna and Roald. "What are we doing? Why did we get off here?"

Sylvan turned around. "Too hard for the horses to carry us. We walk them."

"Are we near the sea?" Nellie asked.

This was like the sand dunes near the ocean in Saarland, only at the ocean there was one row of dunes and then the beach, but here there seemed to be no end to the expanse of sand. Johanna didn't *think* there was an ocean on the other side, because Gelre was a land-locked country and the northern ocean was to the north of Estland. But to be honest, she didn't understand why this sand was here either.

It's a cursed country. That was all she knew.

The group started across the sand in single file. Sylvan went first with his horse, the two bears and the dogs, then Sigvald and a couple of his men leading their horses, then Roald, Johanna, Nellie and Loesie, and finally the rest of the group and remaining horses.

The air became more pressing, while thunder growled in the distance. The horses were skittering, lifting heads and tossing manes. Father always said it was a bad thing to be caught in a field during a storm.

The wind blew in squalls.

Sand whipped around them, biting into exposed skin. But it was more than sand that caused Johanna's skin to tingle. There was *magic* in the air.

Even the hounds stayed close to the group. They whined and squeaked with tails tucked between their legs and preferred to walk between the horses. The bears stopped every so often to sniff the air.

Sand got in Johanna's shoes, in her eyes and in her hair. It bit in the exposed parts of skin. The wind swelled until it took Johanna's breath away and carried sand over the surface in streaks

Sigvald hurried the group along. The horses plodded through the biting sand with their heads held low.

Johanna had to force herself to put one foot in front of the other. Every time she thought they were at the end of this horrible sand, there was another hill. They would sink deep into the sand on the lee side, ploughing through it almost up to her knees.

Nellie collapsed several times, and cried that she didn't want to keep going, but each time a bandit hauled her to her feet, increasingly roughly.

Johanna wanted to shout, *Stop the theatrics. It's not helping.* But she said nothing for fear of getting a mouth full of sand.

Loesie plodded on, her eyes closed. Her mouth moved, as if she was praying.

Roald seemed the only one unaffected. His hair whipped across his face, but his expression was blank as usual.

On and on they went.

Thunder was now close enough to make the air shake. The dogs yowled, and Sylvan yelled at them while trying to keep his horse quiet.

The muscles in Johanna's legs screamed from exhaustion. The wind picked up and blew lashes of sand against her that bit even through her clothes. Sand got under her dress. It got in her eyes and her mouth. She could barely open her eyes to see.

What sort of terrible evil country was this?

CHAPTER 5

THE STORM broke with a few claps of thunder that made the ground shake. A sharp burst of rain halted the drifting sand. The wind stopped as suddenly as it had come. The sky cleared with crisp clouds and even a few patches of blue. The rain had made the sand wet and easier to walk on. The magic had vanished from the air.

Coming over the crest of a particularly tall dune, Johanna spotted a dark row of forest on the horizon, a wonderful sight after all that loose sand and the dunes.

A quick look over her shoulder revealed an untouched landscape of white sand dunes with a few gnarly pine trees. The wind had erased all their tracks.

After crossing a few more dunes, they came to a small village, nested in an alcove between sand dunes that smothered a landscape of heather and small pine trees.

The houses were low structures from rough wood, with no windows, half-sunken in the ground. Like the abandoned house they had seen previously, their slanting roofs were covered with sods of heather, the branches brown and dead, and now all quite sandy from the wind. Johanna counted twelve such houses, each of them surrounded by fields with the most miserable crops that Johanna had ever seen. The plants were pale green, almost yellow, their stems short and uneven, and very sparse. Not even the weeds had made much of an appearance.

A couple of women were working in a field, scooping off encroaching sand and carting it out of the settlement in a wheelbarrow. A small sad-looking paddock with a rickety barn held an ox and a shaggy-haired pony. A man was filling the drinking trough that stood against the barn wall. Two children herded a group of sheep along the main "road", a path pockmarked with puddles and rutted with tracks from nothing but wheelbarrows.

Someone whistled and everyone in the village turned around to watch the newcomers. People stared at the horses. Even if they weren't being ridden, the bandits' horses looked magnificent compared to the village animals.

A couple of scrawny children stood in the doorway of the closest house, dirty, dressed in rags, very skinny and small.

In the centre of the village, a man with a shovel in his hand came out of a barn as the procession came to a stop on what looked like a village square. Sigvald handed the reins of his horse to the young bandit next to him and went to speak to this villager. Sigvald was much taller and broader than the man, and his tattooed head gave him an imposing appearance.

They exchanged greetings, the villager appearing very timid. He didn't look Sigvald in the eye.

His hands were dirty, and when he wiped his face he spread a smudge over his forehead.

A couple of small boys stared at the party from the barn door behind him. A young woman dragged them out of the way with a hissed, "Begone with you, or the magician will change you into a toad."

Sigvald said something about a bed and food.

The man flinched. "The barn is available, as always. But, Lord, we have barely enough to feed ourselves. The winter has not been kind to us."

His speech sounded a bit odd and old-fashioned, but it was surprising how well Johanna understood him, better than she understood the bandits.

Sigvald shouted at him about having an agreement. The man

retreated further, muttering about poor harvests and fields being covered in sand. "It's like a curse, my lord."

"You deserve it," Sigvald said.

"We bring our own food." Sylvan came forward, holding up the rabbits. "If you can cook them."

The man's eyes widened. "Yes, yes, certainly, lord. Lenie, put them over the fire and ready the barn."

The young woman scurried forward, took the rabbits and disappeared after the two boys. Sigvald gave Sylvan a dirty look. Sylvan said something in too low a voice for Johanna to hear and Sigvald replied with an obscenity.

"We will tend to your horses," the villager said.

"Make sure they're well-looked after." Sigvald's voice was a growl.

"Certainly, my lord." He called a few names.

A couple of men came out from the other huts. All of them were skinny, with bony arms and hollow cheeks. They took the horses to the pen near the village's well, which was occupied by the pony and the ox. The horses bunched together in the corner furthest away from those two animals. They held their heads low and showed little interest in their companions. The sand had exhausted them as well.

One man dragged in a wooden trough, while a young woman came to the well.

She lowered the bucket, keeping a wary eye on Sigvald. Johanna could hear the bucket hitting water, not very deep. The woman turned the wheel to bring the bucket up with a squeak, squeak, squeak that sounded ominous in the silence. She emptied the bucket in the trough. The water had a red-brown tinge.

Sigvald snorted. "That's not water, that's piss."

She flinched away from him. "This is the only water we have, my lord."

Johanna cringed at how these people treated him as a highly-ranked person.

The girl trembled visibly when she lowered and pulled up the bucket for the second time. Squeak, squeak, squeak went the wheel into that tense silence. She emptied it in the water trough. *Splash*. The horses gathered around.

"Wait," Sylvan said. He pushed himself between the horses' bodies and stuck his hand in the water. He paused, with his eyes closed. To an outsider, it might have looked like he relished the coolness, but Johanna could read the signs.

Water magic. She'd thought he had wind magic. Was it even possible to have two different kinds of magic in one person?

He turned to Sigvald and nodded. He had judged the water safe. The horses drank and not much later, the dogs and the bears came to join them. The girl brought up a few more buckets of water, doing her best to ignore the gazes of Ludo and several other bandits. A young boy brought a wheelbarrow full of hay.

"I wonder where they cut the hay in this miserable place." Sigvald lifted his face to Sylvan, as if his question was a challenge.

Sylvan snorted, but said nothing.

Someone was spoiling for a fight, but Johanna had no idea what it was about.

Sigvald went inside the barn when the owner called him. The rest waited around uneasily. A couple of the children stared at the group from the door of another house. Johanna met the eyes of a little girl and found herself the subject of the stares of all the children. Most were scrawny, dirty. One had a funny eye that looked in the wrong direction; another's foot was turned awkwardly inwards.

She felt too embarrassed for words. She didn't want to be part of this group that barged into this poor village and demanded favours that the villagers couldn't afford.

Never had Johanna seen poverty like this. There were beggars and refugees in Saardam. Some were sick or had lost limbs in wars, but even if they couldn't find work, there was the church where the poor and destitute could always get food. Even in their plain farm clothes, dirty and tired as they were, the Saarlander travellers looked so much richer.

The farmer called the group into the barn. Johanna, Roald, Nellie and Loesie followed the bandits through a rickety door into the hastily vacated room.

A few lights burned on roughly-hewn pillars that supported

the roof. The floor was covered in heather twigs in a layer so thick it was springy. Rough-hewn wooden planks held up the layer of soil on the roof, but some of the roots had worked their way between the planks and dangled from the ceiling like spider webs. It was surprisingly warm in here. The bandits put down their packs along the side wall. All the saddles and riding tack went near the door.

"The food will be out shortly," the farmer said to Sigvald.

There was a rough door in the back wall that opened a sliver, and the two boys peeped through again.

The farmer turned to them. "Hide yourselves. Don't annoy our guests."

But now the door opened further, and two teenage boys entered carrying a table, which they placed in the middle of the barn. Then the little ones carried in a bench which they placed on one side of the table. They ran back to fetch another bench for the other side of the table. The older ones brought a couple of rough-made chairs that went on both ends of the table. Sigvald sat in one of them, Sylvan in another.

There was not enough room for everyone, and a couple of younger bandits, as well as the prisoners, had to sit on the ground.

Johanna, Nellie, Roald and Loesie ended up next to the saddles, which exuded the smell of horse.

The bandits laughed and talked as if they owned this place and it was their right to be here.

The farmer, whose name appeared to be Otto, called into the adjacent room, "Bring the soup now, Lenie."

Johanna revised her assessment of these people. While this was obviously a barn, the sheep were outside at this time of the year, and the family made money by offering travellers a simple place to stay. She guessed there hadn't been any travellers for a long time. Who would willingly traverse that horrible sand?

The farmer's daughter brought in a large pan of soup that smelled wonderful, which she set on the table with the announcement, "The rabbits will be awhile cooking."

She first served the bandits, starting with Sigvald, and only came to Johanna, Roald, Nellie and Loesie when she had finished with all of the men.

She handed Johanna a battered bowl, their eyes meeting. Lenie's eyes were grey, and she wore her hair tied back in a severe bun that made her look much older than she was. "I didn't know that women rode with Sigvald."

"We're not part of his group," Johanna said, well aware that that Sigvald had his head turned and was listening while pretending to talk to his fellows.

"You're travellers?"

"Prisoners. We're from Saardam."

The girl's eyes widened. "Really? The home of the free church?"

Free Church? "We have the Church of the Triune."

"That's it." She lowered her voice, "We're Free Church members, too. That's why we can't live in Florisheim. You know how they allow magic over there?" She glanced at the bandits. Some had finished their soup.

One of them yelled, "Stop talking, serve us first!"

The girl turned away. "I'm sorry, I've got to go. Will you pray with us later tonight? It would be an honour."

"Hurry up!" Sigvald yelled and another bandit hit the table with a thud.

The girl went back inside and made her round past everyone at the table with a pan of mash.

Johanna watched her sinewy arms as she lifted the heavy pan. She was really incredibly skinny. The Church of the Triune? Here? Really?

When the girl got to Ludo, he squeezed her behind. She shied away from him.

She finished her round and came back with bowls for Johanna, Nellie, Roald and Loesie.

"Be careful of that one," Johanna said in a low voice, glancing at Ludo. "He's been harassing us the entire journey. Don't give him ideas."

The girl gave her a strange look. She picked up her pan and walked out without a further word. No thanks, no questions.

Oh well, at least she'd warned the girl.

The soup was watery, the bread made without butter or salt and the plates were stained and chipped. The rabbit was a little undercooked and the mash very bland. But it was warm and filled her belly for at least a little while. She met Nellie's eyes over the top of Nellie's bowl. "You're all right?"

Nellie nodded. Her cheeks were red from being outside all day.

Both Loesie and Roald had finished their meals. Loesie lay curled up with her head on her hands, not unlike a cat. Her eyes were closed. Roald leaned back against one of the saddles, also with his eyes closed. His mouth was slightly open.

Exhausted. Johanna felt like joining them.

"Isn't it terrible how these people live?" Nellie said softly. "They go to church and are good and honest people."

Johanna wasn't sure if going to church was a quality that defined a good person, but she wasn't going to argue.

From her position she could see through the open door into the other half of the house. There was a single room, now empty in the middle where the table would normally go. In the corner stood a simple stove, where the girl was just putting a block of wood on the fire. The two little boys sat on the ground playing a game by the light from the flames. A smoky rush light burned on a shelf, giving off only a faint glow.

The girl beckoned Johanna to come. The bandits had finished their meal and had taken out the flask again, talking and laughing.

"Come," she said to Nellie. Best to let Roald and Loesie sleep.

Johanna and Loesie had to step over Roald's outstretched legs to get to the door. Sylvan's glare followed them all the way.

The other room was possibly even darker than the barn. Apart from the open stove, there was little furniture. The bandits were using the only table and chairs these people possessed. There were a number of beds around the room's perimeter. One of Lenie's adolescent brothers lay in a bed, looking at the fire. The other sat playing a game with his two young brothers near the stove lit by the glow from the fire.

In the far corner of the room was a small altar with whittled pieces of wood and oddly-shaped stones. A particularly knotty piece of wood looked like a round-waisted woman. Maybe a goddess of fertility. They would need one here.

There was also a stone with a hole in the middle and a blackened tooth. Not human, not like any animal that lived on land. Johanna had sometimes seen teeth like these on fish, but this one was much bigger. Other items included a stick with a plume made from feathers, dangling on a string made from horsehair. Johanna was unfamiliar with the type of bird—it had feathers with light and dark blue spots. She touched the colourful feathers.

"It's for reading the wind," Lenie said.

"Wind magic?"

She frowned. "We do not use that word. The church does not allow magic. Magic is the evil that the duke's men wreak upon us."

"But the wind shows you what's happening in another place?"

The girl frowned at her. "You know this also?"

"Yes, we do." *And we call it magic.* "I don't see things on the wind. I see things in wood."

Johanna put her hand on the figure of the wooden woman. It was pine, but she'd grown used to the fact that in these parts, all wood showed her things, not just willow. It showed her the family gathered around the altar. In the vision, Lenie lit a candle with a burning stick, a proper candle and not one of the horribly smoky rush lights. That candle must have been a real treasure.

There was also another woman, holding the statue in her hands. She was older, with wisps of grey hair, and very pregnant.

Lenie's mother, who had died recently in childbed? Lenie and her four brothers were the only ones in the room. The mother would be here if she were alive.

Johanna cringed inside.

Lenie continued, "The wind tells us when people come or when rain comes. There is always wind here. Without reading of the wind, we could never survive."

They were barely surviving as it was. These people were so poor that she couldn't imagine it. The land was poor, and the fields could never grow much with the battle against the sand.

They even had to trade in their dignity by letting a bunch of rogue bandits use their only table.

"Why don't you move into the forest?" Johanna asked.

"Oh no, that's the duke's land. We can't go there."

"If you offer to work for the duke, wouldn't he allow you to live on his land? You could work on his fields or—"

"No, never. These rich people blame the sand curse on us. They say that wherever we go we bring it with us, because we belong to the Free Church. They use magic and call us mad. They would kill us if we went on their land."

"Have you tried?"

"Many people have. Sometimes we are hungry and don't have enough to eat, especially when winter comes. Sometimes the boys go into the forest to trap rabbits. Other times, people go into the forest to trade things, but they never come back. We've lost many precious possessions that villagers have taken to sell at the markets in return for food. Wherever we go, we always have to cross the duke's land, and no one goes there and comes back."

Johanna imagined the strip of forest as she had seen it before coming into the village. It was just a forest, right? "What do you think happens to those people?" She shivered. There was no such thing as *just a forest*. Forests were full of evil.

"We don't know. Sometimes we see creatures amongst the trees."

"Creatures? Like the bears the bandits have?"

"Them, and others. Sometimes they're people, sometimes they're . . . something else. Magical, evil. The duke is a bad magician."

She let a silence lapse. A chill crept over Johanna's back. People in Saardam didn't believe in magic because they never saw any, because there were no forests in Saarland.

She asked, "What causes the drifting sand?"

"It's a punishment from the True God. Eventually, the sand will batter against the duke's evil magic long enough to break through his defences. Then he will be drowned under huge mountains of sand. You must pray with us and maybe we can make it happen."

Johanna wasn't going to tell the girl that her "Free Church" and the Church of the Triune sounded like very different institutions, or that the Church of the Triune in Saarland considered the ability of being able to see things in the wind or in wood as magic. Their "True God" was probably also not the same as the Triune.

She said nothing about some of those "evil magicians" being right here in the house, in the group of bandits whom they treated as guests. Anyone who knew about magic could see it in Sylvan's eyes.

She was not even going to say anything about the sand not being their friend, and if anyone was going to drown in it, the people in this village would be the first to go.

When you were this poor, there were no easy options.

She sat with Lenie on her knees in front of the altar.

Nellie had taken off her bonnet, and to be honest, it was so dirty she looked much better without it.

Lenie started the prayer in a low voice.

"True God, hear our prayers. We pray for our forefathers and all those who have been taken from us. We pray for our granpa and granma and our ma and our little sister who never took any steps with her little feet. We pray for Jan because his wife is sick, and for Seb, who is still missing two of his sheep. We pray that they may be found. We pray that the harvest might be good this year and that we have enough to eat through winter. We pray for the visitors and their safety, that they will make it safely through the duke's land. We pray that the day will come that magic is defeated and our land will be free of the sand curse." She fell silent and no one said anything for a while.

Then she turned to Johanna. "What do you pray?"

The question hit Johanna in her heart. She started in a low voice. "I pray for my country where many people were killed by fire and fire demons. I pray that whatever evil destroyed Saardam has been defeated. I pray that there are people braver than us who fought the invasion. I pray that my father has survived. . . ." She had to stop speaking because her voice would no longer cooperate. Then she steeled herself. "I pray for my husband who needs all the help he can get to—" She almost said *reign the country* but remembered that no one was to know who they were. "—to help put the country back in order. I pray that I will have the strength to help him."

"I didn't know you were married," Lenie said.

"He's asleep in the other room."

"The young man with the beard?" Lenie frowned. "I thought he was . . ."

"He was what?"

"He's not really normal, is he?"

"Normal enough." Seriously, she was getting annoyed with people pointing out the obvious. "He is awkward around people." And that, when she came to think of it, was a very good description of what ailed Roald. He didn't like people and didn't know how to talk to people except when he was talking about things he knew. He didn't like crowds, didn't like standing out or speaking in public. Didn't like being the centre of attention. He couldn't tell emotions from a person's face. He didn't know "appropriate". When someone forced him to do things he hated or felt insecure doing, he behaved strangely.

It was now Nellie's turn for her prayers. In a soft voice, she said, "Like Johanna I pray for my country and the people in Saardam. I pray that they have the strength to recover and I pray that we will soon be with them again. I pray for my family, my father and mother and for my little brothers. . . ." Her voice wavered with emotion. "I pray for our Reverend Romulus, that he may have survived the cowardly attack and continues to help the common people of Saardam." Her eyes met Johanna's. Tears glittered in them. "I pray for our royal family, and that they will have the strength and support to once again make Saardam a peaceful place again."

"Please, Nellie," Johanna whispered. The royal family wasn't doing any such thing at the moment. The fact that she was now part of that family pressed heavily on her conscience. They should go back to what was left of Saardam as soon as possible. They had been planning to return the moment they were captured but, due to that misfortune, were still moving further and further away from the place where they should be.

The room blurred with the haze of tears.

Lenie, of course, didn't know what had happened in Saardam

so Johanna told her as much as she knew, leaving out the parts about the royal family and Roald's identity. The four boys were listening, and while the younger ones wouldn't understand much, the older ones might.

Lenie turned her head as if to listen for something outside. "You better go back to the barn. My pa has gone to help one of the neighbours. He won't be happy if he sees me talking to you."

The reasons for parents to say things like that baffled Johanna endlessly, but she was too tired to argue. Too tired, in fact, for pretty much anything.

CHAPTER 6

BACK IN the other room, the bandits were singing and laughing like stupid oafs. They were telling jokes, most of them red-cheeked and bright-eyed from the liquor.

All except Sylvan, who sat at the corner of the table, meeting Johanna's eyes when she came back into the barn.

Lenie followed them to collect the plates, bowls and spoons. Johanna spotted her talking to Ludo. She smiled at him.

Johanna wanted to scream, *Don't give that creep ideas*, but there was little she could do.

Lenie left the room again, and came back to collect more plates. She smiled across the table at Ludo.

Johanna cringed and hoped the girl's father would come in soon. She was too innocent and too young to know what he wanted. If the bandits groped the daughter of their host, she didn't know how things would end. She was too tired to pack up and leave again. Too tired to face a duke with evil magic.

The barn door opened, and the farmer Otto came in. He spotted his daughter talking to Sigvald and jerked his head to the other room.

Lenie scurried back into the family's room.

Johanna had trouble keeping her eyes open. Her position, leaning against the warmth of Roald's body, became comfortable and familiar.

Loesie had rolled onto her back, her arm stretched out over her head. Her hand twitched occasionally.

Otto spoke with Sigvald and then Ludo. They seemed to be negotiating, probably the price for their meal and stay. Johanna was too tired to listen. She leaned on one elbow in the heather twigs. The ground was surprisingly soft.

The farmer's four sons sat against the wall, watching the bandits. When had they been allowed to come in and what were they doing here?

Johanna dozed off, but next thing she noticed was Ludo leaving the room for the family's living quarters. The door shut behind him.

In one moment, Johanna was wide awake.

Lenie was in that room, Ludo had just gone in. Lenie's brothers were in the barn, and Otto was still talking to Sigvald. Was this what she thought it was?

She let her hand hover over the wood at her back, the planks whose other side formed the wall in the living room, but then she looped her arms around her drawn-up knees as tight as she could. She didn't want to know and didn't need to see.

A wave of hot anger took hold of her.

That filthy swine of a father of hers still talked to Sigvald, as if selling his daughter to bandits was the most normal thing in the world. Did he even know what this meant to her? She would never get married, never be wanted by a man, never be worth anything.

It seemed like Johanna watched the door forever. She listened to the roaring of blood in her ears. Her backside got sore from sitting in the cramped position. She put one hand on Roald's shoulder and felt the steady rise and fall of his body with his breaths. A few days ago, she had felt sorry for "sacrificing" herself for the kingdom, but she had been so self-absorbed that she couldn't even see how rich she was. Her "sacrifice" would be another girl's dream.

Finally the door opened and Ludo came out. He had the nerve to grin at his comrades.

While he took his place at the table, another bandit went in.

Otto continued talking to Sigvald. The four boys sat and watched, their faces pale and gaunt.

They knew what was going on. *They* didn't like it.

The second man was back fairly quickly and then, fortunately, the four brothers went back into the room.

Their father stayed a little longer, after receiving a handful of coins from Sigvald. Going out the door, his eyes met Johanna's. She gave him the vilest stare she could muster. These people called themselves honest and religious? The same church as the Church of the Triune? No way.

The door shut.

Johanna let her shoulders slump.

Then again, it was easy for her to judge. If her family was as poor and desperate as these people, they might have done the same.

Even women of ill repute are people. She thought of Helena in Saardam, and her infectious laugh and endless source of gossip. To be honest, she preferred Helena to some of the "proper" nobles.

The boys removed the table and benches again and the bandits rolled out their mats. The farmer took the oil light into the other room. When he shut the door behind him, the barn became shrouded in darkness.

Soon, heavy breathing indicated that the bandits were asleep. One of the men started snoring, and then another. A horse made a snorting noise outside and a sheep bleated. One of the dogs grumbled in response.

Johanna fell asleep briefly, but she dreamed of climbing up a steep hill of drifting sand. With each step she took, more sand would cascade down from the top. It reached to her ankles, and then her knees, and then her thighs and her waist. She jerked awake, her heart thudding like crazy. Something heavy and warm lay over her: Roald's arm had fallen across her legs.

Johanna pushed the arm and hot blanket off her and lay staring at the darkness where the ceiling would be if she could see it.

The sighs of the wind over the roof made soft whispering sounds. They were like voices just out of hearing, voices that whispered warnings or spells, but could only be understood by people who had wind magic. Clearly the villagers could hear and see things in the wind, but all its secrets were kept from her.

The more she learned about magic, the more she realised that she knew nothing at all and that her own ability was paltry and insignificant. Maybe the people of the village were right in not considering the ability to see things on the wind and in wood proper magic. No one could do anything with the ability, except leave objects in places and retrieve them later to "read" them. It wasn't an active skill.

These people had experience with far more magic than she had seen in her lifetime.

Sylvan used kinds of magic she had never even known existed.

She remembered the ghost horses in the forest, the images of the murdered farmer and his family, the wrecked water mill. Wherever these men went, they killed and raped and pilfered as they pleased. It was a wonder that the four of them were still alive, a wonder that the men hadn't ripped the clothes off any of them.

That left only one option: their leader wanted them unscathed. She knew almost for certain that this leader was the duke who had tried to murder his half-brother the baron. She wasn't sure whether wanting the group alive was a good or bad thing. Did she really want to be confronted with the man who may have ordered the burning of Saardam? Who had sown death and destruction all the way down the river, just so that he could —what exactly? Was the whole thing about a feud between two half-brothers? She found that hard to believe.

She didn't know anymore. She was not too sure if she wanted to know. The duke might be the necromancer.

Had King Nicholaos really been so stupid as to approach a dark magician to try and bring Celine back from the dead?

Was the reason that the bandits had not tried to find out their names that they already knew? The necromancer might want to exact revenge on the last remaining survivor of the Carmine house.

And since Johanna was certain that there would not yet be an heir, the house that had brought peace to Saardam would die, and war would break out all over again. The Saardam nobles would fight. They had the money to put together an army. In fact, the king had been talking about that even before the burning.

They might fight over religion if the Church of the Triune appointed a governor. They might fight over rights of inheritance if one of the King's hated cousins tried to claim Saardam as his.

Under the king, Saardam had become important as port city. Maybe even Estland or Burovia would try to claim Saardam to stabilise their access to luxury spices and tobacco, which the rich had so come to appreciate.

Johanna's thoughts went around and around in circles, and each time she revisited a particular line of thought, the ominousness of it seemed to have exploded until her thoughts were one big black pool of swirling evil magic.

They had to get away.

That thought was clear as glass to her. Roald could *not* fall into the hands of this duke.

But how? This was a stupid place for trying to escape, far more stupid than the forest of last night. The sand would show every footstep, and would slow them down. They'd spent half a day plodding through the sand, and it would be easy for nimble, able riders and dogs to catch up.

We could go into the forest.

She shuddered at the thought, but the bandits might not expect their captives to flee in that direction.

The saddles were right behind her. They would have to take horses, which were neatly stabled in the pen outside, and then ride until they came to a town. Florisheim, perhaps. That was where the baron had his castle, and the baron would be an enemy of the duke, if Roald's information was correct. If the baron and his son had survived the fire—and she had to assume that or all would be lost—they would have returned home by now.

Yes. That was probably their best chance. What was more, Sylvan had not gone outside after dinner, and would not have put his ward around the barn—probably because the people in the village would notice and would refuse to shelter "evil wizards"?

How to get to Florisheim? Turn west and find the river. Then follow it upstream. It would not be the shortest route, but one the bandits wouldn't expect them to take. They would expect them to go back to the *Lady Sara*.

Johanna rose, carefully, trying not to make any twigs crack.

Roald still lay as a warm presence next to her. She tapped him on the shoulder until he moved.

"Wha—?"

"Shhh." She whispered at the place where she thought his ear to be, "We escape."

"Ohh, I like tha—"

"Shhh. Be quiet." Was it possible for him to whisper?

One of the bandits gave a particularly noisy snore. Johanna held her breath, but his breathing settled again.

She bent over and whispered in the hollow between Roald's shoulder and his ear. "Stay here. Grab a saddle behind you. Wait until I say we're ready to go."

Next, she found Nellie, who woke with a gasp. "What?"

"Shhh. Get up." Fortunately, Nellie didn't protest.

Johanna crawled to Nellie's other side. "Loesie?" She shook Loesie's shoulder, disturbed at how bony she felt through her clothes.

"Hmmmm."

"Come. Be quiet."

As silently as she could, Johanna gathered up the blankets, draped them over the saddle that she picked up, and crept towards the barn door. The gear was so heavy that her arms were screaming. She had to put the saddle down to lift the wooden bar that locked the door. It creaked when she pushed it open and one of the dogs on the other side gave a warning *woof*.

Johanna froze, waiting for the racket of barks that would surely follow. But the dogs only squeaked, sticking their noses through the gap between the door and the doorframe and the saddle.

She stood still for a long time, but nothing moved. She let

the hounds sniff her hand and the familiar smell of the saddle. A tail went *thud, thud, thud* against the outside of the barn wall.

Johanna pushed the door open further and wriggled through, coming out in the cooler night air. The night was clear and the whole sky was so bright with stars that she could see the dark shapes of the dogs by starlight. The sky was never as clear as this in the hazy air of the coast. You could see all the constellations against the firmament of stars, a pale white band that arced across the sky. The moon had only just risen over the horizon, and its low light silvered the trees at the edge of the plain. Johanna waited outside the door until the others came through. The dogs crowded around her. She scratched their heads and behind their ears. In return they slobbered all over her hands.

Roald came out after her, yawning audibly, followed by Nellie. Johanna pushed the door shut after Loesie came out. They walked a little away from the barn, followed by the dogs. The bears were nowhere in sight.

"Where do we go?" Nellie whispered.

"Get the horses," Johanna said.

"And then? I don't want to go back through all that sand."

"We're not. We go through the forest. We ride like crazy until we get to Florisheim."

"Ghghghghgh!" Loesie said and her voice sounded stressed.

"We have no choice," Johanna said. "Quick. Roald, you know how to handle horses." She hoped he understood, because there wasn't the time to explain. She hoped Loesie wasn't going to do anything strange, because they couldn't afford to slow down.

The horses stood in the pen near the well, a mass of subtly shifting, breathing darkness. Johanna wondered why they hadn't been allowed to roam like the previous night. Maybe Sigvald was afraid that they would get stolen, or maybe there was *something* out there that might eat horses.

When Johanna came closer to them, one snorted nervously.

Roald slipped past her, carrying his saddle and blanket.

"Be careful," she said. "They're very big."

"I know about horses."

She hoped he was right. He climbed over the fence and disappeared into that dark mass of animals.

They waited. The night was breathless and chilly. An eerie birdcall echoed in the still air. Nellie's teeth chattered.

"You're cold?"

"Yes. Nervous. I really need to visit the outroom."

"When we're out of here."

Roald also seemed to have quite good night vision, because not much later, he emerged from the group of horses leading an animal by the reins. He opened the gate to the pen and deposited those reins in her hand. It was one of the smaller packhorses.

"Here, hold on tight." He ducked back.

Johanna held on, but the horse was nervous, jiggling and pulling at the reins. The bears were somewhere around here, too, and if this horse kept going like this, the dogs would start barking and then everyone would come out.

Roald brought two more horses, giving the reins to Nellie.

"How are we going to get on their backs," Nellie said through her chattering. "They're so big."

"We'll have to walk the horses out and climb on once we get to the forest. We'll have to walk really slowly, or everyone will hear them."

Roald came with the last horse. "I'll leave the gate open."

That was a good idea. If the bandits woke up and discovered the horses loose, it would take them a while to find out that some were missing.

"Let's go," Johanna whispered. She was looking around for the bears but didn't see them anywhere.

But the horses saw *something*. Her horse was snorting and tossing its head. Another horse whickered in the dark.

Nellie squeaked.

"Calm down. I'll take these two." Roald took the reins from her. He was really quite good at this practical stuff. This place where he had spent the last few years sounded more like a religious farm.

Johanna turned her horse away from the houses of the village. There was now barely enough moonlight to see the outlines of the forest in the distance.

"They'll see our tracks in the morning," Nellie whispered behind her.

"Yes, but we'll ride soon. Once we're in the forest, our tracks will be less easy to see."

They walked quietly in single file. Johanna desperately wanted to go faster, but couldn't, because the horses would make too much noise. They now went up the sand hills and no one had breath for speaking. The horses seemed to have settled and plodded along peacefully.

Johanna could barely believe it, but it started to look like they had finally escaped.

Fields with crops stretched out on both sides of the path, probably oats and barley, but it was too dark to see.

They stopped at the edge of the field where the village was barely visible. The moon had risen over the trees and cast pale light over the world. The forest was a dark wall to their left, silent and brooding. There was not a breath of wind, but Johanna thought she could hear the leaves rustle.

The ghosts are already talking about us. Johanna shivered. All evil magic came from forests, she was sure about that.

Roald went around the horses to fasten and check the saddles on all of them. "Eastern saddles," he said. "I know how they work." He went back to his horse, and swung himself up.

Johanna tried to do the same, but oh, that awkward dress, and this horse was absolutely *huge*. There was no bandit to help her up. Nellie was struggling as well.

Johanna went to help her first and managed to push Nellie on top of the horse, but it fidgeted, and Johanna had to keep hold of the reins. Nellie was not a rider and might have ridden a pony maybe once or twice. She had to hitch her dress up high and now the horse wouldn't stand still for Nellie to get used to it.

"It's so tall. I'm afraid to fall off. I don't know that I can ride that well."

"Neither can I. Just do the best you can."

Just as well Roald had chosen the packhorses. Imagine what those giant black beasts would be like with clumsy riders.

Roald's horse didn't fidget. It stood perfectly still, its ears pricked forward. Roald was a silhouette in the saddle, sitting straight-backed.

With a lot of effort, Johanna managed to clamber up her own horse. "Ready to go, everyone?"

Loesie still stood next to the horse, silhouetted in the moonlight. Her hair was a tangled mess and the moonlight made the outline of it glow like silver. *Like a ghost.*

Johanna shivered. "Loesie, get on."

"Ghghghghghgh."

"Hurry up, we need to get out of here." What was going on with Loesie? Surely she wasn't afraid of a horse? The horses they'd use on the farm were big, too. She would know how to ride.

Loesie reached for the horse, but the moment she touched the reins, the animal stiffened. The ears went back. The head jerked up.

Roald said, "Whoa!"

Johanna's horse snorted and sidled sideways, also tossing its head.

"Calm down, calm down." She patted the horse's neck, but felt the muscles strain under the skin.

Loesie again reached out for the horse's reins. As she did so, the moonlight hit her bare hand, bathed in a silvery glow stronger than moonlight alone could have made it.

She yelled, "Wait."

Loesie's horse reared with a scream that echoed over the field. Loesie retreated, holding her arm over her head, away from the horse's kicking hooves.

Johanna's horse shied back. She had to hold on tightly just to stay on. Loesie's horse broke into a run around the other horses, its tail held high.

"Loesie, are you hurt?" Johanna reached out her hand to her friend. "Come over here." But her horse made unhappy noises and shied away from Loesie.

Roald slid off his horse. He made a grab for the reins of Loesie's horse, but it reared, kicking its front legs.

"Watch out!"

In the distance, the bandits' other horses replied. Some of

them came running through the fields with a thudding of hooves. Men shouted in the village.

"Quick, get out. Hide." Johanna flicked the reins. Her horse took off with a speed she had thought impossible for a boring old packhorse.

CHAPTER 7

T HE HORSE tore down a muddy path, throwing up clods of dirt with its hooves, and then plunged into the darkness of the forest. Johanna had to hold on with all her might not to fall off. The horse wouldn't stop. She had dropped the reins and they dangled somewhere down the sides of the horse's neck, but she couldn't get them without letting go of the edge of the saddle and if she did that, she would surely fall off. She had no idea if anyone still followed her. It was too dark between the trees. She thought she heard the sound of hooves behind her, but couldn't be certain. In fact, the further into the forest the horse went, the less certain she became.

A quick glance over her shoulder revealed only darkness. No sign of Roald's horse. No sign of the bandits. She had no idea where Nellie was, or whether Loesie had been left behind or had managed to climb on another horse. She had no idea and no control over where the horse was going. Only that it was going too fast. Distant voices echoed through the forest. Dogs barked. They would probably catch up soon. Or the bears would find her.

The horse ran and ran. Now they came through a section where it was darker than before, and where prickly branches slapped her sides. The horse's footfalls sounded muffled here.

Trees grew close together here, forcing the horse into a trot and then a walk.

A scent of pine needles hung in the air.

Now that she no longer needed to hold on for life, Johanna fished up the reins which still dangled to the sides. The horse's flanks were wet with sweat. She pulled the reins.

"Whoa, stop."

The horse stopped, panting.

Johanna looked around. They were in a very dark spot between pine trees that grew so close that the tips of branches pricked through her dress.

Johanna listened.

The only sounds came from much further away: the rustling of leaves, the breaking of branches, the footfalls of hooves on the forest floor. No sounds that made it clear if these were bandits or her companions. No barking of dogs either.

Johanna waited, holding her breath to listen better. Whoever had been following her must also have stopped.

She let out her breath and held the next one.

Would Nellie, Roald and Loesie have been recaptured?

Poor Nellie.

What had Loesie done when touching the horse? She had ridden with the bandits for the past two days without much trouble. And then a chill: had she done it on purpose? She had done her best to help Loesie, but no one else had trusted her.

Where was Roald?

Her hand went to the ring she wore under her dress, which hung heavy against her skin. The key to keeping war out of Saardam and keeping the country together.

Johanna waited, but the sounds made by other people and horses faded until they were so faint that it was impossible to separate them from the sighing of the wind in the boughs.

Had they given up looking for her, sure that whatever lived in this forest would finish her off anyway?

She felt cold.

The trees whispered to each other in voices she couldn't hear. Animals scurried up there and talked to each other with little squeaks and squawks. They must be birds or the little long-tailed squirrels that ran up a tree trunk as if it was a horizontal path. Let's stay calm and not see things where there weren't any.

Johanna swung her leg over the horse and let herself slide to the ground. She landed in a carpet of pine needles that was soft and springy. The dense cover of pine trees made it so dark here that it was impossible to see the ground, but a bit further shafts of moonlight penetrated the canopy. The trunks of trees stood as silhouettes against the faint glow. They were strange trees, straight with dead branches at lower levels.

She tied the horse's reins onto a tree and peered between the foliage. The damp and cold air reached its fingers between the gaps in her clothes.

What would she do if no one from the group had escaped? Would making her own way through the forest be out of the question?

She should warn someone in Florisheim.

But you don't know where the bandits are going, the little voice that sounded like Nellie said.

But she knew some of their names, if they were real names.

Who in Florisheim is going to care about some foreign people when they probably have their own problems to deal with?

Nellie's voice was right. Alone, she couldn't do much, never mind convince a foreign baron to send out men to look for a couple of girls, one of whom was a maid and the other bewitched, and a prince no one wanted to know about—all of them foreigners. Add to that the fact that she'd have to cross the duke's land first.

So she waited.

The biting cold made her shiver. She tried to keep herself warm by snuggling against the horse, but this particular horse was not the snuggling kind. It also refused to lie down and was probably more interested in finding a paddock than keeping a miserable human being warm.

Very slowly, morning light returned, first weak and blue, then brightening into the soft grey tones of mist. Johanna's view of the forest expanded with the increasing daylight. In places, the trees stood close to each other, but in other places light reached the forest floor and grass covered the ground. She could see no sign of anyone having passed this way.

Behind her, the horse pulled at the reins she had tied around a tree. Its ears twitched constantly.

What was it hearing? A wild animal? One of the bears? People?

Johanna held her breath and listened, but could make out nothing unusual over the sparse sounds of the forest. A bird chirped in a tree, not a kind she recognised.

Between the trees she noticed the outlines of a hill. Maybe if she climbed up there she would be able to see more.

She untied the horse, but no matter how she pulled the reins, the silly horse wouldn't move.

"Well then, have it your way." She retied the reins. The hill was not very far anyway. The horse could wait and mope here.

Johanna traversed the dense stand of pine trees, pushing low branches aside. The pine forest stopped suddenly and made way for beech trees.

Johanna climbed up the hill. It was bigger than the ancient burial mounds that they had seen yesterday. Much taller, too. As with the beech forest they had traversed, the ground cover consisted only of dead leaves. About halfway up the steep hillside, Johanna slipped in the moist leaves. She groped in the dirt to stop her slide down the hill, and her hands met a piece of wood buried sideways in the hillside. *As if it was a step.*

This hill had not been made by nature. Another burial mound?

When she got to the top, she found a slab of stone about a pace wide and two paces long set in the ground at the highest point of the hilltop. Slabs of stone came from quarries in Burovia or Westfalia. Johanna had seen places where stone came to the surface naturally, but that was further south in Lurezia. Not here. All building stone had to be carried downriver on barges like the *Lady Sara*.

That left the question: why was there a slab of stone in the middle of the forest?

She knelt and brushed away a cover of leaves.

Carved in the stone was a symbol that she didn't recognise.

Two circles surrounded a head of an animal with large, hollow eyes. The mouth bore several pointed teeth. The head had a pair of cat-like ears, but the bottom jaw was missing from the image, either because the stone was age-worn or it had never been there. The carving looked like a skull.

Johanna reached out and her fingers touched the stone at the same time the little warning voice inside her said, *Stone magic!*

A deep chill went through her.

The grey dawn became night again. People screamed, primitive, beastly screams that were nothing like war cries. It was too dark to see, but even just the sounds made her sick. Gurgling death cries, screams of pain.

Johanna yanked her hand away from the stone, her heart thudding.

What sort of sorcery was this? She had no stone magic. Or had someone placed another trap of fear in this area?

She looked around her, but all she saw was trees and greenery, the greenness of the pine forest and the elegant trunks of the beech trees. Again, no sign of anyone having passed here recently. She slid down the hill, where she placed her hand on a beech trunk, but it only showed her tranquil forest. Apparently the pools of churned mud a bit further down were popular with a group of wild pigs. They had a whole bunch of striped piglets.

What sort of evil place had this been long ago?

She circled the hill. On the far side she noticed the narrow passage that led into the hill. It was not a hill, but a cool room or ice cellar of some sort. Or a treasure chamber.

Johanna glanced into the tunnel. Its walls were made from red bricks on either side, the brickwork arched at the ceiling. At the end of this passage, perhaps a few paces deep, was a door. It was a dark, featureless thing with a simple door handle and two latches, one at the top and one at the bottom.

A waft of chill air came from the passage. It was humid, but cold and laced with a tang of decay.

Johanna shivered. She had seen ice cellars in Burovia. She didn't like their rank wetness and the fact that one was here meant that a house or settlement couldn't be too far away.

That would be the duke's house and she wanted nothing to do with this duke.

She had better go back to the horse and get out of here. Find the river and then turn upstream. Beg the Baron to come with her. She *had* to find Roald.

Johanna started walking around the hill back to the stand of pine trees where she had left the stubborn horse, but at that moment, the barking of a dog echoed through the forest. And the gallop of a horse.

The bandits. She had to hide, quickly.

The beech trees surrounding the cellar offered no hiding places at all. There was only one hiding place short of running back to the pine forest.

In that dreadful tunnel.

Johanna pressed herself against the door at the back of the tunnel. The air here was cold and humid, and chilled her deep inside. The scent of cold wetness made her gag.

Through the tunnel entrance, she saw the bottom half of a horse pass close by. The animal's coat was brown, not black. She didn't recognise the boots of the rider.

The duke's men. If she didn't find a better hiding place, they would find her.

Johanna tested the door at her back. To her surprise, it opened.

A foul, cold waft came out. Urgh. She held her nose, inching further into the darkness. Outside, the sound of galloping hooves faded. Someone shouted, but it sounded far off and she couldn't hear the words.

While she listened, her eyes became better used to the darkness.

Blocks of ice were piled in huge stone basins that stood around the walls. Each basin had drainage holes in the bottom, from which melted water seeped into the earth, hence the smell.

Just an ice cellar. Winters weren't that cold in Saardam most years, and people in the city didn't have the luxury of cellars. They built cool rooms with thick walls. Having ice in summer was a luxury that was limited to years when winter was cold enough.

She tried to calm herself. There was nothing to worry about.

But the duke's men would find the horse and see that it was tied up. They would come and look for its rider

She had to find a better hiding spot. Johanna looked around. It was cold in here and the ground around those basins was wet. Some chunks of ice were really big and others had odd shapes like . . .

Hands?

Feet?

White-skinned, waxy. Open staring eyes. Wet hair, hollow cheeks. Naked breasts and buttocks.

CHAPTER 8

JOHANNA STAGGERED back towards the cellar's door.
Now that she knew what she was looking at, she counted at least half a dozen people kept frozen amongst large blocks of ice, some slowly leaking water on the stone floor. Now she really understood where the bad smell came from. Those were just the bodies she could see. It was too dark in the cellar to count the basins and who knew how many bodies were stacked up in each basin?

She heard the farmer girl Lenie's voice *People who go into the forest don't come back*.

Her head reeled.

Slowly, she backed out of the cellar into the tunnel. In between being stuck with dead people in here and live people outside, she took her chances with the live ones.

She closed the door firmly behind her and pressed herself in the little alcove in which the door was set. The cold air that seeped through the stone still carried the cloying scent of rankness. Her muscles shivered uncontrollably and she couldn't stop her teeth chattering.

It had become fully light outside. The mist had become thin enough for pink-tinged sunlight to skirt the tops of the trees.

The forest was full of sounds of horses' hooves and shouting men.

They would have discovered the horse by now. She should have let it loose. Johanna listened, but heard no screams from Nellie or anyone.

Maybe if she stood here very quietly, they would not find her. Surely, the person who kept dead bodies on ice would not want other people to know about this. The bandits wouldn't know that this cellar was here.

It was silly coming out here, because she would be safer inside, but she wasn't going to—

Someone came from around the back of the hill and looked in the tunnel. A guard in unfamiliar green and grey livery. He looked neat, with short-cropped hair and a short beard.

For a moment he froze, surprised. He and Johanna looked at each other. Before Johanna could run, he jumped forward and grabbed her by the arm.

Something clicked in Johanna's mind. In a time that seemed ages ago and a world away, she had heard a male voice tell her, *You hold their other arm and then twist. You have to do it quickly so you take them by surprise.* Johanna grabbed the soldier's wrist and twisted the arm that held her. To her surprise, her arm came free.

She ran. First down the hill, to gain speed.

The man's footsteps thudded behind her. He was so close, he would reach her in a moment. She expected the hand on her shoulder any moment. She swerved sideways through a field of bracken. He hadn't expected that. Sticks pulled at her dress. There was movement in the corner of her vision but she didn't see what or who it was. She ran.

Footsteps again thudded behind her, more than one person this time.

Someone whistled hard.

Johanna came into a clearing and there she faced two snarling bears. She screamed and turned around, but the soldier was close behind her.

One of the bears jumped. Johanna let herself fall in the leaf litter. She covered her head with her arms and ducked. Any moment now and its teeth would grab her by the throat or rip her head from her body. Someone shouted.

Silence.

Johanna waited.

Somewhere close by several people breathed hard. A bear snorted its hot breath into her neck.

"Get up," a harsh male voice said.

It was Sylvan, his face hard with anger. Behind him stood the duke's soldier. The two bears had been the ones that belonged to the bandits.

Johanna clambered to her feet, looking from one to the other. Her heart thudded like crazy against her ribs. Why was the duke's soldier with the bandits?

Sigvald came from behind and tied her arms behind her back. Sylvan watched with his brooding, angry expression. He held his arms folded over his chest.

Sigvald gave him an order, but Sylvan didn't move, and continued to glare instead.

Sigvald finished tying Johanna up. The rope drew tight around her wrists. He pushed her to the soldier, and said something that sounded like, "Take her to the others."

The soldier grabbed Johanna around the upper arm in a bruising grip. His fingers dug deep into the soft skin under her arms.

She protested. "Hey, ow! I can walk myself, you know?"

While the man continued dragging Johanna away, Sigvald stepped towards Sylvan, his hands planted at his waist.

He said something about orders.

"Fuck orders," Sylvan said. "We take all of them."

Johanna's captor stopped and looked over his shoulder.

"Who is the boss here?" Sigvald said.

Sylvan stuck his nose in the air. "No one who doesn't deserve to be."

"Say that again if you dare."

"I will. If you go back on your agreement, the men will distrust you and abandon you."

"And they'll trust you with your filthy magic?"

"Honest deeds go rewarded, always. Foul deeds breed distrust. I know that you've had no trouble—"

Sigvald swung his fist at him, but that was followed by a deep growl and a crack of branches. Both bears had jumped forward and faced Sigvald, poised to attack.

He retreated, his face red.

"Don't think I've forgotten this. I will not forget this, until I get the chance to put my sword through your arrogant heart."

"Dare try it."

There was a tense silence, and then Sigvald whirled around and stomped off to his horse.

The soldier pulled Johanna with him to a place where a group of people and horses had gathered.

Seated on the pine needle-covered ground, their hands tied like Johanna's, were Nellie and Roald. The soldier shoved Johanna down with them. Johanna's first thought was one of relief. The second thought . . .

"Where is Loesie?"

Nellie glanced to the side. Her left cheek showed a red mark in the shape of a man's hand. There was a bead of blood in the corner of her mouth.

Over the back of a horse hung a bundle in black clothing, which Johanna recognised as Loesie's dress. Her hair, dirty and knotted, hung down the horse's flank. Her hands dangled free, the fingernails broken and bloodied. Her heart jumped.

"Is she . . ."

"They gave her a good knock on the head, but she moves."

"She spooked the horses," Roald said. "That's why the thugs woke up."

Johanna nodded. The question remained whether Loesie did it on purpose or under the order of a master.

A couple of bandits joined the group leading the packhorses.

Their regular riding companions lifted Johanna, Roald and Nellie to their mounts. Roald managed to sit up straight even though his hands were tied, but Nellie slumped. Her cheek was growing purple.

The column set in motion, at a slow pace. Sigvald went in the lead.

Sylvan rode to the right-hand side, making his own path in the forest. The duke's man followed him, and the two bears and the hounds loped behind them. Occasionally he glared at the main party. Sigvald would spit in his direction and then Sylvan would increase the pace until all the main party saw was his horse's backside.

They now rode on clear paths, and the horses could go two or three abreast.

When Ludo's horse and Nellie's bandit's came next to each other, Johanna raised her hand to her face to indicate Nellie's swollen cheek.

"Does it still hurt?"

Nellie nodded. A tear ran over her cheek.

"Where did they catch you?"

"Not far from the house. The stupid horse turned back to the village. The creep over there magicked the horse and it ran back to the others."

Next Johanna turned around to Roald, who was behind Nellie. His face looked pale and drawn. He didn't meet her eyes.

"How far did you get?"

He didn't reply.

Johanna remembered that first night when they had fished him out of the water and he hadn't spoken. He'd started banging his head into the wall.

"Please," she said softly. "Talk to me."

Roald continued to stare.

Nellie said, "He tried to protect me, but there were too many of them. That soldier man hit him real hard and then he screamed and he fell down. The bandits kicked dirt over him and laughed. He was frightened."

As frightened as he had been that first day when he went out in the hall and had to give a speech. Emotions didn't penetrate Roald's thoughts often, but she suspected that when they did, they made a profound difference.

Nellie's bandit kicked his horse into a trot so that it went to the lead of the column and out of earshot of Johanna.

Johanna met Roald's eyes. The look in his face disturbed her. "Hey, it will be all right. We're all still alive."

He said nothing. It was not all right.

She worried about what he had seen and what the bandits

had done to Lenie, her brothers and her father. Hopefully, they hadn't blamed the family for their prisoners' escape.

So they rode on for the best part of the morning. Johanna had thought that the ice cellar had to be close to a house, and that the wide forest lanes with straight rows of trees on both sides indicated the same, but she had clearly been wrong, or this was a very large estate. Whatever the soldier was doing with the group, and when he had turned up, was a mystery to her, but he rode with Sylvan, constantly talking and joking. Whenever Ludo's horse came close enough for Johanna to hear their conversation, they discussed things that she wouldn't consider bandits' business: trade, a musical performance.

Sigvald glared at the pair of them.

He rode at the head of the main group, Sylvan at the other. Occasionally, the bears crossed the distance between the groups, but always ran back when Sylvan whistled.

The group startled a couple of deer, which jumped away with great elegant bounds. The hounds went after them, but they soon came back, panting, with their tongues hanging out of their mouths.

Some time after midday, the forest lane with its straight rows of trees opened out into a huge sun-drenched garden.

At the far end sunlight glistened off a lake with a large blocky house built from red clay bricks in the middle, on a small tongue of land. Green-painted shutters covered the windows, each with a stylised flower with alternating red and white petals in the middle. The garden was mostly ornamental, with neat hedges and flowerbeds in straight lines. There were roses and lavender bushes and other flowering plants which Johanna didn't recognise. The vegetable garden had been banished out of sight of the house, behind the stables. Johanna spotted bean stakes and cabbage.

The bandits dismounted at the edge of the garden. Sylvan and the soldier rejoined the group.

"We take them from here," Sylvan said.

Sigvald crossed his arms over his chest. He said something about payment that was not enough.

"You agreed to our terms. From the moment we captured them, you tried to talk me into doing what you wanted."

Sigvald said something about being stupid.

"I have my reasons. I can't help that you are incapable of following simple instructions. If it had been left up to you, they would have escaped."

Sigvald spat at Sylvan's feet. "You need me. You pay me. You don't pay enough, I take what belongs to me." He glanced at Nellie. Johanna didn't know how much she understood of this conversation, but her face was pale and drawn.

"Ha, none of them would fetch a good price. Every town on the river is flooded with people wanting work, even the kind of work no one wants to do. None of this lot are strong enough, or pretty enough, to interest people who can take their pick of hundreds of workers. You may *want* to sell them, but you can't."

Sigvald stared and didn't reply.

Sylvan stared back. Without breaking eye contact, he produced a pouch from his belt, which he tossed to Sigvald, who caught it in mid-air.

Sylvan said, "That's the last time I'll ever ask you to do a job."

"Fuck off, rich boy."

Sylvan balled his fist, but Sigvald had already turned his horse around. He whistled to his men.

"Bye, beauty." Ludo squeezed Johanna's backside and jumped from the back of the horse. The bandits riding with the other prisoners did the same.

They mounted the spare horses and with whistles and the flick of reins, the group left in gallop, leaving Sylvan and the soldier with the two bears and the four prisoners all on the biggest of the bandit's horses. Of course these animals did not belong to Sigvald and his group.

"Untie them," Sylvan said.

The soldier went to Roald first.

"Can you tell us what's going on?" Johanna asked.

"It will be my pleasure, lady, and I do apologise for your earlier treatment."

Having untied Roald, the soldier came to Johanna and used a dagger to slice through the rope. She flexed her wrists when the rope was off. The soldier helped her dismount and then went to help Nellie. Loesie had woken up. She didn't want to be helped, but was a competent enough rider to let herself down without accidents.

The horses stood passive, their heads lowered. One was trying to nibble on a bush, oblivious that a bear nosed around in the garden bed facing it.

Sylvan whistled. Furry heads went up, tails wagged and ears went forward.

"Get Karl to look after the animals," Sylvan said to the soldier.

"Certainly, sir."

The man took the horses' reins and led them up a path to the stables on the right of the garden. Hooves crunched on gravel. The dogs and bears followed meekly.

"I get in trouble when they destroy my father's roses," Sylvan said, while leading the group to the house.

His father? The duke?

Had he come to the river especially to capture the last of the Carmine House to take the group back to his father?

They arrived at a large gravel area in front of the castle's forbidding entrance. A broad set of steps led to the main doors, tall and painted green. Although there was no gate, the steps were the only connection to the castle across the land bridge, and Johanna imagined that those doors were very heavy and reinforced with iron bars.

A couple of swans swam peacefully across the water, followed by three fluffy grey cygnets.

"Look," Roald said, pointing. "Cygnets. Like Cygna."

His mother, the pale swan-like princess from the north.

The door to the castle opened with a mournful squeak and a thin man shuffled onto the forecourt. He was dressed in dark colours and wore his hair in a dark ponytail.

"There you are, master. Your father was expecting you back yesterday."

"We got delayed." Sylvan climbed up the steps and spoke to

the man briefly. After a few words, the man went to the door, and Sylvan gestured for the others to come.

"Meet my father and enjoy the hospitality of the Swandale estate."

Johanna's mind still reeled from the turn of events. What was she supposed to think of this development? What kind of "hospitality" included guests that were brought in as prisoners?

The main entrance hall was a grandiose affair, with marble flooring, a grand staircase and an enormous chandelier. Giant oil paintings depicting severe-looking men with ruffled collars hung on the walls. They were quality paintings, too, looking so life-like that Johanna had to check several times to make sure that the men's gazes weren't following her.

It was quite dark here. The windows were small, and the walls were covered in dark green wallpaper. The few candles that burned in the chandelier didn't dispel a stuffy atmosphere.

The man led the group through the hall into a large room full of clutter: chairs, tables, few of them matching, shelves, book cases full of old works.

In a big armchair by the window sat a man. He was thin, in a well-worn house coat and matching slippers. A walking stick rested against the arm of his chair. He had a grey beard, clipped short, and a ring of hair surrounding his head. The top was bald and shone like a polished stone.

Apart from the fact that he was of the right age, he didn't look one bit like Baron Uti. In fact, he looked stern, but in a friendly way.

"Meet my father, Duke Lothar."

Johanna felt compelled to bow. Nellie did the same, but Roald stared at the duke, his brow furrowed. Did he recognise this man?

Loesie's gaze wandered off to the corner of the room, towards a cabinet with doors that held tiny panes of glass. Her irises had gone cloudy again. *Please, Loesie, behave yourself and stay out of trouble.*

"Father, these are the refugees I told you about."

Nothing about names. The bandits had never asked any of them for their names either.

"Hmph." The duke grabbed his walking stick. With a groan he heaved himself to his feet. Johanna was surprised how tall he was. Like father, like son. He shuffled to the group, looking Johanna in the eye.

"Some are magic-touched," Sylvan said.

"Is that true, hmmm?" The duke walked around the four of them.

From close up, his face was red and pore-riddled. His dark hair hung in greasy strings over the collar of his shirt.

His grey eyes met Johanna's in a flat look. She feared he would sense her magic, but he said nothing and his face remained blank. Then he went to Roald, who looked back at him as if he was a startled rabbit.

"This one's funny."

Sylvan said, "Don't worry about that one. He has as much magic as a farm dog."

The duke stopped at Loesie. "Ah, I see."

"Ghghghghgh!" Loesie retreated, but backed into a couch and fell backwards over the armrest onto the seat.

While Johanna called, "Loesie!" the duke grabbed Loesie's shoulder. The chill of magic spread through the room. Loesie stiffened, her head thrown back.

"Loesie!" Johanna called.

"Be quiet, child," the duke snapped.

He bent over Loesie's prone form and pulled at her eyelid. She spat at him. Her eyes had clouded over to a luminous white.

"Hmmm, possession. That's interesting. I haven't seen any of those for a while." He chuckled, rubbing his hands. "Well, we might be able to fix that."

Johanna shivered. She wasn't sure if she wanted the man who kept dead bodies on his land to do anything to her friend.

He turned to Johanna. "Do any of you know who did this?"

How about: *You*? "We don't. She can't tell anyone. She can't talk."

"I presume she cannot write?"

"No."

Sylvan came to stand next to his father. "The person who has done this is someone strong enough to break open substream layers and infuse his own. He would have needed to win her trust to let him come close enough to do that. It's probably someone from her local area, someone she knows."

Substream layers?

His father turned to him. "Can't. There aren't any powerful magicians in Saarland. I know a few who could do that, but none who would bother with a Saarlander farm girl."

"Unless she was witness to something the magician did not want her to talk about."

Johanna saw Loesie hold the basket out to her. She remembered the images she'd seen when taking the basket—of men crossing the river and a woman's screams.

He was right: Loesie *had* seen something, and not wanting her to talk was why the magician had shut her up. But what was it that she had seen? None of those nightly images were clear enough for Johanna to see much, or identify the attackers.

"This case is interesting, though." The duke stood back, rubbing his chin. "It seems that she has a certain level of innate magic that has clashed with the spell."

"I was wondering about that." Sylvan glanced at Johanna. She feared he was about to say, *That one has magic, too*, but he didn't.

The duke clapped his hands together. "Well, let's not treat them as criminals. They are tired and dirty. You are welcome to share dinner with us. We will try to solve this interesting situation in the morning. Hans!"

CHAPTER 9

T HE SAME thin man who had opened the door for
them now led the group back into the hall. In his prim-
faced silence he preceded the group up the sweeping
broad staircase into an upstairs corridor.

The walls were dark red here, and the doors a very dark
brown. The ceilings had been painted white, but the paint had
yellowed with age. The only light came from a tiny window at
the very end of the passage and the light that fell in was dusky
and didn't do much to dispel the closed-up, stifling atmosphere.

"Phooey, this place could do with an airing," Nellie said under
her breath. Johanna agreed. Apart from the musty smell, the
runner looked dusty, as if no one had walked through this
corridor for ages.

How many people lived in this giant house?

They passed an open door to a room that was empty, except
for a carpet and floor-length heavy drapes that half-covered the
window. The small panes of glass were dirty on the outside and
spiders had built webs in the corners of the window frame.

"Does only the duke's family live in this house?" Johanna
asked, but the stiff servant didn't reply.

He opened a door to the left. Inside, dark curtains hung
before the window, almost blocking daylight. There were three
beds with dark frames and velvet bedspreads. A chair that had

seen better times sat in front of an empty fireplace. A cupboard against the side wall held a variety of handmade dolls. It looked like this had been a children's room.

"Two can sleep here," the servant named Hans said in a clipped, heavily accented voice.

The next room was larger and had a double bed, a hearth and a couple of chairs. The walls were dark red.

"Sleep in this room or this room," the servant said. "I bring water for washing."

The man took them to third room where every bit of wall space that had no window or door was taken up by wardrobes, all of them filled with clothes. Men's, women's, in a variety of styles, but most a bit old-fashioned.

Hans said in his clipped voice, "Wash. Find clothes. Come to dinner. Downstairs." He bowed, turned around and left the group to stand awkwardly in the hallway.

Well, what to do?

Loesie had turned around and was studying a portrait that hung on the wall, depicting a man in a ruffled shirt wearing a hunter's hat. His face vaguely resembled the duke's.

"You and Roald must sleep in this room," Nellie said, indicating the room with the double bed. "We will sleep in the other room." Coming from Nellie, who was petrified of Loesie, that meant a lot.

Johanna wasn't sure if she wanted to sleep in any room. Much as she appreciated a real bed or being free of Ludo's leery stares, she didn't want to be fooled into thinking that they were visitors here.

"I'd rather have all of us in the same room. I'm afraid I don't trust anyone here." *And I don't trust Loesie.* If she was the reason Sylvan had brought them here, he must know more about her than he let on.

"No, Mistress Johanna, you must be with your husband."
Get on with producing an heir.

Johanna resisted the urge to roll her eyes. How quickly Nellie had recovered from the ride through the forest. Dependable, unflappable Nellie.

Instead of arguing about who was going to sleep where,

Johanna went into the third room, with all those wardrobes against all the walls. Nellie opened the door to one of them. It was full of dresses, mostly heavy dark velvet ones of the type that Johanna had tried on with Mistress Daphne but had found unsuitable for the ball. This type of dress, buttoned up to the neck with few frills, must be eastern fashion. She pulled one out and ran a hand over the fabric. It was very heavy and thick.

"Quite old-fashioned," Nellie said, hanging the dress back. She opened another door. Inside was a variety of men's clothing, some of the jackets visibly dusty at the shoulders.

"They are very pretty clothes," Roald said.

Nellie wrinkled her nose. "I don't like this one bit. Who else lives here? Why does he have all these clothes here?"

"For guests?" Roald said.

"Who would be travelling in this area? We've come through the sand. It's horrible. No one goes that way. There is no trade, no farming, nothing of importance out there, only trees."

Johanna couldn't help think of the bodies in the ice cellar. She didn't know whether to bring it up or whether this duke would have some sort of magic that allowed him to listen in on the conversations. Or whether the cellar was even on his land.

She pushed the uneasy thoughts away.

"I think these clothes have been here for a long time." Nellie said. "They're quite old-fashioned and could use an airing. But we better choose something. If we're to go to a formal dinner, we need to clean up. You two are the future of Saardam. You need to look the part."

"Nellie, they might have untied us, but we're still prisoners."

"That doesn't mean we lose our dignity."

"Dignity would mean not using this man's clothes."

"Go to a formal dinner in these?" Nellie spread her hands. Her dress had a tear down the front and was smudged with dirt. Roald had been wearing a farmer's vest, which was extremely dirty. Loesie had refused to change into anything new even after they collected clothes from the farm. She still wore her grand-mother's black dress, now smudged with mud and other substances.

Johanna sighed. Yes. They could not attend a formal dinner

in their own clothes, and there really was no other option but to use the duke's.

They found a blue dress for Johanna and a ruffled shirt and green velvet jacket for Roald. The two of them went into the room with the double bed, where Hans had brought the promised water and cloths. Johanna draped the clothes on the bed and proceeded to take off Roald's filthy garments.

"I should shave. Do you know how to do that?"

Johanna dipped cloth into the basin and wrung it out. "I think a beard looks fine on you, if you can keep the food out of it." She scrubbed his chin, where flecks of white stuff had dried in the stubble

"I know how to eat properly, if we get tableware."

She had no doubt that he did.

"Do you think that I can look at you tonight?" He stood with his arms wide while she dipped the cloth in the water again.

"Is that the only thing you ever think about?"

"No, but I like looking at you. Take that dress off." He reached for her bodice.

She batted his hand away. "Not now. We're supposed to be at dinner with the duke. Do you know the duke?"

"I told you about him. He tried to kill his half-brother several times."

"Yes, I remember you telling us, but have you met him before?"

"He would have recognised me if we met."

True. She washed his neck and chest, his arms—

"Take off that dress. I want to see you."

"I think you need a little cooling down." She thrust the cloth into his crotch, where his member stood up like a crooked stick.

"That's cold!" He tried to push her away.

She tickled his side and he burst out giggling. "Heeee, don't do that. Don't do that!"

They fell in a heap onto the bed and rolled over the cover, scattering pillows.

Someone knocked on the door. "Are you all right, Mistress Johanna?"

"Yes, Nellie, don't worry." She met Roald's eyes. He managed to look surprised.

"You're silly," she said. Silly, inappropriate, but funny. He trusted her. He needed someone to tell him what to do, and he listened to her.

She pushed herself up from the bed. "Come, let's put on these horrible clothes."

She helped him into shirt and trousers, quickly washed herself and wormed herself into the dress. She asked Roald to do up her laces at the back, but he didn't seem to know how to, so she had to ask Nellie.

Roald stopped her when she went out the door. "I love you. I haven't said it yet today." His face was humourless and sincere. She knew he was only repeating what his mother had said to him, and he didn't understand love. But he understood being safe and comfortable.

She stroked his stubbly cheek. His grey eyes met hers in their usual sincere look. "You love me, too?"

"Yes. Yes, I think so."

He smiled, really smiled, while his eyes met hers. A cheeky smile that spoke of silly, naughty and slightly inappropriate things. She had never seen him smile like this and had thought he was incapable. It was beautiful and filled her with hope. They would find safety, they would return to Saardam, they would defeat the occupiers, they would rebuild the city, they would have a big family with lots of little chubby babies.

Tears sprang to her eyes.

"You're crying."

"Because . . . because I think that we can get out of here safely and go back home, and there will be a home to fight for."

She wasn't sure that he understood, but that didn't matter.

She kissed him fleetingly on the lips before going out the door.

In the wardrobe room, she found Nellie going through the dresses and Loesie standing in front of the window. Nellie made every effort not to look at Loesie, and Loesie had her arms crossed over her chest.

"I told her that she needs to change out of that filthy dress, mistress, but she just makes filthy noises at me."

Loesie said, "Ghghghghghgh!" She turned back to the window.

Something in the tone of her voice made Johanna feel cold. The duke sensed her magic. He said there was something odd going on with Loesie, that her own magic had clashed with the magic of the person who had tried to put a spell on her. Did she believe him, that he wasn't that person?

"Yes, well, let's worry about you first, Nellie."

She asked Nellie to do up the back of her dress and then went through the wardrobes in search of a dress for Nellie to wear.

Nellie was both embarrassed and delighted to choose.

"These clothes are much too nice for me. I'm only a maid."

"When we get back to Saardam, you'll have to wear much nicer dresses than this one."

"How so, Mistress Johanna?"

"You don't think I'm going to leave you behind? If I move into the palace, you'll come. You can be my Lady-in-Waiting."

Nellie's eyes widened. "Really?"

"Yes, Really." Nellie was not, and had never been, "only a maid". Then Johanna had an odd thought. Her own ambitions had been to run the Brouwer Company. What about Nellie's ambitions? Maybe they were intertwined with hers. Unable to work for herself, with an unsupportive and religious family, Nellie's future depended on Johanna's.

Nellie had chosen a dark red dress that looked too severe on her.

"I don't like that dress. It makes you look old."

"I agree. It's not the kind of thing I should be wearing. These clothes are all so expensive—"

"Cowpats, Nellie. The duke wants a dress-up party with pretty young girls. He doesn't care about who you are or who I am. I don't even know if he's got any maids himself or if that sour man is the only other person in the house."

"Don't forget the son. He's quite handsome."

"Handsome?" With all the will in the world, she couldn't call

Sylvan and his tattoos and ugly scar handsome. "Don't you feel his magic?"

Nellie frowned. "Magic?"

"He's a dark magician. He may be young or handsome to you, but don't underestimate him. He's dangerous."

Nellie had to settle for the red dress, because there wasn't anything more modern that would fit her slender frame. Johanna combed out Nellie's hair. It was full of knots, but she managed to do it up in a bun. A brooch and necklace completed the ensemble.

Nellie stood in front of the mirrored glass, twisting and turning this way and that.

"You look good, Nellie, stop worrying."

"I'm not sure, Mistress Johanna. What about . . ." Her gaze went to the bonnet that she had left on the arm of a chair.

"No, it's filthy."

Nellie didn't protest, but continued to look at her reflection, as if checking that it was really her.

Now it was Loesie's turn. She stood in front of the window, looking into the garden. Pale light fell on her face.

Johanna took two dresses from the cupboard that looked like they might fit and were of the dour and black type that Loesie favoured. One had no lace at all, but the other had a little bit, and might look quite good.

Then she called, "Loesie?"

She turned around. Her eyes were wide, but no longer clouded over. Johanna wondered if that only happened when there was strong magic in the air.

"We need to get you dressed for dinner."

"Gghghghghgh!" She shook her head so violently that her hair danced around her head.

"Why, what's wrong?" Nellie said. "Look, Mistress Johanna has even chosen a dress for you that looks like that horrible thing you're wearing now used to, before it got so disgusting. Why don't you for once do what she says? You know that she's—"

"Never mind, Nellie." She probably had been about to say that Johanna was the princess now, but that should remain unsaid. There was yet no evidence that the duke knew who Roald was.

Johanna held up the dress with the lace. "See, this one is not so bad—"

"Ghghghghghghgh!" Loesie backed away.

"What's going on, Loesie? It's only a dress. You can't go to a dinner with a duke looking like this."

"Hmmmmmm!"

"You don't want to come?"

Loesie shook her head.

"If you don't want to go to dinner, then what are you going to eat?"

Loesie shrugged.

"Well, you may not care but I do. Try this dress on." She undid the laces at the back.

But Loesie's behaviour made Johanna feel uneasy.

Johanna didn't like any of these clothes and the reason they might be here any better than Loesie did, but the fact was, she had no evidence whatsoever that the duke even knew about the dead people in the ice cellar, or that the cellar was on his land. These clothes might be here legitimately. They were old enough to have belonged to old family members who once lived here and died—

More dead bodies. She shuddered.

She whispered close to Loesie's ear, "Is the duke the person who put this spell on you?"

Loesie shook her head again.

"You're afraid of him?"

Loesie nodded. She made some hand signs that Johanna didn't understand.

Whatever magic had passed between them when the duke examined Loesie downstairs had been strong enough that Johanna could feel it.

"We're all afraid. We can't let them find out who we are. We must make it look like we're just ordinary travellers. Please, put it on, Loesie."

Johanna pulled Loesie's black dress over her head. The fabric felt greasy to the touch, and it smelled terrible. Loesie's underclothes weren't much better, so she had to find a clean chemise and drawers. Loesie's skin was pale and reminded Johanna uncomfortably of bodies, except the near-translucent skin showed blue veins underneath. Her ribs stuck out, and her stomach was hollow.

It was eerie, really. "You're much too thin, Loesie."

She helped Loesie into the dress. It turned out to be dark green instead of black. Nellie fussed over the colour, because Roald also wore green and Johanna should wear the same colour—

"Nellie, it's a game the duke wants to play with us. We're not guests and it isn't the royal ball."

"Just making sure he doesn't get any wrong impressions about who belongs with who. . . ."

"Ghghghgh!" Loesie hissed at her.

Johanna said, "Stand still. How am I supposed to do up your corset if you keep moving?"

Wasn't tonight going to be fun with those two sleeping in the same room?

Roald had come into the room and waited patiently at the door. He looked surprisingly regal in the green jacket and shirt with ruffles.

Finally they were all done and ready for playing dress-ups with a mass-murderer.

CHAPTER 10

B Y NOW the light outside had faded to deep orange and the gloomy hallway had become even darker. Johanna walked first, followed by Nellie and Roald with Loesie bringing up the rear.

In the huge entrance hall, their footsteps echoed against the ceiling. The huge crystal chandelier hung on a chain suspended on a pulley mechanism, so that the household staff could light the few candles up there. The ceiling was painted in dark colours with scenes depicting destruction and a man pointing towards a light.

"Who is that?" Nellie whispered to Johanna, because talking aloud didn't seem appropriate in the intense silence.

"It's the True God from the Belaman Church, I think."

"I thought the Belaman Church was even stricter on magic than the Church of the Triune."

"The fact that the duke's ceiling bears religious scenes doesn't mean that he adheres to the teachings."

Nellie swallowed visibly.

The Belaman Church had many branches, and the Church of the Triune was sometimes considered part of it, but their stance against magic united them all. Instead of believing in the Lord of Fire, they believed in Doom. It was a place without leader, a place where voices were not heard because there was no sound.

In fact, she imagined Doom to be a bit like this hall: abandoned and dusty.

When coming in, she had not noticed the draughtiness of the hall and the dust on the chandelier. Candle wax had dripped onto the stairs in several places, and it was blackened and worn with people having walked across it for some time.

The house was quiet except for a few chinks of porcelain that had to come from the kitchen.

They found the dining room through a door under the stairs. Inside stood a long table with a dark blue velvet cover, gold-rimmed plates and crystal glasses. There were two standing chandeliers, and a lusty fire burned in the hearth. Since it had now started to go dark outside, the drapes were closed, and the room was bathed in a warm yellow glow.

The duke sat at the head of the table. He had changed into a velvet coat which was a rather garish dark purple, and the shirt he wore underneath was excessively ruffled. He indicated the other chairs with an exaggerated gesture of his hand.

"Sit down, friends."

Johanna battled the impulse to say *We're not your friends*, but she didn't. No doubt this man was using his henchmen or his magic to keep his "guests" here.

Sylvan came out of the shadows and took his place at the other end of the table. He had changed into an equally severe blue jacket that made him look more brooding.

Johanna eyed him. *Handsome?* Seriously?

They sat down, Johanna and Roald on one side of the table, Nellie and Loesie on the other.

The duke asked for a moment's silence. "True God, we pray that our weary travellers may enjoy our meagre hospitality and that they may continue their journey safely."

Johanna was getting very irritated with these people's insistence on ignoring the fact that they had been captured.

Nellie was eying Sylvan.

Loesie looked oddly elegant in the dress, and her thin arms and long, spider-like fingers gave her an ethereal presence. Her hair was darker than that of typical Saarlanders. Johanna remembered Loesie telling her that she had only a mother on the farm.

Who was her father? She had never given it much thought. Loesie had told her once that he had died of illness while working at a neighbour's farm. Johanna had never considered that he might have been a foreign guest worker, or even that her mother and father might never have been married. He had probably been Estlander, because there was only one thing that Saarlanders with magic abilities had in common: eastern blood.

A dour-faced woman came in and brought a tray with a silver lid which she placed in the middle of the table. The thin man brought several gold-rimmed terrines with cooked vegetables.

"Time to have the cook's specialty," the duke said. "Roast venison from the forest."

Johanna shivered, thinking of the ice cellar.

They were silent while Hans came forward and took the lid off the tray. He cut a piece which he offered to the duke who tasted it and nodded his approval.

Then he proceeded to carve the meat, doling out steaming portions to all around the table. It smelled heavenly.

Then he poured something that looked like cider.

In Saardam, only the church used wine, and then not much of it. Grapes grew on hillsides further to the south.

When they finished serving, the maid and Hans retreated. The duke lifted his glass. "We drink to this memorable occasion." The candlelight made deep shadows over his old face.

What was so memorable about being a prisoner here, Johanna didn't know.

Roald lifted his glass in turn. "To this occasion." He took a sip of the cider and set the glass on the table. His face remained blank. Someone must have spent a lot of time drilling him in these exchanges.

She thought of the unguarded smile on his face when they were cavorting over the bed in the room upstairs. The man who hid behind this impersonal mask was not dumb at all. Just very, very awkward.

Nellie sat straight-backed, staring at Loesie, who was trying to work out in which hand to hold the spoon.

Johanna could no longer contain her desire for answers. "Can I ask what your interest is in us?"

"Is it improper to offer a meal and a dry bed to travellers?"

"We're not travellers. Those men captured us. We were minding our own business and they took us from our ship." He glared at Sylvan, who glared back at her.

"My men found you wandering on our land."

"We were in an orchard along the river. Do you have land that far away from here?"

"I do."

"Do you do the same to all river traders who stop off?"

"True river traders keep going. They don't stop off at places where no people live."

True.

"We are not river traders. We're refugees with no place to go."

She gave Loesie a sideways glance. Isolated as this estate was, did he know about the devastation of Saardam and Aroden? If he treated all his visitors to a meal, people might have told him in this room.

She put down her spoon and carefully wormed her hand under the table. The moment her fingertips contacted the wooden underside of the table, a rush of cold went through her. Images flowed unbidden through her mind: a fire-lit sky, someone jumping off the quay, Roald, wet and pale, in the cabin of the *Lady Sara*, the skulls and bones in the ash of the burnt farm, the children yelling at the *Lady Sara* at Aroden, Roald looking at her. Somewhere in the background, Nellie prompted, "Say: I do."

And he said, "I do," and slid his ring over Johanna's finger, where it dangled loose because it was much too big.

Johanna gasped and withdrew her hand.

What in all of heaven's name was this? She stared at her plate, her heart thudding. She had expected the wood to show her things, not invoke her own memories. Wait—did that mean the wood sucked out her memories? Did that mean the duke would now know for certain who they were—if he didn't know already?

The duke had asked Nellie a question. She was stammering

something about a farm and selling baskets and cheese. Presumably the question had been about Loesie.

Then another thought: not since they had set foot in his house had the duke asked for their names.

That's because he already knows.

"And what is your relationship to this strange possessed girl?" the duke asked.

"I . . . um," Nellie said, and met Johanna's eyes in a kind of *help me out* look.

"She is my friend," Johanna said.

"It's very odd for a daughter of a rich merchant to have a friend who comes from a farm."

So he knew her father. Well, he might have recognised the *Lady Sara.*

"Yes, well, my mother is no longer alive as you might know, and I help my father, so I go to the markets to buy and sell things. That's where I've met her."

"Hmm, is that so?" He stroked his beard. "Could it also be that both of you share a certain ability?"

"What do you mean?" She was trying to sound as innocent as possible.

"You know very well what I mean. Magic is rare in Saarlanders."

"It is not so rare amongst the river traders."

"Ha, most of them are peddlers. They buy small trinkets: talismans or mistwood. They may have a tiny bit of magic and the wood shows them things. Then they fancy themselves magicians. Ha!"

He put a piece of meat in his mouth.

"Both of you are different. My son says that he could feel your magic quite strongly."

Sylvan nodded.

"Is that a reason to take us prisoner?"

He had been cutting his meat and put knife down. "You do not know anything about magic, do you, child?"

She wanted to say, *I'm not a child, I'm a married woman,* but didn't. Her heart was thudding against her ribs.

"I guess I can't blame you, coming from that ignorant place, full of priests who live in constant denial of what they could see before their very eyes if only they opened them."

Roald protested, "Hey, you don't call—"

"Shhh." Johanna put a hand on his arm, careful not to touch the table.

"Yes, tell him to be quiet. Keep pretending that magic doesn't exist, and my half-brother will overrun the entire coastal plain. You don't believe that I brought you here for your protection, because you need to know about magic, and you need this situation . . ." He flapped his hand at Loesie. ". . . solved. She is leaking so much magic in the substream that all of us can feel her. That's why you're here. She will attract my half-brother. He will use her, and you have no idea what his court magicians can do."

"You mean Baron Uti?"

"The very one."

"But . . ." She remembered the baron in the party of guests walking into the hall with the royal family. She had not sensed any magic around him, but—wait. Court magicians. Kylian.

He had looked at her and picked her out of the crowd. He had tried to seduce her and then when the fire demons hit, he had vanished.

She met the grey eyes of the man who, according to Roald, had tried to kill his half-brother. And he honestly did not look like a killer. He might have tried because he considered his brother a danger to everyone. Or he might not. Even in business, the people who looked least likely to default on their payments sometimes did.

How could she know?

Do not get involved in this feud. It has nothing to do with Saardam.

Except it did, because of Loesie.

"You have brought us here because . . ." She licked her lips, finally putting some pieces of this strange situation together. "Are you an exorcist?"

The duke laughed. "They love words like that in the west, don't they, son?"

Sylvan flicked his eyebrows in a kind of "get on with it" gesture.

"Are you?"

"If that's the kind of answer you want and the kind of language you like to use, yes, I am." The look in his grey eyes was intense. He pushed his chair back, picked up the walking stick that leaned against the edge of the table next to him, and shuffled to a cabinet against the back wall. His stick went *tap, tap, tap* on the floor.

The cabinet was made from dark wood and had doors with small panes of glass through which Johanna couldn't see anything because of the reflection of the candles in the glass.

He fiddled about with a key and opened the door with a creak. From inside, he produced a cup, a signet ring and a gnarled and knotted piece of wood, which he placed on the table. The cup was an odd thing, made of dark glass and heavily decorated with gold paint.

The duke returned to the back wall, to another cupboard. *Tap, tap, tap.*

Next he brought a cage to the table. It was an ugly thing, made out of rusty iron, and big enough to fit a large cat. There was a little door at the front, which the duke opened by lifting a latch that seemed too heavy for a door of that size.

He went back to another cupboard.

Roald frowned at the cage. "What's that for?"

"That's for holding the demon, young man," the duke said, his back to them.

The servant Hans came in and quickly collected the plates and trays. Johanna noticed how he stayed well clear of the objects his master had put on the table.

Nellie met Johanna's eyes and frowned. "What's that for?" she mouthed.

Johanna shrugged.

Loesie glared at the duke's back, her face a mask of distrust.

The duke came back to the table, *tap, tap, tap*, and put a carafe next to the cup. He placed the walking stick so that it leant against the edge of the table and made a show of slowly lowering himself in the chair with a groan.

"What's all this for?" Johanna asked into the silence.

The duke waited until Hans had carried out the last tray of

plates and tableware and shut the door behind him. He poured a dark fluid from the carafe into the cup.

"We must first determine the nature of your friend's possession," he said, swirling the fluid in the cup.

Johanna heard Reverend Romulus talk about goat's blood and black sorcery. That fluid didn't *look* like blood. It looked like very dark wine.

"Should some of us perhaps wait outside?"

Roald watched with an expression of intense interest, but Nellie's face had gone white as a ghost's.

The duke turned to her, surprised. "Why?"

"Because the possession concerns only my friend, and me. Perhaps."

Duke Lothar chuckled. "So, you're afraid, young lady?" He pointed the bit of gnarled wood at Nellie, who bent back, so that the wood didn't touch her. Her were wide. She nodded.

"She's got nothing to do with this," Johanna said.

"What about him?" He poked the wood at Roald, who didn't flinch and gave the knot of wood a cold stare, as if it were a dead fish.

Johanna's heart thudded. If the duke knew who Roald was, he sure did a good job of acting like he didn't. "He has nothing to do with the possession either. Let both of them go to their rooms."

Roald started, "No. I need to protect my—"

Johanna cut him off. "Yes, he's got nothing to do with this."

"All right." The duke leaned back. He seemed amused. "All right, let them go."

Nellie jumped to her feet as if she had been sitting on a spring. Roald didn't move. Johanna wanted to get up and bodily push him out the door. Every minute he remained in this room was one where his identity could be discovered. But if she seemed too keen to have him gone, the duke *would* suspect something.

Nellie said, "Aren't you coming?"

Roald said, "No." And Johanna said, "Yes."

The duke pointed the wood at Roald again. "He's not afraid.

She isn't afraid either." He pointed in the direction of Loesie, and Loesie batted the wood away—

Johanna shouted, "Don't touch it!"

But it was already too late. Magic flashed through the room.

Loesie stiffened. Her eyed widened and went luminous white. She opened her mouth and let out a bone-chilling wail.

Nellie screamed.

Sylvan yelled at her, "Shut up!"

While Loesie slowly fell face first onto the table.

"Loesie!" Johanna pushed her seat back so hard that the chair fell over. She rushed to her friend's side. Loesie's skin was ice cold.

"What have you done?" she screamed at the duke.

Loesie went, "Hmmmmm!" She pushed herself up, her eyes like shining slits of whiteness. She balled her hands into a knot, her fingers white-knuckled.

"Hmmmm! Ghghghghghgh!" She swayed from side to side. Her mouth moved but no sound came out.

"Talk to us," the duke said. "Talk to us, talk to us." In a chanting voice.

Nellie had remained by the door, the doorknob in her hand. Her face was so white that she might faint any moment.

More than anything, Johanna wanted to get Roald out of here. Whatever was going to happen, it wasn't going to be good.

In her mind, she heard the Reverend Romulus' voice talking about quackery and goat's blood. Rituals from the Lord of Fire. Black magic. Necromancy. Dead bodies in the ice cellar.

"Talk to us, talk to us, talk to us."

Loesie gave an animal-like snort.

"It won't work like this." Even Sylvan's voice sounded concerned.

"Talk to us, talk to us, talk to us."

"Father, there is more going on than simple possession. This is not a spell cast by a peddler. You can't break it like this."

Loesie produced a low hum. Her face was tilted to the ceiling, her eyes luminous white, leaking wisps of mist. She swayed in her seat and the duke swayed in the same rhythm. Had his eyes always been so cloudy?

"Father!" Sylvan sprang forward, roughly shoving his father's chair around. The walking stick slid to the ground with a loud clatter. Sylvan nearly tripped over it. "Father!" He shook his father's shoulders.

The duke's eyes re-focused. "Huh, what?" He stared at his son, his expression confused. "What are we—" He looked around.

Loesie still sat swaying from side to side. Her hum made her chest vibrate. Johanna wanted to clamp her hands over her ears.

"Do something!" Nellie yelled.

Roald simply stared, his face in an expression of intense curiosity.

Still humming, Loesie picked up the goblet. Her hand trembled so much that the wine spilled over the sides, first onto the tablecloth, but then on her dress as she lifted it to her mouth. She drank. Wine flowed past the sides of the cup down her chin, down her neck, over her chest, leaving dark red trails.

She put the cup down and sat as if frozen, staring into nothingness.

"What's going on?" Johanna whispered when the silence lasted too long.

Sylvan pushed Loesie's shoulder, but there was no reaction. Her eyes blinked, but the irises still shone luminous white.

Then Loesie sprang up from her chair. With stiff steps, she staggered towards the window. Her hands shook visibly. Her eyes blinked fast. Her bottom lip trembled; even her hair seemed alive. She was shaking too much to keep walking. Johanna glanced at the duke or Sylvan, but they didn't look like they knew what to do either.

Nellie watched from near the door, covering her mouth with her hand.

And Loesie's shaking still increased, until the entire room seemed to be shaking with her. She held her hands out in front of her, her fingers curved like claws. Now even her breathing was coming in gasps.

Johanna couldn't stand it anymore. "Is someone going to do anything?"

Nellie yelled, "No, don't go near her!"

And Loesie let out an ear-splitting cry, that descended into a gasping gurgle, and a cough. She coughed and coughed, and leaned forward.

Johanna patted her on the back. A visible muscle spasm went through Loesie's body, and with a loud burp, a gush of dark vomit welled out of her mouth.

The mass hit the floor with a wet splash and spatters going everywhere. And another lot.

It was very dark-coloured because of the wine. Too dark, really, almost black. And it moved of its own.

Johanna backed away, wiping dark specks from her shoes.

Nellie screamed. "Oh, look! They're spiders!"

It was true. Thousands and thousands, millions of them, spreading out over the floor. Loesie coughed and vomited up more of them, covered in trails of slime. She coughed and vomited, struggling for breath. Gasping. Vomiting into her hands. Gasping.

She was going to faint.

Johanna stepped forward. She had to help her friend.

"No, wait." Sylvan pushed her roughly out of the way. With one hand he grabbed Loesie, who was about to collapse in her own spidery vomit. With his other hand, he made a sweeping gesture at the floor. He spoke a few harsh-sounding words.

A blast of cold air went through the room that blew out all the candles. The curtains whipped up. The fire flared in the hearth. The flames were blue.

Then silence returned.

The spidery mass had turned to water. Sylvan caught Loesie as she collapsed.

He carried her to a chair, her head lolling over his arm.

Then he re-lit the candles on the table. His hand didn't even shake.

"Hmmm?" Loesie said. She opened her eyes and pushed herself up. "Johanna?"

"Loesie!" Johanna was about to hug her friend, but Sylvan held her back.

"Wait. She's not completely cured."

Johanna retreated. The whiteness had gone from Loesie's eyes. "Can you say something to me?"

"What are we doing here?"

Sylvan was right. The voice was Loesie's, but the accent was not. Loesie spoke like a farm girl.

"She's a true witch," the duke said, leaning back in his chair. He wiped sweat from his forehead. His face had taken on an ashen grey tone. "I can't perform a full exorcism here. I will need to tap the magic lines."

Whatever that meant.

"We have to take her out into the forest."

Johanna's unease developed into full-blown panic. No, she did not want to go into that forest again. "We were on our way to town to find someone to cure her."

"You won't find anyone else. I can cure her, but I'll need a rest first. You will have to lift the curse from her before you reach Florisheim. I assume this is where you were travelling?"

Johanna gave him a suspicious look. "Haven't you heard what happened in Saardam?"

"Sadly, I have. A lot of people have come up the river and told us the tales. My own brother was there and managed to escape with his life. He's been back scarcely a day."

Curiosity took over. "You've spoken to him?" The man he was supposed to have wanted to kill. She didn't know that they were that close to the town.

"I have."

"Do you know how much of Saardam was burned? Who were the attackers? Who rules the city now?"

"Word goes that the fire was started by the members of that church of theirs and that they now—"

At the same time Nellie said, "Impossible." Johanna said, "Cowpats!"

And Nellie glared at her in a you-don't-use-that-language-in-presence-of-a-duke kind of way.

Johanna composed herself. "I don't believe that for one moment. A lot of people, especially the nobles, hate the church, but they would never do something like that. Also, they forbid magic, and the fire was started with magic."

"I'm merely repeating what many people have been saying. I can't verify the rumour without going there. The news is also that the church has instated a governor."

Johanna almost said *cowpats* a second time, but didn't think Nellie would survive that.

"Who is this governor of the church?" Next he was going to say *Reverend Romulus* and that would just show how much these rumours were worth—

"A man who calls himself Alexandre."

"Who?" She looked at Nellie. "Do you know him?"

Nellie shook her head. On Nellie's other side, Loesie sat frowning at the duke.

"According to refugees, this man has instated himself as regent. My brother isn't happy about it. If anything, his son could claim the throne if the Saardam royal family does not show up anywhere."

Johanna's heart thudded in her throat. Roald's ring hung heavy against her chest. "Has anyone seen where they went?"

"They fled like cowards."

They didn't.

Johanna met his grey eyes and returned his stare until she had to look away. If he expected her to say something about the royal family, he was going to be disappointed.

She didn't want to stay in this man's house or eat his food, or wear his clothes.

He put his hands on the armrests of his chair. "Go to bed now, my friends. Tomorrow, I will undertake the task of driving the remnants of the demon from your friend's soul, and then you can travel on. You *should* travel on. Many refugees have come from Saarland to Florisheim, and you will surely find people amongst them you know."

Father. Although she didn't dare hope.

CHAPTER 11

SYLVAN ACCOMPANIED the group back through the hall. They walked slowly, with Johanna and Sylvan supporting Loesie between them. She could walk but wasn't very steady on her feet. She kept asking how they got here, and no matter how many times Johanna explained, the answer didn't stick. The voice was Loesie's, but the accent too cultured to belong to her.

Going up the stairs was a struggle, with Loesie unable to lift her feet far enough, and the effort it required rendered her silent.

Johanna's eyes met Sylvan's. "I find it had to believe that your father lets us go so easily."

"Do you? He is only interested in the magical. He's not interested in you, just in the demon. He's wanted to capture a demon for a while."

"And then do what with it?" She thought about the rusty cage on the table.

"My father likes to invent things. It is his dream to make a *machine* powered by magic. He wants a magical creature so that he can force it to lend its essence to moving the machine."

"Does he perform magic a lot?" *Like, try to bring people back from the dead?* Treading into dangerous territory now.

"He likes to. I have to hold him back sometimes. He thinks he's better than he is."

"It sounds dangerous."

"To him, yes. To everyone else, not so much. We're on an estate well outside any town. Most of his constructs wander around the forest for a while before fading away without harming anyone."

"Then what about . . ." She brought her hand to her cheek, and thought it was unwise to ask about his scar. Men could be funny about those things.

"Nothing to do with anything except my own stupidity. I failed to control a newly-acquired bear."

Ouch. "Is that why you came with the bandits? To capture Loesie?"

"There were rumours of a magic-possessed woman coming this way, so he sent Sigvald. Possession is very rare and Sigvald is a brute, so I went with him, because I didn't think that a lone woman in the presence of bandits was going to end happily."

"What did you do to make those spiders vanish?"

"It's just a simple spell that people with air magic can do."

"Didn't look simple to me."

He stopped walking. "You know, you Saarlanders are all so ignorant about magic that even though some of you have a limited ability you wouldn't know what to do with it. One day, someone is going to come who knows how to use magic and wants to take control over your country's strategic location. You will be defenceless."

That may already have happened.

She met his eyes, but said nothing.

"Saarland needs court magicians."

She nodded, really confused now about what he was trying to tell her. Nothing he had said so far convinced her that he didn't know who Roald was. He came to conclusions similar to her own, and now—was he saying *Hey, if you need to employ a magician, I'm available?*

She wanted to believe he was being honest with her, about his father, about his mission to capture Loesie. He sounded too naïve, unbelievable for someone with as many powers as he seemed to have.

The little voice inside her said, *This is all a trap. You need to leave as soon as possible if you don't want to end up dead inside the ice cellar.*

They arrived in the upstairs corridor. Nellie opened the door to the kids' room while Johanna and Sylvan manoeuvred Loesie through. They dragged her onto the bed.

Sylvan left, and Nellie helped Johanna take Loesie's dress off.

Loesie's eyes were no longer white, and followed Johanna's hands as she undid the laces.

"Do you feel better?"

"What are we doing here?" Loesie asked.

"I just told you when we were coming up the stairs."

Loesie frowned.

"She's almost cured," Nellie said.

"I'm not sure. Loesie speaks in eastern dialect, and she doesn't seem to listen to anything we say."

"Well, she's better than before. I'm sure this man can cure her."

Johanna shrugged. She still didn't trust the duke. As some point she was going to have to ask him bluntly what his business was with an ice cellar full of dead bodies. Until she knew, and probably even after, she wouldn't trust either him or his son, who seemed all too keen to offer his services.

"You're sure you can handle being with her in the room?" Johanna asked.

"I can manage. A wife should be with her husband anyway."

Johanna vacillated between telling Nellie off for always worrying about what was appropriate and letting it go. In the end, the easy option won. She was too tired to argue.

Loesie was already half asleep, so Johanna went with Roald to the other bedroom.

Someone had been in to light the fire, which burned with a healthy glow. Neither Johanna nor Roald said anything when entering the room. Roald hadn't said much even at dinner or during that horrible magical performance. She worried about what went on in his head. Eventually, he would have questions about it.

When Johanna closed the door, sounds in the room became muffled. The room had a thick carpet and heavy curtains. It would have been quite cosy if not for the fact that the furniture was sparse and dusty.

Once, many people had lived in this house. What had happened?

A small table with a carafe of wine and two glasses on it stood near the hearth. The church frowned upon the consumption of alcohol, and wine had to be imported in Saarland, so there was rarely any at the table. She found it strange that other sections of the church allowed wine. It was as if all the districts had different interpretations of the book.

Johanna poured wine in the glasses. "I don't really know what to think of the duke. He seems kind enough, but . . ." She shrugged and went to the fire. Her hands were still cold from the magic, and she couldn't quite dispel the memory of those spiders. And then Sylvan's spell. Should she accept the help of the son of a man who had tried to kill his half-brother? He was right in that Saarland needed a court magician. They needed many other people as well. It was high time that they found survivors and started establishing the position of the royal family.

Roald sat staring at some point across the room. Johanna picked up the cups.

"Roald, look at me."

He turned his head. "Oh yes, I love to look."

Not like that. Heavens, was that what he had been thinking all night? "No, that's not what I mean. I want to ask you a few things."

"Oh?"

He took the glass from her.

Johanna sat down and took a sip. The fluid's taste was quite sharp and it made a little burning track inside her all the way down to her stomach. "When you went away with the order in Burovia, were they people of the Church?"

"I don't like going to church. My father says I have to go.

The monks want me to go every day, but I like much better to work in the fields. I get the horses, I feed the horses. I pick the grapes. I weed the garden."

"So this place was a monastery?"

He frowned at her.

"A monastery is where monks live and pray. You said they were monks."

"But it wasn't a monastery."

"There are no women in a monastery."

A slight frown. "Yes, it was like that and it's very sad, because there are no women to look at. You know these monks have never looked at a woman? They don't like talking about it either. Probably because they don't know."

For crying out loud. Was there anything he could get excited about other than women and the family tree of various royal families?

"The monks in this . . ." She almost said monastery again. ". . . place go to church?"

"Every day."

"What does the church look like?"

He frowned. "Like a church?"

"Is there anything in the church?"

"Benches to sit, and for the choir. They tried to get me to join the choir, but I don't like the music. It's boring and too slow, but I can't sing that slow. I get out of breath."

She chuckled. "Are there any statues in the church?"

"Like the one in the big church, with the dog-heads?"

"It has only one dog head, but yes, that's the one."

He frowned. "It has two."

"No, there is one. The other heads are the ghost and the holy god."

"There are two."

"One."

"Two."

Johanna realised: this might well be a different statue of the triune. She had not known Roald to be wrong about anything.

"So there is a statue like that in the big church in Saardam?" Would that church still be standing?

"Yes, I just said so."

"It's at the front of the church, with the pulpit to one side and—"

He shook his head. "It's in the middle and all the benches are around it."

Yes. A different church, obviously. Now she was getting somewhere. "Do you remember the names of any of the monks?"

"Peter."

"They were all named Peter?"

"No, there were others." He held up his hand and counted on his fingers. "David, Johan, Anselmus, Bernhard—"

"Was there one named Alexandre?"

He frowned. "He is not a monk. He is . . . ooohhh, you don't mess with him."

"If he's not a monk, then what is he?"

"He says he's a prince of Burovia, but I don't believe that, because the king has no sons."

No legitimate ones at any rate. Illegitimate ones were another matter.

With a lot of difficulty, she managed to get out of him that someone named Alexandre was also a guest at the order where he had stayed. It had been a church farm of sorts, where they also grew herbs for making concoctions. Other guests included two of Baron Uti's cousins, both of whom, Roald said, spent a lot of time in the dungeons as punishment for *being inebriated and disorderly*.

The place seemed like a home for troublesome royals. The young men were subjected to a punishing schedule of hard work and prayers when they weren't in the fields.

They had an elaborate system of punishments that seemed quite excessive. Lashes for a lot of minor transgressions like being late in church or forgetting to tidy one's bed, time in the dungeons for more serious missteps, such as failing to recite prayers properly or making fun of figures of authority. The most serious of crimes, blasphemy, attracted a punishment of a week in chains without food, and a hundred lashes every morning.

"They used a belt on me, not a chain, because of the scars." He said this proudly.

"You mean they locked you in the cellar and hit you every day?"

He lifted his shirt. "See? No scars."

Johanna looked at that bronzed skin with renewed awe. "Why did they punish you?"

"They said Prince Richert of Estland stole bread from the kitchens but he didn't. I know that for a fact. Because I stole the bread for Tomas, who was sick and couldn't come to the hall to eat. The monk wouldn't believe me so I called him a prick."

Somewhere in that distant mind of his was a very strong sense of justice.

"What was this Alexandre doing there?"

"He was friends with the monks. He never made his own bed. He never worked. I wasn't afraid of him, but many people were."

Alexandre, Roald further informed her, came from the Burovian river town of Lisseau. This was on the Saar River and Johanna had been there. A pretty town, not very big, but it did have a fair bit of money. Apparently the Nielands used creditors in Lisseau to finance their bid to go into ocean trade.

This whole situation was becoming more complex by the day.

Eventually, the fire died and the glasses were empty. The wine had made a warm spot in her stomach. Somehow, the problems of the world seemed far away and not so important. It was comfortable and warm in this room, and Loesie would get better. They would get out of here, and would never know about the bodies in the ice cellar. Maybe the reason they were there wasn't for her to know anyway. She put her glass down. "We should go to sleep."

Roald turned to her, an eager expression on his face. "Now do I get to look at you?"

"If you want." She didn't feel like any awkward acrobatics, but he was her husband now, so it was his right to ask.

She let herself out of the horribly stiff dress. Roald's intense gaze made her feel uncomfortable so she went to the window, dressed in her underclothes, and pushed the curtain aside a crack. It was very dark outside, the sky spotted with stars. The room was at the front of the house, looking out over the clipped bushes and neat beds of the gardens.

"I like looking at you." Roald had come up from behind and put his hands on her hips. His palms felt warm through the underdress. He tugged at the fabric. "Take this one off, too."

Johanna slipped the underdress over her head. A cold draft from the window made her shiver. She pulled the string around her waist and dropped her drawers. Roald stepped a little back, staring at her.

"Yes, I really like looking at you."

Johanna took off his jacket and undid the buttons to his shirt. He sat down on the bed, pulling her onto his lap and pressing his face between her breasts.

"They're so soft." His breath tickled over her naked skin.

He slid his hand over her back, pressing her closer to him. She could feel him through his trousers. The thought of that first night came with a slight shudder.

"Wait." She rose, undid his belt and peeled open the front of his trousers. His member stood straight up, like an overgrown gherkin. And thinking about gherkins made her laugh.

"Heeeee!"

He pulled her back on his lap, nuzzling the white skin on her belly. She breathed the scent of his hair. It was getting quite long and unruly.

"You're quite tanned. Did you spend a lot of time outdoors?"

"All the time. They had cows. Real ones, not sea cows. I learnt to milk them. I worked in the field, harvesting grapes. The monks make wine."

"You liked that kind of work?"

"It was nice. My father says I have to be nice to all these boring people. Do I really have to? They don't like me."

Johanna chuckled, and then a feeling of sadness came over her. "Yes, you have to be nice to them." At least the ones who were still alive.

He leaned back on his elbows. "I want you to touch me now."

"Shift a bit further back."

He did. The whole thing was strange, an oddly rational and mechanical process. People said she was meant to feel something while doing this. *Like you really want it,* Augustina had confided, but she felt nothing.

Johanna climbed onto the bed, put one leg over him, took his member, lifted it up in the right position and pushed down. He went deep into her. He groaned.

"You find that pleasant."

"Ooooh, very nice." He rocked his hips.

"Don't do that, because it hurts me."

He frowned. "It hurts?"

"Not like this, but it does when you try to lift me in the air."

"Oh." He frowned. "Does that mean we can't do it anymore?"

"No, it doesn't mean that at all. Just that I would rather you didn't try to lift me off the bed anymore."

"Oh." His frown deepened.

A waft of cold air drifted through the room, making Johanna's naked skin crawl with goosebumps.

"But hurting people is bad."

"It doesn't hurt if you stay like this." She leaned on her outstretched arms on either side of his shoulders and rocked backwards and forwards. For a while neither of them said anything. Roald leaned his head back in the pillow, his eyes closed and mouth slightly open.

Each time she rocked, he gave a soft groan.

She wanted to feel what he felt, because she didn't understand this. Helena said that it was easier if you pretended to enjoy it, and that pretending to enjoy it sometimes led to enjoying it. And Johanna figured that she'd better learn to enjoy it or otherwise this part of her life would be very miserable.

She didn't want to be miserable, she wanted to enjoy it. She wanted to feel something.

Johanna kept rocking her hips. She closed her eyes. Why hadn't she noticed how tight it was, and how each time she pushed forward, she rubbed a very sensitive spot?

Roald grabbed her thighs with white-knuckled hands. He groaned with each time she rocked back. Johanna remembered the noise he had made the previous time. She had the vague notion to tell him to be quiet, but part of her didn't care, and that part was taking over her mind. She rocked harder and faster, because it was pleasant, and because she was married and they could do this.

And then Roald arched his back and did his *huhhhh!* thing, almost lifting her. It would have hurt but she didn't feel it anymore, he was that deep inside her.

He relaxed, his chest heaving with fast breaths.

"That was good," he said.

She nodded. She didn't think it was as good as it could be, but this was obviously something they could work on. Something that didn't require him to use words.

She went to sleep next to him, in the warm hollow made by his body in the mattress and enveloped by the peculiar smell of his seed that flowed out of her and made wet patches on the sheets and her underdress. She didn't care. He might have snored, but she didn't notice. She had done her duty. The future of the Carmine House would grow inside her.

JOHANNA WOKE up sometime in the night when it was still pitch dark. She lifted her head off the pillow, aware of the coldness on her back. Roald sat up in bed.

From somewhere outside came an unfamiliar *crunch, crunch* sound.

"What's that noise?" Her tongue wouldn't cooperate.

Roald didn't reply, but she recognised the sound. Footsteps on gravel. Horses.

At this time of the night?

She climbed out of bed and tiptoed over to the window. A cold draft worked its fingers around her legs and under her underdress.

A half-moon had come up. It faint blue light silvered the perfectly-tended garden, the hedges, the clipped trees, the benches and ponds. A group of people stood on the drive, one of them leading a horse by the reins. The animal tossed its head and snorted as if it had been running.

The other two people looked like they were house servants,

but not Hans or the woman Johanna had seen. The three spoke with raised voices, too far away for Johanna to hear.

Roald came to stand behind her, a warm presence at her back.

"Who is that?" he asked.

"I don't know."

"Does he always receive guests in the middle of the night?"

"I have no idea, but it's odd." Especially since there would have been little light for the traveller's horse to see by.

One of the servants took the horse in the direction of the stables; the other accompanied the traveller up the steps to the house.

At the top of the stairs another man came out of the house. Johanna recognised the long hair of Sylvan. He met the newcomer on the paving in front of the door. The two spoke briefly. Sylvan gestured wildly with his hands and then the other man raised his voice. Sylvan shouted something at him. The visitor walked past him towards the main door. As he did so, he raised his head, and Johanna could see his face.

It was Kylian.

CHAPTER 12

JOHANNA AND ROALD went back to bed. Roald fell asleep immediately, but Johanna was too disturbed to sleep. What in all the heavens was Kylian doing here?

She still saw him on that night Saardam burned, first when their eyes met across the crowded hall, when she could feel his magic, then him wanting to dance with her, having followed her, perhaps, into the deserted gallery. Admitting that he could sense her magic. The kiss—no, she didn't want to think about that. Then he'd asked her to come with him to Florisheim. And then, when the fire started, he'd jumped over the wall and disappeared without trace *while his father was still in the hall.*

She could still feel the moment his lips touched hers. Her overwhelming reaction had been one of disgust, and then fascination. Wanting to know more, but knowing that the knowledge was forbidden until she was married. She had never questioned what he was doing there or why he had fled so quickly.

Or why the memories made her feel hot.

Now that she was married, any thought of him was fraught with danger. If she came face-to-face with him here, he might bring up their nightly encounter at the palace. So mysterious, dangerous, inappropriate . . . Whatever she did, those thoughts would just not die.

You're better off never seeing him again, said the little voice inside her that sounded like Nellie.

She clamped the pillow over her head. She didn't want to think about him. She never wanted to see him again. Why couldn't she just go back to sleep like Roald?

Johanna forced herself to calm down, but those thoughts would not go away. Roald snored and kept jiggling his leg. The mattress was so soft that she kept sliding into him. Johanna tossed and turned and grumbled under her breath that she was going to sleep on the floor, all of which had precisely no effect. She might as well have been talking to a sack of grain for the notice he took of her.

Eventually she fell back asleep when a faint glow of dawn coloured the little strip of sky she could see between the curtains, and a few birds made tentative warm-up noises for the morning chorus. She woke up with a shock when the sunlight flooded into the room. She rolled onto her back and lay staring at the plaster flowers on the ceiling.

Oh, by the heavens, her head felt like it was stuffed with wool.

This sleeping in the same bed thing would have to improve a lot or she was going to get her own bedroom. A blackbird sang on the roof with another one answering further away. There were no city noises, and no noises from within the house.

Someone walked *crunch, crunch, crunch* on the gravel of the drive.

Roald gave a startled snore.

Johanna threw back the cover with more vigour than necessary and pushed the heavy curtain aside, but it was only the stablehand Karl carrying a bucket of scraps down the lane, out to the chicken coop. The sky was soft blue and sunlight beat down on this side of the house, edging Karl's hair in a golden glow. He had sail ears.

Johanna let the curtain fall and went in search of her clothes. Would the duke expect her to wear his dress again today? She picked up the heavy fabric, cringing at the stiffness of the bodice. The farm dress which she had worn since the day after the burning of Saardam needed mending and washing, and she couldn't imagine wearing that to breakfast with a duke, especially if Kylian might be there.

Kylian.

Now, in the brightness of morning, it seemed like a dream that she had even seen him. She must have been mistaken. After all, if the duke had tried to kill Kylian's father, and even Roald had learned of that plot while he was in Burovia, why would he visit the duke's castle alone in the middle of the night?

Because Kylian wants his father killed as well?

So—to sum up: the burning of Saardam was an attack on Baron Uti after several failed assassination attempts by his half-brother. The burning was magical, and she had seen and felt Kylian's magic. He could have—no, he couldn't. The fire demons had been leaping over the roofs before Kylian ran. He could never have been in control of those beasts all the way from the palace.

That was a comforting thought. See? Kylian had nothing to do with it. Maybe even the baron had nothing to do with it. They were just guests of the royal family.

Oh, her head hurt from thinking about all this. Why didn't Roald worry about all this? Why did he lay there snoring when she couldn't sleep? Worse, why did she let this stuff keep her awake?

She should go and check on Loesie.

Never mind the duke's fancy clothes, she flung on her old farm dress and went to the door.

"You need to help me." Roald had gotten out of bed and stood with his arms wide, like a doll wanting to be dressed up.

Johanna whirled around. "Can't you dress yourself at all?" Seriously, he expected her to be available for him, kept her awake all night with his snoring and expected her to dress him as if he were a toddler?

He managed to look confused.

"It's not that hard to learn. I have to go and check Loesie." She went out the door and she had to do her best not to slam it.

As she entered the corridor, Nellie just came up the stairs, looking awfully awake. "Oh, I was just going to check if you were up yet."

"How is Loesie?"

"Still asleep. I left her like that. No need to wake her up."

"You're very cheerful, Nellie." *Way too cheerful after such a night.*

"Isn't the weather nice today?"

"Uhm . . . yeah?" *Have you forgotten that we have an exorcism to do today, somewhere in that horrible forest?* "How long have you been downstairs?"

"I got up just after sunrise, as I normally do. I went in search of a chapel or shrine for prayers of thanks that we've survived so far. I couldn't see any in the house so I went into the garden. I met a very helpful young man there—"

Kylian. "Did he have hair the colour of autumn leaves? And chestnut brown eyes?"

"Why, yes, he did. Do you know him?"

"He's Kylian prince of Gelre, Baron Uti's son."

Nellie's eyes widened. "You're kidding."

"Do I ever kid?"

"All the time, Mistress Johanna."

"When it's serious?" Then she thought about something else. "What did you tell him about us?"

"What do you mean?"

"Did you tell him where you are from and how we got here?"

"Well, he wanted to know, so I said we came through the forest."

"Did you give him our names?"

Nellie's cheeks had gone bright red. "No, I didn't. You said that we shouldn't, days ago, so I didn't."

"Did he ask?"

"He asked if I was alone and I said that a few friends had come with me. Is there a problem, Mistress Johanna? Why do you mistrust people so?"

Johanna really, really didn't like Nellie's red cheeks. That was a sure sign that something was going on.

"Is he downstairs at breakfast?"

"Oh no, he said he had to go."

Go where? "He didn't even speak to the duke?"

"I don't know. Why are you asking me all these things? I

don't know anything. I met him, I talked to him briefly. He was kind and I had no reason to question him."

"Did the duke say anything about his visit?"

"No, he didn't." She gave Johanna another *what do you need to know this for* stare. "Anyway, breakfast is ready."

"I'll check on Roald." Because *he* hadn't come out of the room either. And someone needed to wake up Loesie or bring her some breakfast.

Johanna went into the bedroom where it smelled of male sweat. Roald sat helpless on the bed, looking at his shirt which he held in white-knuckled hands on top of his knees.

"Come on, let's go to breakfast. The duke is expecting us downstairs. Are you hungry? There will probably be honey."

He said nothing and that was strange, because the mention of honey should have him jumping at the door.

"Roald?"

A sob.

Johanna closed the door and crossed the room to him. He sat with his shoulders hunched. When she knelt in front of him, he pressed his balled fists to his face, still clutching the shirt.

"What is the matter?"

He wailed. "You're angry with me."

"I'm not angry with you."

"Yes, you are!"

"Shhh, quiet. Behave like a prince. You don't want people to hear that you're crying." Or worse, Kylian to realise who was upstairs and tell the duke.

"I don't care. You're angry with me. I'm a bad husband."

"No, you're not."

"Yes I am!" He was swaying from one side to the other as if in a trance.

"Roald, please." She eased the shirt from his hands, forcing him to look at her by manoeuvring herself into his line of vision. She grabbed his shoulders so that he would stop that horrible swaying.

His eyes focused and widened.

"Don't do that, please."

He said nothing. His entire body shook with sobs.

"Keep calm. No one is angry with you." *Please, keep yourself together. I need you to be calm.*

She closed her arms around his shoulders. The naked skin felt cool to the touch. "Come, hold your hands out. I'll help you put on your clothes."

Roald calmed a bit, but his hands still trembled. One day, she would teach him how to dress himself, but for now, it wasn't worth worrying about. Johanna wrestled him into his shirt and jacket. The farm clothes he had worn coming here were too dirty to wear to a duke's breakfast. She would ask if their clothes could be washed.

Not much later they both met Nellie in the corridor. While Nellie wore the duke's dress, Johanna had opted to stay in her old farm clothes.

Nellie's face was disapproving. "Mistress Johanna, are you going to breakfast like that?"

"I don't trust this man and until I know where all these expensive clothes come from, I'm not going to wear them anymore."

"They used to belong to his wife. He told me."

And where was his wife now? The ice cellar?

She didn't want to think about it. She needed the duke to return Loesie to her normal form, but after that, they'd be out of here as soon as possible.

In the dining room, they found the duke alone at the dinner table. The dour-faced woman had just brought in a tray with boiled eggs, jam, bread, yellow butter and honey, which she was setting out on the table.

Everyone sat down in the same positions as last night.

The duke smiled at her. "I hope you slept well." Like this, he looked so much like a friendly old man that it was easy to see how Nellie was fooled into trusting him.

"There was a lot of noise outside the window last night," Johanna said. "I heard a horse coming up the drive."

"Karl the stablehand goes out to swim the horses most mornings."

And he was going to lie about it, too.

"Nellie said you had a visitor?"

"Did she?"

Nellie's cheeks went red. "I met this nice young man this morning when I went in search of a chapel or shrine."

"Oh, that was just my nephew."

"He arrived in the middle of the night?"

"He comes here at all hours so often I almost consider him part of the furniture." The duke chuckled. Johanna studied his face, but saw no sign that he considered this an uncomfortable subject for discussion.

"Did he bring any news? Did he come from Florisheim?"

"He did. He says that many refugees are still arriving in town and things are a bit crowded over there. I'm sending some people with him to help keep the order."

"People from Saarland?"

"Yes, many, and also Estland."

"We'd like to join them as soon as possible."

"It would be unwise to travel into the forest with your friend in this state."

"We were going to do something about that today, right?"

"Yes, certainly." He looked uneasy. "Understand, though, that exorcism is not a precise science. Even if she is completely cleared, there is some danger of lingering traces of magic. There are bands of rogue magicians in the forest. There are people who would kill you and eat you. I'm not even talking about the ghouls and other magical creatures."

"You could send some bandits with us."

"It's not that simple."

"They work for you, don't they?"

"They don't. I pay them sometimes to keep an eye on who enters this area and what they are doing here. As you can see, we are only a few in this house and I am quite poor in health. I cannot ride anymore, and have to rely on others to check my lands. Our holding is very large and much of it is useless forest."

Johanna cast a sharp glance at Roald, in case he was going to divulge his vast knowledge about the Baron's family's sordid family details. She couldn't help but think how he'd lain in bed under her, his eyes closed. It was scary and wonderful that she could do this to someone who was socially awkward and incapable of dressing himself.

Roald remained silent.

"What about your son?" After last night, Johanna hadn't seen him anymore.

"He cannot do these things alone. He has a need to go into the forest. His magic of living things needs him to roam in nature. I suspect he's gone riding this morning."

Or maybe he just had a profound dislike for Kylian.

"What are you going to do today?"

"Yesterday, I was able to break some of the demon's wards that affected your friend. What we'll do today is try to coax the demon out of her."

"How does that work?"

"There is passive coaxing, which we tried yesterday with the wine. Demons love wine. Unfortunately, they're usually determined to stay where they are. Sometimes they've been inside that person for such a long time that they're afraid to come out. At other times they're under specific orders to stay. Just offering something they like doesn't always have the desired effect."

"Vomiting spiders? Is that a desired effect?" Johanna shuddered.

"It is part of breaking a ward that magicians often use to secure their demons. Really, child, you know so little about magic. It is a wonder you have survived the trip here."

I'm not a child. "Then tell us."

"Well, it is like this: magic belongs to nature. It resides in wood, in water, in wind, in the soil—"

"In fire?"

He gave her a sharp look. "Yes, fire, too. The original people with those kinds of magic lived on land where the elements displayed these types of magic. The magic itself is contained in lines that run through the land. They may be in the soil or in the water or in the air. The creek you would have followed for much of your journey has a strong water magic line. The people who lived on its banks and drank its water became imbued with magic, which they passed on to other generations. But as people move around more, magic has become muddled. People from different estates have moved elsewhere and intermarried."

The sour-faced maid came in, asking if they had finished eating.

"Yes, take all the plates away."

"We need some breakfast for our friend who is still upstairs."

"Certainly." The maid set aside a plate with two thick slices of bread and a little jar of jam.

The duke waited until she was gone. "On this estate, we have water lines crossing with earth lines and tree lines. My grandfather built the living tunnels that lead up to the junction. Everything converges in this one point. He was such a strong tree magician that to this day, the trees obey his spells."

A chill went down Johanna's back. Was tree magic the same as willow magic?

"And this junction is where we have to take Loesie?"

"It is, because that is where I can best tap the magic that I need to fully drive the demon from her soul. Let us go." He picked up his walking stick and used it to push himself from the table. Nellie tried to assist him but he would have no help. "What do you think I am? An old man?" He smiled and winked at her.

He shuffled into the hallway, where he started explaining to Roald about all the portraits that hung there and who was related to whom and who had built which part of the house.

Johanna and Nellie climbed the stairs to get Loesie. Nellie was carrying the plate with the bread and the jam.

Behind them, the duke's voice echoed in the cavernous hall. ". . . and then that one over there, that's my great-grand-uncle Willem, who bought the neighbouring landholding . . ."

"Do you think we're doing the right thing?" Johanna asked in a low voice as soon as they were in the upstairs corridor.

"I thought you knew about all this magic?"

"I know enough to know that I know nothing. Should we trust him?"

"It seems to me that if there is anyone who can help the poor girl, it's this man."

"I'm not so certain that he does it to help us. He wants the demon, and I'm worried about what he wants to do with it."

"He told us: study demons. He's certainly a bit odd, but I can't see him doing any harm. He's an old man, and not good of health. You're very distrusting, Mistress Johanna."

"Well, yes. I want to like him. He *seems* a nice old man, But Roald told me that the duke has tried to murder his half-brother Baron Uti a few times and . . ." She hesitated, but could not bring herself to mention the bodies. Loesie needed to be helped. In her current state, Loesie was a danger to everyone, including herself. Loesie knew who had done this to her. Likely, Loesie knew who led the people who had burned Saardam, and telling Nellie what she knew might not only make Nellie afraid, but the knowledge might end up in places where it would be harmful. Kylian seemed to have a knack for extracting information out of girls.

They found Loesie on the bed, staring at the ceiling.

She looked up when Johanna and Nellie came in.

"We're going to help you today," Nellie said in a voice that sounded too cheerful.

Loesie gave Johanna a hard and cool stare. "What are we doing here?" That same question again. How many times had she asked it already?

"We're going into the forest," Johanna said. "Let's get you dressed."

Loesie just repeated, "What are we doing here?"

Johanna shivered. Somehow, she preferred Loesie unable to talk but with some of her wits.

Loesie's old black dress was definitely beyond wearing outside, so they dressed her in one of the duke's dresses. Nellie had put the bread on a little table next to the hearth, which Loesie ate while Nellie tried to bring some order to her hair.

Loesie sat like a doll while Nellie yanked at the knots. "You're going to have to cut some of these out. This is just terrible."

Where previously Loesie would have gotten angry, because she didn't like anyone commenting on what she looked like, she only repeated, "What are we doing here?"

Nellie managed to get Loesie's hair into some sort of bun, and then they helped Loesie down the stairs. It was as if every time Johanna touched Loesie, she seemed more fragile.

This thing is killing her, like having wasting sickness.

In the hall, the duke was still talking to Roald about his family. Roald let his gaze wander over the walls and ceiling, but Johanna had no doubt that he heard—and would remember—everything the duke said.

"Ah, there you are. Karl has brought the wagon. Come with me."

He started for the door, but Johanna held Nellie back.

"You don't have to watch this, Nellie. You're probably better off waiting here. It could get really nasty."

Nellie didn't protest.

"I will go with you," Roald said.

"Stay here with Nellie," Johanna said. Whatever was going to happen in that forest was not going be pleasant.

Roald didn't protest either. The two of them looked forlorn in that huge and empty hall.

An open wagon with a single horse stood in front of the steps. The stablehand Karl came up the steps and helped Loesie into the back seat. He offered her a cloak, but she didn't want it.

Johanna gladly took the offered cloak. The sun might be out, but the air was crisp. Next, Karl helped the duke into the wagon. He settled on the bench next to her, with a blanket over his legs and clutching the walking stick between his knees.

Johanna turned around to check on Loesie. In the space between the seats stood a crate covered with a dark red cloth and the cage made of rusty iron.

Karl jumped into the driver's seat. With a flick of the reins, they were off, along the gravel drive and the tree-lined path. This was why the network of lanes was so extensive: so that the duke could go for rides.

They rode out into the forest to the far side of the castle. A fine haze still hung between the trees and over the water of the lake. A swan glided gracefully over the water, barely stirring the surface with a ripple.

Oak trees grew on the sides of the lake, big ones with twisted and knotted trunks. The field between the trees was a riot of buttercups, daisies, dandelions, wild carrot and soft purple flowers on slender stems.

The horse trotted at a brisk pace, so she guessed that their destination couldn't be too far away, but it was hard to judge distance in this undulating country.

They went over a hill and into the forest. Pale sunlight made the fresh leaves on the trees look bright green, although a haze still lingered between the trees. Johanna looked for signs, but saw no traces of magic.

Loesie sat in the back of the wagon, observing the countryside. Her face was pale and drawn, the skin on her bone-thin arms grey and ghost-like. She had given up asking what they were doing here and Johanna was glad about that. She couldn't imagine how frightening it must be to have something else possess your soul and drown out your own thoughts. Then a disturbing thought: Loesie was meant to survive this exorcism, wasn't she?

The horses followed a path that ran along a creek that fed the lake. The watercourse meandered between trees, through thickets and marshy bogs. The water was so clear that you could see the white sand at the bottom.

They came to a field with a farmhouse. The orchard bloomed on the far side of the house. Cows grazed in the meadow. It was all so peaceful that it was hard to believe that there were major veins of magic nearby.

Then up another hill between huge gnarled oak trees with thick and knobbly trunks. Several trees were hollow and had lost large branches over the years, leaving gaping maws of darkness where Johanna could almost see pairs of eyes staring back at her.

"These trees are older than the estate itself," the duke said. "They are hundreds of years old."

Johanna believed it, too. In the back of her mind rose the soft whisper of voices. The very forest was alive with magic. A breeze brought a chill wind that made Johanna shiver.

"The tree line passes here," the duke said. "This is why those trees get so old. The line goes from here, through the field over there to the other side of the hill." He pointed with his walking stick.

"Do all trees have memories? In Saarland, it's just the willow trees and willow wood."

"That's because they grow close to the water, and that water comes from here. Magic spreads all over the world."

"Does all magic come from around here? Everything seems to have magic."

"No, magic is a far eastern thing. You may think that this countryside is alive with magic, but we have few strong magicians. In the far east, everyone is a strong magician."

Johanna thought of the tales told by seafaring traders of the evils that lay around the horn. "But the stories of sea creatures are fables, certainly?"

"I don't know about sea creatures, that's the domain of the sailors, but I do know of some people who attempted to go to the east overland. I don't know the names of the creatures the easterners have, but they are made of pure magic. If they want ill —and why not, because who can stop them?—they can overrun the entire world and reduce us to slaves. We do not want that to happen, right?"

Johanna thought back to the ball on the night of the fire. Father's colleague Master Deim had been saying similar things.

Everyone was saying it: *If the people from the far east came . . .*

Well, if they did, they would find this region's main port in a big mess, ruled by a puppet from a church that taught that magic didn't exist.

The wagon crested the hill and entered an area where five tree-lined lanes joined. Between the straight and slender beech trunks, Johanna had a view over a green meadow which sloped down on the other side. Karl pulled the reins and the horse slowed.

Johanna looked around. "Is this the place?"

A cold breeze blew in from the opposite direction, and it contained a prick of magic. Wailing voices that cried of misery and death.

She shivered despite the nice weather.

The five-point intersection looked an extremely unlikely location for a magical junction.

"No, not here, but most of us will have to continue on foot. We need to go down there." The duke pointed at the meadow.

A network of dark hedges ran through undulating grassy land, all joining at a hillock in the centre. No, they were not hedges. She followed the closest of them uphill, where it branched off a lane that joined the intersection. They were *paths* hidden under living tunnels of branches. Trees forced by magic to grow in tunnel shape to hide the path underneath. All these tunnels met up in a larger, dome-shaped junction, also formed out of tortured trees.

Johanna shivered. Who treated trees like this? She wanted to run to the trees and free them if she knew how.

At the mouth of the tunnel waited a man on a horse, his face shaded inside the hood of his cloak.

"You came," the duke said.

The man lowered the hood. It was Sylvan, his scarred face humourless. "Did you ever think I wouldn't?"

"I can never be sure with you."

Karl brought the wagon to a complete halt. He got down from the driver's seat and helped the duke down, and then Johanna. Sylvan also dismounted.

Karl took care of Sylvan's horse.

Loesie in the wagon couldn't walk and now Johanna understood why he had chosen such a simple wagon. A bigger one would not have fitted through this tunnel.

Sylvan took the horse by the reins and led the way into the tunnel.

CHAPTER 13

A S SOON AS Johanna set foot on the path, voices whispered with the wind, the words lilting and mysterious. The leaves rustled as if reaching for her. They were bursting with stories. They were in pain. They struggled against their magic-enforced shape. They wailed *Set us free, set us free.*

The chill that took hold of her went to her bones.

The duke, walking behind the wagon, concentrated on where he put his feet and his walking stick on the uneven ground. Both he and Loesie in the cart showed no signs of being affected; neither did Sylvan.

Johanna had to restrain herself from running away. She had to get out of here. Something bad was going to happen.

But the duke kept walking slowly, with his cane going *tap, tap, tap* on the uneven ground. Once the path had been paved, but the baked clay bricks had crumbled so that the surface was uneven and pitted with holes. He tapped the ground with his walking stick, as if seeking out safe places to put his feet.

His breath came quite heavy and at times he had to stop for a while.

"I ask my son to come here, usually," he said during one such stop. "He can do most things that need to be done regularly."

"What sort of things?"

"Setting wards and renewing protections. Seriously, girl, what do they teach you in that so-called enlightened town of yours? Does no one protect the town or even their property with wards? You have the gift. Are you going to tell me that all of your life, you have never done anything with it?"

"The church forbids magic."

"The church forbids *dark* magic. There is a big difference."

"In Saarland any magic is dark. Also, isn't that what we're coming out here for? Exorcism? Isn't that dark magic?"

"Yes. Dark magic has touched your friend. There is no way to undo dark magic other than with dark magic. In fact, the term dark magic is a poorly-chosen one. It simply means magic that requires active involvement. Not all of it is dark, or bad. The darkness is not in the magic, it is in the user."

A gust of wind made the branches whistle in high-pitched voices. It was as if someone screamed a warning. *Get away from him! He'll turn you into a toad!*

"Nooo!" Johanna clamped her hands over her ears.

Set us free, set us free, set us free.

Sylvan said something to his father which Johanna didn't hear. Neither of them laughed, as the bandits would have done.

She didn't know what to think anymore. One the one hand, she wanted to trust this man. On the other hand . . . she and Loesie were at his mercy. If he wanted ill, there would be no stopping him.

They had come to the top of the hillock in the middle of the web of tree tunnels. Seven tunnels met each other here in a space that could best be described as a cathedral of trees.

In the middle was a circle of stone paving with, in the middle, a stone altar. It was an old-looking thing, made from ancient stone. The top bore carvings, but age had worn away at the stone, so it was hard to see what the image depicted.

"This is where the magic lines meet." The duke smiled. "The water line runs from here to there." He pointed. "The earth line runs across the meadow. The wood line runs down the path we've just come on. I trust you've heard voices or felt magic?"

Johanna nodded. The whispering voices in the back of her head would not go away.

"My grandfather had this planted. My wife and I were married here."

The voices screamed in her ears, the words no longer audible. The chill of the wind took her breath away.

But the sun was still shining and the leaves on the trees didn't move visibly. The horse showed no signs of being disturbed by magic, and horses were normally very skittish. Loesie was also not more disturbed than usual. Was it just her?

Sylvan stopped the cart. The duke took the reins while Sylvan helped Loesie down from the wagon. He picked her up in his arms and set her on top of the stone table, then he lifted the cage and crate out of the wagon and put them on the ground.

He took the reins from his father and led the horse away. The wind carried the sound of the horse's footsteps on the eroded brick paving.

"Well, we may start," the duke said, breaking the tense silence.

He uncovered the crate and unloaded a number of items. A tall, long-necked bottle, half-filled with a dark, sloshing fluid. A gold-encrusted goblet. A sheep's skull. Johanna remembered the face of the Reverend Romulus. *You want an exorcist,* he had said. Well, she had found one, and now that he was about to start, she wondered if this was such a good idea. Actually, she was sure it *wasn't* such a good idea, because even Sylvan admitted that his father didn't always get it right.

But it was too late for all of that now.

The duke unstoppered the bottle and poured some of the fluid into the goblet. Then he slowly walked around the stone table, pouring drops of it on the ground until he had emptied the goblet. The wind brought a scent of sourness that made the hair on Johanna's arms stand up. *Like vomit.*

The duke met her eyes. "Dark magic is nothing more than us using the magic we have been born with to create more of the same. Your magic is wood, so you should be able to make things grow in whatever fashion you want."

"It that what your grandfather did? Force the trees to grow this way?"

It was a most hideous thing to do. Tree torture.

"It is up to us to control nature, or else nature will control us."

He hobbled back to the cart, leaned his walking stick to it, and produced a box. Inside lay a couple of burning coals. He held a dry stick against the heat and blew. The wood started smoking. He lifted the stick in front of his face. A curl of smoke rose from its tip.

"I need to warn you. My magic is fire, so you may see some strange phenomena soon."

Fire magic. There had been fire demons on the roofs of Saardam on the day the city burned. Kylian had jumped over the fence as soon as he saw those. Had the duke been in the city? He said he rarely travelled except along the tree-lined lanes of his estate. Maybe they weren't as far from the river as she thought. Maybe he'd come with his half-brother—the one he'd supposedly tried to kill? The situation was getting more confusing all the time.

The duke turned the burning stick upside down. An orange flame erupted from its burning end, and crept over the length of the wood.

The duke blew and fanned the flames. Fire licked his fingers, but it didn't seem to bother him. Sylvan gave him a torch made from a stick with oil-drenched straw. The flames went *wooof* when he held the burning stick underneath. He swung the torch from side to side to fan the flames, scattering bits of burning straw on his clothes and in his hair. Smoke rose from a patch on the shoulder of his jacket, that was spreading now, with a ring of tiny flames.

Just as Johanna wanted to say something about it, he flung the torch into the air towards the "roof" of the tree cathedral.

Something made a terrible screeching noise, like an animal about to be killed. Johanna clamped her hands over her ears. "Stop it!"

The duke held his outstretched hands towards the torch, which hung in mid-air, spewing flames in all directions. He spoke harsh-sounding words in a low voice.

As the torch fell, the flames detached themselves from the wood end and shaped themselves into some kind of *creature* that moved of its own accord. It grew a long bushy tail, an elongate body and four short legs, and a rounded snout with two pointy ears with tufts of fire-hair at the top.

A squirrel. It hopped through the air, and paused on the duke's outstretched hand to look around. The tail twitched, leaking bits of fire. Then it ran down his arm, setting fire to his jacket in its wake. It ran across the ground, leaving a trail of singed grass, to the trunk of one of the imprisoned trees.

There was that horrible screech again and now she understood what it was: the wood's fear of this creature. Johanna shivered. A gust of wind tore between the trees, making the branches whistle.

The squirrel stopped, sat on its hind legs and sniffed the air.

The duke called a few words in that harsh, magical language and the creature ran back to the stone table. It sniffed the ground where he had poured the wine, following the trail of drops around the table. And around and around.

Loesie sat up, her eyes wide, more alert than Johanna had seen her. Her gaze followed the fire squirrel around the table, quite alarmed, Johanna thought.

Why were Loesie's clothes and the stone around her wet?

Wait—water dripped from above. *From the trees.* Loesie's magic was wood, and the trees were keeping her safe from the fire.

The single squirrel had split into two squirrels, running around and around with fire trailing from their bushy tails. The trees leaked water. Whenever it fell on a squirrel, there was a hiss and a cloud of steam.

The squirrels ran faster and faster until they merged into a blur of fire. With each round, their numbers doubled. There were eight and then sixteen, and then she lost count. Their fiery bodies blurred into one another. The air chilled. It was as if the sun dimmed and the wind picked up, whipping up the flames erupting from the many squirrel tails. Loesie sat motionless in this spectacle.

Johanna became aware of a strange noise, like a colony of bees trapped in a box. The extinguished torch had fallen on the ground next to the stone table. It trembled and jiggled. Little buds sprung from the handle of the torch. They grew into tendrils. Leaves sprouted. The twigs curled and twined around the base of the table. The vines pushed themselves up the side of the table and grew to the top of the heavy slab that covered it. They grew around Loesie's legs, around the bottle that still stood there, up her arms and through her hair.

The fire squirrels ran up the vines, seeding flames in their wake. The vines grew and grew as if trying to outpace the squirrels. Each time a vine burnt, a new one sprang up. They covered Loesie in layer upon layer of tightly-twisted vines. They grew up her legs, covered her body, her arms, grew through her hair, until her entire body was covered in vines. The squirrels ran up and down the vines, leaving fire in their wake. The vines regrew each time the fire had passed.

The duke stood with his hands outstretched and his eyes closed. His face was red, glistening with sweat. He urged the squirrels on, faster and faster. They still multiplied, but not as fast as before.

The vines combined into thicker branches that no longer had leaves. A solid cage of wood protected Loesie and the demon that possessed her.

"Sylvan!" the duke yelled.

A gust of wind fanned the flames, eating through the foliage. Sylvan stood with his hands outstretched. The wind obeyed him as it had when they were crossing the sand dunes.

The flames spread until they covered the entire tangle of vines. The fire belched thick clouds of smoke. The duke stepped into them, yelling incantations at the top of his voice. The roaring of the fire almost drowned him out.

He sang and chanted, waving his arms. The fire grew. Something soft hit Johanna's shoulder, and then her head, and her arm. Dead and shrivelled leaves rained down from the tree roof. The heat seared her skin.

"Loesie!" she called.

Her friend was in the middle of that inferno, protected by a layer of vines that were slowly and certainly eaten by flames. Great gouts of sparks gushed from the fire.

"The cage! Get the cage!" the duke shouted.

As soon as Sylvan stopped fanning the wind and picked up the iron cage, the fire dimmed.

His father took the cage from him, heavily leaning on his walking stick. "Go, keep the fire going." He inched forward until the flames swallowed him.

Johanna turned to Sylvan, but he took no notice of her. He waved his hands. He chanted at the top of his voice. The fire roared. Gouts of flame erupted from the burning vines. Even the stone slab burned.

Then there was a rush of air towards the fire, followed by a sharper rush away from the fire. With an almighty roar, the knot of vines exploded. A huge fireball tore around the tree cathedral, dragging a white-hot object behind it. The fireball burst free through the cathedral roof and into the air. The glowing object bounced along the ground a few times and came to a halt. It was the metal cage, its door open, empty, glowing orange-hot and hissing steam.

The vines around the stone table had exploded into thousands of shreds of wood. Loesie sat on the table, looking around with a deep frown on her face.

The duke sank back against the cart, panting. "I let it escape." He balled his fist at the overhanging trees where a burnt hole in the canopy indicated the place where the demon had burst to freedom. "I let it escape!"

Johanna had no idea why he had thought that he could capture a magical being in a tiny iron cage, but she was glad that it had gone and that the duke could not harm anyone with it.

"Johanna? What we be doing here?" *That* was Loesie's voice. She rushed to her friend and closed her arms around her shoulders. Loesie felt cold and frail. The hand that reached up to Johanna's arm trembled. Her fingers were so thin and bony, her lips cracked and bleeding.

"Did the fire hurt you?"

"I din' see no fire. What sort of place is this? How'd we get here?"

"It's a long, long story. We better go back to the house. Are you hungry?"

"I could eat a horse."

At that moment, Sylvan just came out of one of the tree tunnels leading the horse and wagon. "See, there be a horse. Someone's listening to me." She laughed.

That was the old Loesie.

"Is she all right?" Sylvan asked.

The duke said, "She is very strong. I don't know who did what to her, but it must have been a strong magician. I think we got most of the spell, but there may be a lingering effect. She'll have to come back here if that is the case."

Loesie frowned at Johanna. "Why do these people talk funny? What's this with spells and magicians? I thought ye city folk din' believe in magic."

"We're a long way from the city." Johanna helped Loesie off the stone table. She might have been cured, but her muscles were very weak. She leaned on Johanna's shoulder and was breathing heavily by the time they reached the cart.

"I be no magician, Johanna. Tell them that. I want not a thing to do with magic anymore. It's evil."

Johanna agreed with her, but the problem was that magic would happen no matter how people denied or forbade it. She climbed in the wagon and sat next to Loesie on the back seat. Sylvan helped the duke in before leading the horse through the tree tunnel back up the hill.

Karl waited at the end of the tunnel with Sylvan's horse. He climbed in the driver's seat while Sylvan mounted his horse. He looked tired, too.

He stared over the meadow and into the blue sky. "Did you see where this thing went, Karl?"

"All I saw was a sudden ball of fire that leapt in the air. It went higher than I could see, and then it was gone. Nothing I could do."

The duke shook his head. "I didn't expect you to do anything. It's all right, even if it's a pity that I couldn't catch it."

The horses broke into a slow trot down the hill. Loesie leaned against Johanna. Her head rested on Johanna's shoulder and grew heavy and warm.

No one said anything on the way back, but the bird song seemed more cheerful and the sunlight brighter than before.

When they arrived at the house, Karl helped get Loesie down from the wagon. She woke up enough to support her own weight, but that was about all. Considering how long it had been since Loesie had slept properly, she had a lot to catch up on.

The duke said. "She will probably sleep most of the day. Longer, if she has been under this spell for a while." He rubbed his face. "I'll probably sleep for a while, too."

Sylvan helped Johanna take Loesie up the stairs to the front door. She could see Nellie's face behind the upstairs window.

They entered through the front door into the cavernous hall that had dispelled most of its eeriness and had become plain stuffy.

"You'll have to forgive my father," Sylvan said when they were slowly walking up the stairs. "He hasn't done any of this for a long time. We don't see many people who are this badly affected by magic."

Did they see many people here at all? "I've . . . never seen anything like this. Is fire magic common?" She wanted to keep him talking. As yet, this place raised far more questions than answers.

"Not common at all."

"That is an extremely powerful type of magic." *Powerful enough to burn an entire city*.

"It's not the most powerful. Destructive, yes, but not easily controlled and not hugely useful in everyday life. Do you know that you can always tell a fire magician by the creature his apparitions take on? It's the only type of magician you can identify from their magic signature."

Was he trying to tell her in a roundabout way that the duke hadn't been in Saardam? Was it even true what he told her? "Do you know anyone whose fire demons look like giant cats?"

Sylvan turned to her. "Leopards? With spots?"

"I don't know. I wasn't close enough to see spots. Do you know who that could have been?"

"Cats are common as fire creature. I would really need to know if there were spots to tell who it was. Where did you see this?"

"Fire demons caused the burning of Saardam."

He gave her a sharp look. "My father has nothing to do with that, before you ask."

"According to what you've just told me, I gathered as much." *If it's the truth.* "That's why I'm asking about large cats. Can you give me some names of possible people?"

"I am not allowed to, unless I have evidence to clearly identify the person."

"Allowed? Who doesn't allow you to give names?"

"The magician's guild. They control the practices we adhere to. There is enough rumour and untruth circulated about magic without us adding to it."

"A magician's guild?"

"They're normally fairly quiet and don't draw attention to themselves. It is a place of knowledge and academia, where people learn about magic. I recommend that when your friend is ready to travel, you go on to Florisheim to seek out the guild. You will need any knowledge you can get." His eyes met hers in a penetrating way that made her certain that he knew who she was, he knew who Roald was, and he had known this all along.

And it would be really nice if she understood why the duke had sent men to get them off the *Lady Sara* before it reached Florisheim. Surely *Giving weary travellers a bed* was not the reason.

CHAPTER 14

THEY CARRIED Loesie into the bedroom. Nellie opened the door and folded back the covers. "Oh, that dress is disgusting. We should really do some washing, Mistress Johanna."

"Let me know what you want washed and I'll ask Gertrude to take care of it," Sylvan said.

Gertrude, presumably, was the dour-faced servant.

Johanna sank down on the edge of the bed when Sylvan had left. After all the excitement of the morning, she felt really tired, too.

She straightened the blankets over her friend. Loesie was asleep, on her side, with her knees drawn up and her hand curled up into a relaxed fist and pressed against her cheek. She looked peaceful, like a child.

Nellie watched from the other side of the room, as if still afraid to come close. "Is she going to be all right?"

"Maybe." Johanna wasn't sure that Loesie was entirely cured yet, and wouldn't believe it until she had spoken with Loesie and knew that she remembered everything that had happened to her on the farm. "It will be a few days until we know for sure, but it looks promising."

She remembered the vines growing over Loesie and the fire-ball bursting from them. All those things seemed to be such a long time ago already, as if they had happened in a different time and different place.

"Where is Roald?"

"Oh, my excuses, Mistress Johanna. I discovered that the duke has a really amazing library and I showed him. I've been unable to get him to come out, even to see you."

"That's all right. I'll go and see him later."

"He never even asked about you."

"That's fine. It's the way he is. No one can change that."

Johanna went to her own room and tried to sleep, but there was too much to mull over in her mind.

The most important thing: the duke and his son had been unfailingly kind and helpful. And yet she couldn't shake the feeling that they were somehow lying to her or trying to lead her —and Roald—into a trap. She worried that they were walking into this trap with their eyes open, or had already done so. But if they had, she couldn't see it.

After a while lying on the bed staring at the ceiling, she got up and went downstairs in search of the library.

It was eerily quiet in the house. Her footsteps echoed in this horrible dark hall. Even the servants seemed to have disappeared. The paintings of the duke's ancestors on the wall were so lifelike that in the dim light, Johanna sometimes thought that the people in the paintings moved. She stopped several times to read the notes engraved in small plaques in the frame, giving the painter's name and the name of the person who had commissioned the work.

The duke's grandfather had been a tall man, like Sylvan, with penetrating blue eyes. Johanna could almost feel the magic radiating from the painting.

She found the library at the end of the downstairs hallway where the dining room was. It was a high-ceilinged room with the walls covered in bookshelves. Because the ceiling was so high, a wooden gallery ran along the walls to have access to the top shelves. Father had a couple of shelves of books, beautifully written, with coloured plates and bound in gold-embossed leather. Some of them, such as Rinius' *On the Movement of Stars*, had been Father's presents to her. To have as many books as they had at home was considered a treasure. She could barely comprehend what this library must be worth.

Roald stood in the very corner of the gallery, reading a thick book. He didn't seem to have heard her, so Johanna padded up the wooden stairs, sliding her hand over the railing. The wood showed her the tranquillity of the room. The duke seated by the fire, reading. Sylvan copying diagrams. Gertrude dusting the shelves.

"What are you reading?"

Roald gasped and looked over his shoulder. He turned around. The book in his hands was a copy of *The Anatomy of Man* and he had it open on a page with the title *The Woman With Child*. It displayed a drawing of a woman's body with a swollen stomach, cut open to show a child inside.

Roald's eyes met hers. Another man would have looked guilty, but he simply eyed her stomach, which was distinctly flat.

"That's what's going to happen, right?"

"Um, yes."

He continued to stare, first at the book and then at her, as if comparing the two. "It says here, 'The woman should not exert herself, should not expose herself to the elements, or ride a horse.' You should be careful."

"Later, yes." When it became obvious that she was with child.

Johanna stared at the page, but succeeded only in making herself feel sick at the sight of the woman's cut-open stomach.

Being married meant bearing children. It wasn't just about having no fun. It was about the ordeal and the pain and the fact that many women didn't survive. Her own mother had died while with child, although not in childbed. How could she tell if she was with child? Not for a while yet, that was for sure. Way back in Saardam, so long ago that it seemed another century, Augustina talked about quickening. Johanna had been disgraceful enough not to show any interest. She didn't want babies, right?

She was saved from an uncomfortable discussion when the door to the library opened and two people came in. One she recognised immediately as Sylvan.

The other was Kylian.

He looked up at the gallery, turned to Sylvan and nodded.

There was no longer any question about their identity.

"I'd like you to meet my cousin. He is a physician and he insisted on seeing the young lady afflicted by magic."

"She is asleep."

"So I heard from the other young lady." His eyes met Johanna's with renewed curiosity.

Johanna made sure that she went down the stairs first, to protect Roald. Now that her and Roald's identities were in the open, she felt strangely relieved. That was one thing she no longer needed to worry about.

She met Kylian's brown eyes.

He gave a small bow. "Fancy meeting you again here."

Funny, that, seeing as the last time she had seen him, he'd vaulted the fence at the palace, just before it burned.

"One could say the same about you." Haughty, detached. Yes, maybe she could do this royal thing.

"The duke is my uncle. I regularly use his estate as a way house."

"So I've heard." *Do you know of the dead bodies?* "You spoke to my maid this morning. Why didn't you come into the house for breakfast? You could have met us all there."

"I had my own matters to attend to. I presume you saw the farm on the way to the crossing point? I run those farms for my uncle. I arrived very late last night. My uncle told me of the possessed girl he had as guest. He said he was going to attempt an exorcism and asked me if I would like to have a look at her when it was done." Then he saw Roald. "Oh." He laughed and bowed. "Your Highness." He bowed to Johanna, too. "To you, too. I heard about your interesting marriage."

So much for Nellie not telling him anything.

"When your friend recovers, you must come with me to Florisheim where we can have a proper ceremony. My father will be most happy to host it, as he is already hosting many of your citizens. Several had told me that they had seen the heir to the throne escape the palace—one man even helped him—but he had not turned up at Florisheim with the others. So when I heard the rumours of a halfwit man with three women travelling upriver, I guessed it was you."

Sylvan gave him a cold look.

"Let us go and see this friend of yours."

"She is fine. She was very tired when we came back and she is resting now."

"I only need to see her briefly. I can feel if she has any residual magic in her."

There was no dissuading him from seeing Loesie, and to be honest, she wasn't quite sure why she didn't want him to see her, so they went up the stairs. Sylvan again came with them. She met his eyes while walking up the stairs. His eyes were penetrating. Johanna had no idea what he was trying to tell her.

Upstairs in the corridor, the sunlight came in through the window at the far end.

Nellie sat by the window sewing the holes in Loesie's old dress and rose as soon as they came in. "Kylian." She curtsied for him, with a very strange expression on her face.

Kylian gave her a cursory glance and sat on the edge of Loesie's bed. He reached out for Loesie's cheek.

As soon as his fingertips touched the skin, Loesie's eyes flew open. She inhaled a sharp breath and held it. Her eyes widened.

A chill breeze went through the room.

Kylian laughed. "You can't harm me with magic, little sorceress."

Loesie fell back into the pillow, looking dazed in a *why did you wake me up?* kind of way.

Kylian bent closer. "Do you remember who did this to you?"

Loesie frowned. There was no lingering magic now.

"Do you remember someone casting a spell?"

Her frown deepened.

For a long time, Loesie said nothing. Johanna only heard the thudding of her heart.

"Well," Kylian said eventually. "I'm sure the memory will come back." He rose. "She'll be ready to travel within two days. I'll accompany you to Florisheim."

He rose again and left the room. Sylvan ran after him.

After he had shut the door, Nellie smiled at Johanna. "Isn't he absolutely handsome?"

Loesie said, "He be a strong magician. No good fer church girls."

"Any better for farm girls?"

"I weren't saying that. I were saying that he'd be looking fer a noble girl."

"What's this about?" Johanna looked from one to the other. Nellie, studiously pushing the needle in and out of the fabric of her dress, and Loesie with her arms crossed over her chest.

"Nothing," Nellie said.

Loesie snorted. "Ye want that man fer yesself. That's why."

"I don't," Nellie said, a bit too abruptly. "And if you're going to come with us, can you at least learn to speak properly?"

"I'll learn no townsfolk talk."

They glared at each other. Nellie stuck her chin in the air.

"Be nice," Roald said. "My mother says we all need to be nice to each other."

Loesie snorted. "Well, that be tough luck, because life isn't nice."

"Don't speak like that to the prince."

Loesie frowned at Roald. "The prince?"

"Prince Roald," Nellie said in a prim voice. "That will be 'Your Highness' to you. Same as Mistress Johanna. She's married to him now. Show some manners and respect."

Loesie frowned at Johanna. "You're kidding, right?"

Johanna shook her head.

"Holy cows. I missed the party."

CHAPTER 15

TALKATIVE AS LOESIE had suddenly become, she did not seem to have any recollection of how she had ended up mute, no matter how Johanna asked.

Johanna asked her about the demons which the basket had shown her, and Loesie just gave her a blank look. She asked about Loesie's family but the mention of them didn't seem to evoke any emotion from Loesie.

Kylian had declared her *fit to travel*, but what had really passed between him and Loesie?

There were more questions than answers.

The nice weather held for the next couple of days. Roald insisted on spending most of that time in the garden. There were wilted flowers on the roses, he said, and he simply could not tolerate that. Johanna wandered around the gardens and the lake, looking at the swans and the duke's ducks and peaceful sight of Roald pottering in the rose beds.

Loesie came outside on the third day. Even in three days, she had gained in health. Her skin was no longer ghostly white and her hollow cheeks were starting to fill out. During each meal, the duke urged her to eat more.

Johanna still didn't have a satisfactory answer to the question of whether he was more than a friendly old man who happened to have powerful magic. She spent some time in his library trying to find books about magic, but there weren't many, and those he had covered things like recipes for potions. Magic books, he said, were extremely rare, since most magic lore was never written down for fear of persecution.

The only one who still seemed tense was Sylvan. The duke laughed when she mentioned this to him, and said that Sylvan was never at ease when sleeping in a house. His son's bedroom, the duke said, mostly went unused because Sylvan slept in the stables with his bears. He said Sylvan was greatly disturbed by his bear magic because it could so easily be used for evil.

Johanna tried very hard to believe that these were good people, but could not dispel her unease completely. They might be perfectly friendly mass murderers.

She was glad when, on the fourth day, Kylian brought a coach to the front of the house. They packed up their meagre possessions, bolstered by some clothing which the duke insisted they take with them.

The most welcome bit of news was that Kylian said his men had brought the *Lady Sara* into Florisheim. The sea cows, he said, were all fine.

The duke and Sylvan insisted on coming with them on the ride to Florisheim which, Johanna gathered, was much closer than she had thought.

They rode out over the estate's main lane. Johanna sat next to Roald near the window. The duke had insisted that they dress well and take those visible positions in the coach, because *there might be some fuss*. Refugees from Saarland had learned that their prince had survived.

The duke had also lent Johanna some of his wife's jewellery, because *you simply cannot face your citizens wearing a farm dress*. That had really hit home to her that from now on, nothing in her life would be either a secret or the same.

Before getting on the coach, Johanna had stood in front of the mirror in the bedroom saying to her reflection, "You're a princess now."

She agreed she didn't look like one. So, she needed jewellery. Heavy gold pieces with glittering stones. She had insisted that she would return them to the duke as soon as she could, but he just waved his hand and said something about rather seeing the pieces being worn than stowed away in some wardrobe.

So here she was, dressed up like a slightly old-fashioned noble woman, facing Nellie, who was dressed up like a slightly less noble woman and sitting next to Roald, who looked distinctly uncomfortable in his stiff nobleman's clothes. The duke sat next to Nellie, explaining about all the places they passed. The estate's farms and what he grew there, the wineries, the creeks, the water mill, the estate's boundary and the village.

Sylvan sat on Johanna's other side, dressed in black and staring out the window with a brooding expression on his face. Loesie sat opposite him, making faces at him, to which he reacted by looking angrier.

They hadn't been travelling for long when the coach rounded a bend in the road and Florisheim spread before them. The town lay on a slight slope, a mass of terracotta roofs and stone that covered the undulating land on the left bank of the Rede River, whose mirror-like surface reflected the town.

The castle stood at the highest point, a grey stone building with two forbidding round towers and a high wall, overlooking the town like a protective mother duck.

The curved line of the quay hosted a good number of barges. Low, flat, *Saarlander* barges, many flying the flag of Saardam.

Johanna's heart beat faster.

Father.

What she wanted more than anything was to check on the *Lady Sara* because surely if Father was here, that's where he would stay.

The duke told her that the baron had allowed the refugees to camp in a piece of land close to the river, a bright green meadow on which stood a collection of mismatched tents. A couple of boys in typical Saarlander trousers played sword-fights with sticks between the tents. A couple of women stood talking to each other, their long and wide skirts achingly familiar. Johanna even spotted a couple wearing clogs.

As the coach entered the grounds, people stopped their activities to watch. They called other people, who came to the tent entrances.

The coach came to a halt in the middle of the camp. By now, a veritable crowd of refugees had gathered. The wobbling of the coach signalled the driver getting down and coming to open the door.

"Look, look! It's prince Roald!" someone shouted.

Johanna's heart beat faster. Roald sat with his hands clamped between his knees.

"Let me go first," she whispered to him.

He didn't react, but she put her hand on his. His skin felt clammy with sweat. He swayed from side to side ever so slightly.

"Shhh, calm down. You don't have to speak. I can do that." She fished the chain with the ring from under her dress, undid the clasp and slipped the ring on her finger. Her hands, too, were trembling. What would people say about this?

The door opened. The driver reached in. "Your Highness."

Roald went first.

A great cheer went up outside. Holding onto Roald's arm, Johanna could feel him tense up.

"Prince Roald is alive!"

"Three cheers for the new king."

He had frozen completely, still on the coach steps.

She whispered to him, "Roald, take one step down, then I can come out, too. I will talk to them." *Please don't start swaying or banging your head into something.*

The muscles in his arms were so tense that she could feel their hardness through his jacket.

"Roald, please?"

She pushed him gently, and he took a stiff step to the ground.

People cheered and clapped.

"Three cheers for the new king!"

"We are saved!"

But Roald stood there frozen, his face a mask of terror. Any moment now and he would start screaming, or rolling on the ground, or laughing like an idiot.

She pushed past him, waving her hands. "Give him some room! Please, people."

Then their attention turned to her.

"Why, it's Johanna Brouwer."

And then a woman said, "Is that the Carmine crest she's wearing?"

A voice behind them called out, "Make way for their royal highnesses, the prince and princess of Saarland." It was Kylian, standing on the driver's seat of the coach.

The people retreated and formed a path. Johanna held onto Roald's arm.

"Just keep walking," she whispered to him, while guiding him. "Stay calm. Keep walking."

In the crowd, she met the eyes of Julianna Nieland, in simple, dirty clothing, with hollow cheeks. She came forward and dipped a curtsy to Roald. And another to Johanna.

"Please, Julianna."

Julianna looked up with tear-filled eyes. "Is my brother with you?"

"No. Have you seen my father?"

A look of mutual pain went between them.

Then another familiar face met her in the mayhem. "Master Deim!"

The merchant wrestled through the crowd. He gave her a big hug. "Oh, child, I didn't think I would see your happy face again!"

"Where is Father?"

"He was upset that the *Lady Sara* was gone. He took the *Lady Davida* and that was the last I've seen of him."

"He's not here?" A black hole opened inside her. Father, dead?

Master Deim shook his head. "So many people are gone. The king and queen, the mayor, Reverend Romulus—"

"The reverend? Was he killed?" The thought made her sick. Who would kill a priest? "Is it true that Saardam is in the hands of a religious brother called Alexandre?"

"We've heard people say that, yes. We don't know how much of it is true."

A nobleman on Johanna's other side was speaking to Roald. "Your Highness, you must come with us. We must decide our next steps." He met Johanna's eyes. "Um, Lady, I'm unsure what the baron's son meant when he said . . . are you . . ."

"Married before the eyes of the Triune," Nellie said, behind Johanna. Dear old Nellie and her appropriateness.

The man swallowed. "Well. We, um, must . . . make it official."

He didn't like it, not at all.

The procession came to the edge of the field, separated from the riverbank by a road. At the jetty on the other side a welcome sight greeted Johanna. The *Lady Sara* lay amongst a couple of barges, most of them Saarlander, but one was a local ship with a large cabin, similar in build to the Burovian ship that had brought Roald to Saardam.

The duke said, "The baron provides you with one of his ships to use as accommodation. I guess this is where we say goodbye."

"Thank you so much for helping us," Johanna said.

The duke took her hand in a weak, paper-skinned grip. "It is nothing, child. One day, when you're settled back into your home town, think of us and do my son a favour."

Johanna met Sylvan's eyes. The look in his eyes alone was enough to stab someone through the heart.

The driver was already helping the duke back to the coach, but Sylvan stayed behind.

He leaned close, giving Johanna a much closer view of his tattoos and that horrible scar, far closer than she had ever desired. His expression was just as humourless and morose as before. "Look, I need to tell you something. I know you don't trust us. Given all that has happened, I can't blame you. It's probably a good thing. You are going to need all the wits you have to get through this and survive."

Kylian sat in the driver's seat of the coach, looking directly at the pair of them.

"My father and I survive in the same way. We keep standing in the face of daily betrayal, evil and worse. I'm not telling you to trust us, but I hope that our actions will speak for us instead. I hope that you at least trust us enough to believe what I'm going to tell you now. It's about my cousin, Kylian. Don't ever trust anything he says. As heir to the throne, he takes betrayal and reigning by terror to a new level. Once he has you in his sights, he does all he can to get whatever he wants. For the men, that is usually money or power. He will find something that you have done wrong in the past, and threaten to make it public. Then he'll come to you at all hours and act like he's at home. He'll demand favours—"

"Like an ice cellar full of dead bodies?" Johanna had said it before she could stop herself.

Sylvan gave her a blank look. "Like—what?"

"Discover something his victim has done wrong in the past, like an ice cellar full of dead bodies."

The look of total puzzlement on his face was very convincing. "I have *no* idea what you're talking about."

Johanna was by now shaking so much that she had trouble speaking. "On your father's land, not very far from where you recaptured me after we ran from the village in the sand, there is an ice cellar."

"Yes?" He frowned. "I think there might be. It used to be used by my uncle who owned that land before it turned into a useless desert."

"Go there, and have a look inside. Remind yourself what's in there."

"Whoa, why do you think we—"

"You're right. We don't trust you." She pulled off the heavy brooch and golden chain she wore around her neck and dumped them in Sylvan's hands. "Here. I'd take off the dress, too, if I had anything else to wear."

"But hang on. You turn against us after we've helped your friend get rid of—"

"Your father did that for his own aim. We were brought to you as prisoners. Somehow along the way, you found out who we were and became all friendly. We don't need you, Sylvan."

She started to turn around to catch up with Roald and the others who had proceeded onto the jetty, but he grabbed her arm. "Listen to me. All right, distrust us. Believe whatever you want, but listen to this one bit of advice: please seek out the magician's guild before Kylian can take you there. We need to stay strong against him. There is one thing, one very important magical thing you should know about him." He fixed her with his grey eyes.

"And that is?"

"He's the most powerful dark magician you are likely to come across in your life. He's a necromancer."

Then he let go of her arm, climbed into the coach and was gone, leaving Johanna to stand reeling amongst the adoring citizens. The breeze that touched her skin seemed colder than the coldest of midwinter.

THE IDIOT KING

Book 3 of the Ghostspeaker Chronicles

PATTY JANSEN

CHAPTER 1

THE LETTER was written in cramped, barely literate hand. The writer had used cheap paper which turned pen strokes into blobs and did not improve its legibility. Neither did the poor light that fell into the boat shed through the open front.

Fleuris LaFontaine had given the letter to Johanna only after she had specifically requested to see it, twice, and Master Deim had asked him to give it to her and Fleuris could no longer go on ignoring Johanna's presence. He had pushed it across the rough wood of the simple table with his be-ringed, delicate hand, wrists barely protruding from the lace cuffs—*dirty* lace cuffs to be sure. Nothing in the refugee camps was still pristine.

Johanna had taken the letter, coolly, chin in the air, and said, "Thank you." She'd unfolded the sheet, making sure that the men in the room wouldn't notice that her hands trembled. Those men continued their discussion, as if she weren't there, about the occupation of Saardam, and people who had or hadn't made it out and assets that may or may not have been destroyed.

Most of it was pure speculation, but they spoke as if those statements were fact.

Johanna had just calmed down from being angry about being told that the Council of Nobles meeting was for *men of import* and not for *wives or consorts*, and now she got angry again. This was how stupid rumours started in the camp of refugee Saarlanders, because the nobles speculated idly, and then the other people took their words for fact, *Because they were important men.* Because people had been waiting for news for weeks and the waiting and endless days of no news were getting on everybody's nerves.

"What does it say?" Roald, who sat next to her, leaned over her shoulder to read.

She smoothed out the letter.

In loopy writing, it said at the top,

To the Red Baron of Gelre and all he deems notifiable in matters of the city of Saardam.

The date at the top said 14th June, which was barely a week after the fateful day that Saardam had burned. Apparently this letter had been delivered to the castle in Florisheim over two months ago, so evidently the Baron didn't consider the former citizens of Saardam immediately notifiable. And that in itself said something about what the Baron really thought of the survivors.

I hereby notify the barony that as of today, I have taken up the position of Governor of the city of Saardam on behalf of the Belaman Church and its rightful supporters. All heathens, disbelievers, disciples of treacherous beliefs and followers of dark witchcraft have been purged from the city. Most of the other citizens have been spared and have in fact welcomed our move. No commerce or ships were harmed. We will do our utmost best to resume the river trade as soon as possible.

Your friend,

Alexandre Trebuchet

"What does he mean—no commerce was harmed?" Roald asked, his too-loud voice cutting into the genteel talk of men that was going on around them.

They stopped talking, most of them looking annoyed.

Johan Delacoeur pursed his lips. He stroked his moustache. "He means that no shops or other businesses were harmed in Saardam, Your Majesty." He dipped his head, but his voice had a tone as if he were speaking to a small child.

"Everything he writes is a lie," Roald said. "A lot of businesses were burned. All along the harbourfront. I saw it."

Fleuris LaFontaine had been drumming his fingers on the table and now thudded his flat palm on the tabletop. "He means that no stock was harmed."

"It's still a lie. The whole city was on fire."

"Shh, Roald." Johanna put her hand on his arm. After weeks of begging, the Council of Nobles, who effectively ran the refugee camp, had finally run out of reasons not to allow Roald to attend. The begging had been Johanna's, under the encouragement of Master Deim, who sat at the far end of the table and who smiled at her every now and then but had been mostly silent during the meeting.

Roald, though, was unaware of the intricacies of the situation. "The whole city was on fire. I saw it. My parents are dead. Everyone is dead!" His voice rose to a squeal.

"Shhh, I know. Calm down." She spoke softly, but was acutely aware of the penetrating gazes of the rich and influential men of the council, those who had been King Nicholaos' advisers and those who, along with the rest of the kingdom, had been unaware of the condition that inflicted his son.

Roald jammed his hands between his knees and sat stiff as a board. The continual tensing and relaxing of his muscles told Johanna that he would probably start swaying soon, or that he'd bang his head into the wall if he got close enough to one.

Master Deim said, "Your Majesty, we are sure that a lot of people in Saardam, most of them in fact, are still alive—"

"But I have never seen any proof," Johanna said. In fact, the only proof she'd seen pointed in the opposite direction. Stories from people in the camp about raiding bandits killing everyone who got in their way or setting fire to houses with entire families inside.

"Everyone is dead! There was blood everywhere and fire everywhere."

"Roald, please, calm down." She put an arm over his shoulder, if only to stop him swaying.

His distress brought back memories of their flight, of the chaos in the palace where she had lost Father, of the buildings on fire in the harbour, of the munitions depot being blown sky-high. Of the dead king and queen, and she hadn't even told Roald that she had seen their bodies. Maybe he had seen them, too. He had never spoken of what happened to him that night and how he came to be in the water in the harbour by himself.

Ignatius Hemeldinck rolled his eyes. He was easily the youngest of the nobles, with his pale hair tied back in a ponytail at the nape of his neck. "Seriously, do we need to hold these important meetings in the presence of an idiot? It's hard enough taking difficult decisions on our own."

"This idiot is your king," Johanna said, primly.

Or Roald would be their king once the coronation ceremony had been held. But that had been put off until the time that the King's sceptre and crown could be retrieved from the cleaning cupboard where Johanna had hidden them. If that cupboard, in fact, still existed.

And the council wasn't making any decisions and hadn't made any for about two months. All that happened in these meetings, according to Master Deim, was that they speculated and pontificated about what had happened and said little about how to go forward.

Ignatius said, "It's not necessary for him to be here. King Nicholaos would allow us to deal with day-to-day issues." He seemed to be making a point of not looking at Johanna.

If that's the case, then it's no wonder that King Nicholaos got into trouble. "The occupation of Saardam is not a day-to-day issue."

"King Nicholaos would also never have allowed interfering women to our meetings."

"I am your Queen according to the law. I accompany my husband."

Ignatius' mouth twitched.

Johan Delacoeur gave his colleague a wary look that seemed to say *shut up while you're still ahead.* He was the oldest of the nobles, grey-haired, thin, wary and suspicious. An old army commander who Johanna didn't particularly like, but had come to respect.

Ignatius took the unspoken advice, leaning back in his chair while heaving a sigh. He wasn't going to repeat what, according to rumours, he'd said the other day about Johanna's marriage to the prince. Not in the presence of the few powerful supporters

Johanna had in the camp: Master Deim; the mayor of Saardam, Joris DeCamp; and Captain Arense of the Nielands' ship *Prosperity,* which had brought most of the nobles to Florisheim. The Shepherd Carolus, a young man by the name of Dirk Goedthart, who had been training under Shepherd Romulus, was also meant to be there, but according to Fleuris LaFontaine, he was always late *doing some bleeding-heart thing for the children or something.*

The secretary was busily scribbling in the corner, noting down what people said. He sat against the wall of the boat shed, which was made from clay-daubed wood, with the big notebook on his lap.

"Let's keep talking about this letter," Johanna said. "Like why the Baron has taken so long to show it to us, and what we should do now."

"We have already drafted a response," Johan said, and the secretary in the corner nodded. "Will you read it to the meeting?"

The man leafed through his papers, until he found what he was looking for with an "Ah, here it is. It says: Esteemed colleague—"

Johanna said, "He's not esteemed. He's head of an occupying army."

The man eyed her sideways and continued reading, "Esteemed colleague, thank you for your correspondence—"

"—Thank you for invading our city and burning it to the ground."

"Please, can you let the man read?" Fleuris sounded annoyed.

Johanna crossed her arms over her chest.

The secretary lifted the paper so that he couldn't see Johanna. "Thank you for your correspondence. In light of the recent events, we would like to send a delegation to negotiate the return of authority of the city to us. We would be most delighted if you could meet with us—"

"I was thinking we should say something like: stop killing our families. You're nothing more than a bandit. Get out of our city before we chase you out, and, if you resist, string up your heads over the city gates."

Roald clapped his hands. "Yes, yes, yes. It's our city."

Fleuris rolled his eyes. "That is plain bluff and he will know it. We are too few to amount to much of an army."

"We are, together, the richest people of Saardam and the entire low country. Surely we can hire an army?"

Johan Delacoeur scoffed. "Fight a battle for your homeland with a mercenary army? Who has ever heard of such folly!"

"King Ivan of Bresnia had no problem with it."

He snorted. "What do you know about armies and fighting? A woman, young enough to be my daughter." But his attempt at derision did not hide the impact made by her knowing of the Battle of Dravik, and of how a young king had bought his troops' loyalty. *Thank you, Father, for forcing me to read all those boring history books.*

"Fighting is not how we like to do business," Fleuris said. And doing business, of course, was all that mattered.

"Do you have any business with this man Alexandre?"

He scoffed. "Of course not." In a *what-do-you-think* kind of way. "But he seems to have gotten the marauding savages under control."

"I was under the impression that he *brought* the marauding savages. He invaded. He used fire magicians to burn down much of the city, and then he took possession of it. So, in the light of those things, the king is not going to sign a letter addressed to Alexandre Trebuchet that has the word *esteemed* in it."

Fleuris went red in the face, but before he could say anything, there was the sound of running footsteps outside, and a moment later a man in a brown robe came into the shed: Shepherd Carolus. His cheeks were red, his blond hair stood in all directions, he had smudges on his cheeks and his habit was covered in straw. He sat down at the far end of the table next to Joris DeCamp, panting. "My excuses. I didn't know you'd started already. We bought some straw. I wanted it inside before it started raining again." He wiped his face. The golden chain with the symbol of the Triune dangled around his neck.

His sheer bulk dwarfed poor Joris DeCamp, who was a very slight man. The Shepherd's hands were huge, with thick fingers covered in freckles and hair—very dusty hair to be sure. He was like a normal man, but one-and-a-half times the size, who never shied away from helping people with his sheer strength.

Johanna smiled at him.

The interruption had leached the redness from Fleuris LaFontaine's face. He continued in a milder tone, "Let the correspondence be handled by men who are well-versed in conversing with people of Alexandre Trebuchet's standing. He is a direct cousin of the Burovian king."

"Are you afraid of him?"

"Alexandre Trebuchet has many connections."

In other words: *yes.* And the nobles probably had some business connections tied up with him.

"Whatever letter we write is not going to change our immediate situation here. We need to do *something.* People in the camp are suffering because they don't know what has happened to their families. We have been here for months and we've heard nothing. Winter is coming and most of them are sleeping in tents. I'm sure most of us would like to return."

"We don't know that it's safe to do so. The Red Baron has assured us that he's in discussion with Alexandre, and he's sent messengers to Saardam."

"The Baron's men? Why should they care about *our* city?" She gestured at the letter. "It's really simple: I want this man, this Alexandre, this fire magician, gone. I want to rebuild. I want to know if the people who didn't make it out of the city"—*Father* —"are safe. I want to go back before winter comes."

Fleuris snorted in his *Dumb woman* tone. "You don't understand anything about the situation."

"All right, then. I've given you my thoughts. What do you think we should do?" *Sit here and eat the Baron's food while we wait until he tells us what he wants from us in return?*

"Well . . ." Fleuris placed the fingertips of both hands together. His many gold rings glittered in the light that fell in through the open door of the boat shed. His fingers were pudgy and looked like sausages. He was in his middle years, with a face that had lost none of its pudgy roundness in the camp. His cheeks were full and made him look younger than he really was, and made his eyes look piggy. "We have been in contact with the

Baron and have it from his authority, and that of the leaders of the Belaman Church, that they are restoring order in the city."

"The Belaman Church does not rule Saardam," Shepherd Carolus said, and he wiped his face again. His cheeks were still red.

"He's right. What business does the Belaman Church have in Saardam? And if the Baron has sent people to Saardam, why haven't we heard any news? Why haven't we heard anything from any of our families and contacts?" Seriously, what was wrong with these men? Why were they happy with other people sorting out the trouble? "Are you happy with the Belaman Church taking charge of our city?"

"Of course not."

"Then why aren't you angry that we've been waiting here for months while the Baron has had this letter for all this time?"

"Young lady, you are presuming far too much. The Baron probably only received it recently. He is our friend—"

"I am your queen and you will address me as such."

Fleuris gave her a hard stare. He didn't say anything, but his expression held a *We-will-see-about-that* warning. "The Baron has his reasons which he has already revealed to us, his trusted friends." He breathed in through flaring nostrils. "Contrary to your assertions, the Baron is helping us a great deal."

"The Baron has lent us tents and given us items of furniture. I'm grateful for that. But what other help is he giving us? He hasn't visited the camp for weeks. I've seen him once since we arrived, and he never even spoke to Roald. Has anyone spoken to him recently? Have there been any signs that he has even sent people to Saardam to talk to this Alexandre? And on the off-chance that I missed their departure—which would be hard to do, since we're camped right next to the river—but on the off-chance, why hasn't he come here to ask for our representatives? Why, for that matter, should *he* negotiate on our behalf?"

"Because he knows Alexandre Trebuchet much better than any of us."

"Isn't that a reason to keep an eye on both of them?" She spread her hands, frustrated.

Fleuris said, "You can't possibly understand. This is a thing between men of certain standing and influence."

And so the bottom line was that, besides being female, Johanna didn't meet the criteria of "standing", and hadn't earned the trust of the circle of nobles that stretched across borders and involved many royal families and their wide and entangled family trees. Alexandre Trebuchet, Roald had informed her, had been a fellow guest at the work farm for difficult royal sons where Roald had spent most of the past few years and which seemed to be the source of much of the trouble.

Johanna said, holding her back straight, "I think the time that we rely on others to do things for us has passed. Baron Uti may mean well, but his concern is his own land. We will make our own investigations. We will write back to this Alexandre." Her eyes met those of the secretary. "We will let him know that his occupation of Saardam displeases us greatly and we will return to resume our rightful position. We will use stronger words that still carry your approval."

She met hard stares around the table. "Or does anyone here actually like that a foreigner sits in our palace?"

"Of course not," Fleuris LaFontaine scoffed, but he sounded less than genuine.

"Then I will see to it that it is done." She rose. She would have the letter delivered by two volunteers who would go to Saardam and report on the situation there. Men from the camp, not the Baron's men.

Roald was staring at the boat shed's dark ceiling and appeared to have been counting ceiling beams, probably to stop himself sliding into a screaming fit. "Come." Johanna pulled him up gently by his arm. Then she looked at the ceiling again. The undersides of the ceiling beams were exposed. If the singing in her blood was anything to go by, they were made of willow wood. She had an idea.

"Her Majesty the Queen declares the meeting finished," Ignatius Hemeldinck said, his voice sarcastic.

"I'm glad that someone here recognises my status," she said, equally sarcastic. She strode past him out of the shed.

CHAPTER 2

"MY CHILD, you're playing with fire," Master Deim said when the meeting had finished. They were slowly walking back from the boathouse along the riverbank.

A bit further along the curve of the Rede River, the *Lady Sara* and the *Prosperity* lay moored at the jetty that would normally be used by the river ships that came to pick up milk. The cows normally grazed in the paddock that had now become a jumble of mismatched tents. It was almost midday and trails of smoke rose from cooking fires between those tents.

The path along the riverbank was quite narrow, so Master Deim walked first, turning around when he spoke. Johanna had hooked her arm through Roald's. He was distracted by some animal in the reeds and she held him so that he didn't trip. His tenseness had abated a bit and he no longer shook or swayed.

"Would you have let them talk over your head as if you didn't exist?" Johanna asked Master Deim. "I don't know what's going on, but those men have done nothing for us. The people are getting unhappy. They want to know when we're going back, or, if we're not, what the reason is, but we've heard nothing and they're doing nothing. Why do they think that the Baron can sort it all out for us? Do they know something we don't?"

"Yes, they probably do. There are many gentlemen's agreements between noble families. They're not going to divulge those agreements to others, not even to their peers." Master Deim shook his head. "They have only barely allowed you to be present. Do you really think it's a good idea to turn them against you already?"

"They were never going to be helpful."

Roald said, "I heard them talking. They were laughing about me. They called me The Idiot King."

"They did indeed. It's disgraceful."

"I'm not an idiot." He pronounced the word *idiot* slowly as if allowing it extra time to sink in.

Johanna shook her head. Whatever you wanted to call Roald, an idiot he was not. With his simple way of looking at relationships, he often understood matters well enough, even if he was clumsy at voicing those thoughts. "Those men are insufferably rude. They're far too used to getting their way. If they were merchants, they would have not a customer left."

"But they are not merchants. They are dangerous men from the most connected, most experienced noble families."

"And that's the reason I have to be grateful to them that they let me come to a meeting where we should have been invited in the first place? I have to be grateful for every word they say? They've always been against us. They have no respect, not for their wives, their fellows or their king. I don't think they ever did." She suspected they had played games with King Nicholaos, and the king, stricken by grief over the death of his daughter, had not seen it.

This was what Father had been talking about when she was with him in the coach underway to the ball. This was why the King's envoy had asked Father, and not the nobles, for a loan.

Master Deim said, "Yes, they were probably happy with Nicholaos as figurehead king, as long as he didn't get into their way. They were born into power. They like their power and will do whatever they can to hold onto as much of it as they can."

"But then why haven't they done anything about the occupation? Why do they just accept whatever scraps the Baron throws them?"

He spread his hands. "There are many possible reasons. Because they are comfortable doing what they're doing? Because they don't like to risk themselves and their wealth in fighting conflicts they're not sure they can win. Because they hope to be given a position at the Baron's court? Some of them are distantly related to the Baron and other nobles in Florisheim."

"I don't think I'll ever understand that world." She had been exposed to it a little bit through her mother, a minor royal of the Aroden court. When Mother was still alive, Countess Josafina, Mother's great-aunt, would sometimes visit her house. Johanna would have to dress up and sit on the stiff couch in the formal sitting room, while the Countess gossiped about who said what and who was marrying whom, while Mother looked on and occasionally smiled at Johanna or brushed her hair to the side or reminded her to sit still.

"They expect patronage. If you look after your peers, they will look after you."

Of course she knew about patronage, of the arts, usually. The Burovian king had been a patron of Rinius for most of his life. But the habit of noble families to send their unruly and entitled sons to other noble families in order to get them straightened out was not one she understood.

Master Deim added, "Also, child, don't forget that most of them are afraid of magic. This Alexandre appears to have rather a lot of it, and is not afraid to unleash its full force onto the common people. Saardam has always been so poor in magic that most people would never have seen a fire demon, let alone had any idea how to defeat it."

Johanna spread her hands. "Then we hire magicians. Every ruler does it. I don't understand the problem. Anything has got to be better than sitting in this field. They act like they've got their feet stuck in tar. It's impossible to get them to do anything."

"They're not in a hurry to make decisions. They're comfortable—"

"They may be comfortable. They've got the best tents. They got first choice of the items the Baron lets us use. Many people aren't so lucky. Winter is coming." It had rained a lot recently, and the lower part of the field had become very muddy.

"I know, I know, child. You don't have to explain it to me."

Then why did he keep making excuses for these men?

Captain Arense and Joris DeCamp had come up behind them.

"I enjoyed that," the captain said, smiling at Johanna. He was a jovial fellow, with a huge beard, the typical ship's captain.

Joris chuckled. "Yeah, I don't think I've ever seen Ignatius Hemeldinck so restrained and angry at the same time. He's a piece of work, that one."

"Do not speak ill of other people," Shepherd Carolus said, coming up behind the Major and the Captain. "You never know when you need their help."

"Have a blessed day, Shepherd," Captain Arense said and gave an exaggerated bow.

"You jest, my friend."

Captain Arense clapped him on the shoulder. "Dirk, you are allowed to loosen up sometimes."

"I take my vocation seriously. Men who do not believe will watch like a cat and pounce when the opportunity arises. I'm the mouse. I try to stay out of their way. But like the mouse, I can go places where the cat can't come."

They all laughed.

Captain Arense said, "You, Dirk, look about as unlike a mouse as any person has ever looked."

"It is the metaphor that counts." He smiled and bowed. "But you have to excuse me, Your Majesty. I am expected to teach some children."

He continued along the riverbank and into the camp. Like a mouse. What a strange statement. She knew the nobles didn't particularly like the church, but was he suggesting there had been hostilities? She guessed that shouldn't surprise her, although making threats to a priest seemed tasteless to her, even a priest who was as apt to defend himself as the Shepherd Carolus.

Captain Arense said to Johanna, "We completely agree with

you, by the way. We should make preparations to leave this field. I don't understand what is holding back the nobles, either. Maybe we'll find out, maybe we won't. I think you'd get quite a lot of support in the camp. Most people are sick of waiting for news that doesn't come. I'm rather sick of it myself. I'd rather be on the water. You should talk to my mistress about the use of the *Prosperity* for that reason."

That mistress was Julianna Nieland, Johanna's old rival, but the bite seemed to have gone off that rivalry, which had mostly concerned clothing and other trivial things. Like Johanna, Julianna had left her entire family behind in Saardam and hadn't heard a word from them since.

"I'll think about it," she said, still looking at Master Deim. His face didn't give away what he thought of such a plan. "Would you know some adventurous young men who would like to go downriver to deliver a letter and check out what's going on in Saardam? We'll find a boat for them, and they can use two of our sea cows to come back upriver."

The animals in question grazed, as usual, in the shallows near the riverbank, where occasional bubbles rose to the surface. Sea cows seemed to like work.

"I think you'd find plenty of young men who would do that. Most youngsters are sick of being idle in this camp."

"Find names and recommend two to me."

The captain bowed. "It will be a pleasure, Your Majesty."

The men continued into the camp and Johanna walked with Roald and Master Deim up the gangplank of the *Lady Sara*. Two men stood on either side and they greeted the group with polite nods. They were supposedly royal guards, right now lacking a uniform. Johan Delacoeur had instated them *Because the royal family always has guards*, he'd said, and that was true, but suddenly Johanna wondered about these men and their motives.

They were ex-soldiers who Johan Delacoeur trusted and had served under him. But what if Johan Delacoeur's motives for posting the guards were not entirely honest? They might be employed to spy on the king as much as to protect him.

She hadn't thought to question it until now. Roald was the

king and kings had guards, simple as that. Most of the men in the camp had little to do anyway, so guarding the king seemed a good thing to do. But Johan Delacoeur wasn't a friend, really, and he and his cronies had not been strong supporters of the royal family for quite a while.

Johanna, Roald and Master Deim stopped walking on the deck.

The day was brooding, and fat thunderclouds already gathered on the horizon. Pearls of sweat beaded on Master Deim's upper lip and forehead.

"It's very hot," he said, wiping his forehead. "There's a thunderstorm coming."

They watched the darkening sky in silence for a while. Even the birds seemed to be affected by the oppressing weather. One came strutting along the riverbank with its beak open.

"Look, a heron," Roald said. "You know they catch fish and frogs by spearing them with their beaks? The heron is from the sea-bird family, but do you know how far away from the sea we are? Isn't that strange?"

"Yes, very strange," Johanna said. They'd even seen seagulls the other day.

He went on to talk about other birds he saw. Larks, fluttering high in the sky, a pair of coots on the water, swallows skimming the surface so closely that occasionally their wings brushed the water, swifts in the sky, flying so high that you could hear their screeches only when you were very quiet.

Wouldn't it be amazing to be so lost in knowledge of birds and nature that you didn't see the terrible things that happened in life? Johanna met Master Deim's eyes.

"I'm so glad that you are here," she said. "You're a voice of reason, someone I know I can trust."

He sighed. "Not a word from your father or anyone else. I'm beginning to doubt the veracity of the claims in that letter. If the citizens of Saardam were well, certainly someone would have sent a letter, or someone else would have made the same journey up the river as we have, even if only to look for us."

Johanna had wondered the same thing. "Maybe they didn't come up the river far enough." Or maybe they, having seen the destruction of Aroden, had concluded that the whole world was dead. "The letter didn't actually say in so many words that the people were safe. It just said most of the citizens 'have been spared,' but it didn't say anything about their condition."

"It didn't. It's also strange how it mentioned business interests but not people. As if there was some sort of pre-arranged deal between Alexandre and the Baron about the spoils."

Johanna laughed in a hollow way. "And then he found that the King's coffers were empty, having spent all his money on the church."

"A nasty surprise, I'm sure. I wonder how much the Baron endorses this 'friend' Alexandre."

"I think Alexandre only calls the Baron a friend because he wants to be the Baron's friend. It seems to me that if he were really the Baron's friend, the Baron would have thrown the letter into the fire, and not given it to us even months after it was sent."

"True." Master Deim gave her a thoughtful look.

Something he hadn't considered, perhaps? "I'd really like to know what's going on in Saardam. I'm going to write that letter. I want to have it ready when Captain Arense finds some boys to go to Saardam."

He nodded and they stared over the churning water for a while.

Roald announced that he saw some ducks. He walked back down the gangplank past the impassive guards and kneeled, peering into the reeds. A young boy came to him, and Roald pointed. The boy kicked off his shoes and went into the water.

"The kids like him a lot," Master Deim said.

"Yes. They're not full of judgement, like adults." And Roald seemed to have remained stuck in that phase where boys find information interesting and want to learn about the world.

"True."

"Are you going to be at next week's meeting? I want to find volunteers to travel down the river to report on what's happening in Saardam."

"Just be careful. Don't anger the nobles. I haven't heard them say so, but they might well be disappointed that you survived. If that is so, I dare say they will try to get rid of you as soon as they can."

"They can't. I'm legally married to Roald."

"Yes, child, but I doubt they recognise the validity of the marriage. They may be patient for now, but that might change if you don't produce an heir soon."

CHAPTER 3

THAT DISTURBED Johanna more than anything, and as she watched Master Deim walk down the gangplank and wave to the guards with his usual jovial manner, a chill came over her. Because every night except those where she bled, she had slept with Roald and she had noticed no changes in her body. Her last bleeding was three weeks ago and it had disappointed her.

How long did it normally take for a woman to become with child?

She thought she had heard rumours that it had happened to some girls after being with a man just once.

Maybe she and Roald were doing something wrong.

A couple of young children were running between the tents, to a mother who had called them for the midday meal. All those people obviously knew how to do it right.

Was there anyone she could ask?

In Saardam, young women would ask Helena about being with men, about what to do the first time, about their husband's expectations, about how to tell when you were with child before you started swelling. But Helena, of course, had not been considered worthy to be taken on Captain Arense's ship.

That thought brought a pang of pain.

What would have become of Helena? Did sailors still come

to Saardam and did they still have the money to pay to spend the night with her? Did young women still come to her with questions?

Johanna looked over the camp. The Captain was a supporter of the royal family and friendly to her, but he had taken far more men than women. The women who had made it onto the ships were mostly nobles. Johanna certainly wasn't going to ask them for advice—they'd be horrified to be asked about these things.

Roald's interest in books had provided him with access to the fabled library of the monastery of the Jeromist Order in town. Men with a love of books often formed bonds. He had a penchant for books of human anatomy, and in one of those she had spotted a drawing of a couple engaging in the reproductive act. The woman lay on her back and the man on top. That was how Roald had wanted it originally, but she found it uncomfortable. Maybe it was wrong for her to sit on top of him, because the seed came out as soon as she got up.

Maybe next time when she came to the library she should find some books on what she was doing wrong, or about magic or herb lore that she could use.

The stems threshed in the reeds and a boy yelled, "I got it! I got it!"

Two people waded through the reed bed back to the river-bank. First the boy, jumping up and down. Then Roald, carrying something in cupped hands. He climbed up the bank and walked past the guard up the gangplank. The man broke his normally impassive expression to frown at the thing in Roald's hands with a *good-heavens-what-now* look.

"For you," Roald said, slightly puffed.

In his hands he held a tiny fluffy brown and yellow duckling. It peeped.

In the water below, the mother duck quacked.

Roald couldn't have looked any less like a king had he tried. His pants were wet and muddy up to the knees and there was a green smudge on his cheek.

Johanna laughed. "I think it belongs with its mother."

Just then, that mother duck flew up onto the deck and

walked, flat-footed in Roald's direction. She quacked and shook her tail. The duckling peeped.

"Put it down," Johanna said.

Roald bent. The duckling jumped out of his hands before he had lowered them onto the deck and scampered to its mother. The mother duck then flew back down into the water to the rest of her brood, and the little one jumped all the way from the edge, landing sideways with its little feet flailing, but bobbing back onto the surface.

Roald laughed.

Johanna went up to the cabin where she found Nellie in the galley and Loesie busy sewing while seated on a roll of rope in the shade of the cabin, with the summer breeze coming in through the open door.

Since Nellie had made this cabin hers, she had put up lace-edged curtains—from the underwear that they had taken from the burnt-out farm along the Saar River—and crocheted a bed spread from coarse wool which she had bought at the local markets.

Loesie was squinting at her work, and the tip of her tongue poked out between her lips in concentration.

Johanna laughed. "I didn't know you could sew, Loesie."

"I can't. She's teaching me," Loesie said. "I was bored. I can make apple baskets, but there's not many apple baskets to be made."

"And? Are you turning into a seamstress?" Johanna eyed Loesie's work, by far less neat than Nellie's, which lay on the bed.

"Nah, not a chance. Give me some cows to milk any day."

"Are you ready for the midday meal, mistress?" Nellie asked from the galley.

"I think so. Bring it quickly before Roald runs off to catch some other animal."

"Yes, sure. I'll do it now."

Johanna sat on the hold cover, turning her face into the humid breeze. The sun had vanished behind the fuzzy edges of the top of the thundercloud that was coming closer at alarming speed. Squalls of wind tore at her clothes and already thunder growled in the distance.

Roald's catches had been an endless source of amusement. Over the past week, he'd brought a small rabbit, little fish in a jar and a tiny mouse. She didn't mind those so much, but drew the line at the frog he'd caught. She did *not* like frogs. They were green and wet and cold and—eeeeew.

He'd held up the frog enclosed in both his hands, with its head poking out, and told her all about its life cycle and about the different kinds of frogs. He had put it on the desk so that he could draw it—he was quite decent at drawing. Unfortunately, the frog had other ideas, so he'd spent the next hour chasing it around the hold.

Whatever you wanted to call Roald, he wasn't an idiot. He remembered things he read in books. He understood them, as long as those things were facts, as long as people left him alone with his books.

It was only now that she began to understand how stressful it must have been for him to speak to the highly critical nobles of Saardam at the ball and dance with strange girls who expected some kind of Prince Charming. He'd made inappropriate comments not because he was lewd, but because he was scared and didn't understand what people expected of him.

Nellie was just coming out of the galley with a tray when the first clap of thunder hit. She flinched and ducked, but managed to hang onto the tray.

"It's getting close, mistress."

They quickly made their way down the stairs, where Roald gave Johanna an alarmed look.

"Thunder," he said, his eyes wide. "The little duckies will be all right, won't they?"

"They'll be fine. They'll shelter in the reeds."

"But they'll get wet if it rains."

"They're ducks. They're used to getting wet."

Nellie put the tray down on the tiny table at the bottom of the stairs and left again, shutting the cover behind her.

"Dinner," Johanna said. She set the plates on either side of the table and uncovered the tray. Legs of rabbit, applesauce and carrots. The food smelled heavenly. How did Nellie manage to get all these things?

One of the things that worried her was that Roald tended to forget to eat if no one paid him any attention. He got distracted and somehow just didn't feel hungry. But he loved Nellie's applesauce, so she gave him a big dollop of that, some carrots and a good chunk of rabbit meat. For a while they sat eating happily.

The hold that had carried many a load of grain down the river and spices upriver was long and narrow. They had made a small sitting room near the stairs that had replaced the ladder. It held a carpet, a small table, two mismatched chairs and a tiny desk where Roald sat reading whenever he wasn't roaming the riverbanks. A fat book lay open there.

"What were you reading?"

"I'm reading a very interesting book about the night sky and the phenomena in the heavens. The writer says that there are other worlds like the Earth and that they all go around the Sun."

"Rinius."

He gave her a sharp look. "Yes. You know him?"

"No, but Father brought me a copy of that book." It was in her room, likely burned in the fire. The thought of her comfortable room and house constricted her chest. What would have happened to Father or Koby or Master Willems?

"It's very interesting. I like this book a lot. He says that the Moon is a world like ours and that people live there."

She laughed, remembering that last chapter of the book with its strange speculations. "Maybe, but I doubt we'd ever see them, if the Moon is really as far away as Rinius says it is."

"How far is that?" He turned around and reached for the book. He opened it at a page with diagrams. Johanna had studied them, but had to admit that she found Rinius' calculations hard going.

"Here it says." He pointed at the page and moved his finger down as he read. "It says that it is four hundred and twenty-eight times the length of the Saar River. That is a long way indeed."

"You couldn't travel that far."

His face went thoughtful. "You would have to get free from the Earth."

"What do you mean?"

"The Earth and the Moon are both worlds floating in the air.

To get to the Moon, you have to free yourself from the Earth and cross the air."

"You mean fly? That's impossible."

"A bird could do it."

"People don't fly," Johanna said, uneasily. "Isn't there this story of a father and son who both strapped on wings, but the son flew too close to the sun so the wax that held the wings together melted and he fell down and died?"

"That's a myth. People can't fly when they strap on wings. They're too heavy. Birds have hollow bones and they're light."

"Then people can't fly."

"They could use a machine."

A what? Where did he get these ideas?

"The eastern traders have machines." He went on an extended explanation about these machines, which, apparently, ran on wood and steam and could make carts move by themselves, and could do things like saw wood and grind grain if there was no wind for windmills.

"But there is always wind."

"In Saardam there is, but not in the eastern forests."

Guess he had a point there. "Roald, listen. We have to be careful. Don't ever let Shepherd Carolus or the nobles hear you say things like this."

He gave her a blank look.

"Rinius' book is considered heresy by many in Saardam." Especially the Church. She also wasn't sure about the Belaman Church's position on the subject of Rinius. A large part of his book argued that the beliefs and gods were a figment of human imagination. Why a book like that would be owned by a monastery was beyond her.

"But what he says is true."

"True or not, nobody can prove it."

"Yes, we can go to the Moon and measure how far it is."

Sure. We can do that tomorrow. "Just be careful with the things Rinius says." Johanna sighed. "Your father was very close to the church. I'm not sure what went on just before the ball and just before you came back, but he didn't get on well with the nobles and they were very angry with him."

"Oh." Another blank look.

"Did he tell you anything about it?"

"Father said that if I became king, all the men were mine."

He really didn't understand. Where did that leave her? Alone and isolated. Without too many friends in this camp, or outside it.

In a way she was glad that the Baron had been conspicuous by his absence. She wasn't keen to speak to him and she could still hear the last words Sylvan had said to her about Kylian: *he's a necromancer.* Of course no one in the camp had mentioned anything about it, nor, fortunately, had she seen Kylian.

She hadn't been able to do anything about contacting the Magician's Guild, as Sylvan had suggested. Whenever she had been in town, she had looked for the guild, but Florisheim was a warren of narrow streets and slate-roofed houses that all looked the same. Somehow, she had expected the Magician's Guild to be easy to find, because this whole area was rife with magic, right?

Rife with magic, it certainly was. Often, a breeze would waft past that made her skin prick, despite her inability to see things in the wind. Often, too, she would see misty shapes lurk in the reed beds, only to vanish again when she looked closely. They were ghosts and other beings, and they were watching, ready to pounce.

She and Loesie were the only Saarlanders in the camp with as much as a shred of magic. If magic pounced, there would be no warning.

CHAPTER 4

B Y THE TIME Roald and Johanna finished their meal and Johanna went up to the deck, the sun had well and truly disappeared behind thick clouds. The sky towards the west had darkened to the colour of ash, leaden, almost dark blue. Gusts of wind whipped at Johanna's hair. Nellie rushed across the hold covers behind the cabin, where she pulled flapping sheets and shirts off the washing line before they blew into the water.

"It's sure going to rain, mistress." Her cheeks were red with the effort.

Nellie had to give up wearing a bonnet when her only one became too torn and dirty during their foray with the bandits and now wore her flaxen hair in a bun.

"I look like a peasant girl," she had complained.

That might be true, but a very healthy and good-looking peasant girl. Her skin was much better than Johanna's, her shape was better, and living on the ship had brought out a no-nonsense streak in her which Johanna liked. Through the terrible events that they'd experienced, Nellie had been unquestionably loyal. Nellie deserved to be married.

Loesie now also came out and helped Nellie. A squall of wind almost blew a sheet out of Nellie's hand. Both women scrambled to hold onto it, and then laughed.

At times like this, Loesie looked almost normal albeit still a bit dark for a Saarlander. Her skin bronzed a lot more, too. She had never regained her peasant's accent after the demon had been driven from her.

Loesie and Nellie now got along quite well, and Johanna wasn't sure what to make of that. The Loesie she knew from the markets in Saardam wasn't such an open, laughing creature. She was mysterious, she would deliberately frighten little boys, and sometimes bigger ones, who came to beg or tease her. She would pretend to curse young men making lewd comments to her. All of that was gone. Did people's characters change after they had been possessed by a demon?

A couple of fat drops started to fall, and Nellie and Loesie rushed back into the cabin. Nellie shouted to Johanna, "Better stay dry, mistress!"

While the first rain hit the covers, Johanna descended the narrow and steep steps into the hold, where Roald had settled in his usual chair with a book. He'd sit there all day if she let him.

She came up behind him and put her hand across the page.

He protested. "Hey! I was reading that."

"Roald, I need you to do something for me. It's a secret."

He turned around and his frank eyes met hers. "Oooh, I love secrets."

"Put on your peasants' shirt and trousers. We're going out." She cringed. His pants were still wet from this morning's escapade into the reeds. She hoped he wouldn't catch anything.

"But it's raining," he said.

"That's good. People will be inside." Although the rain was really pelting down on the hold covers now. A clap of thunder made the ground shake.

Roald gasped and then he said, "It's all right. I'm only scared of thunder at night. We will stay away from trees. You know that if lightning hits a tree, you can die from the presence of the fire demon that comes down with the lightning?"

Just then a lightning bolt hit somewhere close, followed by a sudden clap of thunder.

Thanks, Roald, that's really helpful information right now.

In the semidarkness of the hold, Johanna searched for her

peasant dress. Nellie had washed it since coming here, but every time she put it on she thought of the burned-out farm where they had found these clothes, and their bed sheets, and other things. It still felt like stealing, even though the blackened bodies of the woman and baby in the burned-out kitchen were unlikely to ever need these things again. She thought of the thriving vegetable garden outside, the poor cows bursting with milk, the ruined mill. And she thought about the ruins of Aroden castle and the nearby town, where people had run along the riverbank with the *Lady Sara* begging for help. How were those people coping now?

She pulled on the drab dress and then helped Roald get dressed in his decidedly damp trousers and, not much later, they climbed up the narrow staircase out of the hold. A good amount of rain came in when Johanna slid the cover aside. The drops were large and stung with cold.

There was another crack of lightning followed by rumbling thunder.

Roald gasped.

"It's only thunder," Johanna said, trying to cover her own unease.

"Yes. I'm not scared of thunder." But his eyes were wide. "It can't hurt you. Except when you're under a tree."

"Aren't we lucky that there are no trees between here and the boat shed?" Nowhere to shelter either, and the rain was coming down in sheets. She could barely see the other side of the river.

"Is that where we're going? The boat shed? You know that there is a swallow's nest right up the top against the far wall?"

Johanna shut the cover and they ran across the deck to the gangplank. As quickly as she could, she let herself slide to the jetty and helped Roald.

A few more distant cracks and rumbles shook the ground. Johanna held her breath with each one. It was easy to pretend that you weren't scared of thunder when you were not in the middle of a storm, and this one was really getting very close.

Those sullen guards by the sides of the gangplank both stood hidden deep within the hoods of their army-issue cloaks.

"Are you going out in this weather?" one asked.

"No need to come. Roald is going to show me some frogs."

She hoped that excuse would work, although they would remember that fuss over the escaped frog, and know that she did not like frogs.

The men nodded.

They were sure to report to Johan Delacoeur that "the king and his consort" had gone out in the pouring rain for "catching frogs". That was not to be helped.

Johanna and Roald slipped and slid over the path along the riverbank. A squall of wind blew the rain in their faces.

A nearby thunderclap cracked through the sky and shook the ground. Roald yelped and dropped to his knees, holding his arms over his head.

"Are you all right?" Johanna pulled him up, feeling the tenseness in his muscles.

"Maybe we should go back. The thunder can harm you, right?"

"It's exciting, an adventure," Johanna shouted over the noise of the pelting rain. They were both soaked all over. Cold rivulets of water were running down Johanna's back.

The boat shed along the river was a dark shape against the grey sky. It was hard to see where they were going with water running in her eyes. The sudden snap of cold air made mist rise from the water. Was it her imagination or was there a peculiar smell to the air? Her imagination certainly didn't play tricks with her as far as the swirling shapes in the mist were concerned. The ghosts watched, and waited.

Inside the shed, it was almost too dark to see, but at least it was dry. The wooden table and benches where the nobles would sit for their meeting stood forlorn in the middle of the compacted earthen floor. The rain made such a racket on the roof that it would be impossible to hear if anyone came. Better be quick.

Johanna walked along the walls, looking up at the ceiling beams. "Here it is. Lift me up."

Roald lifted her by her waist, but she still couldn't reach the timber, only the rough clay of the walls.

"Not high enough. Can I stand on your shoulders? Wait."

She took off her shoes and then her overdress. Even the fabric of her underdress was so wet that it stuck.

Roald giggled and put his hands on her sides. She could feel the warmth through the soaked fabric. "It's a pity I can't look at you here."

"Not now. We have to do something first. I have to reach the ceiling." She tried to climb on him by pushing herself up on his shoulders. He held his hands together so she could put her foot in them to boost herself up, but she almost fell.

She let herself down. "It's too wobbly. Wait. I'll stand with my legs apart on the bench. Then you put your head in between and I'll sit on your shoulders. Then you stand up and I'll use the wall to climb up."

So it was done, and finally she stood on Roald's shoulders and she could reach the wooden beams in the ceiling. As soon as she touched the wood, the images rushed to her.

She heard a familiar voice, that of Ignatius Hemeldinck.

"I'll go and see him." He sat at the table in the shed with the two other nobles from the council. They were wearing the same clothes as in the meeting this morning and this discussion had probably taken place after Johanna, Master Deim, Captain Arense, Joris DeCamp and Shepherd Carolus had left the shed.

"Let me come with you," said Johan Delacoeur.

Ignatius snorted. "What? Don't trust me?"

"Well," Johan said, "You don't seem yourself lately. I've not known you to give in to a woman."

Ignatius' face twitched. "It just seemed best not to escalate it further."

"Since when have you ever said that? What is wrong with you, man?"

Ignatius glared across the table.

"I think we should all go." Fleuris LaFontaine said. "Remind him of the promises he made us."

"Just the three of us, right?" Ignatius said.

"Yes, that goes without saying. I don't trust the captain or the mayor. That merchant, too, is much too friendly to her. I was waiting for him to reveal all we've been talking about."

"Rest assured, the only reason he didn't do that in the meeting is that he has already told her everything."

"He knows nothing." This was Ignatius again. Then he snorted. "I have to admit that we don't know much more either. It's like that meeting with the Red Baron at the castle never happened. 'We'll keep you informed,' he said. I'm tired of waiting."

"I agree I'm sick of it. And now we have this woman who is far too probing, but she's right about this. I've been unhappy that the Baron seems to have forgotten about us. It's all very fine for us to make excuses, like 'He's too busy,' but they're excuses, nothing more. We don't even know if he really is too busy, because we haven't seen him. And I don't like this business any more than she does."

There were headshakes around the table.

Ignatius pushed himself up from the table. "No need to panic. Let's just say that it's time to go into town and employ my contacts."

"And what are you going to do? Magically make the Baron appear and parade him through the camp?"

Ignatius smirked.

"You're kidding, right?" Johan said.

"Nope. I think the time is right."

"You're crazy."

"Don't let anyone see you, especially the captain or that priest. Those two are everywhere," Fleuris said. "If she finds out, you'll never hear the end of it. She'll think she has made us nervous."

Johan said, "She already has. She's a lot smarter than most women."

Ignatius snorted. "Bah, a woman. Nattering, gossiping, seductive creature."

"Don't underestimate her."

"No woman can match me. No woman will rule me."

They rose from the table and left. Johanna slowly withdrew her hand from the ceiling beam. The vision faded for the semi-darkness of the shed.

Well, that was certainly interesting. Master Deim had been

right. They had made secret arrangements with the Baron. Maybe she should try the other beam to see what it had to tell her. She reached out—

A huge thunderclap shook the ground and made the walls of the shed rattle. Roald squealed and ducked. Standing with her hand outstretched, Johanna lost her balance. Her foot slipped off Roald's shoulder. She tried to steady herself against the wall, but Roald stood too far away from it and she hadn't the strength to keep herself up. She fell. Roald toppled over under her weight and they ended up in a tangle of limbs on the dusty floor.

Oof.

She had landed with her head on Roald's chest. "Are you all right?"

"We fell." Roald started laughing. "We fell."

Johanna scrambled up, brushing dust from her underdress, but as wet as it was, she ended up smearing dirt across it.

She started laughing as well. They were both so wet and dirty and looked so much like a couple of children who had been playing in the mud. And it was raining so hard outside that getting back to the ship involved yet another dunking.

"I haven't told you that I love you yet today," Roald said. He put his hands on her shoulders and met her eyes. His beard had been trimmed that morning. It seemed to have grown fuller recently, and despite his condition and the childish innocence of his mind, he looked not unattractive. "I love you."

He slid his hands up over her shoulders until he cradled her head in both hands. Johanna stroked his hair and the sides of his face. His beard scratched her palms. She pulled him closer until she could kiss his lips. He remained unresponsive, but when she pulled back, the expression in his eyes showed his interest.

"Maybe I could look at you now?"

"What? Here?" She eyed the shed's empty interior, the table and benches, the bare ground with gouges from where people had dragged boats that would now be on the water. And would probably be filling up with water from the rain outside.

He pulled at her underdress and peeped inside through the gap between her neckline and her chest. "Ooh, I can see something."

Johanna laughed. Well, why not? People did sillier things than that. She slowly undid the buttons at the front. He tried to poke his hand in, but she slapped him away, teasing

As the thunder rolled over the banks of the Rede River, and the rain pelted on the roof of the shed—and found its way inside by the sound of the drip-drip-drip on the floor—they came together. Johanna clung onto Roald's sweaty body while the edge of the table bit into her backside. The thrum of the rain masked any noises, and she wasn't ashamed that there were some noises.

She wouldn't really be a queen in the eyes of those men unless she had a child.

When it was done, after Roald had done his *hunhh!* thing and they clung to each other breathing fast while letting the glow ebb, they got dressed and ran through the rain back to the *Lady Sara*. Nellie had started wondering where they were. She fussed over the wet clothes and having nowhere to dry them.

Johanna said, "That's why we wore the peasant clothes." She wondered if Nellie would recognise the smell of seed that had ended up all over the back of the underdress.

"Still, mistress Johanna, did you have to go out in this weather?"

Yes, she did have to go out, and the wood had told her useful things. The nobles were concerned about her influence. They had made some sort of deal with the Baron, and now the Baron was ignoring them. Why? Because the Baron had what he wanted and didn't need the nobles anymore? Worse: what was Ignatius Hemeldinck planning to do?

CHAPTER 5

WHEN CRACKS of daylight leaked between the hinges of the covers, Johanna could no longer stay in bed.

Roald was still asleep. He lay on his side, with his face to her, his eyes closed, little slivers of blond eyelashes. He was so peaceful that she didn't want to disturb him.

She got dressed as quietly as she could, took her basket with the leather cover and climbed up the creaky stairs. Roald groaned and turned over, but didn't wake up. A peek from underneath the heavy hold cover gave her a glimpse of wet boards and little circles where raindrops fell in a puddle.

Dang it. Still raining.

She crept down the creaky ladder again to get her woollen cloak.

Out on the deck of the *Lady Sara*, it was still very quiet. Not even Nellie and Loesie appeared to have risen. In the camp on the river bank, a few trails of smoke rose from people cooking breakfast, but not even the boys were out to play yet.

It must have rained a lot in the foothills of the mountains because the river was high with muddy churning water. Sticks and bits of grass drifted downstream at a good pace. The drop from the deck to the jetty had increased quite a bit and the *Lady Sara*'s gangplank had become quite steep. She had to shuffle down carefully, holding the rope to make sure that she didn't slip.

At the riverbank, the guards stood hidden in the depth of their woollen cloaks, their hands in their pockets.

"What a miserable day," she said.

One of the men turned around sharply, as if she had startled him. "Good morning, mistress. It's a lousy day to be out."

"I have a need to visit the library to get some new books for Roald." She patted her basket, looking as innocent as she could. "He's getting bored."

She wasn't sure how convincing the excuse was on a rainy day like this; after all, the precious books might get wet. But on rainy days there was lots of time to read, as well, and he made no protest.

"Do you want someone to accompany you?"

"Thank you, but I'm fine with going alone. I know where the library is. And it would be a very boring place for you, I'd wager." Why were they asking this all of a sudden? They had never shown any concern for *her* safety. In fact, they'd mostly ignored her. Was it because of things she had said yesterday?

The man nodded. "As you wish, mistress."

Johanna drew the hood of the cloak over her head, debating if she should tell them to address her as *Your Majesty,* as was appropriate. But she didn't like this renewed attention from the men at all, and would do best not to push them.

She walked quickly over the path between the tents, looking down so she didn't step in the puddles. Some of them were very deep, and already parts of the field were becoming sodden with the high water in the river.

The field of the camp lay in an outer curve of the Rede River. The path that led to the boat shed continued upstream through a swampy thicket with willow trees. Someone had put two rows on logs on the ground and filled up the space between them with sand to make a path, but today, even that was half-flooded, so Johanna had to walk past the back of the swamp, where the little path went up the levee where it joined the main road into town.

The town of Florisheim lay stretched out along the eastern bank of the Rede River, snug between the water and the forested hills. Those hills were too steep to build on, she'd been told, so the town took up only the somewhat less steep riverbanks and the lower part of the slopes.

Because of its strategic position along the river, Florisheim was foremost a fortress town, with thick city walls as the first line of defence. The quay, in the bend of the river, was a plain, barren place, with another forbidding wall at its back and a single gate that provided entrance to the city. There were also a couple of entrances at water level, closed off by heavy iron gates, now half covered in muddy, churning water.

Baron Uti's castle stood on the highest point within the walls, an ancient, menacing building, having thick walls with slits for the guards to shoot their arrows. If you came in from a certain angle, you could see the top of a catapult poking in between the parapets. The castle had one fat and stumpy tower on the corner overlooking the town. The main gate was in the western wall, next to the tower, and the castle was separated from the rest of the town by a drawbridge over a little creek that ran from the hills into the Rede River.

Johanna entered the town through western city gate, where a bored sentry looked miserable under his wet cloak.

The town's houses were mostly made of clay-daubed wood, painted white or red, while the wooden framework was painted black. The patchwork walls made neat patterns that, today, were darkened with rain that was again increasing. The streets were almost entirely a single, muddy puddle. Water dripped off the straw roofs. Smoke curled from chimneys and hung low over the town, spreading tendrils of fog and the scent of burnt wood and cooking. Most people stayed indoors by the fire and she met only a goose-herder boy driving a flock of ten or so birds, which waddled ahead of him, with their orange feet going splash, splash, splash in the puddles.

Johanna picked her way through the narrow and winding streets. Since arriving at the camp, she had come into town a number of times, usually to visit the markets or the bakery, but occasionally the barber or tailor, and she knew the way. Today, it was so early that a lot of the shops hadn't opened, and the market vendors hadn't set up all their wares. In fact, it looked like many weren't going to be here today.

One side of the market square was dominated by an elaborate stone building with a belltower. It had pillars with carved gnomes and trolls and gargoyles on the corners. There were little winged devils and ugly faces. It was, of course, the main building of the Belaman Church, and she had walked past, gazing at the stained glass window many times, wondering what it would be like from the inside. People had told her about its splendour.

Today, the elaborate doors stood open and the sound of singing drifted to the street. A choir of young voices, singing in beautiful harmony. Johanna climbed the few steps to the porch and entered a dark foyer that gave access to the main church hall. A broad aisle with mosaic tiles went to the front, where there was a stone altar, also with elaborate carvings on the side that faced the many rows of pews. The Belaman Church did not depict their god. It believed that each person held the god in their hearts and pictures of a bearded man, like the one in the Church if the Triune, were unnecessary. The wall behind the altar held a huge mural of a hand that appeared out of the clouds, and this hand was the only part of the god that made it into paintings. It pointed an index finger at the sun, which cast brilliant rays of light in response. The sun and its rays were painted in gold and the sky in radiant blue. All along the edges of the mural, there were flowers and vines with fruit, and ears of grain heavy with seed.

Wow, she'd never seen a church this big, or this beautiful.

A bunch of choirboys stood on tiered stands and the choirmaster was talking to them, his voice echoing in the emptiness.

Immediately inside the hall stood tiered tables with hundreds of candles. Tall ones, stubby ones, white ones, carved ones and coloured ones, all of them with flickering, flapping, smoking flames. The faint scent of soot and wax laced the air.

High in the walls at both sides were windows of brightly coloured glass. One depicted a trio of men lifting their hands to a bright light in the sky. The colours were beautiful, bright and clean. Amazing reds, oranges, yellows and greens. The brightest of blues. Purple even. Didn't they make that dye from some sort of shell?

The church was so big that, besides the central aisle, there were two more aisles between the rows of pews and the outer walls. Johanna walked to the one on her right, past the many rows of candles, which flapped more vigorously in her wake.

Each candle came with a little sign made from parchment or cheaper paper. She bent over to read the curly script. Names, mostly. Of people who had passed away, she guessed. One card had flowers drawn on. Another a young woman's face. A lot of cards had been written in the same hand, probably written by a church attendant on behalf of mourners.

While she stood there, the choir started to sing again, and the voices of young boys filled that giant hall with a hymn in chilling harmony. Johanna's skin puckered into goose bumps.

She walked past huge paintings of giant men with wings, and statues on pedestals. At the base of some, people had put bunches of flowers. The Belaman Church might not depict their god, but they sure loved their many saints. Some statues were old and plain, others elaborately painted. But even the old ones —and one of the statues was very old and worn, as well as greasy from the touch of many hands—had elaborate pedestals and velvet-covered benches for worshipers to kneel and pray.

If King Nicholaos had spent a lot of money on the Church of the Triune, it was a mere drop compared to the flood of money this church must have at its disposal.

The final statue in the row was a white marble life-sized figure of a woman. She wore a long cloak, held her hand, palm up as if begging, and had her face turned to the sky. The hood of her cloak half-covered her hair. She looked quite young and was also visibly pregnant.

This statue was surrounded by a stepped pedestal, and every step was covered in flowers, little toys, some baby socks even. Each one told a little story of itself. Of lost children, of children hoped-for or mothers lost in childbirth. Johanna looked for, but didn't see, a sign with the saint's name.

She sat on one of the benches surrounding the shrine, jamming her hands between her knees.

The voices of the choir rose into a crescendo, a multitude of harmonies.

In her imagination, the marble woman saint looked at the sky and pleaded *please, grant me a child. Only one will do and I care not if it is a boy or a girl.*

In her imagination, she knelt on the steps and prayed.

Certainly, it was not proper to pray in a church that wasn't yours?

A male voice said, "I would not have expected to see you here, child."

Johanna gasped. She hadn't heard the brother come up from behind. He was very tall, with a short stubble of hair on his head.

Johanna rose. "I'm sorry. I didn't mean to trespass—"

"No one trespasses when they come into the house of the Lord. All are welcome." He spoke with faint eastern accent. "I'm Brother Velespius, and it honours me to have you as a guest in our church."

"But I'm not a member."

"I know who and what you are. All are welcome in the church, day or night. It's never too late to pray to the true God and convert."

"I think I already believe in the true God."

"Do you?" He fixed her with an intense look. His brown eyes held an intense expression that made her feel uneasy.

"I think we all believe in the same God, because we are all people of the same land. We all know what is good and what is bad."

"You have a very generous spirit."

The choir had stopped and the choirmaster was yelling something at the boys about going to the midday meal.

"They are very good," Johanna said.

"People come from far and wide to listen to the choir. It's an honour for those boys to be in it. The abbot travels the country to scout for good voices. I was a member of the choir myself, but that was many years ago."

"You've lived in the monastery ever since?"

"Yes. I was a teacher and scribe before becoming a librarian and running the printing press."

Johanna looked up at the marble face of the young saint. "Who is this woman?"

"She is the holy saint Magdalena, the mother of all mankind. Women come here to pray for a child, for an easy delivery or to pray for children they have lost. Am I guessing that this is the reason you have come here also?"

"Um . . ." How did he know this? "I came because I walked outside and I heard the singing. It was so beautiful that I had to come and listen."

"While you're here, do pray to Saint Magdalena. She is the saint of mothers and motherhood. I'm thinking you will be joining that group soon."

CHAPTER 6

J OHANNA ENDED UP making a short prayer to Saint
Magdalena. The Brother seemed friendly and she couldn't
see the harm, because they were all part of the same
church, right? If Saint Magdalena was fair, she would look
kindly upon every woman, not just those who lived in town.

She left the church again not much later, unsure what to
think of it. The singing was beautiful, but while the display of
wealth was very pretty, it seemed unfair to her, and she disliked
the suggestion that she should convert. Why should these
people care? It was all these same church.

The library belonged to the old monastery next to the castle,
which had a water mill feeding off the same creek that ran
underneath the castle's drawbridge. The monks made paper and
operated a bookbindery on the ground floor. The back of the
building held a huge collection of books, which she'd been told
had belonged to a former abbot with a love of the written word
who had bequeathed his collection to the order.

Johanna went in through the huge double doors with the
snake-headed door handles. In the foyer, the familiar old monk
sat writing at a small table by the light of a flapping candle. A
proper wax candle it was, too, one that would not produce as
much greasy soot as the tallow candles. He wrote on a large
sheet of thick parchment, beautiful letters in intricate strokes.

Right now, he was colouring in the margins with lines of blue and red, a true work of beauty.

He nodded a greeting to Johanna without lifting his head from his work. The light from the candle reflected in the bald skin on top of his head.

He said, "He's in the paper press room."

The "he" would be Brother Reginald, the monk who looked after the library.

She went through the room to the left, where the rattling and clanking and creaking sounds of a working mill were loud. A couple of monks worked here, scooping ground-up cloth onto mesh sieves. The resulting layer of fluff in the bottom of the sieve would be press-dried into paper. It was noisy in the room with the constant rattle of the giant wheels and shaking of the sieves. It was stuffy in here, too, even though the door was open.

She continued through to the main room, where a couple more monks greeted her with nods. Both wore drab grey habits, tied at the waist by a simple rope. The older one was Brother Reginald.

"The day is blessed, lady," he said. Johanna had grown used to his thick accent and strange turns of phrase.

With the wrinkled skin that hung off his face and arms like an ill-fitting suit, Brother Reginald looked older than time itself. But his eyes were sharp, and the expression in them not nearly as old and tired as his body suggested.

Johanna laughed. "I've certainly seen more blessed days than this. The weather is awful. Does it often rain like this?"

"Not oft-times. The sun will come out again soon and you will beg for the rain to come back." He placed his hands at the edge of the table and pushed himself up from his desk. "Has your husband finished his books again? He reads a lot, certainly."

"He does. He is a wise man." In case they thought Roald was stupid. "I will return the other books when it has stopped raining."

"There is no hurry. What would he like to read now?"

"Do you have any books on magic and herb lore?"

That earned her a wary look.

"He is interested in the plants and their properties." Last

time she'd asked for books on the heavens so this was not too much of a stretch, she hoped. Roald *was* very interested in how nature worked.

"Herb lore, I can give you, although you had better ask the herb women in the markets. Magic is the domain of the Magician's Guild. We are a monastery." Brother Reginald's voice was prim.

"I was told that the Belaman Church allows magic. I'm sorry if I'm wrong. I don't know much about it. I'm after the magical properties of herbs."

"The church allows only certain magics, such as the magic of the holy spirit. That magic is considered sacred and the domain of men of the church. It is not the same as herb lore."

"Isn't herb lore magic?"

"No, not at all. Herb lore is the domain of herb women."

All these different definitions of magic were getting very confusing. "That means that you would have books on it?"

"We have some on herb lore."

"And magic?"

"Yes, we do have some of those, but we keep them locked away for the sake of safety of our citizens. Magic is a dark, evil subject, and people would do well not to meddle with it."

"I only wanted herb books for my husband."

He gave her a thoughtful look and stroked his beard. His eyes had an *I-don't-believe-you* look in them, but to her surprise, he nodded. "All right. Come with me."

He led her up a narrow winding staircase with uneven steps that came out in another large room filled with books. Between the two floors and the downstairs bookbindery, Johanna had never seen so many books in one place. At home, Father owned a few cabinets of books. That was considered a treasure. She hated to think how much all these books were worth. That abbot must have spent all his life collecting them.

Brother Reginald began pulling books off the shelves. He spread all of them out on a large table in the middle of the room. Johanna opened some of them and turned a few pages.

There were books about the different herbs and where they grew. There were books with intricate coloured-in drawings of plants. One book contained maps of places where these plants grew. Roald would love this.

She wondered where the magic books were hidden. She could see another winding staircase through a door across the room from where they'd entered.

A man's voice called downstairs.

Brother Reginald put another couple of books down. "If you will pardon me, I have to talk to a customer about his paper that we're making." He winked. "We wouldn't let the mayor wait, now, would we?"

He went back down the stairs and the sound of jovial voices drifted up.

How are you today?

Never better.

That sort of thing.

Johanna waited, leafing through the books on the table. Brother Reginald and his customer appeared to have moved into the papermaking room.

It was amazing how many books were here. The shelves covered every bit of wall in the room. Leather-bound books with gold-embossed titles; thinner volumes with paper covers; large, heavy books; small, fat books. Books in numbered series, books in languages she couldn't read and some in languages she didn't even recognise.

While she stood there, she noticed movement in the corner of her eye at the top of the staircase. Someone was coming up the stairs and she had been so absorbed in all these books that she hadn't even heard footsteps.

But the slender figure that came out of the stairwell wasn't Brother Reginald. It was a woman in a heavy cloak with the hood pulled over her hair, her face hidden within the shadow of the fabric.

Johanna was about to say something, but the words died on her tongue at sight of the woman's sickly pale hand. She had heard that there was a disease in this region that disfigured people's faces. Would this woman be suffering from it?

The woman didn't look up or seem to notice Johanna at all. She crossed the room, gliding around the table in the middle as if she barely touched the ground. Her footsteps made no sound even though the floor was made of wood. For a moment, Johanna thought she was a ghost, but she looked far too solid.

Yet the tingle of magic wafted in her wake.

The woman went to the entrance to the second staircase and disappeared up the steps and out of sight. A glow of light flickered into being on the floor above, casting a golden triangle of light on the wall in the staircase.

Were the magic books up there?

Brother Reginald was still talking to his customer. Their voices echoed from one of the rooms downstairs, mingled with the rattling and clanking of the mill wheels.

As silently as she could, Johanna crept up the stairs.

The light from the flapping candle flame cast long shadows over the wall. The stone was pitted and the wall was curved, so the shadows were rough and distorted, making it hard to see where the woman was and what she was doing up there.

Johanna crept up a step, and another one, until the room came into view. As she had expected, this was yet another room full of books, except this one was much messier than the one downstairs, with books stacked on top of each other and on the floor.

The woman stood looking at the shelves. She held both her hands on the back of a chair. The skin was very pale, but unaffected by disease. She looked quite young.

Johanna wasn't sure what to do. She could talk to the woman, but she might not understand her. If she was important, Brother Reginald would have introduced her. If she wanted to speak to Johanna, the woman would have introduced herself.

Maybe—and she felt cold—this woman was the abbot's personal plaything. That was an embarrassing thought, but something she'd sadly come across more times than she cared to remember. She never knew who she felt more sorry for: the poor girl or the man who couldn't get a girl in any way other than to "buy" a poor wrench and feed and clothe her in return for certain services.

Anyway, she'd better go down before the Brother came back.

But as Johanna retreated a step down the stairs, the woman

turned around so that the light fell on the side of her face. The straw-blond curly hair that poked out from under the hood was familiar. The freckles were familiar, too, and so were the dark blue eyes.

It was Princess Celine.

Johanna had never forgotten Celine's face. There was a painting in the church hall that was an exact likeness of the princess as she had been just before her death. This woman matched the likeness down to the little mole on her cheekbone, down to her pale yellow dress with the tiny buttons and the lace frills.

She raised her hand to her mouth to stifle a gasp. That was impossible. The princess had been dead for a number of years.

"Ah, little princess," the woman said in a voice that sounded like the rasping of millstones.

Johanna wanted to run, but she couldn't. She stood petrified on the stairs, and might even have fallen had there not been the wall at her back.

"You have a problem, right, little princess?" The apparition laughed, a breezy sound.

Johanna retreated. Whatever this *thing* was, princess Celine, it was not.

"Come on, answer me."

Ghosts never talked to anyone. Sometimes they imitated a voice, but they never recognised people, they just went about their ghostly business without regard for who watched them.

"Tell me, what is your problem? Why have you come to the library?"

An ice-cold draught made the candles flap. It was so dark up here that if the flame blew out, Johanna wouldn't be able to see her way back down.

The apparition laughed again. "I'm going to have so much fun with this. Go on, try to take all the herbs and other quackery. Raspberry leaves, stinging nettles. Make the tea and drink it every night. That's why you're here, right? To see what you are doing wrong? To see why the idiot prince cannot get you with child. Keep trying. Go and stand upside down after he has fucked you. It will not help, but it will be good to see your despair. The reason is: because you're cursed by the deepest, darkest magic there is. You can never take the place that is rightfully mine. They will never accept you as their queen, because I am the queen!" She laughed, a horrible rasping sound.

"Get away from me! You're not real," Johanna yelled.

"I'm not real? Do you want to feel the cold of my curse?" She floated towards the top of the stairs, threatening to come down into the stairwell.

Johanna did her best not to scream. She launched herself down the stairs as quickly as she could, but the steps were narrow and uneven. She tripped, fell against the curved wall and tumbled a fair way.

The apparition whooshed past her with a rush of freezing air, leaving the sound of evil laughter in its wake. Johanna sat with her arms covering her head until she was sure that it was gone.

Her heart thudded like crazy.

Ouch, her wrist.

When she stumbled back into the other room, Brother Reginald just came running to the top of the stairs and stood there panting. He was not young, and many of his age would have given up climbing stairs long ago.

"What was all that noise?" His gaze rested on Johanna's arm.

Johanna looked. She was bleeding.

Oh. "I . . . fell down the stairs." She glanced at the entrance to the stairwell, but there was no sign of the apparition.

"Not much point being curious, young lady." He panted for breath. "There is nothing up there but spiders."

"That's not true. I saw—"

"That's just Liesel. She is always harassing people. She is harmless."

"Liesel?"

"Liesel the house ghost comes out sometimes when she is curious. She was the daughter of the original owner of this house, who gave it to the Order. She threw herself out of the tower window because of a spurned love affair. Don't those women all go funny when they think a man loves them?" He chuckled.

"But this was not a ghost. She was touching the chair. She was talking to me. She was looking at the books."

"There are no books up there. No chair either. You must have taken a spell."

Johanna looked from his bony frame to the entrance to the stairwell. She had *not* imagined this.

"I see you have doubts. Go upstairs. You'll see."

Johanna did.

The stairs came out into a dusty attic where cobwebbed items of furniture stood spread out in a haphazard way. There were no shelves with books, no desk with a chair, no piles of books on the floor, no candle, no table and no young woman.

That was the strangest thing ever. The library room had felt real. It had smelled real.

When she came down, Brother Reginald was nodding at her shocked expression. "It is a strange thing, and if I'd known that she was in this part of the building, I wouldn't have left you alone. Ah, Liesel, why do you make our lives so difficult?"

"Does she ever speak to everyone?"

He shook his head. "She doesn't speak at all. Not that anyone has ever heard."

"But she spoke to me . . . I don't think I saw the same ghost."

He gave her a brief *dumb woman* look, and she decided to leave the subject. The back of her neck pricked as if the ghost were still hanging around in the shadows.

From the table, Johanna chose a few books with pictures and lots of diagrams. Roald spent a long time figuring out text, but he loved illustrations and he was very good at deciphering their meaning, too.

She thanked Brother Reginald and left the library again, without books on magic, and without any potions to solve her problem.

CHAPTER 7

E VEN WHEN SHE was in the street, Johanna felt the eyes of Celine's ghost on her. She heard that raspy voice *You will never take the place that is rightfully mine*, which chilled her to the core of her bones. Why had Brother Reginald thought this was the ghost of a common girl? That did not look like a common girl to her at all. Her hands were clean and unblemished and unscarred from manual work. Her clothes were rich, with little pearl shell buttons and embroidery that common people couldn't afford.

She didn't look like a ghost, she didn't behave like a ghost. Yet she was not Celine, but someone's magical minion.

Johanna clutched the basket and made her way down the streets.

She didn't dare go back to the camp. The camp was full of Saarlanders who were unused to open displays of magic.

Some of the rich and influential people were said to believe that Celine was still alive and had been hidden away from the people to keep her pure. Those people said that the grave was empty and that the king's grief was a farce.

She checked over her shoulders many times and saw nothing except the wet street. But the trouble with a ghost was that if you didn't see it, that didn't mean it wasn't there.

It would be watching her and following her wherever she

went and whatever she did. Watching and waiting for revenge. The nobles might even blame Johanna for bringing magic back to the camp.

Master Deim's family's house was in one of the higher streets of the town, close enough to the castle for the walls to loom menacingly over the roof.

When Johanna knocked, an adolescent girl opened the door and said something that Johanna didn't understand.

"I'm here to see Hieronymus Deim," she said.

The girl frowned and then repeated Master Deim's first name with such a different pronunciation that Johanna would never have picked it up if she'd heard it in a conversation on the street. The girl beckoned for her to come inside. She preceded Johanna through the dark corridor and into a warm living room where a number of people sat by the fire: a grey-haired woman with embroidery work sitting next to an oil lamp, two young boys playing on the floor, a man in his middle age—Master Deim's cousin?—and a woman of the same age. His wife or Master Deim's wife?

The merchant's eyes widened when he saw Johanna.

"Look at you. What brings you here in weather like this?"

He rose and took Johanna's hands in his. His skin felt like it was on fire. She hadn't realised up until now just how cold she was.

"Child, you look like you've seen a ghost. What's wrong?"

"Master Deim, please, I need to talk to you." And she *had* seen a ghost.

On the wall above the fireplace hung a large painting of the harbour of Saardam. Johanna recognised the work of the artist Claudius Verbeeck, whose commissioned works graced the walls of the town hall in Saardam.

His portraits of important Saarlander men were stiff and their likeness dubious at best, but his landscapes were beautiful, done in tiny little brush strokes and displayed so much detail that she could see Father's office. Was one of the ships in the harbour the *Lady Sara* or *Lady Davida*?

Then a disturbing thought: how many of these old buildings had survived the fire? The palace loomed over the houses. That was definitely destroyed. Probably a lot of the very old houses, too.

The middle-aged woman saw Johanna looking at it. "We will rebuild it," she said in slightly stiff but perfect Saarlander dialect.

Johanna turned to her. "You're from Saardam?"

As Johanna met the woman's eyes, the woman dropped to her knees. "My name is Hilda. I came from Saardam when I was young and beautiful. My family is at your service, Your Majesty."

It was the first time that someone addressed her like this and it took Johanna by surprise. She wanted to tell the woman to get up and stop being silly, but knew it was absolutely the right thing for her to do. Roald needed support as a king, and that meant people should treat him as a king. She said, "Thank you. I will do what I can, too, but it may take a while so you may have to be patient."

"We can be very patient. Whatever it is we can do, let us know. I will send my sons to fight, if they're old enough."

The young boys looked up from their game, clearly well-versed in the language.

"Thank you."

It was a strange and emotional moment to have someone promising her the life of her sons. The idea of going back to Saardam to free the city with an army abhorred her, but it might be what needed to be done. Although how an army could defeat strong magic wasn't clear to her.

"Actually, you can do something for me right now. I need to visit a woman who is well-versed in herb lore."

"You must go and visit Magda. She is simply the best."

Master Deim said something to her in the local language, and she replied in a somewhat annoyed tone.

Master Deim snorted.

"My brother-in-law says that Magda is an old witch."

"I can tell her that myself, and she *is* an old witch. Hilda, I know you don't have a shred of magic in you, but that woman is not half as harmless as she looks."

"She is the best. If you need her, you will find her house on the other side of the markets. It's a grey house, a bit dirty-looking, and there are strange things on the windowsills, but don't let that, or the sight of her face, frighten you."

Master Deim still didn't look happy about it.

"But will she understand me?" Johanna asked. She wondered what could be wrong with Magda's face.

"She will, even though she will grump about it, and pretty much everything else, too. Always making out that whatever you've asked is a big deal. She's not an inviting person, but just ignore the complaining. She'd be complaining a lot more if no one came. She'll know who you are, too, but she'll be rude about it—"

Master Deim said, "Hilda . . ."

She glanced at him. "What? I'm just warning the queen."

"Thank you," Johanna said.

"It is a pleasure." The woman curtsied and that was even more embarrassing than being called Your Majesty.

Master Deim snorted and led Johanna into the corridor, where it was very dark and cold.

The floor was covered in worn tiles that seemed to have been untouched for the last hundred years.

"This is a very old house," he said. "This part of Florisheim goes back all the way to the time of the Belaman invasion. Florisheim stood strong against their armies."

The Belaman religion had been much more successful.

Master Deim led her to the end of the corridor, up a narrow staircase and through a small doorway. It came out into a large room with windows along the far side that looked out over the slate roofs of the town and, beyond that, the river. Drops of water ran over the outside of the glass panes. All the roofs were dark and glistening with rain. The river had broken its banks in the low-lying areas on the opposite side, which was in Burovia.

"Look at all that water," Johanna said.

"It rained a lot in the foothills yesterday. There will be more to come. Those Burovian farmers should get their animals to higher ground."

A couple of cows stood on a patch that had become an island. They all faced the same way, with their backsides into the wind.

"Isn't that the religious order's land?"

"Not that," he said. "They own everything you can see to the north of here, but not further upstream."

"Who lives there?"

"No one. It's wild land and forest as far as the eye can see."

Johanna stood so close to the window that her breath fogged on the glass.

Forest with magical creatures, good and bad. She had only seen small parts of the forest, even when riding through with the bandits; there were always lone farmhouses and tiny villages along the way. *Forest as far as the eye can see* was not something she could comprehend. She didn't like forests. After her trek to Duke Lothar's castle and his explanation about magic lines, she liked it even less.

Master Deim said, "There are mountains to the south of the forest and other strange lands on the other side of those mountains."

"Father often told me about the strange lands and people there." He had not travelled there himself, but those people travelled up the rivers to Lurezia and he did business with them there.

"Have a seat."

Johanna sat on one of the cloth-covered chairs. Along the walls stood many wooden shelves filled with books, big leather-bound volumes and cheaper board-covered texts.

"I didn't know you had this many books."

"Many of them came from my brother's collection. This is his house."

"I thought the man in the living room was your cousin. I didn't know you had a brother."

"He is my cousin. I had a brother. He used to run half of our business, but he went to a trip down south and never returned."

"What happened?"

"No one knows. We never heard from him again. For this trip, he had chosen not to travel on one of the company ships, because he intended to travel south of the rapids. He was not alone, but rode with our company accountant. Neither of them were ever seen again."

"That must be a terrible thing to have happen."

He nodded. "Hilda is devastated. I'm helping her out with the boys. I'll probably end up marrying her." Master Deim's wife, she remembered now, had died a few years ago from wasting sickness. He told her that she'd already been thin when they married. Not even the best medics had been able to stop it. They never had children.

That thought made Johanna shiver. Some women just never had children. Maybe there was something wrong with her.

There was a knock on the door and the maid came in with a tray with tea. Johanna and Master Deim were silent while she set out the cups and plates. Master Deim only spoke when the maid left.

"So what happened this morning that has you so out of sorts?" he asked while sitting down.

"It's a bit of a story. I went to the library to get new books for Roald to read."

"It's an odd time to go to the library."

"I know, but he ran out of books, and it's raining so he's driving me crazy doing nothing and fidgeting. Brother Reginald took me up to the library room. He was called away and while I was waiting for him to come back, and leafing through the books that he was going to give me, a ghost came up the stairs."

"Oh, that's Liesel. Everyone knows her."

"It was not Liesel. It was Celine."

He frowned at her. "Are you sure of that?"

"I know what Celine's face looks like. It was Celine. She was wearing that pale yellow dress with the tiny buttons that she wears in the painting of her that hangs in the church." She had to check herself. By all accounts, the Church of the Triune in Saardam had burnt to the ground. "Celine went up into another tower room that was also full of old books. She spoke to me. Her voice was like rasping millstones, not human at all. She said that I was a usurper and that only she could be queen."

His frown deepened. "Ghosts don't normally speak."

"No, they don't. They don't look solid either."

"Are you sure it was a ghost?"

"No, but it was some sort of magical apparition. After she'd made her threats to me, I ran down the stairs and fell. Then Brother Reginald came back up from talking to his customer. I told him what I'd seen and he said there was no library room up there. I went back upstairs again and it was just an attic with lots of dust and spider webs. The ghost or apparition created an illusion around itself that was strong enough for me not to notice that it wasn't real."

He shook his head, the expression on his face worried. "I have never heard of anything like that."

"No, I haven't either. That's why I need to see a magician. Do you know that there are rumours that there is a necromancer in town?"

For a moment, an uneasy expression hovered in his eyes. He didn't deny the question. He didn't confirm it either.

"Hmm." He rubbed his chin and then repeated, "Hmm. Let me make some inquiries for you. But please don't go and see that woman Magda. She's harmless to people like my sister-in-law who just come to buy herbs, but her knowledge goes much deeper than that. She's rumoured to have been an accomplice for Duke Lothar's attempted poisoning of his half-brother. I presume you know about that."

She nodded. "Roald knows all these things. He's like a walking compendium of royalty."

Master Deim raised his eyebrows. "Is he, now?"

"Like you told me to do with Magda, you shouldn't underestimate him. He sits and reads all day, and he remembers all of it. He's just really awkward with people. He doesn't like meetings and doesn't like to be in the spotlight."

"Hmm." He let a small silence lapse. "All right, I guess I shall keep that in mind then. But I repeat: don't see Magda. She is not just a herb woman."

"What if the reason I wanted to see her is just for herbs?"

He seemed taken aback by that statement. "Oh. Sorry. Just for herbs, then, but I would prefer if you bought them from any other herb seller at the markets, if you can."

"I will try." But Johanna was curious about this Magda now. If she was a friend of Duke Lothar's then she might have useful information. No matter what people said about the duke, he was the only one to have given her serious information about magic and the only one to have helped her with the matter. She didn't want to take sides between the Duke and his half-brother Baron Uti, but the Duke at least had taken her seriously, even if she was only a woman, while the Baron had so far done his best to ignore her.

Master Deim repeated his promise that he would talk to someone about the apparition of Celine, and repeated his warning against Magda a third time.

Then she asked him the question that she had never dared ask when they both still lived in Saardam. "Do you have some magic?"

He hesitated only a moment. "I do. I have very limited water magic. The water in the tea tells me that the young maid who opened the door for you has been kissing the neighbour's coachman in our kitchen again. I'll have to talk to her about that. He's from a family that's no good, and if she keeps going like this, she'll end up in trouble and then she'll have to marry him."

Johanna wondered why so many young women got *in trouble* while she could not end up *in trouble* no matter how often she and Roald shared the bed.

"The water in the river tells me how much it has rained upstream."

"Do raindrops tell you what it's like to fly?"

He frowned at her like he'd never considered that angle. "I guess they could. How did you come up with that thought?"

"Roald. He says a bird could fly to the Moon by crossing the air."

"He's been reading Rinius." It was not a question.

"Yes. He's fascinated by all those things."

"You are aware that most churches consider Rinius heresy? The Church of the Triune is one of those churches. Your father often lamented that you went to it."

"There are more reasons than one to attend a church. I liked how the church teaches that people are equal regardless of their wealth. I like how they help poor and unfortunate people. I don't like their position on magic. I'd like Saardam to be a place of free thought and inquisitive minds."

The more she thought about it, the more convinced she became of this. The crime was not that Rinius had some strange ideas. It was that he had been hanged for voicing them.

CHAPTER 8

B Y THE TIME Johanna left Master Deim's house, the rain had intensified and didn't look like letting up any time soon. The sky was leaden grey and wind lashed at trees.

She ran through the narrow streets, empty except for puddles, through the gate, where the bored sentry still sat being miserable in his little hut, and along the by now very muddy path to the camp. The books made her basket heavy. The wind kept pulling at the leather covering. She must have eaten something bad because her stomach cramped.

At the camp, some people were still attempting to cook dinner, but even the wood that had been stored under shelter was wet, and most refugees hid inside their tents.

The gangplank of the *Lady Sara* had become even steeper and slipperier than when she left.

When she opened the hold cover that provided access to the stairs, a good amount of rain came in. They should get someone to make a cover for this entrance.

A couple of people were talking in the hold. It was too dark to see who they were, but one of the voices was Nellie's. "No, you can't see him." She sounded distressed. "My mistress has told me that no one can talk to him unless she is there—oh! Mistress Johanna, there you are."

The people who were with Nellie at the bottom of the stairs looked up and by the grey light from the rainy day, Johanna recognised their faces: Johan Delacoeur and Fleuris LaFontaine. What were they doing here?

"Good morning, gentlemen," she said, while climbing down. She made sure that her annoyance came through in her tone, which wasn't hard when she was wet and cold and desperate to get changed into dry clothes.

Since when did citizens encroach on the King's freedom? She had told Nellie that she wanted no visitors here, which was Roald's domain, where he was safe from prying eyes. The guards would know that, too. They should have stopped the men.

Roald sat at his desk, studiously ignoring the nobles, but the way in which he jiggled his leg showed that he was already pretty distressed, even though outsiders wouldn't pick up on it.

Johanna had arrived at the bottom of the stairs and now faced the men, both of whom were much taller than her. "Do you have a pressing reason to bother the king in his private quarters?"

"The matter is quite urgent." Johan Delacoeur's manner was so distant that he didn't even look into her eyes.

"Ah, I see. You have come here to discuss the details of the coronation ceremony that we must hold soon."

"Um . . ." They clearly had not.

"Well, come down, and we'll discuss it."

"Miss Brouwer," began Fleuris LaFontaine, and that was not a good beginning at all.

"Why the 'Miss'? Am I not your queen?"

"That's what we're here to talk about."

"I don't understand." Her heart thudded in her chest. Why discuss this now? They'd had two months to question her status. What had changed?

"None of us witnessed the ceremony that you say took place on the deck of this ship near the ruins of Aroden castle. The only witness appears to be the maid who performed the ceremony and a demon-possessed witch. We cannot verify the young maid's claim that she is authorised to conduct such a ceremony—"

"Well then, it's easy, we must hold the wedding ceremony again. As long as it's organised quickly, because it would look improper if I attended it looking like I swallowed a water bag."

It was all bluff, but Fleuris gave her an uncertain look. "But certainly it's a bit early to . . . Are you certain? We cannot hold the ceremony then, in your condition . . ."

"It's early days yet. We have time. But if you would like to see an official ceremony, then we must hold one." A chill came over her. Would they really cast out a woman who carried the king's first-born? Would they cast out any woman in that condition, knowing that she would have nowhere else to go?

Johan Delacoeur was looking at her with an *I-don't-believe-this* expression on his face. "I would like to see a ruling from a physic before we make any rash decisions."

"I have been with Roald since we fled Saardam. I saved him. I helped him all that time." *I dressed him, I fed him.* "There is nothing 'rash' about this decision."

"Yes, but I think it would be more appropriate for the new king to be wed to a girl from a good family."

"I am not one of your approved candidates, is that it? Can I mention that at the ball on the night before the fire, all of the approved candidates danced with him, and most of the girls thumbed their noses at 'the idiot prince'? Some even ran back to their mothers crying. They would not have fished him out of the harbour. They would not have put up with his strange comments."

Neither of the men she faced had unmarried daughters of the right age anyway, and the problem had been deeper than that: the king had fallen out with the Council of Nobles over the king's encouragement of the Church of the Triune.

And she realised something even more terrible: maybe Roald was *meant* to have died in the fire or drowned in the harbour. She had assumed that he had jumped in the water to escape fire and that, being a strong swimmer, he'd judged the water a safe escape. Could it be that someone had pushed him? Maybe this was all part of a plot to get rid of not only the Church of the Triune, but its most vocal supporter. Maybe they had wanted to replace Nicholaos with one of the king's Burovian cousins.

Heart thudding, she looked into the old and haughty faces of the two men opposite her. They *appeared* quite civilised, but especially with nobles, appearances never told the entire story.

"Why don't you ask the king what *he* wants."

Johan Delacoeur scoffed. "He's not in a state to—"

"He is *not* dumb if that's what you were going to say."

"No, I wasn't."

Yes, that was exactly what he was going to say. "Roald?"

He sat bent over his book, but his eyes weren't moving. He held his hands clamped between his knees, and a muscle in his forearm kept alternately tensing up and relaxing.

"Roald?" She put an arm over his shoulder. Drops of sweat pearled on his forehead. He smelled sweaty, too.

"I was rude to them," he said.

Fleuris LaFontaine snorted. "He was, too. I don't know where a prince learns that kind of language."

"They were rude to *my* women," Roald said. "The maid and the witch. No one is rude to *my* women."

"I know. It's all right." She spoke very softly, hoping that the men couldn't hear her well enough to understand.

"You're mine. Nellie is mine. They can't be rude to you."

"It's all right, really. Calm down, please."

"Your Majesty," said Fleuris LaFontaine.

"Tell them to leave," Roald said.

"They won't listen to me. You're the king. Tell them."

"I can't talk to them. They're rude. Father says I can't talk to rude people."

Johan Delacoeur cleared his throat. "Your Majesty . . ."

Johanna turned around. Why couldn't he see that she was busy? "The king will talk to you if he wants. Right now, he asks me to tell you to leave."

Johan ignored her. "Please do tell us, Your Majesty, if you would prefer to wed a woman of your status—"

Roald got up from the table so suddenly that Johanna had no chance to stop him. He faced the two men.

"They are *my* women! You can't take them away from me. I forbid you to take them away from me. I'm the king, you have to listen to me and do what I say. I want you to leave. This is my room for me and my women."

"Roald, it's all right. Calm down."

"No, it's not all right. They are here to take you away. I don't want you to go. You're mine. I love you." His cheeks had gone red.

"Roald . . ."

He turned back to the men, whose eyes were wide. Johan Delacoeur's mouth hung open.

"You hear that? I love her. Now, you leave. Get out of here. This is *my* ship. Go, go, go." He more or less pushed them up the stairs, Johan Delacoeur first and then his colleague.

Fleuris LaFontaine stammered, "Your Majesty, I'm sorry to have caused offense. It was not my intention—"

"Go, go, go!" Roald was almost shrieking now.

"Come, my friend," Johan said from the top of the stairs. "We know we're not wanted." He met Johanna's eyes. "I can only say, young lady, that this is a very bad move—"

"Go, go, go! Stop talking. Stop making noise. Yap, yap, yap, yap. Get out of here."

Fleuris LaFontaine had reached the top of the stairs, his face red from exertion. Men of his standing did apparently *not* run up narrow and steep stairs.

They pushed the cover shut, and Johanna was left alone with Roald.

They looked at each other.

Johanna stifled a snort of laughter.

"You think that's funny?"

"I think you were brilliant." There would be consequences, but the sight of those two portly men scrambling up the steps was not one she'd forget quickly.

"You liked it." He said that in a tone as if he could barely believe it.

"Yes, I did."

He started laughing, too. "Did you see how scared they were? How I chased them up the stairs?"

Johanna laughed out loud. She put on an arrogant voice.

"Your Majesty, wouldn't you prefer to wed a woman of your status?"

Roald giggled and snorted.

"They could hardly be more crass about what they wanted. And you know what the funny thing is? Ha, ha, ha. They don't even have any daughters."

Roald squealed with laughter.

Nellie poked her head in. "Well, I'm glad you're having fun. Those men were *most* rude."

Johanna was laughing too much to reply.

"Well, I'm getting dinner ready," Nellie said, and closed the cover to the hold.

Poor Nellie. When was the last time she'd laughed?

Johanna let herself fall on the bed and Roald dropped next to her. She heaved a satisfied sigh, staring at the rough underside of the hold cover.

Then wriggled an elbow under her so that she could look at Roald.

"You're all wet."

"Yes, the weather outside is horrible."

His eyes were fixed on her. The light from the lamp fell sideways on his face. His beard had gotten a lot denser, which made him look more like a king every day. She stroked the rough hair. There were blond hairs and darker ones and fox-red ones.

She whispered, "I love you."

"No, you got that wrong. I should say that to you."

"Yes, but I love you, too." And strange as it sounded, it was the truth.

He frowned. "No one has ever said that to me."

"Not even your mother?"

He shook his head. "You really love me?"

"Yes."

His expression was so shocked that it made her all weepy. "Come on, Roald, you're making me cry."

"You can't cry. I'm supposed to make you happy."

"You do make me happy. They're happy tears." She kissed him softly on the lips.

From one thing came another, and when Nellie came a bit later to say that dinner was ready, Johanna and Roald weren't quite ready for dinner.

CHAPTER 9

I N THE NEXT few days, it rained a lot more. The river broke its banks on the eastern side as well as the western side and started encroaching on the camp. Some people in the lower parts of the meadow had to move their tents, which made the higher side of the meadow very crowded.

With the help of Captain Arense, Johanna found two young men who agreed to be scouts and check on the situation in Saardam. Master Deim helped organise a small dinghy, and Johanna leant them a harness and two placid sea cows so that they could come back again.

Johanna watched them go with a pang of apprehension. The river was an expanse of churning, muddy water and the men had to harness the animals just to be able to control the little boat. If they were hit by a floating tree trunk, they would have no chance. But both men assured her that they could swim and she knew both of them had experience with boats. Still, who knew what they'd meet in Saardam?

Johanna attended one more Council of Nobles meeting where she proposed that to cheer up the people, there would an official wedding ceremony at a date to be announced soon.

The nobles didn't like it, but there was nothing they could do when Master Deim, Joris DeCamp and Captain Arense all supported the idea. She sure hadn't seen the end of their protests, but for now the nobles were outmanoeuvred.

A few days later, Johanna was in the camp talking to some of the women about things the refugees collectively needed to barter in town, like better clothing for the wet weather, shoes, and a cart and horse. A young lad came rushing in to tell her that a man in the Baron's red livery had gone to the *Lady Sara*. Johanna's first thought was: news from Saardam. She hurried back, sidestepping puddles and areas of mud. By the time she came to the jetty, the man was just coming down the gangplank. He nodded to her when meeting her coming the other way. Wet and bedraggled as she was, he probably thought she was a maid.

Roald sat staring at a piece of parchment on his desk.

Her heart jumped. Bad news? Please, no. "What is it?"

He said nothing, so she looked over his shoulder. No, it was not from Saardam. The letter bore the Red Baron's family seal. In elegant, curly script it said,

It has come to my attention that Your Royal Majesty and the consort are planning to hold an official ceremony to celebrate your holy matrimony. We simply cannot allow for a ceremony of import to be held in a cow paddock. We offer the use of our grand hall in the castle for this purpose. Please send your personal servants around to talk about the arrangements.

The letter was signed Baroness Viktoriya, whose name she had never heard, but who had only been referred to as "The Baroness" whenever people spoke of her.

Johanna frowned. They hadn't even set a date yet, and nothing about this wedding was official. If nothing else, this confirmed that someone in the camp was close to the Baron, even if the Baron seemed to avoid her and the nobles of the council.

"I don't understand," Roald said. "We can't get married. We are already married."

"I know, but the nobles want another ceremony because they couldn't be at the first one."

"Oh." Roald said, and he frowned. "Why? I don't like ceremonies. I don't want another ball."

"If I have anything to do with it, there won't be another ball."

But if the Baron's family insisted on having the ceremony at the castle, there would be a ball with lots of unfamiliar important noble people.

Worse, she couldn't see a polite way to refuse the offer.

Worse still, Kylian would be there.

And the letter absolutely needed replying to, so Johanna wrote a polite reply that she'd be delighted to visit the next day, but she had to force herself to write that word *delighted*. Who in the camp had told the Baroness this?

Johanna wasn't going to let Nellie go to the castle by herself, so she decided to go with Nellie and two guards the next morning. Both Johanna and Nellie got dressed in their best outfits, which still left a lot to be desired. Nellie was nervous, wanting to know if it was really necessary for her to come, because she was only a maid.

"A lady-in-waiting," Johanna corrected, "and you absolutely should come, because I can trust you."

Nellie looked nothing like a maid in the old-fashioned dress they had taken from Duke Lothar's castle. The dark colour of the fabric made her skin look pale and ghost-like. Johanna promised herself that as soon as they were out of this camp, she would get Nellie some proper clothes that did not make her look like a walking corpse.

Fortunately, the rain had let up a bit, even though the streets in the town were still muddy. The townsfolk wore raincoats of oiled cloth and tall boots. Some children played barefoot in the mud. A couple of foreign guests doing their best to avoid puddles in their best clothes drew a certain amount of attention.

At the castle, they walked across the heavy drawbridge and announced themselves at the gate, where a guard told them to come with him to meet the Baroness. From inside, the castle looked as austere and plain as it did from the outside. Walls were made from bare stone, and mostly unadorned. Passages were high-ceilinged and empty. Any furniture was made from heavy oak, stained dark. Dark and menacing suits of armour lined the corridors where their footsteps echoed hollow. What little light fell through the windows looked washed out and wan.

"It's creepy in here," Nellie said in a low voice, glancing over her shoulder. "As if those suits of armour are going to come to life and jump on us when we're not looking."

The guard led them into a huge but very dark hall, where many long tables and benches stood in rows. Johanna could imagine wedding guests seated at those tables, laughing and eating. The air smelled of stale beer mixed with a faint waft of roast meat.

A couple of dark wooden chandeliers hung from the ceiling, but none of the candles burned. Johanna's first thought was that the hall had nothing like the splendour of the gorgeous ballroom in the palace in Saardam. But it was a hundred times better than holding the ceremony in the muddy field of the camp, which might well be half-submerged if this rain kept up.

Still, she did not want to accept any more of the Baron's charity.

This whole idea of having a wedding was silly. It would be much better to have it when they were back in Saardam.

But the nobles would see that she'd lied about being with child.

The sound of a clear female voice disturbed her thoughts. The woman who walked towards her between the tables had the figure of a matron: broad-hipped and large-breasted, with her greying hair piled on top of her head in a bun, held in place by a jewelled net. Her dress was made from thick velvet in the darkest of red.

"You are the princess Johanna, right?" She spoke with a heavy and very unusual accent.

"I am. It's an honour to meet you. Thank you for your hospitality."

The Baroness waved her be-ringed hand. "Oh, it is nothing. I'm so excited to host a wedding. My son, he will not get married. I tell him about which girls is looking to marry. Nice girls. Rich girls, but he just say nothing. Every time I ask him, he change subject."

Her accent was really unusual, as were her dark brown eyes.

"Is a pity that you're already married. I say to him: what is happening to castle and land when your father dies? But he just laugh. Now we receive letters from Aroden, from Burovia, even from Lurezia. The parents tell us: 'At his last visit, your son was besotted with our daughter. I think it might be beneficial to let them marry.' Oh . . ." She spread her hands and looked at the ceiling. "By the Holy Spirit, we get one at least every month. Rich men's daughters, princesses even! My son, he is a nice, decent young man. He does not go break the hearts of all these girls."

She sighed and shook her head in a *what-has-the-world-come-to* kind of way. Johanna thought of Kylian's attempts to seduce her, and decided not to pierce the Baroness' bubble of delusion about her son's decency.

The Baroness talked and talked and talked. She had the whole thing planned out already. What Johanna would wear, what Roald would wear, where they would sit, which dances would be played, the guest list, and so forth and so on.

Johanna could make use of the kitchens, she said, as well as the courtiers. It would be a joint festivity for the Saarlander refugees and the esteemed citizens of Florisheim.

Johanna had been afraid of that.

But her carefully-worded suggestion to invite mainly people from Saardam "to keep costs down" was swept aside with, "Oh, but don't worry about the money. It will all be on our account. We *love* a good feast. It's at harvest time, so we will have plenty." And, "Don't worry that you don't know many people. I will personally introduce you to citizens of Florisheim. They will be delighted to meet you."

Johanna gnashed her teeth in frustration. She didn't *want* to be introduced to all the citizens of Florisheim. Maybe some other time she would, but right now, she just wanted to go home.

The Baroness' plans were like a spider's web: once you were stuck, you could not get free, no matter how much you tried. The Baroness herself sat like a big fat spider in the middle of the web. Sickly sweet, dressed up like a favourite auntie, but impossible to escape from.

Was there such thing as magic through words?

Not to mention that the Baron's feasts were fertile ground for feuds and poisonings, and she wanted nothing more than to get out of that dark room. She glanced at Nellie, who hadn't been able to get a word in at all, and who looked as desperate to leave as Johanna felt.

She didn't want to hold the ceremony in the Baron's castle. She didn't want the nobles of Florisheim to be there, because not only did she know none of them, but she would have no idea if any of them would be there for other reasons. The Baron would probably be there, as well as his son who she was trying to avoid.

Yet she knew she couldn't politely refuse this offer.

Worse, this woman just kept on talking.

FINALLY, Johanna managed to cut off the visit by politely refusing tea "because I have to be back to help my husband with the midday meal." It was only a half-lie. Roald would happily eat by himself— just the applesauce, and he'd leave the rest—but it finally did the trick. After asking Johanna about her earlier unofficial wedding, and announcing, "We can't have a king be married in old farmer's clothes and dirty jacket," Johanna and Nellie were finally allowed to go. The same guard who had brought them in—and who had been waiting patiently by the door—accompanied them to the gate.

Johanna kept her silence until they were safely in the market square.

"Why in all of the heaven's name does that woman think she owns me?"

Nellie frowned at her. "What do you mean? I don't understand. She is just being friendly and helping us. We can hardly hold the wedding in a muddy field."

Not you, too. "Nellie, she has no reason for doing this. We are not her relatives. If I'm correct, she comes from the east, the land of wolves. She has no connection to Saardam—"

"Does she have to have a connection to us? Why can't she just help us? Why do you always expect the worst of people?"

Johanna spread her hands. *Because people try the worst on me when they think I'm not looking?* But that argument was lost on Nellie. One day, someone would betray poor Nellie so badly, it would break her heart, and then would she still find it in her to forgive this person? Yes, she probably would.

Nellie's tendency to trust everyone had always infuriated her as much as Johanna's tendency to distrust people had infuriated Nellie. It really could not be helped. It was engrained in Nellie's character.

And there was nothing she could do to refuse the Baroness' hospitality, even though the thought of having to see that woman again made her skin crawl. She did not want to be ensnared in this web of stickiness masquerading as hospitality. She did not want to see Kylian. But for now, she could see no escape.

She asked Nellie how much she wanted to be involved in the wedding preparations, which was quite a bit, but she said, "I'll need a lot of help, mistress."

So later that day, Johanna set about getting that help. Mistress Daphne or any of the modistes from Saardam had been below Fleuris LaFontaine's status to offer them a place on the *Prosperity*, but some of the noble women knew about fashion, and a lot of them complained bitterly of having too little to do. She went in search of Julianna Nieland, who lived in one of the tents with a distant uncle of hers and whom she hadn't seen much since coming to the camp.

Johanna announced herself at the door.

"Wait, I'll get her for you," said the young man who came to see what she wanted.

He made a small bow, and Johanna could see the loyalty to the royal family written on his face.

A moment later, another man pushed aside the tent flap. He was older, dressed in a velvet coat and riding pants. Julianna's uncle was a horseman, she remembered. He gave her a suspicious look before bowing stiffly and turning back inside.

"Don't make too much useless women's gossip," he said inside the tent.

"I'm all right, uncle," Julianna replied. "I won't bother you." And she finally came to the entrance.

Julianna had always had a full figure that Johanna secretly

admired, but the young woman in drab clothing who shuffled into view was as thin as a skeleton.

"I've been unwell," she said in response to Johanna's shocked look.

Unwell and unwelcome, if her uncle's strange behaviour was anything to go by.

Now she felt sorry for not having checked up on Julianna earlier. "I need some women to come and help me with the wedding. I thought you might like to do that." She had to do her best not to cringe.

Julianna put her finger to her lips and pulled Johanna away from the tent. Her grip was both strong and seeking support in holding herself up. Johanna put her arm around Julianna's shoulder, feeling Julianna's bones through her clothing.

"I've been really sick. Ate something bad and couldn't keep anything down for days."

"I heard that it was going through the camp." Several people had been very ill. "I hope your family are all right."

"They are. My uncle says I'm blaming my aunt for bad cooking, even though I never said so and I would never say anything as ungrateful as that. He says I was faking illness, but I wouldn't even know how to fake something like this. Please, let me do something for you, because these people drive me crazy."

"Then come to the *Lady Sara* every day to help Nellie and Loesie sew. A couple of good servings of Nellie's food will sort you out."

So Julianna came to the sitting room in the *Lady Sara*'s hold. She had trouble with the stairs, and Johanna worried about what "I've been unwell" really meant. Clearly a lot more than just a simple illness for a couple of days. Nellie brought cakes and biscuits, but Julianna ate only half a biscuit.

To Johanna's plans for an official wedding, she made an effort to show enthusiasm, but the tone of her voice wasn't convincing. Moreover, she didn't like Julianna's coughing, big, heavy wet coughs.

"Please, Julianna, let me help you. If you want a medic to come, I have the name of a herb woman who is supposed to be really good."

"It's all right. I'm a lot better already." She illustrated this with a coughing fit.

If that was "a lot better", Johanna didn't want to know about worse parts. "You must come here every day, and I'll make sure that you eat enough. You have to get well again."

Julianna looked down at the thin hands she held clenched in her lap. "What does it matter? All my family are dead anyway."

"You don't know that."

"I saw my house burn. No one can survive a fire like that. No one of my parents' age anyway."

"Octavio was at the ball. You were there with him." She remembered how he'd been condescending to her while begging Father for her hand. Octavio Nieland was good friends with Ignatius Hemeldinck, she remembered.

Julianna's face tightened. "It's Father and Mother I worry about. They're not young."

"I am really sorry. I'm pretty much in the same situation. I don't know where Father is. I have no idea if he's still alive."

Julianna shook her head. "You're not in the same situation. You got out during the fire. You weren't there for what happened after the fire. Octavio . . ." She clamped her hands between her knees and shuddered visibly.

"What happened to Octavio? I saw him outside the palace that night."

"He doesn't really care about me or about any of us. He only cares about power. I should have realised that long ago. You know I used to think that he was stupid about wanting to marry you, because you weren't from a noble family?" She looked down. "Well, I'm sorry about that. I was really stupid. I didn't see that it was all about the Brouwer Company, which he wanted. I just didn't want to see how important money was for him."

Johanna's heart jumped. "*Was*? Did something happen to him?"

A tear glistened in Julianna's eye. "Something happened all right. He joined Alexandre Trebuchet. Apparently, they knew each other from when Octavio lodged with Mother's cousin in Lurezia and they were friends there."

"You *met* that man? What is he like?"

Julianna shrugged. "Just another young man. He's got a sharp face and dark brown hair, which he wears in a ponytail, not unlike my brother. He keeps saying how he saved Saardam and how good he is."

"Saved? What from?"

"Isn't it obvious? That church that got all of the king's money. I guess it's all irrelevant now, but they were not bad people. They didn't deserve to be killed in the street, to have their houses burnt and possessions stolen."

"Just the church people?" Johanna thought of several church families she knew—Nellie's family and Master Willems—and wondered if any of them had been victims. "When you saw Alexandre, did you see any evidence of magic?"

Julianna gave her a *what-do-you-take-me-for* look. "He has bands of rogues helping him silence people who disagreed with him. There were men with bears and other animals. One of them had a big cat with spots. They went around all the houses and dragged everyone out. If they didn't like you, they burned your house."

Johanna had heard a bit about those days. Apparently the survivors had been taken to the town hall, which had survived the fire, as had many stone buildings surrounding the market place. In the town hall, Alexandre had addressed them in a long and rambling speech mostly incomprehensible for people unfamiliar with Burovian.

Several people in the camp had spoken of Alexandre's orders to hand over any remaining church supporters or face death. The Saarlanders had been asked to betray their fellow kinsfolk, the people they had grown up with, their neighbours. Some people in the camp, especially the women, had spoken of how appalled they were. They were glad, they said, that the young Shepherd Carolus had made it onto the ship, even though no one was sure how he had managed that, presumably because he was mostly still known in town under his given name of Dirk Goedthart and he had been well-known in town as a well-off merchant's son until he joined the church and went to the seminary.

"If only Father had been there. He would have told Octavio exactly what he thought." Julianna's eyes brimmed with tears.

Johanna didn't know what it was like to have a brother, but she imagined not having a brother was better than having a brother who betrayed his town like this.

Julianna launched into another coughing fit.

Poor Julianna. Johanna told her to be careful and get plenty of fresh air. After making Julianna promise that she'd be back the next day, Johanna watched her climb up the stairs with all the mobility of a woman of eighty.

Johanna had to go up and close the hold door, because Julianna wasn't strong enough to do it. Rain still fell, so she went back down into the sitting room.

It was a sign of Roald's condition that he had continued to sit and read through all this, and had completely ignored any mention of his name.

Johanna dropped onto the bed and lay staring at the rough and dusty undersides of the hold covers for a while, but staring wasn't going to get anything done.

She pushed herself up and went to Roald.

"I am going to need your help." She put an arm over his shoulder.

He continued reading.

"Roald?"

He glanced at her. "This book is interesting. It says that if you keep sailing a boat around the Horn, you will find a whole other world like ours. I wonder if people live there."

"They do. That's where the eastern traders are from."

"Yes, everyone talks about them, but has anyone seen these people?"

"Some have." She believed Father and Master Deim had, or at least some of the seafaring captains.

"Then why do books like these contain no diagrams of what they look like?" He held up the book. The front cover said, *On the Travels of the Known Lands.*

"I'm not sure."

"Are they dangerous?"

"I don't know." Father talked about the eastern traders a lot, because they brought the spices that he sold. He told her that they were smart people who sailed on big square-looking ships with red sails. The ships were big enough for the men to take their entire families. Many of them lived at sea and didn't go home after each voyage. They were nimble and independent, unlike the seafaring captains of Saardam, who returned with their wares to sell, to pay their investors and to rustle the next lot of investors to outfit their next trip.

Some people suggested that the eastern traders could become dangerous if given too much freedom to sail along the coast, but she didn't want to go into that discussion now. She put her hand over the book. "Roald, look at me. I need your help."

"Oh?" His expression was startled.

"We need to hold an official wedding as soon as possible."

"But we're already married."

"I know that, but the people in the camp won't accept it until we hold the ceremony before their eyes." She now understood how much stress ceremonies placed on him and it pained her to ask him to be present at another one. "We also need to hold an official coronation ceremony."

"Oh." He gave her a blank look. "Do I have to do anything for that?"

You're the king, for crying out loud! "I want you to write a proclamation. We'll set a date and make a formal announcement."

"Oh." He looked confused. "Can't you do those things for me?"

"They won't listen to me unless we're officially married in their eyes."

"Oh."

"That's why I need you to write a proclamation that we will hold a wedding. They can all see that it's official."

"All right." And after a brief silence, he added, "She suffers from bad air."

"What on Earth are you talking about?"

"The woman who was just here. She suffers from bad air. Many people in the camp have it. It's from the cold and damp and having many people sleeping cramped together in tents."

There wasn't much that Johanna could do about that other than try to get out of this camp as soon as possible. This was summer. Conditions would get much worse in winter. People said that, in these parts, snow fell almost every year.

There was no way they could stay here for winter. She decided for herself that she would take the *Lady Sara* with whomever it could carry back to Saardam after the wedding, at the very latest.

How she would do it, she didn't know, but the people would not spend winter in this cold and damp field.

More importantly, she would not stay here where Roald had little support and where either of them might get sick at any time.

Most importantly of all, she would not stay because her bleeding was late.

JOHANNA HELPED ROALD WRITE A DECLARATION. He took a long time, but his handwriting was beautiful and he signed it with a loopy signature. Master Deim put the parchment up on the wall of the boat shed that was fast becoming the equivalent of the mayor's house. The wedding ceremony would be held on the first of the month of October. Johanna hoped that she would show the signs of being with child by then.

She went to see the Shepherd Carolus, who announced that he'd be "most delighted" to conduct the ceremony and then looked at her with misty eyes. He had a youthful face, with freckles on his cheeks and playful blond curls of hair that, no matter how much he smoothed them down, always found a way to stand up.

"Shepherd Romulus would have loved to do this," he said in a voice filled with emotion.

Johanna nodded, silently.

"They killed him. They burned the church. They stole all the clothes and food we kept stored for winter to give to people in need. Why? I don't understand."

Johanna put a hand on his shoulder. "We will go back. We will rebuild. They can try to wipe us out, but they can't kill us."

A few days later, the Baroness Viktoriya heard about the

wedding date, and announced that the grand hall would be at their disposal. Johanna reluctantly agreed to hold the ceremony there, much to the approval of the nobles.

Julianna came faithfully every day. She sat at the table in the hold and ate whatever Nellie brought. At first, Johanna had to force her, but after two days, her appetite started returning with her chattiness, which made Johanna remember why she had never liked Julianna much. Rather than get annoyed at it—a major achievement—Johanna asked Julianna to casually chat to people in the camp and listen to what they said. Julianna took to her task with enthusiasm and reported back every day.

"Everyone wants to go back to their houses," she said.

"Why do they think we're not returning?"

"Because the council says it's too dangerous. Alexandre is a strong magician. They are afraid because they have never dealt much with magic before. Some are happy to wait, but some are saying that magic or no, we should go back and drive him out. Some of the young men are prepared to fight."

Julianna mentioned a list of names, most of whom were merchants or nobles who weren't involved with the ones who made decisions in the council.

Then she worried about the two scouts she had sent. They should have been back by now, although it might be taking them longer because of the high water.

Unfortunately, Julianna said that she had been unable to dig up further information about what kind of deal with the Baron was keeping the nobles in Florisheim. But Johanna had heard some rumours while listening to the older children tag behind Roald in his frog-hunting.

A boy had said, "My father says that we can't go back until the whole of Saardam has been cleaned up, and he says Alexandre just wants to do a good job."

To which a younger boy had said, "Well, *my* father says that your father is crazy."

After which they started an *is-not—is-so—is-not* word fight, which only stopped when someone in the reeds shouted for them to be quiet. "You're scaring the frogs!"

And with the wet weather frogs were, unfortunately, everywhere.

But that little snatch of conversation got Johanna's thoughts off to an uncomfortable tangent. Because what if the nobles had *asked* Alexandre to drive out the church, and now Alexandre, and his friend the Baron, would no longer speak to the men?

Johanna and Julianna stood on the deck of the *Lady Sara*, overlooking the camp. The rain had eased somewhat and the water level had dropped a little bit.

"There are lots of young men in the camp who want to return and fight," Julianna said.

"There is little point in fighting magic with arms," Johanna said. "We need to fight magic with magic."

"But we don't have magic."

"That's why we must find a court magician."

And that meant making deals with possibly unpleasant people. Out of all the magicians she knew, Duke Lothar and Sylvan were the ones she trusted most, but she doubted they'd help her. By association, she *should* have more trust in Kylian than she did, but as yet she didn't understand all the different sides to the assassination attempt by the Duke of his half-brother Baron Uti. The strange thing was that many of the locals seemed to consider this attempt a great source of hilarity. Johanna struggled to make sense of the relationships of the Baron and his family. If Kylian was welcome at Duke Lothar's castle, did that mean that he supported the attempt to kill his father?

She had considered asking the duke to help her, but he and his son were pretty much unreachable from here. She'd asked couriers to take a letter to him, but they all refused to go into the forest.

Probably because people go missing in those woods. And ended up in that ice cellar.

Johanna desperately didn't want to get involved in the case of the ice cellar. But she needed a magician.

"We also need ships," Johanna said, pushing away uncomfortable thoughts about magic and having to rely on people she didn't trust. "I've got the *Lady Sara*, but that's not enough for everyone."

She looked up the river, still swollen from the recent rain. From here to Saardam was all downstream. They didn't need animals, although they would take them regardless, and getting to Saardam from here would probably take less than a day on the strong current.

"We can have the *Prosperity*," Julianna said. "Captain Arense supports us and the ship can carry many people."

"We're going back as soon as we can," Johanna said. "Don't tell anyone, just try to gauge who would come if we gave them the word." If she had sorted the magician problem.

"When?"

"As soon as possible after the wedding." Maybe even before. Maybe she needed to keep up the illusion that there was to be a wedding and that nothing would happen before that time, in order not to raise suspicion from the nobles or the Baron, or anyone else. Because the more she thought about it, the more she was convinced that she didn't want to hold her wedding in that gloomy castle, attended by the Baron's guests and family: Baroness Viktoriya the fat spider in her web, and Kylian the Necromancer.

The next morning, she woke up to find her nightshirt drenched with blood.

CHAPTER 10

THE BLEEDING came with strong cramps, and Johanna stayed in the cabin for a day. Master Deim and Julianna came to see her because they were worried. At their subtle hints that she was with child, she could only laugh. If only. She didn't understand why this happened. She *thought* they did everything right.

Loesie was not helpful when she said, "Didn't happen for Annette's ma until she'd been married three years. Never happened to her since. They got Annette, which must have been a mistake, because she was much too pretty for the farm."

Annette was Loesie's neighbour. Loesie's mother, of course, had been with child after a dalliance with a foreign visitor.

There *were* women who never had children, but Johanna was determined not to have that happen to her.

"I'm going into town," she said to Nellie the next morning.

"Do you want me to come, mistress Johanna?" She and Loesie were peeling and cutting apples for the applesauce that Roald liked so much.

"It might be a good idea, but I'm visiting a herb woman who is said to have magic, so it might be better if Loesie came."

Loesie gave her a sharp look. "Don't want to have anything to do with magic. Nothing good ever came from it."

"We're just going to visit this woman. You don't need to say anything. I want you there because you are the only one who could tell if she's using magic. And I also want you to see what the wood says about who visited the house and what was said in any of the rooms, wherever we get the chance."

Loesie grumbled. "There is never anything 'just' about magic."

"I'm going to ask her for herbs."

Loesie gave her a suspicious look. Seen from this angle, her father's foreign blood became obvious. People in eastern Estland, Gelre and Burovia tended to be darker and taller than the Saarlanders. Loesie was not soft, friendly and feminine. She was lanky and all angles with deep-set, intense eyes. "We can just as well ask for herbs at the markets."

"This woman is supposed to be very good."

"This is not still about the bleeding, right?"

Nellie cut in, about to start peeling another apple. "Loesie, it is really important that the mistress has a child soon."

"Bah, children are annoying and too much trouble." Loesie threw a hand full of apple pieces in the pan and took off her apron. "But I'll come, because if I don't, she will get us into even more trouble." She went into the cabin.

Nellie's gaze followed her, and her mouth twitched. Not happy, clearly. Maybe she considered it her duty to come with Johanna.

Johanna said, "Do keep an eye on Roald so that he doesn't go wandering off too far."

"Yes, mistress. Certainly." Still not happy by the tone of her voice.

Come to think of it, Nellie had been pretty unhappy the last few days, and Johanna couldn't quite work out why. Compared to when they were with the bandits, the ship was comfortable, and Nellie even had her own bed. There was enough to eat and Nellie's status had vastly improved.

She would worry about her family, but then again, everyone did.

Not too much later, Johanna and Loesie walked down the rickety jetty to the riverbank. The water level had fallen a bit, but the water was still only an arm's length under the walkway.

The guards who stood there gave friendly nods, but didn't ask if they should come. Roald was still on board, and they didn't care about her.

Johanna and Loesie walked quickly along the path. Because it was so wet, people had made tracks through the tall grass higher on the riverbank to avoid muddy areas. Those tracks were narrow and they had to walk behind each other. The weather was muggy, and building clouds on the horizon heralded more thunderstorms. Would the rains ever stop?

The track joined the main road in the curve of the river, and when she could finally walk next to Loesie, Johanna wasn't sure what to say. Loesie had been distant since the demon had been driven out of her, saying about the incident only that she "didn't remember much", but never quite meeting Johanna's eyes when she said this.

Her attempts to deny magic and turn into an obedient domestic maid would be funny if Johanna didn't expect that there was a more sinister reason behind them, and she had no idea how to find out what that reason was.

"I'm going to need your help, Loesie," she said after a long and uncomfortable silence.

"I'm already helping."

"Yes, and thank you for that. I love your lace. It's really pretty." They walked another distance before she added, "But it's help of a different kind I'll need."

Loesie raised her eyebrows.

"Alexandre Trebuchet who rules Saardam is a fire magician. People from the camp want to go back there and drive him out. Some of them are offering to fight, but we can't get rid of Alexandre with an army. We need magicians. My magic is weak and insignificant. You are the only other person in the camp with any magic. I would like you to go to the Magician's Guild here in Florisheim to receive training so that you can be our court magician."

"Didn't I tell you that nothing good ever comes from magic?"

"You did, but in this case the bad things have already happened. We need to fix them."

"You don't understand at all."

"Then explain it to me so that I can help you."

"I do not want to be helped. We should not be using magic."

"But Alexandre is using magic! We have no hope of defeating him with an army, no matter how many men we get and how good they are." Johanna tried to push down her frustration. Getting angry wouldn't achieve anything. "At least tell me why."

Loesie pressed her mouth into a thin line. Her gaze shifted to somewhere over Johanna's shoulder on the opposite riverbank. Johanna turned to look, but saw nothing that caught her attention.

"Please, Loesie. I don't want to hire a foreign magician and I will have to if you don't do it. We don't know who we can trust."

"You don't want to go hiring magicians at all."

"No, I don't." At least they could agree on that.

"Not me, and no one else." Loesie met Johanna's eyes with that intense look. She let a long silence lapse. Johanna thought she wasn't going to say anything, but then she added, "Someone or *something* has messed with the magic lines. I can feel it in my bones, and everyone who's got more magic than me would feel it even more."

"Duke Lothar was talking about magic lines, right?" She thought of the tunnels made from tortured trees and then remembered that Loesie would not have seen them because she'd still been possessed. Johanna had felt no desire to visit that place after the exorcism was done, and Loesie would not have had the strength to do so had she wished to see it.

"Magic lines are everywhere. There is a strong one under most of the Saar River. Sometimes the willows grow so stunted that you can't even find branches to cut for making baskets. The horses that try to swim across the river grow webbed feet and they turn into water horses. And the grazing cows get so mad from eating the grass that they dance through the meadow."

Johanna nodded, a shiver running over her back. She had seen cows do that, especially in spring when they first came outside. Horses, too, although she wasn't too sure about the webbed feet.

"All those magic lines join up and split again, like a giant . . . fishing net under the ground. Sometimes they come to the surface. That's where you get trouble. Like across the river from my granpa's farm . . ." For a moment her eyes misted over. "Like the ghosts, and the funny trees and water horses, and all the evil magics, like bear magic."

"Necromancers?"

Loesie nodded, clamping her arms around herself. "That's what the rumour says anyway. I think ghosts happen because people die while having unfinished business, I don't think magicians have anything to do with it. But by us using the magic, more of the lines come up, like a tailor unravelling a thread. Once a thread is up, you can't put it back into the ground. We shouldn't be using magic."

"That's all very well for you to say, but should we just sit like ducks and let magicians rule us and kill all of us? Shouldn't we learn about magic so that we can defend ourselves, or just save ourselves?"

That earned her another suspicious look.

"Loesie, please. I have no one else that I can trust."

"I won't do it, and you shouldn't be trusting me anyway. You're a nice, pretty, innocent girl, like Annette. She's dead now, and it's my fault. I'll do your washing and your sewing until you have better people to do it. But do not ask me to do magic for you, because you have no idea what you're asking."

"I'm not innocent."

"Yes, you are."

"Then why won't you tell me what is going on? Why did you even wait so long to tell me this?" She spread her hands in frustration.

Loesie whirled around. "Because I don't want you to die as well!" Her eyes were wild and there was more colour in her cheeks than Johanna had ever seen. "And you deserve better than that. Annette deserved better. It all happened because of me, and because of evil magic. I don't know how many times I have to say this: if you want herbs, buy herbs. Don't meddle with magic. Don't even think about that Magician's Guild or whatever. Don't write to the duke for magic help. Don't ask his son to help us. Don't ask the Baron, or his son or anyone else. You don't need magic to have a child. You need to go back and wait until it's your turn. I'm not going to come to this magic woman's place and you shouldn't be going either." She stopped walking and crossed her arms over her chest.

Johanna glared at her and she glared back.

"So that's it? You don't care about our safety?"

"Have you listened to anything I said? About magic, about *my fault*?"

"I'm going to see this woman," she said, slowly, while looking into Loesie's eyes. "I understand that it could be dangerous. I understand that she is not 'just' a herb woman. But magic is happening whether we like it or not, and I can't see how not using it is going help us. In fact, I think it's going to be dangerous for us, because there is no place where we can hide where there is no magic. So you can show me that you care and help me deal with this magic, or you can go back to your sewing."

Loesie said nothing.

Johanna took a few steps in the direction of the town and looked over her shoulder. Loesie hadn't moved. Another few steps. She still hadn't moved.

Oh well, it was not to be helped.

Johanna continued towards the town without looking back.

THE HERB WOMAN'S house was on the other side of the markets, an old house that was so narrow that its façade had room only for a single door and one window. The walls had once been painted black, but much of the paint had flaked off, showing the stone underneath. This was a pretty common state of affairs for the houses in the town, and it was a very unremarkable house. So unremarkable, in fact, that it would be easy not to notice it at all. That was until you got close and saw the line of animal skulls and teeth on the windowsill. There were bird skulls with the beaks still attached, rabbit skulls, deer skulls with antlers, and skulls of larger animals. There was also, on a little shelf halfway across the window, a line of blackened triangular teeth. Some were smooth, some had serrated edges. Some of them were as long as her thumb. She wondered what kind of animal those teeth belonged to. Even the teeth on the bear skull were smaller.

The room on the other side of the window was too dark to see more than a few shapes inside. A couch and a formal sitting room chair, she thought.

The place felt a bit creepy, she had to admit. Maybe that was only because of all the warnings from Master Deim and Loesie. After all, anyone who studied the ways of nature would have skulls and bones from animals, and a herb woman studied nature, right?

Johanna put her hand on the wooden door. It showed her a woman going into the house carrying a child with a snotty nose. Another image showed an old man entering, leaning heavily on a walking stick.

See? Nothing to worry about. Just people going to see Magda with illnesses.

Johanna lifted the knocker in the shape of a deer skull and let the heavy metal thing fall on the wood. It made a heavy *thunk* that echoed in the hollow space beyond.

For a long time, nothing happened. Johanna was about to turn away. Perhaps the herb woman had gone out, but then there was a sound of shuffling footsteps behind the door.

A bolt was drawn back and the door opened, revealing a bent figure in the doorway, dressed in a grey cloak with a woollen scarf around her neck.

To Johanna's surprise, the face of the woman inside the shadow of the hood wasn't old at all. It was just badly stained with dark wine-red blotches, which were slightly raised, making the skin look like a giant lumpy strawberry. Johanna had seen people with these patches before, but never in such a prominent way. Her lumpy red skin surrounded one eye, covered her cheek down to the corner of her mouth, and it was also on the wrist and part of the hand that stuck out from underneath her cloak.

"Are you Magda?"

The woman replied in the local dialect, the tone not particularly friendly. Hilda had warned her about that.

"I'm sorry, I'm from Saarland. I don't speak your language. I was told to come here by Master Deim's sister-in-law Hilda."

"Ah. Hilda. Come," she said in a heavy accent.

Johanna went into the corridor, and Magda shut the door behind them, pushing the bolt back. It got very dark in the corridor, with just a faint glow of light coming in from a door that stood ajar at the end. Johanna presumed that this was the sitting room.

Magda grabbed her arm when she walked past and pulled her close. Her long nails dug into the soft skin on the underside of Johanna's upper arm. "Ow. There is no need to—"

"I know who you are. I can smell scent of betrayer on you."

Betrayer? "Sorry, I don't know what you're talking about." Her heart thudded like crazy. "I haven't spoken to anyone in town." Did she mean Duke Lothar, or the Baroness or Sylvan or Kylian?

"You ignorant girl. Don't think I don't know that you spy on me."

"Please, I'm not here for anyone except myself," Johanna said. "I . . ." She was going to say *need your help*, but after that exchange wasn't sure that what she'd be getting would qualify as "help" and even less whether she'd need it. "Hilda said that you were good with herbs."

Magda let go of her arm with a snort, muttering something in her dialect. The look in her eyes was pure venom.

"Hmph." She stepped back and regarded Johanna with her red-blotched face. "Herbs, huh?"

"Yes. For making tea. Raspberry leaves, and stinging nettles."

"Herbs," she repeated, her face still suspicious. "Well then, let's talk about herbs."

Johanna followed her down a dark corridor where their footsteps were muffled by a series of bearskins on the floor, the fur all matted and dirty. Dusty tapestries on the walls depicted a family tree, a hunting scene and a castle in the forest which could have been Duke Lothar's, but it was too dark to see. They came out in a dark room with a single window at the back of the house. It looked out over the house in the next street, across a narrow alley.

The light was so dim in the room that even in daylight it was hard to see. The ceiling and the floorboards and threadbare carpet were all dark. Around the walls were shelves to the ceiling filled with jars and pots. Each contained some powder, leaves or various dried items or items preserved in fluid. The air in the room smelled stale and dirty, with a tang of dried leaves and a waft of something dead.

The shelves left just enough room for a round table and a couple of chairs, all very well-worn and dusty.

At Magda's invitation, she squeezed between the shelves and the chairs.

Magda sat opposite Johanna with her back to the window. She slowly lowered the hood of her cloak. Her red-rimmed eye was blue, but her other eye was all white, like Loesie's had been when she was struck by magic. The wine red stain extended across her face, her neck and chest. Likely it covered all of her shoulder and left arm as well.

Johanna didn't know where to look. Staring would be impolite, but purposely looking away would be impolite, too.

When sitting down, Johanna made the mistake of touching the table. A stream of images went through her. The people who had sat at this table were mostly men, and they weren't sick. They came to talk. They were monks and priests and men in plain clothes. Men in dark clothes with long beards. Johanna withdrew her hand from the table, her heart thudding.

Magda was smiling at her. "Ah. I see. There is a pitiful amount of magic in you. Well, let's talk, then. About *herbs*."

Johanna took a calming breath. "I've been with my husband for over three months. I am still not with child."

"Three months, huh?"

"I've lain with my husband every day. I thought for a while that it worked, but my bleeding started yesterday. It's very important that I have a child as soon as possible. There are . . . people who don't accept our marriage unless there is a child and they want to do everything they can to prevent that from happening."

It seemed so long ago that she'd been adamant that she didn't want to get married, but now she could see why Father had said that society wouldn't accept her. Once the marriage was declared invalid, she would never marry again, and without a business to run—was there even anything left in Saardam?—she would have no income. "It's really important. You have to understand."

"Oh, I understand important. Important means you want something and you believe someone can give it to you."

"Well, I . . ."

Magda pointed a red-skinned finger at her. "Important means that you believe you should get something. But forget that some things are not ours to give."

"I know that. I just thought you would have some herbs that might help."

"Hmm. I could give you some herbs for tea, yes." Magda rose and started rummaging on the shelves. She took off a large jar and then another one. Then she unfolded a triangular paper bag from a drawer and put a scoop full of dried leaves in each.

While this was happening, Johanna looked around the room. There was a stone tile leaning against the wall with writing on it in a language Johanna didn't recognise. There was also a carving depicting a head of some sort of creature.

"Here are herbs," Magda said, pushing the folded bag across the table to Johanna. "Make tea. Drink every morning and every evening."

"Thank you."

And because there seemed nothing else to say, Johanna gathered up the paper bag and made to get up. To be honest, she felt keen to get out of here.

"That's all?"

"What do you mean?"

Magda's form was backlit by the window. "Is that all you come to talk about? Herbs?"

"Well, I . . . ." She had intended to ask about the Magician's Guild and getting a court magician, but in between Loesie's strange behaviour and Master Deim's warning, she was not so sure anymore. If there was one true thing about Loesie's words, it was that Johanna really knew nothing about magic and she didn't know what she was playing with.

"Well . . . what if it doesn't work, the tea?"

Magda gave Johanna a sharp look. "First you ask for herbs. Then you say herbs don't work?"

"I'm sorry, I—"

"Herb medicine have two parts: one is the herb, two is the belief that it will work. No belief, no work."

Johanna frowned.

"If you want to know if you're doing it right with your man, then I can't help. I know nothing about being with a man. Do you see a man here? Do you think I can get man ugly like this?" She angled her face to the light so that the red lumpy skin was more visible.

"I never said—"

"No, but you *think* and I can see what you think because I seen it all my life. I seen people not know where to look."

Johanna decided to plunge in anyway. She hadn't come here only to chicken out again. Saardam was facing hard issues, and there weren't going to be easy solutions. "I was wondering if my inability to get with child could have a magical cause because I'm pretty sure we're doing everything right."

"Ha! Magic! You know nothing about magic." An odd, happy, vindicated tone crept into her voice.

"That's why I'm here: to ask you."

"Magic comes with life and nature. Magic is all around. You people talk about *believing* in magic, but it is not something you can *believe* in. Magic is still going to be there, even if you don't *believe*. Because magic is real." Magda waved a finger in front of Johanna's face. "You people, people from Church, they just scared. Church says they can't use magic and magic people are bad. Bah. But yes, magic is cause of not being with child, because magic is cause of *everything*. Magic is why we alive."

"Then . . . could you use magic to solve it? I understand it will cost more."

Magda laughed, not a pleasant sound. "You understand nothing, little queen. You do not understand at all." She got up from her seat. She squeezed past Loesie and went to a cupboard along the wall. When she opened the door, Johanna could see rows of jars of substances: bright yellow powder, rust red powder, white things that looked like little twigs, curly things that looked like lizard tails, a jar full of blue and grey spotted eggs, another full of frog skulls and many other strange things.

She took out a stone basin on a stand, an earthenware pot with a lid and a blue glass bottle with a clear liquid sloshing inside.

She placed the basin in the middle of the table, unstoppered the bottle and poured in a small measure of fluid. It looked like water, but spread a sharp scent through the room that made Johanna feel dizzy, like strong spirits. Then she took the lid off the pot and sprinkled some of its contents, a fine white powder, in the water. Whatever the fine powder was, it made the fluid bubble and smoke.

Magda leaned over the basin and breathed the vapour. She had closed her eyes. The lumpy red skin even covered her eyelid.

For a while, nothing happened. Johanna glanced over her shoulder at the door. It was still open, in case she wanted to get out quickly.

Then Magda opened her eyes. Both of them had gone white.

Magda started speaking. "Give me your hand, so I can read your magic lines." Her voice sounded rough and intense, and made a chill run down Johanna's back.

Johanna hesitated. If there was some dark magic to keep her from becoming with child, she wanted to know about it. That was why she had come here.

She held out her hand.

Magda gasped. The white mist fled her eyes. "Who is your master?"

"I have no master. I've met Duke Lothar and I watched while he exorcised a demon from my friend. Maybe you can feel that—"

"You disturb the magic lines. Who is your master?" Her voice was more intense now.

"I have no idea what you mean. I'm sorry."

"You ignorant people. Then what is your bloodline?"

"My mother came from the Aroden court." She didn't think there were any strong magicians in that family. Just some people who, like her, could read things in wind or wood. She wasn't even sure that her mother could do this.

Magda said nothing for a while, breathing the fumes from the basin until her eyes went white again. "I feel, I feel . . . could be the betrayer's presence. Could be, could be. Don't know why it would be so strong in you. Maybe you care for the betrayer, huh?"

"I'm afraid I have no idea who you're talking about."

"The one with the two faces." The white eyes met Johanna's, causing a chill to run over her back.

"Who is this person? Do I need to be careful of him? Is it someone in the camp?"

"Ha. You do not know anything."

"I don't. Tell me who this person is."

"The mention of the name would kill me. Magic so strong that none of us can fight it. That's what happens when you disturb magic lines. When you dig up magic from soil where it should never be disturbed."

That was exactly what Loesie had been talking about. "How have people disturbed the magic lines?"

"They dug it out of the soil."

"Where?"

"You do not want to know. It is an evil place for innocent girls. It is no good talking about it because we cannot do anything about it. Even we are powerless."

We? Wait— "Are you from the Magician's Guild?" That would make an awful lot of sense, including the visitors in dark clothes she had seen sitting at this table.

Magda hissed, which Johanna took as an admission. She said nothing in reply, but didn't deny connections with the Magician's Guild either.

"Please, we need your help. The king needs a court magician."

Magda laughed, not a pretty sound. "The king needs a court magician as much as he needs a jester. A court magician *is* a jester. We do not perform *tricks*." She held up an ugly, red-skinned finger.

"Then whatever you want to call it. We need help."

"Every person in this world needs help."

"I would like you to help us."

Magda was silent for a long time and after a while Johanna

feared that she wasn't going to respond at all. She was constantly moving her hands over the bowl.

Johanna stared at those hands, wondering what Magda was doing, wondering if it would be impolite or dangerous to interrupt her and ask her more forcefully. She just wanted an answer. Yes or no, a reply she could act on.

But now something was happening in the bowl. The trails of vapour thickened around Magda's fingers and dripped off back into the basin, forming shapes. Misty forms coalesced into buildings and boats, and people. Her hands were weaving a town out of mist. Was that Saardam? If so, what was that strange ship in the harbour? It was much bigger than any of the local ships, even the seafaring ones, and two really thick masts.

The white vapour had added a building to the town with a dome that towered over the surrounding houses. That had to be either the re-built palace or a new church. The Church of the Triune didn't go for splendour, so it was either the palace or . . . a place of worship for the Belaman Church. She shivered. "Is that mist showing me the future?"

"What mist?" Magda withdrew her hands.

The vapour dissipated and the city of mist fell back into the basin. Johanna stared at the mirror-like surface of the fluid. Not a ripple.

"You did not see any mist," Magda said.

"Um, I'm not sure."

"When people ask, you saw no mist. You saw no buildings and you saw no ships."

"All right, yes."

"I showed this because you will understand danger. Now go and don't play with magic ever again."

"Sure." Johanna rose, taking the paper bag with dried leaves off the table. "Thank you for the leaves. I'm . . . I'll make the tea as soon as I get back." She couldn't think. It was as if that mist had gone straight into her head. Magda rested her hands on the table, the fingers interlaced, but Johanna swore she could still see the fingers weaving the mist over the basin.

She saw the large ship in the harbour, and such a panic took hold of her that she couldn't breathe.

This was the future or something that was happening right now. With all her mind, she wanted to be back home, to look for Father, to help Roald take up his rightful position, to save the town from whatever evil had come in that ship. Loesie said that the magic lines had been disturbed. That ship was the disturbance. She and the others were wasting her time here. They were needed at home.

Johanna stumbled from the room. Magda said something, but the sound of her voice became lost in the roaring of blood in her ears. She walked through the dark corridor, tripping over one of the bearskin mats and into the street.

When she was at the porch, she realised what Magda had said: "You will have two children."

CHAPTER 11

I T WAS NOT until Johanna was in the market square that
the fog lifted from her mind and she could think clearly and
tease out the things that Magda had told her. Most of it was
more or less what Loesie had said: something disturbed magic
lines and no one is powerful enough to fix it. But someone had
done this while digging. And there was a strange ship in the
harbour in Saardam, possibly belonging to Alexandre.

That was more information than she'd had before, but it was
still very incomplete.

The sky was darker than it had been when she came in, but
right now, only a steady drizzle fell from the solid layer of clouds,
whipped up by squalls of wind that chased the low-hanging
clouds over the jumble of slate-covered roofs.

The heavy clouds promised more rain, and she had better
hurry up if she wanted to stay dry.

She was about halfway along the riverbank when the clouds
started disgorging their contents. Big fat drops fell. Johanna ran
close to whatever little shelter the meagre bushes along the path
offered, but quite a few drops still fell on her scarf. Wet spots
were starting to seep through.

Then the rain struck in all earnest. The wind whipped up. So
much water fell down from the sky that it was hard to see.
Within a few paces she was soaked through.

On this part of the path from the outskirts of town to the camp there was no shelter at all. Sheets of rain lashed the trees.

Shards of mist rose from the river and drifted over the field. They *moved*.

Johanna stopped. She stood staring at the river, with the rain pelting down and water dripping from her hair. The water churned like it was boiling.

Johanna retreated.

Out of the mist rose an animal: a white-winged swan that glided over the water.

Then another one.

Both birds looked real and yet they did not. Their feathers were too bright, their beaks too orange.

Swans built their nests in the reed beds on the riverbank and she would have noticed their nest when coming this way. Swans were usually very defensive of those nests. There would have been cygnets, by now adult-sized but still with their grey feathers, aggressively defended by both parents. She knew a boy who got bitten by a swan so badly that his pants needed mending.

As she watched, both birds took to the air with a grace she had never seen from birds this large. She had only ever seen swans run over the water before they flew. It usually happened with much splashing and flapping of wings.

There were no ripples on the water. Already, both birds had vanished from sight.

But now something else appeared out of the mist: a figure of a woman, dressed in a light-coloured cloak with a hood covering her head. She was floating towards the shore, appearing to walk over the water.

Before she reached the riverbank, the ghostly figure veered to the left and floated in the direction of the camp.

Johanna felt cold.

If this was the ghost of Celine again, she could only imagine the mayhem and panic that would cause in the camp.

She quickened her pace and ran through the mud. The ghost had disappeared between the reeds, which had combed deposits of grass and twigs out of the water.

Was Johanna imagining things or had the river level risen a lot since she'd come here on the way into town?

A scream echoed over the water, a woman or a child.

Johanna ran, but that wasn't easy in the sodden clothes. Her muscles were stiff with the cold and the rain had made the path muddy and slippery.

In amongst the reeds stood some boys. Against the advice of the adults, they had gone to play by the river, and one of them was pointing in the direction of the water.

Another boy picked up a stone and threw it at the ghost. The projectile fell far short. He picked up another stone.

"No, don't!" His friend held his arm back.

"Why? It's a ghost."

"Don't you see? It's Princess Celine!"

The boy let his arm sink, staring open-mouthed at the ghost.

One of the younger boys started to cry.

The woman turned and she met Johanna's eyes squarely. It was indeed the same apparition she had seen in the library. Johanna wanted to run, but a strange fascination kept her standing on the riverbank. She wanted to run and . . . what? No one would help her. No one even believed that this ghost existed, that it recognised her.

There was a voice behind her. "Don't get close to that one. That's not a normal ghost."

Loesie stood higher up the riverbank, her arms crossed over her chest and her hair whipped up by the wind.

"That's the witch!" a boy yelled, pointing at Loesie.

"Shoo with you," Loesie called. "Run to your mothers. This is no sight for little boys."

"Leave Celine alone. She's our princess."

Johanna said in a kinder voice, "This isn't Celine, it's an apparition. A ghost. It could be dangerous. Please do as the lady says."

One of the oldest boys said, "What do you know? That's a witch, not a lady, and you're not even the real queen anyway. My father says so." He was at that age where boys are tall and gangly, all angles and awkwardness, with a mop of unruly blond hair. He looked like a ragamuffin, but the shirt he had gotten covered in mud was well-made. This was no ship's boy.

A younger, soft-faced boy said, "Is that why she's all white? Because she's a ghost?"

Johanna said, "Yes, and also why she won't answer your questions."

The older boy said again, "She can't be a ghost, because she already answered our questions. She says she's the real princess and you and the Idiot King can't take her place."

Another boy added, in a quiet voice, "My mother says ghosts don't exist anyway and they're all figments of the imagination of witches to scare us."

Johanna wondered where he had learned such big words.

They descended into an argument, their shrill voices echoing over the water.

The blond boy gestured at the apparition, which had retreated a bit from the riverbank. "If she's not a ghost, what do you think that is, then? Isn't she walking on the water?"

"Yes," the shy boy said.

"Can you walk over water?"

"No, but she's a princess. Maybe she can."

"The king can't walk on water."

"How do you know?"

"Oh, come on, stop being silly. People can't walk on water. Ghosts can float wherever they please."

"Oh, look!" A little boy pointed over the water.

The ghostly woman was now coming towards the riverbank, her eyes burning with anger.

Johanna pushed the younger boys up the river bank. "Please listen to us and go to your mothers. It's not safe here."

The boys moved a bit up the riverbank, but stopped there to watch.

The ghost kept coming for Johanna. The closer she came, the more the flesh of her face sagged. The folds and canyons in the skin deepened, the skin pitted and scarred. She no longer looked like Celine, but like a skull with two gaping holes from which green light radiated.

Behind her, the boys screamed and ran, but Johanna stood

rooted to the ground. Her knees felt like they would collapse on her if she took a single step.

"There you are again," the raspy voice said. "You usurper. You common girl. Let you be cursed!" She pointed at Johanna with a discoloured, bony hand, uttering guttural sounds that resembled no spoken words. Green light flashed along the fingers, dripping off as if the skin itself turned liquid. Strands of silver-green coalesced into a giant spider web.

Johanna ducked. She landed on her knees in the tall grass with a loud *splosh*. Cold water seeped through her dress.

Loesie retreated against the trunk of a sapling. She broke off a twig at her back and waved it before her.

"I will get you, little queen." The ghost laughed, a wheezy sound that made a chill crawl over Johanna's back. The form of her was still changing. She discarded the grey cloak and the pale yellow dress. The skin underneath was lumpy and scarred. Her legs had turned into sticks. Buds sprouted from her waist, growing into long and thin legs with hair along the sides. The head grew two big fangs. The body inflated until it was fat and round, like that of a spider, but many times bigger.

A spider that was throwing out its sticky threads to reel in its victims.

Loesie lashed out at the web. The willow twigs went straight through the threads without leaving a mark but the twig ignited in Loesie's hand. Threads of spider silk wrapped around Loesie's chest, pinning her arms to her sides.

"Loesie, no!"

Johanna stumbled to her feet, but no matter how much she tried to grab the strands that held Loesie, her hands kept going through the material as if the threads weren't there.

Loesie's eyes had gone white again, rolled back into her head. Her back was rigid like a plank of wood.

Johanna called out, "Help! Help me!"

But the boys had run, and the camp was too far away for anyone to hear.

Then without warning, the spider-ghost vanished. The web retreated. Loesie dropped into the grass causing Johanna to fall on top of her.

Oof.

Johanna lay there for a while, dazed, while the trails of mist were reabsorbed back into the water.

"Loesie?"

Loesie's eyes had returned to normal. She wiped her face.

"Loesie, are you all right? Do you know why it disappeared suddenly?"

"That was no common magic." Loesie's voice sounded hoarse. "That was no proper ghost."

"Did it leave because of something you did?"

Loesie laughed. "Like I wave a willow twig and all the evil in the world flees from my sight? Wouldn't that be handy?" She coughed.

They sat silently in the grass while a steady drizzle came down. Water was seeping into the back of Johanna's dress.

"Loesie, can you see now that I need a magician to help men, and I'm asking you to be that magician?"

Loesie's expression closed. "Can't you see that magic is no good, and you don't want to meddle with it?"

"Please. I don't have anyone else I can trust. Even if you just take the position until we can find someone else."

"I'm no magician. I'm struck mad by magic. And you shouldn't be trusting me. That's the last I'll say about it."

Johanna didn't understand it. For years, Loesie had come to the markets flaunting her magic. Loesie's magic ran much deeper than the little tricks she used to scare off little boys. She had never been one to hide it, talking about the warnings against magic by the church as *They don't know what they're talking about* and *Magic is not something you can stop. It's there or it isn't, no matter what the gibbering priests say.*

Johanna used to talk with her about that, because the preachings of Shepherd Romulus about magic didn't sit well with her, either. Now it seemed like Loesie had completely closed to magic. What had changed her mind?

Surely it wouldn't really be about magic lines and increasing magic, because she didn't believe that for one bit.

She helped Loesie up and the two of them continued along the riverbank, Loesie moving like an old woman.

CHAPTER 12

THE STORY that the boys had seen princess Celine went around the camp like wildfire.

By the end of that afternoon, a group of people, mainly women, had gathered at the spot in the reeds where the boys had seen Celine, and they stood on the bank, staring over the water. A steady drizzle of rain fell from the sky, but that didn't seem to bother them.

At first, Johanna had tried to explain that what the boys had seen was an evil construct of magic, but although the women listened politely, none of them said anything or asked any questions, and none of them went back to the camp.

Johanna looked around that circle of tired-looking, pale faces and empty eyes, wet and bedraggled clothes that had seen better days. A shiver came over her. No one had seen the green light coming from the skull-like eyes. No one had seen the spider. No one had seen how it had grabbed hold of Loesie and turned her rigid. And Johanna didn't know how to alert people to the danger. Most people tolerated Loesie while she behaved normally, but Johanna had heard some rumours about her that indicated that people knew very well who she was.

Waiting and doing nothing had turned these people numb. Or so she hoped, because the empty look in their eyes reminded her uncomfortably of Loesie's expression when she had first met Loesie in the market, when Loesie had been possessed.

What did it even look like when a demon entered a person's body?

Or was it something in the air? Magic lines coming to the surface? Where did this magic even come from?

Johanna went back and watched the group from the deck of the *Lady Sara*, with frustration growing inside her.

"What has gotten into these people?" she said to Nellie who had come out of the cabin. "They never wanted to have anything to do with magic before." They were mainly women and children, but also some younger men, staring at the water with dreamy expressions in their eyes. Occasionally one would point and the others would squint into the mist. A woman folded her hands as if in prayer.

Nellie said, "I've never seen these people inside the Church of the Triune."

"No, there is only one church they follow: that of money."

"You shouldn't say things like that, mistress Johanna. These people have lost everything. Their safe houses, their servants, their nice furniture, their beautiful clothes. They don't know how to look after themselves. They're looking for guidance."

"And they're getting that from a ghost that's a spider in disguise?" Johanna spread her hands. "Sometimes I really can't believe how dumb people are, even those who are supposed to know better."

"The people are desperate. They do desperate things."

"Nellie, I love you and you're a much better woman than I am, but sometimes I wish you could just believe that sometimes people do things for stupid reasons. Or evil reasons, or selfish reasons."

"I'd rather be accused of being too good than being too selfish and inconsiderate. Anyway, I came to look for you because we need to take some measurements for your wedding dress."

Johanna followed Nellie into the cabin.

It turned out that Nellie had been able to get some nice fabric from a seller at the markets. She got it for a good price because, according to the seller, no one was sure what to do with the fabric. It was quite stiff but of rough weave, like linen. Nellie showed it to her just outside the door to the captain's cabin, because *it's too dark in there to see it properly*. Johanna ran her hand over the fabric. It was rough and well-made at the same time, if that was possible, and it made her think of the exotic markets she had visited on her trip to Lurezia with Father. Those fabrics spoke of strange lands where the sun rode high in the sky and where the land was covered in sand dunes as far as the eye could see. It was rather odd that something as exotic as this had been cheap, and they might discover that there was something wrong with it, but what could be wrong with a piece of fabric?

There was one problem: it was red.

"Then we shall have to make red lace," Nellie said.

Judging by the pins and cushion on the table, she had already started the tedious work of making lace.

"Oh no, that's Loesie's," she said when she noticed Johanna looking at the work.

"It's nice."

"Yes, she is getting much better, and making a lot of effort to learn, too."

That was Loesie these days: doing everything to prove that she was just a normal, non-magical farm girl so that she could go on resisting Johanna's pleas to learn about magic and be Roald's court magician.

Loesie herself was on the deck hanging out the washing. As if she felt Johanna looking at her, she turned her head so that their eyes met through the little round window.

Nellie had managed to collect a gathering of sewing things, for which Loesie had made a basket. She bustled about with measuring tape, taking measurements across Johanna's back both lengthwise and sideways. She measured around Johanna's waist. "We shall leave a spare fold of fabric here that we can take out in case you need it."

Yes, yes, she got the hint.

"Nellie, do you know what is going on with Loesie?"

"Going on? Nothing. Since we left that horrible house of the

Duke's she has been extremely helpful and kind. I can see her turn into a very useful servant."

But that was just the problem. Johanna didn't *need* another useful servant, and *useful servant* had not ever been words anyone would use to describe Loesie.

"Well, I guess you never knew Loesie before the . . . accident."

"I guess not, but I'd say that she's finally seen sense and quit that childish teasing and making fun of boys." Nellie's voice was prim. "Is it wrong to teach her sewing?"

"No, not at all."

"I just thought I'd teach her to be useful."

"You're doing fine, Nellie. I'm sure the dress will be beautiful."

After some talk about arrangements for clothing for Roald, because *What he wears is completely unsuitable for a king. No wonder people don't take him seriously*, Johanna left Nellie to continue with her work.

To be honest, she didn't really want to have an official wedding; she wanted to return to Saardam. She wanted to know what was going on there. And she was getting quite worried about those young men who had taken Master Deim's dinghy and had still not returned, and she had become even more worried with Loesie's explanation, which had been confirmed by Magda: magic was leaking out of the ground. Loesie said that the Saar River had always been rich in magic and she wondered if, since water came out of the ground, magic could come up with the water. Magda said someone had been digging.

Why would anyone dig for magic? Or if they weren't digging for magic, what would they dig for? What would they do about the magic now that they'd found it?

A strange thought came to her: *use it*. Use the magic to defeat all their enemies.

If you couldn't fight magic without invoking more magic, then wasn't the next logical step to use that magic?

Johanna slid open the hold cover and descended into the darkness and its perpetual smell of dust.

Roald sat writing over the tiny desk, his silhouette gilded by the light. It didn't look like he had moved since she left him here in the morning.

Johanna took off her wet cloak and hung it on the hook under the stairs.

Roald didn't even glance aside, so she went up and looked over his shoulder at the book he was reading.

On Magickal Creatures Of The High Lands, The Sea And Orient, one of the books she had borrowed from Brother Reginald.

The page showed a couple of illustrations of huge lizards with wings and strange, snake-like beings that devoured ships. "What strange creatures."

"They're sea dragons and land dragons," Roald said. "It says here that dragon magic is the highest form of magic and rules all others."

Johanna studied the scaled creatures, with huge spiky heads and lots of sharp teeth. "I've never seen creatures like this."

She would have said that they didn't exist, but after seeing the magical spider, she wasn't sure anymore. There were lands unknown beyond the Horn that harboured the strangest of creatures. She also didn't know if "exist" was the right word for a being that was a figment of magic. If magicians could create what they wanted, then the ghost-ether could be shaped into any form.

"They had a small dragon at the farm," Roald said.

"Did you see it?"

"I had to feed it. It was about this big." He held his hands about an arm's length apart.

"Did it fly?"

"No, but it bites."

"Where did it come from?"

"The lands beyond the Horn. The abbot bought it from some peddler who came to sell silk and linen."

"Why was it there? Was it a magical being?"

"Brother Lucius keeps it as a pet. It sits on his shoulder. It warns him if the air is starting to go bad."

"Go bad?"

"Sometimes the air explodes. The dragon makes noises when it smells the bad air so the people can get out."

"What sort of place is this?" She had never heard of exploding air.

"At the farm."

"Yes, but what sort of place at the farm?"

"At the chapel in the valley behind the fields. Mist comes out of the ground. They're building an oracle room to surround it."

"Mist or ghosts?"

"Never saw a ghost in all the time I was there."

Johanna pulled out the map of the town and surrounding forest that Roald had bought from a mapmaker at the markets. She rolled it out on the desk. The map was a thing of beauty, precisely made with the finest pen strokes.

The town of Florisheim was on the eastern bank of the Rede River, while the lower areas on the western side, part of Burovia, were mostly wild land of marshes and forests. To her, this very much started to sound like the people there had been digging up the magic lines and Roald had either not seen it or dismissed it as something he didn't want to deal with.

On the map, the farm was marked with only a little black square. Underneath, it said in tiny letters: *Order of the Guentherites*.

Johanna pointed at the spot. "Is that what they're called? The Guentherites?"

"Brother Guenther was the abbot. He was very old and died while I was there. I didn't see him much because he was always sick. He's the second cousin of Baron Uti. He inherited the land to the south of here, and had to battle Duke Lothar for the rights to the castle. He lost, so he started the farm."

"Did he build it? Did no one live there before?"

"No. Because the land was haunted."

She would ask him whether this order was officially recognised by the Belaman Church, but he probably wouldn't understand the intricacies involved in church relationships. So she let the topic rest, but she was becoming more and more certain that a lot of the trouble in the world came back to this farm and its magic lines.

"Would you want to go and visit the farm?"

Roald turned to her, frowning. "Why?"

"Well, because . . . because you know people there. Because you have friends there?"

He stared at her, as if his brain was processing the concept of *friends*. "Does that mean I would see Selmus?"

"That depends on if he's still there." She had no idea who this person was, but found some relief in knowing that Roald had made at least one friend. "Do people from the farm visit Florisheim?"

"They do, if the abbot lets you go. You need two strong rowers."

And rowing across the river was not going to happen while the water was so high. But they had sea cows and could use them. "Do people visit?"

"Only important people."

"That's easy, then. As soon as the water calms a bit, we will announce a visit so that you can see Selmus."

BUT THE RAINS KEPT UP, and although the water levels dropped a bit, the river remained a churning mass of water. Visiting that farm seemed like it might create more problems than she could deal with. Over the next week increasing numbers of people came to the riverbank where the boys had seen Celine. Someone put up a wooden post in the water with a platform on top and the next day a little statue appeared there, whittled from wood, and depicting a woman. It was a rough and coarsely-made thing, but the long hair and cloak made it clear that this represented Princess Celine. People stood at the riverbank and gazed at it. Some people even brought small offerings: flowers or whatever scraps of food they could spare. The riverbank became muddy and trampled, and the ever-rising waters came closer and closer to the platform.

"I didn't think that the nobles were this superstitious," Johanna said to Master Deim while watching this strange going-on from the deck.

It had stopped raining and the river was still high, only a few hand-widths under the deck of the jetty, but when the sun broke through the clouds, it didn't look as threatening.

"It's a feature of the Belaman Church to worship ghosts. They call them saints, but it's all the same thing."

That same Belaman Church that had a saint for mothers and babies, the church that was ever-present in all of life in Florisheim, and an institute that Johanna didn't understand. There had been a small Belaman Church building in Saardam, but it was modest, nothing like the magnificent construction in the market place.

"Are you ready to go to the council meeting?" Master Deim said.

"I'm ready. I got Roald ready earlier this morning. I'll go and get him." She went down into the hold where Roald sat with his head buried in a book as usual.

Until Nellie and Loesie had made him new clothes, his best garment was the red velvet jacket that he had worn on the night of their escape from Saardam. These days, it was more brown than red. The dunking in the harbour hadn't done it much good, and the dirt had become so engrained in the fabric that even Nellie's scrubbing wouldn't budge it. On a day like this, it was also quite hot, but one of the oddities about Roald was that he never, ever, removed or put on an item of clothing by himself.

"Come, Roald, we need to go."

He ignored her.

She went down the stairs and put an arm on his shoulders. "Come. The council is waiting for us."

"The meeting is stupid."

She agreed with him, but if she said so, he was likely to blurt it all over the camp. "We have to go."

"I don't want to."

"Please, Roald. You're the king." She gently pulled his arm.

"No." His muscles stiffened. "Those men don't like me and I don't like them. They talk about me behind my back and laugh at me. They call me The Idiot King. I am the king, and I am not going to talk to people who are rude to me."

There was nothing Johanna could say to that. She wasn't going to assure him that no, this was not the case at all. The men *did* talk behind his back and they *did* call him The Idiot King. How to change that would be the big challenge, but it probably wouldn't be fought in the Council of Nobles. The rot had probably started with King Nicholaos and his son wasn't going to change anything.

"Is there a problem?" Master Deim asked at the top of the stairs.

"He doesn't want to come."

"The meeting is stupid! I want to go catching frogs." He had that determined look in his eyes.

Johanna glanced at Master Deim. What to do?

"Leave him," Master Deim said. "He wouldn't do our cause justice. Not like this. We'll go by ourselves and say that he's unwell."

Johanna could agree with that, but what would the nobles say? Worse, how bad would the gossip get?

Johanna followed Master Deim off the gangplank. The sentries posted there greeted both of them. Every time Johanna passed these men—and there were four taking turns—she felt less easy about why they were here. They were Johan Delacoeur's men and the aims of the nobles and of Johanna and Roald started to diverge increasingly.

It might be time to speak to Julianna again about finding guards in the camp who were more loyal to the throne.

By the time Johanna and Master Deim arrived at the boat shed, Master Deim's high forehead glistened with sweat. Big clouds built again on the horizon, so it was likely that there would be more rain.

All the council members were already seated around the table. They had been talking, but fell silent when Johanna and Master Deim came in.

Fleuris LaFontaine raised his eyebrows.

"The king is indisposed," Master Deim said. "There has been an illness of the stomach going around the camp."

There were some nods around the table. Johan Delacoeur seemed happy. He eyed Ignatius Hemeldinck, and a smile ghosted over Ignatius' face.

Johanna sat down at the position that would normally be

Roald's. "The king has authorised me to take care of his affairs." She looked around the table, and it struck her that someone else was missing. "Where is the Shepherd Carolus?"

"Late, probably," Fleuris LaFontaine said. Yes, it was true that he'd been late at the first meeting, too.

"Should we send someone out to get him?" Johanna asked.

"I'll ask Pieter," Master Deim said.

He rose from the table. Pieter was one of Johan Delacoeur's men, and this meant that Master Deim had to walk back to the *Lady Sara* and would be gone for a while.

Johanna made sure that the first subject of discussion was something relatively harmless: the upcoming wedding.

The Baroness Viktoriya had sent her servants to inform Johanna of the arrangements, and frankly she felt that the entire ceremony was out of her control. She had even supplied a priest, because *You have to be married in a civilised church*, and somehow Johanna expected a summons to appear that the day prior to the wedding, she'd be expected to come to the Belaman Church to convert.

"I'd like to hold something more intimate for our own people as well. I'd like the Shepherd Carolus to conduct a ceremony."

Distaste flickered over Ignatius' face. "We will lose support from the Baron if we persist with that church."

"It is *our* church," Johanna said.

It was the church of Saardam, the church of the common people. Not the nobles. Not the Baron's church. Not the church of pomp and ceremony and the church that was richer than many royal families.

"I would like a brief ceremony just for our people, held on the deck of the *Prosperity* or if there is not enough room, in the camp. We can hold it on the day of the other feast, or the day before."

"I'm not in favour of holding it on the riverfront," Johan Delacoeur said. "These days, gatherings of people along the waterfront seem to attract an increasing number of ghost sightings."

Johanna's heart jumped. "Have there been any more apparitions?"

"If my wife is to be believed, yes. She says if you go out at dusk and look into the reeds at a certain angle, you will see where the ghost sleeps."

Ignatius laughed. "And you believe this, too?"

"Apparently, a lot of women have seen this apparition of Celine," Johan Delacoeur said. His voice let little doubt about what he thought of this development.

"It is rumoured that King Nicholaos was trying to have her resurrected," Fleuris LaFontaine said.

Ignatius laughed again. "Nonsense."

Johan held up his finger like a teacher. "Whether it's true or not doesn't matter. It's what the people believe and we'll have to deal with it."

"Can't we just . . . remove the whole damn shrine thing overnight?" Ignatius Hemeldinck said. "Kick it over so that it falls in the water?"

"No, we can't." Johanna was surprised by the amount of anger in her voice. If she had learned anything from Nellie, it was not to disrespect what other people felt, or at least not in public.

He harrumphed. "It's a thing to keep the women busy. Nothing substantial."

And you wonder why you're not married?

Fleuris LaFontaine said, "You can't take it away and not have a lot of trouble and protest. I don't like it either. My wife is taken with the thing, even though she never saw the apparition of Celine. If you take it away, all the womenfolk will be angry with us." He might be a boor, but he wasn't stupid.

Ignatius snorted.

"You will *not* take it away." Johanna met his eyes, a hard expression in them. Oh, he hated to be ordered by a woman. He didn't think Roald should be issuing orders, but he thought even less of her.

Master Deim returned a bit later, without Shepherd Carolus. "I can't find him anywhere. He's probably gone harvesting somewhere."

This was met with comments of *probably*, and the meeting continued.

Besides the wedding, and the "proper" ceremony, the council

discussed arrangements for the running of the camp. With the wet weather, straw was becoming short in supply, and so much of the field was muddy that some tents had been moved to the other side of the road. This land belonged to a grumpy farmer who wanted a heavy payment for the use of his paddock. The council discussed options: move to yet another field or move to more permanent housing in town. The latter option confirmed Johanna's suspicion that many of the nobles had little interest in returning to Saardam.

By the time the meeting ended, Shepherd Carolus had still not turned up.

"Does he often completely forget the meeting?" Johanna asked Master Deim while they were walking back along the riverbank.

"He usually remembers at some time. He's not been this late before." Master Deim gazed over the curve of the river, as if expecting to see the Shepherd come running towards the boat shed with hay in his hair but the path ahead was and remained empty.

"I saw him this morning," Captain Arense said.

"Did he mention the meeting?"

"No, but he did say that he was going to meet someone from town to speak about shoes for children."

"That sounds like him," Master Deim said. "He's probably just forgotten."

They passed the shrine to Celine. Three women stood watching it, one of them holding the hands of two children too young to play. None of the women prayed or cried. They just watched. Bathed in sunlight, the scene didn't look so disturbing. Johanna was reminded of the statues of the saints in the church with the flowers and the candles and velvet-covered seats. Most of the nobles had grown up with the Belaman Church and might view it in the same way. To them, Celine had turned into a saint.

If Johanna hadn't seen the apparition turn into a spider-like monster, she would have thought nothing of it.

The women greeted Johanna and Master Deim with polite nods of the head, and one of the children said, "Oh, look. It's the queen."

The mothers greeted her with polite nods and Johanna returned their greeting. When she and Master Deim had passed, the women went back to staring at the shrine.

"I still don't know what to think about that thing," she said to Master Deim when they were walking around the reed bed.

"It gives them hope," Master Deim said. "Something to pray to that their families are still alive."

"I'm afraid that one day, that monstrous thing will return and kill all of them." She looked into Master Deim's eyes. "This land is soaking in magic. We're not equipped to deal with it. We need to go back to our own land as soon as possible. Before winter comes."

He nodded.

"You will come with us, won't you?" The thought of leaving him here made her chest constrict with panic. With Father not here, he had become like a second a father to her. "I wish we got some news about what is going on in Saardam. Why do you think those scouts we sent haven't come back yet?"

Master Deim gazed over the churning water of the river. "There could be any number of reasons, but I have to admit I don't like it much."

"No." Johanna shook her head.

They looked over the river for a while. Two women walked down the path along the riverbank. They were probably going to visit the shrine. "I feel something is watching us. Watching and stalking, like a sea serpent under the surface of the sea, stalking a ship that does not know the danger it's in."

CHAPTER 13

THE THUNDER rolled in not much later, and Johanna went down into the hold. Nellie brought dinner and Johanna stood patiently for Nellie to take more measurements, while the rain pelted on the hold covers. Loesie had made good progress on the lace and declared that the dress would be ready on time.

Johanna was just getting dressed again when there were footsteps and the sound of voices from outside.

She went to look. The brief shower had come and gone. Julianna Nieland was on the jetty in the presence of a group of children.

"There she is!" one of them yelled.

Another one called out, "Can His Royal Majesty please come outside? We want to catch frogs."

Julianna pulled a face. "They've been spending too much time inside with all this rain. They've been driving us all crazy."

Roald must have heard the word "frogs" because he came to the top of the stairs carrying his net, to much cheering from the children.

He led the group of boys into the reed bed with much chattering and excitement, in which terms of *Your Majesty* were often forgotten.

Julianna smiled. "They love him so much and he's so good with them."

He deserved a family of his own, and that brought Johanna back to the painful thought that this was not happening.

Julianna said, "I really came here because you had a council meeting this morning and I was wondering if Shepherd Carolus had said something to you about going somewhere. He was meant to come and teach the kids, but he didn't show up. He's often late, but he always comes."

Johanna's heart skipped a beat. "He wasn't at the council meeting either. Master Deim went out to find him but he couldn't. Someone seemed to think that he'd gone to harvest."

"In the rain?"

They looked at each other. An expression of worry hovered in Julianna's eyes. There was no need for words. They both thought the same thing: something has happened to him.

"Pieter!" Johanna called out to the guards at the jetty.

The man on question turned.

"Have you seen Shepherd Carolus at all today?"

"Yes, I remember seeing him—no, I remember wrongly. That was yesterday."

"He was meant to come to the council meeting, but he wasn't there. He was meant to teach the children, but he didn't show up. That's not like him at all. Could you check his tent? In fact, I'll come with you."

Pieter accompanied Johanna across the camp. Shepherd Carolus didn't have any relatives in the camp, and shared with a group of single men. None of them had seen him.

A young nobleman's son said, "I thought it was funny that I got up early this morning, and it didn't look like he'd been there all night. You know that we keep quiet about that sort of thing, and I thought it was a bit strange, him being a priest and all that, but you know . . ." He shrugged. His cheeks turned red. "I'm sorry, this is not an appropriate subject for a lady."

Well, thank you for thinking so much of him. "Why didn't you say anything earlier?"

"Because he's often away. He does a lot of things."

"He'll be all right," another man said. "Likely, he got so

smitten with a girl from town that he's still with her. He's a big and handsome fellow."

"But not turning up for teaching a class?"

"A bit odd, I have to confess." He looked uneasy. "Although he did say something about going into town for shoes for children."

"Have you seen anything unusual?"

"No. I don't think so." But something made him hesitant.

"Would you help me check around the camp just to make sure?"

Master Deim came as well, and they walked over the road at the back of the camp and then up and down the river bank several times, past the reed beds and the little shrine that stood further from the bank than it had been when it was erected. They went as far as the boat shed and then back in the other direction. In places, the path had been claimed by the rising waters and they had to walk through the tall grass.

There was no sign of Shepherd Carolus, no sign that someone had been this way.

"He probably just went into town and got held up," Pieter said.

Johanna met Master Deim's eyes. It was probably not wise to say anything about magic in Pieter's presence. He would only report it to the nobles and they would use it against her at the next meeting.

They checked the shed, the reeds and the river. If Shepherd Carolus had gone to town, he would have come this way.

But there was no one on the path. The vast churning surface of the water remained empty. The riverbanks were deserted, the tall grass undisturbed.

With the low clouds, it started to go dark quite soon and veils of mist rose from the water.

"We better go back," Master Deim said. "He's obviously not here."

"I'll go and ask in town tomorrow," Pieter said. "If he hasn't returned by then. But he will probably turn up soon."

Johanna wished she could believe that, but the cold fingers of magic were reaching for her again. She brushed her hands over a few tree trunks while they walked, but they showed her nothing significant, except ducks. One showed the two scouts setting off in their dinghy towards Saardam.

They haven't returned either.

Shapes swirled in the mist but every time she thought she saw ghosts in the corner of her eye, they disappeared again once she turned her head to look in more detail.

Yet, there was *something*. Watching, waiting.

Johanna shivered.

When they came back to the *Lady Sara* it was dusk. Loesie and Nellie stood on the jetty, talking to Captain Arense.

"There they are!" Nellie called out. She came towards the shore. "Oh, mistress Johanna, we were so worried about you!"

But it was Loesie who drew Johanna's attention. She was sitting on the hold covers, her arms around her legs which she held drawn up to her chest. Her eyes were vacant.

"What happened?"

"There were ghosts," Nellie said. "In the reeds over there." She pointed.

"Did Roald see them?" That was where he had been looking for frogs.

"I don't think so. The children had already gone. We were looking for you because we didn't know where you were. We worried that you'd fallen off the deck and no one had noticed. Loesie saw the ghost first. She's been sitting like this since then. It's like she went back to being bewitched. I'm afraid, Mistress Johanna."

Johanna climbed the gangplank and joined Loesie on the hold covers. Loesie was shivering and muttering to herself.

"What did you see?" Johanna asked.

"Must not talk to it. Must not look at it. Must not talk to it. Must not look at it." Loesie stared into nothingness.

"Not talk to what?"

"Must not talk to it. Must not look at it."

"Loesie?"

Loesie faced her. Her eyes were still alert, too alert for her to have become possessed again.

"What did you see? A ghost?"

"Must not talk to it. Must not look at it."

"Loesie, answer me."

Loesie screamed and clamped her hands over her ears. "Don't talk to it! Don't! Don't! Leave me alone. Push me in the river. Put me in a boat without oars. Let me go, please!"

"What are you talking about?"

"Get away from me!"

Johanna slid back off the hold cover. Loesie went back to her previous position, with her arms wrapped around her legs. No amount of coaxing could bring her down.

"I don't understand," Nellie said. "She was doing so well."

"I don't think she was ever completely cured from that demon," Johanna said. "She never went back to the way she used to be. I'm sure you remember that she always spoke with a strong dialect and that she always used magic to scare boys in the marketplace."

"Yes, I do remember. Thankfully, she stopped that."

"It's not as simple as that. You can't just learn to speak differently overnight. The demon changed her personality. It's still changing her."

That brought a chill and neither of them said anything for a while.

"What can we do about it?" Nellie finally said in a low voice.

"Nothing. Wait until she calms down. Go to your cabin. Maybe she'll be fine once we stop fussing over her. There is not much point in arguing with her in this state."

Nellie turned, and then looked over her shoulder.

"Mistress Johanna, do you think she could be dangerous?"

"I don't know, Nellie. I really don't know."

Johanna felt guilty letting Nellie go back to the cabin alone. Maybe she would have to let Nellie sleep in the hold away from Loesie, but that would mean that she and Roald would lose whatever privacy they had. Somehow, that suddenly seemed important, that little home they had made for themselves.

She descended the stairs in that familiar, somewhat musty, smell of the hold. Roald sat at his desk, drawing a frog which he had caught in a glass jar. The drawing was so beautiful and detailed that she forgot all her objections about *no frogs in our bedroom*.

Roald was pleased that she liked it and from one thing came another. They moved from the desk to the bed. With all the worry about Shepherd Carolus and Loesie, she didn't care about doing it the right way, and she sat on him because she much preferred it this way. And something else happened that she had not experienced before. A lot of the time when she was with Roald, she would feel that there ought to be more to it, and that it seemed unfair that just he found it pleasurable. In fact, some of the books suggested that the woman should find pleasure, too. That experience of intimate pleasure crept up on her unnoticed, grabbed hold of her and took her so much by surprise that she cried out, perhaps a bit too loud. Roald thought it was so interesting that he probed her soft flesh with his fingers until it happened again, and then he wanted to do it a third time, but she was a bit sore and tired, and there was sticky seed everywhere.

Tomorrow, she said, and he was happy with that.

Before drifting off to sleep, she realised that she had forgotten to drink the raspberry leaf tea.

CHAPTER 14

JOHANNA WAS WAKENED by rustling noises in the hold. They'd had mice in the room before, but this sounded bigger and too close for comfort. She got out of bed and found that last night they had forgotten that the frog still sat in the glass jar. During the darkest part of the night, it obviously remained quiet, but now it was rustling around in the leaves, trying to climb out of the jar. Poor thing.

Much as she disliked frogs, and she disliked them less since Roald had explained all about their strange life cycles, she didn't think it would be very happy in the jar, so she took the jar up to the deck of the ship—

And found that the morning dawned with mist rising out of the river. The sky above was pale blue, but all around, mist shrouded the land.

A bite to the air heralded the coming of autumn. The guards stood huddled in their cloaks. Loesie had evidently decided to go to bed well before midnight, because the hold cover was empty and the dew had coated the timber covers evenly with no trace that anyone had been there recently.

Johanna went down the gangplank carrying the jar. The guards gave her strange looks but said nothing.

She waded through the tall grass to the water and upended

the jar. With a giant leap, the frog went *splash* into the water, leaving ripples as it went below the surface.

She was about to turn back and ask the guards if by chance they had heard whether Shepherd Carolus had returned when there were alarmed voices from further downstream.

Johanna's heart beat faster. That was coming from the direction of the shrine. The apparition of Celine hadn't shown itself since that day the boys had seen her. Johanna had hoped that it had been a one-time appearance, some magician's idea of a joke, but had always known that hope was for fools.

Johanna made her way around the reed bed walking as fast as she could without running.

A number of people stood there, staring at the water. People shrank back to make a wide path to let Johanna through to the water's edge. They said nothing. Mothers pulled children out of her path.

The platform on top of the post had been smashed; the flowers and the little crude statue were gone. Scraps of wood lay between the reeds along the swollen river. Someone had stomped all over the offerings laid out on the riverbank. Big, booted footsteps over crushed flowers.

"Does anyone know who did this?" Johanna asked.

Fearful silence was her only response, a crowd of pale faces and wide eyes.

After a while, a little boy said, "This is how we found it this morning."

His mother shushed him.

"Did anyone see people here?"

Now another boy said, "We were out playing this morning, and we saw no one." This boy's mother tried to shush him, too, but he turned to her and said, loud enough for Johanna to hear, "What? I'm telling the truth. We saw no one."

Johanna addressed the adults. "What is going on here? Do any of you know who did this?"

People shook their heads, but no one said anything.

"Wait. Does anyone think I did this?"

There were some more shakes of heads, most not very convincing. Some people looked away.

A woman fell to her knees in the grass.

"Celine! Speak to us! This is not our fault. Please forgive us."

Another was crying as well, wailing like a young child.

These were nobles, people who normally prided themselves on being business-like, sensible people who tut-tutted if someone displayed overt emotions. The same people who had ridiculed King Nicholaos for being incapacitated with grief at his daughter's funeral.

"I assure you that I had nothing to do with this act of destruction. I will do everything I can to find out who did this."

The looks that met hers seemed to be of pity more than anger.

Wait—had someone destroyed the shrine because they wanted to make her unpopular? She knew who might do something like that.

Johanna hurried along the riverbank to the camp. She had enough and was going to get to the bottom of this despicable act.

IGNATIUS HEMELDINCK STAYED with the family of Johan Delacoeur. They were well-prepared, with sturdy tents. This part of the camp was also higher up the riverbank and not as muddy as the lower areas. Again, the men of power looked after themselves well enough. Never mind the sick and very young people, and the school, where Julianna worked in a tent where the floor consisted of muddy straw.

She ran up to the tent and announced herself with a loud, "Hullo!" as she would normally do when visiting warehouses for her Father. She had not come here to be polite.

An old man pushed the tent flap aside.

"I'd like to speak to Ignatius Hemeldinck."

"Wait here, missy."

He let the fabric drop.

Missy? She was married to their legal king. What did he think he was that he could call her that? In fact, what did all of these pompous idiots think they were doing?

The sound of male voices came from inside the tent and not much later the man himself pushed the tent flap aside.

His eyebrows rose.

Johanna launched straight into the problem. "This morning the shrine to Celine was destroyed." Johanna had to do her best to keep her tone civilised.

He gave her a *yes, and?* look.

"Do you know who was involved?"

"Pray, why should I know?" In that usual *dumb woman* tone of his. "Ask some of those ratbag boys. They probably know more."

"You wouldn't happen to have told them to destroy it?"

"Why should I do that?" He half-turned, as if the conversation was over, as if she wasn't worth his time, and to be honest, that was probably what he thought about her all along.

"I will explain it to you." Now she definitely let her anger colour her voice.

He gave her a mildly surprised look.

"You may not remember it, but you said you wanted the shrine taken away when it first went up. You wanted to, in your own words, *remove the whole damn thing overnight* and you didn't seem to care much about what the people would have to say about that, because *they were only women.*"

"For a merchant girl, you're starting to become incredibly irritating."

That was it. She was through with the lot of them. "I do not appreciate talk like that. I'm still married to your rightful king, and I'm starting to think you are setting up a plot against my husband. Maybe all of this is part of that plan. Engaging your magic friends to create ghosts that look like Celine—"

He opened his mouth—

"No, don't tell me that there isn't any magic. This place is stiff with magic. This town is full of magicians. Don't blame me for destroying the shrine. Don't address me like I'm your daughter because I am not." She hated this man so much. Him, and Fleuris LaFontaine and Octavio Nieland who was said to have joined the occupiers. These were not men who cared for the citizens of Saardam. They didn't even care about their families. These men only cared about themselves.

He looked taken aback, a puzzled frown on his face.

Johanna went on, "Next time we have a council meeting, you will apologise to Roald for the things you said about him."

"Do stop making such a spectacle of yourself. Look at it, everyone has come out to watch." Indeed, a lot of people had come out of the surrounding tents.

"So, I am 'making a spectacle of myself' when I protest about you constantly ignoring me, belittling me and acting as if I'm stupid. I've had enough of this behaviour. I will not be talked down to! You will either listen to me or Roald, or I will no longer consider you loyal to the royal family."

He laughed, but his expression was uneasy. He glanced around at all the onlookers, meeting the eyes of one group behind Johanna in particular. Johanna glanced over her shoulder. Julianna Nieland stood there with Captain Arense's wife and three sons.

Ignatius bowed, equally uneasy. "As you wish, lady."

"Your Majesty." Johanna disliked pomp, but it seemed the only thing that would impress these men.

"Your Majesty." It sounded like his words came through gritted teeth.

Good. There would probably be trouble about this later, but she had tried being friendly with them, and it had failed.

"I shall now call a meeting of the council. I will inform you what we are going to do to return to Saardam, to reinstate Roald in the palace, to rebuild the palace, and drive the invaders out. You are free to advise us. Unless you wish me to go ahead with my plans without informing you."

Johanna whirled around and met the eyes of a bunch of women standing in the entrance to the next tent. She didn't know them by name, but they were all smiling. Oh yes, there was support for her in the camp. The women, the quiet and civilised men, the merchants. She just needed to give these people the courage to act.

NOT MUCH LATER, the Council of Nobles convened in the boat

shed. It was not their usual meeting time, and Fleuris LaFontaine had to be hunted down from some place in town. He came into the boat shed muttering and protesting and sat down at the table with a heavy sigh.

His face was red from the wine he had evidently consumed with his midday meal.

Johanna had thought it wise to let Roald stay at the *Lady Sara*. He'd been teaching some boys how to catch butterflies without damaging them, and had gotten wet. He had sticks in his hair and smudges on his cheeks and, when she called, had looked at her with such disappointment that she couldn't bring herself to drag him along to a meeting, let alone one where tempers were sure to get heated. He hated it when people raised their voices, because he didn't understand that they weren't talking to him. He might start fidgeting, laughing or screaming, and that would be unacceptable.

So she had watched him trundle back into the reeds with his butterfly net, wishing she could be with him. Instead, she had changed into in her best dress, put on the necklace, brooch and earrings that she had brought from Duke Lothar's castle—much as she hated wearing other people's property—and then went to look for Nellie to put up her hair.

She couldn't find Nellie or Loesie and concluded that they were probably looking after the laundry, so she did her own hair and asked her guard escorts to walk her to the boat shed. Johanna was nervous and her insides squirmed, giving her cramps in her stomach. She took up the position at the head of the table that would normally be Roald's.

Johan Delacoeur gave her a look icy enough to make water freeze. He was a powerful man, an ex-army general with connections in armies all around the low lands. In their return to Saardam, he would be an asset, if she could win his support, no matter how reluctantly given. If.

Master Deim smiled at her from the other end of the table, which made her feel a bit more confident. Shepherd Carolus was still absent, reminding her of another painful problem that needed to be solved. That meant that she was down two supporters in the council.

Now that she'd called this meeting, there was no going back, so she might as well jump in before she lost control of the moment.

"I've called you here, because I want to ascertain your loyalty. I want all of you to swear loyalty to the royal family. When that is done, I want your honesty about your plans for the future of all those camping in this field. We cannot stay here over winter and I want to return to Saardam with whoever will come."

Fleuris made scoffing noises. "Well, I don't know that it's safe—"

"Staying here is safe? Where every time it rains, water rises into the lower areas of the camp, bringing filth and disease? Where our citizens are assailed by magic, seeing ghosts, being struck with apathy? I know that many of you are not aware of this, but this town soaks in magic, and someone or something is waiting to pounce on us. Whoever it is, they know who we are. They know about Roald. But every time I've raised the issue of returning home, you have tried to push it aside, tried to ignore or deflect it—"

Fleuris LaFontaine said, "If you want the truth of it, Alexandre uses filthy magic, that's why."

"Then why haven't you tried to find a magician to deal with him for us?"

He snorted.

"All of the courts around here have magicians." She looked around the table, meeting a collection of hard stares.

"I will tell you why. Because some of you have made a deal with the Baron. You didn't like the influence the Church of the Triune was having on the people and on your royal family. Some time long before the fire, some of you came here to ask for help, where you have friends, and the Baron suggested that he knew a way to get rid of this church for you. He sent Alexandre Trebuchet who adores the Baron so much that he'd eat dirt if the Baron asked him. But things got very much out of hand for you, because I doubt you knew about fire magic, and I doubt you asked for the whole of Saardam to be set on fire, but you could not control or stop him, especially since some of your peers joined Alexandre. So you came here because your main reason was to complain to the Baron. He has allowed you to camp in this field and made you feel important and welcome, but now he won't listen to you anymore, because you served his purpose."

There were several gasps around the table.

At the same time Johan shouted, "Nonsense!" Fleuris shouted, "And what purpose would that be?"

Ignatius said nothing and looked distinctly uncomfortable and Master Deim's eyes were so big that they were in danger of tumbling from their sockets.

All of which told her that she was right about all her assumptions.

Johanna remained quiet and let the men rage.

While Johan heaped protest on protest, going *Whatever do you think you are?* and *Do you know what the Baron has done for us?* and *You have no right to be so ungrateful to our best friend*, Fleuris fell silent and eventually Johan ran out of protests to hurl at her. He crossed his arms over his chest and breathed through flaring nostrils. His face had gone red.

Because I'm right, and he doesn't like the way the Baron ignores him either.

When the nobles had fallen into an angry silence, she said, "There are a number of things we can do."

Captain Arense rarely spoke in these meetings, but he said, "Have you talked to the Baron?" His soft and civilised voice made everyone look at him.

"I have tried to. I have spoken to the Baroness several times, but I don't think there is a point in talking to the Baron. Even if we manage to get an audience, he will continue to ignore us. He clearly thinks that he has better things to do than listen to our complaints. We don't need him to return to our own city."

They didn't even need the Baroness' help in organising the wedding. They didn't need the Baron's prying guests at what was a Saarlander ceremony.

"We need an army," Mayor Joris DeCamp said.

Johan Delacoeur snorted.

Johanna said, "I'm not even sure that an army would do much good against magic." They needed stealth. They needed to disguise themselves as peasants. They needed to come into the city one by one, like farmers going to the markets. Loesie could help with that. They also needed magicians.

"I said several times that going back is ridiculous," Fleuris said. "I'll say it again. I, for one, am not going to take your accusations lightly. You accuse us of disloyalty—"

"This is why I called the meeting. I want to know where you stand: with the Baron or us."

Fleuris spread his hands. "By the heavens, woman, why don't you see that the Baron is on our side?"

"Then why won't he talk to any of us?"

"He doesn't talk to women."

"He's not talking to you either."

"What do you know about the meetings we've had with him? He has assured us that he is on our side." He crossed his arms over his chest.

"If you're so friendly with the Baron then, I ask that you go and talk to him and ask him for assistance to return to Saardam. Because certainly, you agree we can't stay here for the winter in this wet field, and I don't think Florisheim has enough spare houses for us."

He harrumphed. "All right."

"We will meet again here next week and you'll report what the Baron said."

He glanced aside to Johan, whose face was impassive, and then to Ignatius, who looked like he wanted to have her for dinner. Neither said anything.

He said again, "All right. I make no promises." Because he could make no promises, because the Baron wasn't even in town. For all she knew, the Baron was in the palace in Saardam with Alexandre.

"I happen to think that the people of Saardam are owed some promises. They are also owed an explanation of who you think the enemy is and why exactly a foreign magician was given the opportunity, encouragement even, to burn much of our home town."

He gave her a hard stare.

"Also, I want someone to find out who destroyed the shrine to Celine. Like you, I am unhappy about its existence, but there is no need to disturb the people further. We will also contact anyone who can shed light on the appearance of this ghost, and will talk to people who may know about King Nicholaos' involvement in dark magic. The Magician's Guild in Florisheim will probably know more about Alexandre Trebuchet and his masters."

They looked uneasy, but Johanna had enough of being dictated by these men only to be waiting for things they said they'd do but never did. She'd probably made a number of enemies, but they were never going to be friends in the first place.

She was fully prepared to go to the Magician's Guild herself, but at least she had notified them about her intentions and reasons for doing so.

They broke up the meeting, and one or two people actually called her *Your Majesty*. Not any of the nobles, though. But they had stopped calling her *just a merchant girl*. That was progress of a kind.

The meeting broke up and Johanna left the shed with Master Deim.

"I don't like the thought of asking for magical assistance," he said, while walking along the riverbank.

"I wish we could get by without it, too, but we have little choice. We have to act. I hate just sitting here and waiting for something to happen. I wanted to train Loesie as court magician, but she doesn't want to have anything to do with magic. I think we *need* a court magician, or someone to advise us on the subject of magic," she added, after remembering what Magda had said about court magicians being jesters.

He nodded again. "Yes, probably."

"Where would I find a person like that? I thought you were going to make some inquiries?"

"I was, but—"

But what he was going to say would have to wait, because a young boy came running up the path. "Look, look, Your Majesty, what I've found. Mother said to show it to you."

From his fist dangled a golden chain on which hung the

medallion with the symbol of the Triune. The last time she had seen this it was on Shepherd Carolus' neck.

Johanna took it from him. The chain had broken and parts of the medallion were covered in dark mud.

"Where did you find this?"

"In the grass on the edge of the forest."

Johanna's heart jumped. "Can you show me?"

CHAPTER 15

JOHANNA AND Master Deim followed the boy, and one of Johan Delacoeur's guards came as well. As they crossed the camp, several people noticed that something was going on and they followed at a distance.

The boy's name was Gijsbert, and he was the son of one of the merchants in the camp. While he led them across the camp, across the road on the other side and down a narrow track towards the forest, he chatted incessantly about how he and his friends had been playing on the haystack when he found the Shepherd's medallion. Of the Shepherd himself, he had seen no trace.

Squalls of wind made Johanna shiver, even though it was quite warm. Master Deim looked uneasy, too.

The path ran between two paddocks. One contained a couple of horses that were trotting around tossing their heads and with their tails held up so that the soft part of the tail flowed behind like a banner.

"What are those crazy horses doing?" the guard muttered behind Johanna.

But she knew what disturbed the animals: they were much more sensitive to magic than people.

The dark forest loomed at the far end of those paddocks, mostly oaks trees with dense foliage and dark canopies.

The sun chose that time to disappear behind the building clouds. A gust of wind made the leaves rustle in soft whispers. Ghosts waited in that forest. Waited and prowled, ready to pounce on anyone who dared step into their domain.

Gijsbert ran ahead.

Johanna fought the urge to yell at him to come back, to stay with the rest of the group. What business did Shepherd Carolus have in that forest anyway?

At the boundary between the field and the forest stood a wooden barn with one open side. A multitude of cart tracks led through and around the puddles in front of it. This appeared to be where a lot of the hay and straw had come from.

"This is where I found it," the boy said, pointing at the ground.

There was nothing much to be seen except mud and tracks: deep ruts from wagon wheels and churned-up mud from horse hooves.

Everyone in the group walked around for a bit, examining the ground.

"This is the most recent one," the guard said, kneeling. He pointed at a set of tracks that led not back to the road, but into the forest.

The forest that surrounded the group on three sides was full of whispering leaves. The sky had gone leaden grey over the tree line.

Slowly, Johanna walked to the closest tree. She put her hand on the trunk.

The gloominess in the forest disappeared and was replaced with dappled sunlight falling through the trees. There was the clop-clop-clop of horse's hooves and a cart came past. The driver wore a dark brown cloak with the hood draped over his shoulders. He had an unusually heavy brow and his dark hair fell loose over his shoulders. The man next to him was Shepherd Carolus. As the cart passed, the Shepherd looked over his shoulder directly at the tree, as if he knew that Johanna could see him. He moved his mouth like a fish on land, but Johanna couldn't make out words.

The driver flicked the reins and the horse took off. The back of the driver's hood had an embroidered symbol that she hadn't seen before: a yellow key.

🌀

THE BARONESS VIKTORIYA sat down on the couch with a sigh. She had accompanied Johanna to a garden room with doors and windows along one side. The flowers in the castle garden outside looked bedraggled from the rain.

"Unfortunately, my husband is not at home, so I will help you, right?"

She was wearing a dark green dress today and a black vest, a sombre ensemble without lace, which, apart from the rather low neckline, would not look out of place in church in Saardam. The only spot of brightness was a gold and jade brooch that held her shawl in place. Her dark hair was piled on top of her head, held in place by a hair net with tiny glass beads.

They were both silent while a maid brought some tea and a plate with dainty little cakes. She set a cup on a little table next to Johanna. The brew was dark and smelled sweet.

"Thank you for seeing me," Johanna said. "I'm sorry for imposing on your time."

"Oh, don't be so modest. Of course I make time to help my friend. Do help yourself to some cakes."

"But you're obviously busy." She wasn't too sure that she'd call the Baroness a friend either. But she did take a cake from the plate.

"Pfa." The Baroness flapped her hand. "Busy, busy. It's always busy. My husband spend so much time away lately, is getting really tiresome. So much work to be done! Harvest fields, sell geldings, move cattle . . . is all boring. I have to check, check, check all the time that everything gets done. Then it rain, rain and rain and people have to check the water mills and take hay to other barn, and . . ." She sighed heavily. "And my son is no help. I don't even know where he is. Gallivanting with his friends from across river, I guess, but I wish he grow up. I want a woman in family. That's why I invite your wedding at castle. I get best cooks. Hans Salter and his music troupe will play. There will be much dancing. I have big feast so my son will see what a wedding is like. Maybe he get jealous, he wants a wedding, too."

Knowing what she knew about Kylian, she doubted it.

"I'm sure you're doing your best, and thank you so much." And now she felt guilty for not wanting the festivities in the Baron's big hall. The Baroness was doing a lot of work for this ceremony, and obviously, she led a very lonely life.

A young man in the Baron's red livery came into the room, but stopped when he saw Johanna.

He said something and the Baroness replied, her tone somewhat annoyed. Then he bowed and left the room.

"I see you're busy," Johanna said. "I won't take much of your time. In all truth, I didn't come here to talk about the wedding."

"Oh?" The delicately painted eyebrows went up. "I like talking about wedding. We must talk about guests. I've made a long list of people to invite."

Johanna had been afraid of that. "I'm very sorry to have to mention this to you, but one of our people went missing from the camp yesterday. I was wondering if you could offer any assistance in finding him."

"How dreadful. What happened?"

Johanna told her of the Shepherd's absence and the chain they had found and the fact that he had been taken away in a cart. She described the cart driver's cloak and the symbol of the key on the back of the hood. She had drawn it on a piece of paper that she had taken from Roald's desk.

While she spoke, the Baroness' eyes widened. "But that is just awful. If my husband was here, he'd come and help you find this man personally and punish those who abducted him."

"Do you know which group uses this symbol?" Johanna held up the paper.

The Baroness squinted at it. "No. Have not seen that before."

"I'd be happy if you could lend me some people to help us ask around in town." A group of men had gone into town that morning, but had not found any sign of the Shepherd, nor of the shoemaker he was supposed to have gone to see. But they'd run into trouble because some of the townsfolk were suspicious about their presence, which was why she needed the Baroness' help.

"I will send some men, definitely. I'll see to it as soon as you leave this room. They will go through entire town and will not leave a house unvisited. They will find this man."

"Thank you so much." Johanna would have preferred if the Baroness just lent her someone who could explain to the townsfolk who they were looking for, but she guessed it would be impolite to complain.

So she drank tea and listened to the Baroness' plans for the wedding. Both the tea and cakes were really sweet to the point of making her feel a bit queasy. This room was strangely luxurious compared to the austerity of the rest of the castle and a world away from her little room in the *Lady Sara*'s hold.

They discussed dresses and food and guests, most of whom Johanna didn't know. She didn't want to ask if Duke Lothar and his son would be there, but she guessed not if history was anything to go by. She wanted to go back to the camp, but didn't want to be rude. The Baroness just kept talking and talking and didn't give Johanna an opportunity to leave. The wooden armrests of her chair told her that noble townsfolk visited this room often and that there would be much tea and chatter, all in the dialect, sadly, so Johanna had no idea what they talked about. Meanwhile she still tried to steer the discussion to more useful subjects.

"I'm a bit worried about what happens *after* the wedding. Because much as we appreciate your hospitality, winter is coming and we need more permanent quarters—"

"Oh, but you can stay longer. Plenty of room for you in castle."

"Thank you very much, but I would prefer to return home. Maybe some people would like to make further use of your hospitality, but many of us have family in Saardam that we're worried about. We should return home. I and my husband should return."

"I understand." She gave Johanna a sympathetic look, but said nothing further.

"But I don't want to return to a dangerous situation. Do you have any more news from Saardam?"

"No more than what you already know. It will be dangerous to go there, I'd say."

"We sent some scouts to see for ourselves what was going on, but they haven't yet returned. Has your husband said anything about what is going on there?"

"Dear, my husband is barely ever home, and he does not talk about politics to me. He knows I'm not interested."

"Do you know Alexandre?" Johanna promised herself that she would never be one of those women "not interested" in the dealings of men with power.

"He is a most snivelling man," the Baroness said. "I like him not at all." She wrinkled her nose as if an unpleasant smell wafted past.

"Does your husband like him?"

She laughed. "What do you think? That he would make serious discussions with this little man?"

"He has rather a lot of magic."

"Bah, it's fire magic—all spectacle."

"To the citizens of Saardam, it certainly wasn't just a spectacle." Johanna couldn't help letting some anger seep into her voice.

"I do apologise. It was terrible for you. But fire magic is nothing. Not important. Setting fire to a city, it is what cowards do. I could do it. He think he is important, but he is not."

"He seems to think a lot of your husband."

"Yes, but only because he is a snivelling little man. I said to my husband many times to shut him up. Not to listen to him. This man is up to no good, I'd say, but my husband, he is stubborn. One day, this priest might be useful, he'd say. So he invite Alexandre here, in our own castle. And I have to make talk with him, and be polite to him while he behave like a drunk ship's boy."

Johanna had visions of rowdy fests in the big hall with its

many long tables and benches. A Shepherd of the Church of the Triune would never come to an occasion like that. The church abhorred overt displays of wealth. Shepherds dressed plainly. The citizens coming to church dressed in their best clothes that were still modest.

"And he is a dirty little man, too. I wanted to slap him in the face all the time he tries to put his hands up my dress."

She felt a jab of sympathy for the Baroness. "Oh dear, that sounds awful."

"Nothing as awful as what happened to you, but yes, it was quite dreadful."

"Why do you think he went to Saardam?"

The Baroness spread her hands. "If we knew, it would be the end of troubles. Maybe he want money. Maybe he want blond-haired girls. Maybe he want ships. I don't know." The baroness sighed. "Let's leave that for the men to solve. One more thing about the wedding. I would like the Holy Father Lucius to conduct the ceremony, but I don't think you are baptised."

"No." There was a small Belaman Church building in Saardam, if it was still there, but Johanna didn't know many people who attended services there. Mistress Daphne was one, and a few other foreigners.

"You would need to become a member of the church."

No way. Just no way. If there was to be a ceremony, Shepherd Carolus would conduct it—after they found out where he was. "But I think I am already a member of your church? Aren't we all part of the same church?"

The Baroness gave her a sharp look. "My dear, you haven't heard?"

"Heard what?"

The Baroness raised her hand to her mouth. "You really haven't heard about the Most Holy Father's decree?"

"No, I don't think so." That would be the Most Holy Father Severino of the Belaman Church.

"Well . . . he decreed that there were . . . differences between the holy scriptures as understood by us and as interpreted by your Shepherd. Differences that needed . . . investigation." She frowned and then her expression cleared. "An inquisition. That's it. And he had the results of the inquisition."

"And that means?"

"I don't know how to say precisely in words of the church, but it means that the Church founded by Brother Romulus is no longer welcome as part of the Belaman Church."

CHAPTER 16

I N ONE HIT, Johanna finally understood the cause of all
the problems. While Saardam had fallen under the Belaman
Church, the church fathers had thought of the Shepherd
Romulus as an eccentric. Now that it was no longer part of the
Belaman Church, the Church of the Triune was a threat. The
Shepherds were a threat. They helped common people who
ended up liking the Shepherds for that reason. They won the
respect of citizens that way. All the citizens, not just the nobles
who could buy sympathy from the church. They did not insist on
donations by the wealthy, who expected special services in
return, and did not flaunt wealth. And that frightened the leadership of the Belaman Church, because there were so many more
common people than there were nobles.

And with that thought, she became very concerned for Shepherd Carolus' safety.

She had no idea how she managed to get out of the room
without promising anything, but one thing she knew: they
needed to get out of here as soon as possible. And find Shepherd
Carolus, *without* help from the Baroness' men. If the Belaman
Church was behind the abduction, then the conflict stepped up
a whole new level, and all their lives were in danger, unless they
converted.

Johanna hurried through the streets of the town back to the

Lady Sara, but when she arrived there, only Roald was home, seated at the desk, reading.

She noticed wet footsteps on the stairs. "Your shoes are wet."

He didn't react. Johanna dumped the drawing of the key symbol on the desk and kneeled at his feet. His shoes were indeed wet and covered in duckweed. "Let me take them off, then I'll put them outside to dry."

She wriggled his shoes off his feet. His socks were wet, too—and very smelly—and his toes had gone wrinkled like dried gooseberries. Phew, the smell was strong.

"Do you know where Nellie is?" She didn't hold much hope for a reply.

"There was some . . . thing going on."

Her heart jumped. "What sort of thing?"

"They were making a lot of noise up there. I told them to be quiet."

"Who is 'they'?"

He shrugged and went back to his book.

Johanna climbed back to the deck and went into the cabin to look for signs of where Nellie and Loesie were. Just then, Nellie was coming towards the jetty carrying a basket from which carrot greens protruded.

"Oh, mistress Johanna. You're back." The tone in her voice didn't sound happy.

"Yes. Roald said that there had been noise on the deck. What happened?"

"It was not my fault."

"What happened, Nellie?"

"I swear it wasn't my fault, mistress Johanna. Don't be angry with me."

"Just tell me what happened."

Nellie led Johanna back up the gangplank. In the cabin, she took a basket that stood on the bed which contained the dress she had been making. She lifted it out of the basket and the bottom of it was torn to shreds as if a wild animal had taken to it.

Nellie's eyes brimmed over with tears, her hands trembled so much that she could barely hold the dress up. "I didn't do it."

"I believe you, Nellie. Do you know who did?" But she already knew the answer before Nellie told her.

"That witch. She was sitting on the floor and poking a knife through the fabric and then tearing it."

"Loesie?"

Nellie nodded, sniffing. "I really thought she was getting better, mistress Johanna. Learning how to sew and cook. I'm so sorry for trusting her. It's my fault that you won't have a pretty dress—"

"Nellie, stop it." Johanna prised the dress from Nellie's hands. "I like a pretty dress, but it's not so important that I want you to—"

"But what about the wedding?"

"If things keep up like this, there won't be one until we're back in Saardam, and when we are, I'd be happy to get married in this dress. It is not important. Where is Loesie now?"

"I don't know. I told her to get off the ship. I wasn't very nice about it, mistress Johanna. I'm sorry." Her chin trembled.

"It's all right, Nellie. I probably would have done the same. But we do need to find her, before anything really bad happens."

Nellie nodded, her eyes wide. "Someone needs to look after her. I have to apologise."

"Whatever for?"

"I might have used some bad words. I was very upset when I saw her sitting there destroying the dress. But she is obviously not in her right mind. No healthy person would do that."

"I have to find her." With dread, she also realised that Loesie was probably responsible for the destruction of the shrine, and whatever still ailed her was buried deep in her soul.

Johanna walked through the entire camp a number of times, but didn't see Loesie anywhere. She asked everyone she met, but none of those people had seen her either. She ran into Master Deim, and together they widened the search to the surrounding fields and reed beds. They didn't find her on the riverbank to the south of the camp or anywhere near the boatshed. They didn't find her on the main road into town or in the fields on the other side. The horses that grazed there came to the fence and walked with them to the hay shed where Shepherd Carolus had disappeared. There was no magic to upset them today, and Johanna knew they weren't going to find Loesie at the shed long before they got there. Indeed they didn't.

They returned to the main road and walked north of the camp. This was an area even more marshy than the part of the riverbank between the camp and the boat shed.

The water had invaded low-lying stands of willow trees, which now stood with their trunks in the water. Most of the trees were saplings and they grew very close together. Branches had fallen haphazardly in between the trees and reeds and vines had grown over the dead wood, turning the area into an impenetrable thicket. The occasional bramble bush didn't help either.

Johanna and Master Deim walked along the narrow path that ran halfway up a row of hillocks, peering into the vegetation tangle.

If Loesie had gone in there, they had no hope of finding her. In the water, she wouldn't even have left tracks.

"We're not going to find her here," Master Deim said. "Would she have gone into town?"

"Unlikely. Loesie doesn't like people. Not unless someone forced her." And that was a thought she didn't want to entertain at this point. Although the demon likely belonged to someone and that someone would come for it at some point. This place was stiff with magic and if there was a magician tied to Loesie's demon, that magician might well live in Florisheim.

Johanna heard Magda's voice talking about *the betrayer*. She might well have been talking about Loesie. Since Loesie had been with the group from the beginning, she might have been like a burning beacon of magic to those who could see it, letting everyone know where they were all the time.

Johanna's chest constricted with panic. She didn't watch where she put her feet and tripped over a branch. She fell on her hands and knees.

Master Deim rushed to her. "My child! Are you all right?"

"I think so." Johanna brushed mud from her hands and dress. It would need to be washed once again.

"Let's go back. We're not going to find her here."

"Maybe we should try going to town, unlikely as it sounds."

But as she pushed herself up, she caught a glimpse of fabric between the trees ahead. She pointed. "There."

Master Deim peered into the thicket. "I do believe you're right."

He pushed a couple of branches aside. "There is a path of sorts here."

Path was a big word for the animal track that led over the faintest rise between close growing willow saplings. Following Master Deim's broad back, Johanna grabbed the braches as she went, and they showed her Loesie running over this path, wildly crashing into willow trunks. Her eyes were wide, but still had their normal colour. She ran bent over, as if she'd hurt herself.

Master Deim shouted, "By the heavens."

He stopped and Johanna peered around him.

Loesie sat cross-legged in the middle of a patch of grass, her back straight. In one hand, she held a blood-stained knife, and she was using the sharp point to score her skin. She had already made a network of bleeding cuts on her left arm.

She had discarded all her clothes, and was meticulously cutting the skin of her upper left leg, her face unemotional.

Tracks of blood trailed over her pale skin and dripped onto the ground.

She was so absorbed in her task that she didn't notice Master Deim or Johanna, but just kept cutting, her face scrunched in concentration.

Then she looked up, turning to Loesie and Master Deim. She had also scored her cheeks. Blood dripped down her jaw onto her chest.

She slowly wiped her hands over her stomach, smearing blood on the pale skin. She *massaged* her stomach, arching her back, all the while moaning.

"By the heavens," Master Deim said again.

Loesie laughed.

No, the demon had not gone at all. The demon might have been asleep for a while, but it had been with her all that time. It had probably been awakened when Loesie tried to drive off the magical apparition on the riverbank.

"Come," Johanna said, holding out a hand.

Loesie just stared, resting her hand on her stomach. Trails of blood had run between her fingers over the back of her hand.

"Put down the knife," Johanna said.

Loesie looked at the hand that held the knife, the point still poking at the skin. A flicker of disturbance went over her face as if she saw her bleeding arms for the first time.

She dropped the knife in the grass. Her face went pale.

Master Deim rushed in behind her and picked it up.

Loesie dragged her dress over her naked body, her eyes wide, her mouth open. Her hands trembled and the skin had gone purple. She smeared blood everywhere.

"I think I'm going to be sick," she said weakly, and illustrated it by vomiting all over one side of the dress. It was mostly slime and blood, but made even more of a mess of the garment.

"Oh, look at it now," she cried and she vomited again. In her effort to miss the dress, it went all over Johanna's hands, mostly brown foamy slime.

"I'm sorry, I'm sorry." She let the soaked dress drop to her knees.

"I don't mind," Johanna said, looking at Loesie's bloodied skin.

"Come, let's go home." She picked up Loesie's discarded dress and held it up. Apart from the fact that it was wet, the bottom part had been slashed into ribbons. But it would have to do.

"Try to put this on. We're going back to the *Lady Sara*."

Although she wasn't sure if she wanted Loesie sleeping in the same cabin as Nellie with knives in the galley next door.

The wildness had gone from Loesie's eyes and Johanna managed to get Loesie back into the dress. Her cloak, muddy as it was, covered most of the gaping rips in her dress where the skin shone through. In a shallow part of the bank, she made Loesie wash herself, shivering and in stiff and jerky movements.

Very carefully, with Master Deim helping her, they guided Loesie along the path. While she complained of being cold, her skin felt hot and dry. When they came close to the camp, Master Deim ran ahead to get a blanket, but still they got plenty of stares.

Nellie stood on the deck of the *Lady Sara*. She watched with wide eyes and covered her mouth with her hands while Johanna and Master Deim shuffled up the gangplank with Loesie between them.

She retreated once they were on the deck, her face pale.

In the cabin, Johanna cleaned Loesie's cuts. Most of them were shallow and would heal by themselves. She put ointment and bandages over some of the deeper ones. Nellie stood by the doorway, her face still pale. No one said anything.

The uneasy silence lingered until Nellie asked how Loesie got all those cuts and in response to being told exclaimed, "She did it herself? Who cuts their own skin?"

Loesie snorted and Johanna intervened before it could come to an outburst. "Maybe you would like to bring Loesie some tea."

"Yes, mistress Johanna, immediately."

Johanna sat on the edge of the bed watching Nellie's back as she ran from the cabin. *Nellie, one day your trusting nature is going to hurt you badly.*

A bit of colour had returned to Loesie's cheeks.

"Is there anything we should know about?"

Loesie shook her head.

"You're sure about that? Then why *did* you do this?"

Loesie shook her head again.

Johanna's heart jumped. This was so much like when she had first met Loesie at the markets, when she had lost her voice. "Can you still speak?"

"Yes, just not about that. Not his name. I don't know his name, all right?" Her eyes went wide again.

"Calm down, calm down." This was the closest Loesie had come to admitting that someone had bewitched her. She must not lose Loesie's trust. "When did this happen?"

"In early spring, before the trees started sprouting leaves."

"At the farm?"

She nodded. Her lip trembled. "Annette is dead because of me. Ma is dead because of me. Granpa and Granma are dead because of me!" He voice rose.

"Shhh." Johanna held Loesie's shoulders. She felt hot and dry. *Like a demon's fire.*

"Please, if you care for me, leave me alone," Loesie whispered. "Give me the knife and let me kill myself."

"Don't be silly. We'll find someone to help you."

Nellie came with tea and after having made sure that Loesie drank some, Johanna left to go to the hold. She felt so tired. Being here, in this place infused with magic, tired everyone out. They would have to move soon, or risk staying here forever.

In the hold, Roald sat at the desk by the light of a flickering oil lamp, intently staring at a piece of paper. In typical fashion, he didn't look up when she came in.

"What are you doing?"

"That's the symbol of the Burovian royal family."

"What is?"

He showed her the sheet of paper. It was her crude drawing of the key on the back of Shepherd Carolus' abductor's hood.

Johanna's heart thudded. "Is there anyone from the Burovian royal family at the work farm?"

"Prince Hugo," Roald said, pulling a face. "I don't like him at all. He whips the horses and kicks the piglets."

"Does he have dark hair that he wears in a ponytail?"

He frowned at her. "I think so."

"Is he still at the farm?"

"Yes, he is one of the bosses."

Johanna couldn't believe that the answer they had been looking for had been here all the time.

The Baroness had lied about the symbol. She would have recognised it and known who it belonged to. Likely, the nobles knew it, too. So they had taken the Shepherd to the farm? If they were magicians then what did they want with him? A chill went over her back.

"Could you . . . help me get there?"

CHAPTER 17

JOHANNA GOT UP very early the next morning, and went into the misty pre-dawn to ask Master Deim for the loan of a boat, which he said he'd bring along later.

She rushed back to the camp and in the cabin of the *Lady Sara*, she got herself and Roald dressed *for another adventure*. Roald asked if they were going to listen to wood again, and Johanna said they might, but nerves knotted in her gut. She could eat only little of the porridge brought by Nellie. Loesie was still asleep, Nellie said, and it was probably better to leave her like that.

The problem of Loesie was one Johanna would have to solve later.

Out on the deck, the mist still hadn't lifted, muffling sounds and keeping animals silent.

Two people were walking up the jetty towards the *Lady Sara*. When they came up the gangplank Johanna recognised the first one as Master Deim, and the second one turned out to be a young man.

"This is Karl," Master Deim said.

The young man nodded a greeting. He had a severe face that looked too old for his age, all planes and angles. He wore local dress.

"Karl is a cousin of mine by marriage. His family is not in the pay of the duke or the Guentherite order, and his uncle is the Holy Father Lucius of the main church. If anything goes wrong or the Guentherites make threats to you, they won't want to give his uncle a reason to complain. The Guentherites are not on good footing with people in the town, but they rely on us for many of their supplies. Karl will be your shield."

"Thank you."

"Karl has also visited the Guentherites and worked for them, so he is well-versed in their ways."

The young man didn't look old enough to have had those experiences. "Thank you," Johanna said again. "You are really a most useful friend. I do hope that when we return to oust Alexandre, you will come with us."

Master Deim smiled, but said nothing. What did that mean? Was he coming? Was he staying here? There was no time to talk about it.

Last night, Johanna had tied up two sea cows in preparation for this expedition and now she reeled in the ropes of both. The animals were strong males, placid if a bit lazy, but they came to the bank for the cabbage leaves she held in the water. Their big snouts with the rough whiskers brushed her hand. She tied both in the small harness which had hung at the back of the cabin for all of the journey, and tied the ropes to the small rowing boat that Master Deim had brought.

On a whim, she threw the rest of the cabbage in the water and reeled in the ropes of all the animals. She met Master Deim's eyes while doing so. He nodded in silent understanding. *Just in case we'll need to get out of here quickly.*

Roald climbed into the little boat, taking the reins from her. With a bit of training, he would probably be much better at handling sea cows than she would ever be.

Karl seemed a little uncertain about the animals and sat on the bench as far as possible from them.

They set off.

At first, no one spoke. Water slapped against the sides of the boat. Johanna didn't dare look too deeply into its murkiness. She didn't need to study the water to see the ghostly forms swirling underneath. Occasionally one of the animals would break the surface with a flipper or snout, or would come up to take in a deep and noisy breath. She had to steer the boat upstream first so that they could drift back to the jetty on the other side with the current.

From here, it was clear that the Guentherite farm lay on a slight hill and that its buildings and belltower overlooked the surrounding land.

The boat came past the run-off of a creek where a lot of cloudy water joined the river. The creek ran between a couple of paddocks into the Guentherite order's land. Thin veils of mist hung over those paddocks and the banks of the creek.

Upriver from that branch, the colour of the water became darker and clearer.

"A branch of the river splits off and goes around the back of that hill," Roald said. "The abbot got the workers to dig a new creek so that they could build a water mill there."

"So the cloudiness is run-off from mud?" Johanna asked. From where they were, upstream of the creek, the change in colour was very clear.

"Is that mill working now?" Karl asked. It was the first thing he said in their presence, although he still seemed a little uncertain about how to relate to Roald. "Last time I saw it, they were still building it. They had some strange problems with it, I understand."

"The mill is working," Roald said.

The boat turned back downstream, and then drifted back to the jetty.

Johanna caught the post, and Roald threw the rope over and pulled the boat in. A rickety wooden ladder showed that the monks were prepared for times of low water, but those stairs were not needed today.

Johanna loosened the harness and the two bulls wandered off to graze.

A gravel-paved path ran from the jetty to the low buildings of the order set on the hill. The belltower of the chapel that Roald had talked about overlooked the fields.

The place looked completely peaceful, with rows of grapes with yellowing leaves and cows grazing in the paddock. A faint mist hung over the fields. From here, Florisheim looked pretty with the Baron's castle and its fat, stubby tower protruding from the jumble of slate-covered roofs. From here, the quay looked barren and menacing, with the city wall and its iron gates at the back. While the city gate that Johanna passed on the way into town from the camp had always been open, these gates facing the river were always closed. Two ships lay there, low river freight vessels like the *Lady Sara*, but less pretty.

The gated entrances to the cellars underneath the quay were also closed, and most of them were too far under water for any type of boat to enter.

Behind her, Roald said, "Uh-oh."

Johanna's heart jumped and she looked back at their side of the river, expecting to see someone coming down the path. But there was no one. Cows grazed. A group of geese came waddling down the hill.

"What's the matter?"

"Don't like geese," he said, nervously looking over his shoulder. "You know that I once got bitten by a goose?"

Johanna laughed. "You're afraid of geese?"

"You'd be afraid, too, if you knew these geese. They are not nice."

Meanwhile, the geese waddled, honking down the path.

"Let's go this way." Roald pulled her sleeve.

He led them onto a side path between two fields of grapes. The path was narrow and muddy, and they had to walk single-file. The grapes grew in rows on trellises that reached above their heads, so that they couldn't see what happened elsewhere. Johanna thought of the tunnel of interwoven trees on Duke Lothar's land. The vines were heavy with fat, dew-covered red grapes. Roald picked a small bunch and shared them around. "The skins are touch, but just spit them out."

The grapes looked sweet, but they tasted sour. The skins were indeed quite inedible. Roald ate and spat, but she felt like she had to be more civilised about it, and wormed the skins into her hand before dropping them onto the ground.

"Who would want fruit as sour as this?"

"They're for making wine," Roald said, and went on to

explain how wine was made. Apparently, it involved men stomping through grapes with their bare feet.

Then they came over the crest of the hill where the vineyards stopped.

Here there were orchards full of apples, that would soon need to be harvested, and stands of berries bleeding into pine forest.

Johanna couldn't help but think that some of these fruits should have been harvested in the past few days when the weather had been warm.

A couple of horses grazed in a paddock.

Roald whistled.

One of the animals, a brown stallion, pricked up his ears, and turned his head in Roald's direction.

Roald ran to the fence and slapped his hand on the top bar. "Come here, Selmus! Come here, come here."

Silly. Of course his friends on the farm had been animals. Johanna should have known that.

The horse clopped to the fence. Roald climbed on top so he could better reach the horse's face. It nuzzled his face, whickering. Roald petted its head and scratched between the ears. If he could rule the animal kingdom, Roald would be the best king ever.

"Shouldn't we go?" Johanna looked over her shoulders, nervous that someone would come. The plan was to try to find Shepherd Carolus, without being discovered, and smuggle him out.

"They feed the animals in the mornings," Roald said. "No one comes here for most of the day while they're all working."

"Aren't they working in the fields?" Although by the neglected look of the vineyards, she should have known the answer. And neglecting the harvest seemed the most stupid thing to do ever. If the religious order sold wine and dried fruit, then what would they eat for the rest of the year if they didn't get those grapes in?

"You'll see."

Roald jumped down from the fence. They continued down the hill. The horse followed them as far as it could. Most of the mist had cleared, but veils of it still hung in the valley, covering a little thicket of oak trees, where a small tower protruded from the canopy of leaves. Water pooled in a small lake in front of the trees. The surface was smooth as glass and reflected the trees and the chapel on the far bank. It was all so peaceful that Johanna couldn't imagine that people who lived here did any ill.

But when they came close to the chapel, it was as if the mist increased and the day grew darker. There were also . . . strange noises. Hammering, the grinding of millstones.

"Is there a water mill here?"

"I told you they diverted a part of the river to go through the fields so that they could have a mill here."

Yes, he had told her. It just seemed an unlikely place for a water mill, right next to the chapel, supposedly a place of prayer and solitude.

On the other side of the chapel, trees had been cleared from an area that covered both banks of the creek. The water fell down a man-made drop, operating the watermill at good speed. The silence of the forest was broken by the steady slosh-slosh of the water in the scoops and the creaking and clanking of the mechanism. Whatever the mill operated was under the ground, connected by a large beam and two gear wheels and a second beam which went into a hole at least twenty paces across. Johanna couldn't see over the edge, but sounds of clanking and rattling mill wheels rose from below.

"Do they make paper here?" It was a strange place for that, with not even a roof overhead.

"No. This is where they make iron."

Iron? Wasn't that something people got . . . from the mountains?

Johanna crept closer, but even when she could see the mechanisms and moving mill wheels in that hole in the ground, she still couldn't see the bottom of the pit. The beam went deep into the ground, still turning, to whatever mechanism it operated down there. It squeaked.

The pit appeared to be man-dug, with walls fortified with trunks of pine saplings. A ramp made from crude planks of wood zigzagged down into the pit. The air was moist here, and misty.

It smelled of wet earth and reminded her in a disturbing, unpleasant way of the ice cellar.

She could almost smell the faint rank scent of beginning decay.

A monk in a grey habit came up a ramp wheeling a barrow full of what looked like black gravel. He went a short distance into the shelter of a roof on the other side of the pit and upended his load on top of a heap of similar material. Someone else was shovelling rocks from another pile into another machine that looked like grinding stones.

There was a huge brick furnace at the back of the shed. Another set of beams and wheels went in that direction, coming from a second water mill, and moved a giant bellows up and down that fanned the flames in the furnace. The entrance of the furnace was open and a monk was shovelling in scoops full of the black dirt.

On the far end of the furnace, another monk lifted out a long pole with, on the end, a stone bowl with red glowing fluid inside. Another came to help and they poured it into a stone mould.

Wait—she recognised these two. They weren't proper monks. They were the two men she had sent downriver as scouts. She raised a hand to her mouth to stop herself shouting out. All that time the people in the camp had been waiting for them to return.

Both men looked dirty. The hollow expressions on their faces spoke of days of hard work and little chance of escape.

On the floor lay finished blocks of metal, sheets and strange shapes. Some monks were fashioning glowing shapes with hammers before they cooled down too much.

In this open shed, Johanna recognised Shepherd Carolus, dressed in one of the grey gowns, stacking blocks of iron on top of each other. His arms had several raw wounds and bruises. His face was sweaty with the work.

"There are three of our people here," she said in a low voice to Karl, who had not met the Shepherd. She wasn't afraid of being heard. The noise of the mill and the rushing water would down out their voices.

"Are there people guarding this place?" Karl asked.

"It's easy to escape work," Roald said. "Not so easy to stay away from punishment. The forests on all sides are full of dangerous things, and the monks will hunt you down and punish you."

Karl nodded.

Shepherd Carolus now stood with his back to them, lifting another heavy piece on top of the pile.

"What in heaven's name do they need that much iron for?" Johanna asked. She knew about swords and various farming tools, but couldn't think why anyone needed huge piece of iron, flat sheets, curved sheets, and chunky pieces with holes, presumably for handles, but the pieces looked like no tool she had ever seen.

"It's for making machines," Roald said.

"What kind?" He'd talked about these *machines* for a bit, and like many things Roald said, she had not taken him seriously. Did that mean that birds could indeed fly to the Moon?

"The black rock is what makes the fire burn so hot. They find it in the ground in that hole over there. It's extremely deep. There are tunnels down there and it's very wet and dirty. When people come out they're black all over. The iron rocks they get from a little way up the river where they've made another hole. They put those rocks on a barge and let it float down the river. Then they crush it and heat it up in the furnace and they can pour the iron."

A couple of monks were now lifting a platform full of hexagonal shapes that still glowed with heat. One of the monks only had one hand, which he used to lower the platform in the water with rope and pulleys. The water boiled and hissed, releasing a cloud of steam that hid the monks from view.

Johanna pulled Roald back and Karl followed a little bit into the forest.

"How are we going to get them out?" She looked from Roald to Karl and back again. "Maybe at night? Can you show us where they sleep?"

Roald shook his head. "There are geese near the main buildings."

"Do we have to worry about geese?" Karl asked. "They're only birds."

"They make a lot of noise," Johanna said. Besides, if Roald didn't want to do something, it was best not to do it.

Karl gave her an incredulous look in an *and-you-believe-that-we-should-be-afraid-of-geese?* way.

"What is the path they normally use to go back to the buildings?" Johanna asked. "The same one we've used?"

"No, there is another path. I'll show you."

The area behind the chapel was covered in thick forest. Roald led the group over various animal tracks that led through the tangle.

The sound of the thumping mill wheels and falling water faded before becoming stronger again.

They arrived at the top of another waterfall, this one not yet with a mill, although a hollowed-out area in the opposite bank showed that one was planned there. The water that tumbled over the edge into a deep pond was murky, as if someone had spilled milk in the creek upstream. A fine mist spread at the spot where the waterfall hit the pond's surface, and swirls of fine silt formed cloudy shapes under the surface. This was where the river downstream obtained its muddy colour.

It was as if the clouds consisted of tiny particles of silver that, when they swirled, reflected the light like schools of tiny fish. Johanna crouched and reached for the water, wanting to stir it up.

"Don't touch," Karl said. "The water is bad. Don't touch it and don't drink it."

All right. She straightened.

But then, a thought: what about the camp? It was downstream and people had been drinking this water for months.

They had also behaved too passively for months. She had wondered what made them like this and now she knew why.

"Magic," Johanna said, softly. She stared at the pond, watching the swirling shapes under the surface. At times she swore she could see people or faces.

Roald said, "When I was here, Alexandre fell in and the ghosts nearly killed him. That was why they said he went mad."

Johanna couldn't stop looking at the water. It called out to her, making the magic in her blood sing.

Someone has disturbed the magic lines. The meaning of that warning was now clear.

The digging in the ground by the monks had done this. Magic bled out of the ground with the water that the monks used to cool their iron and rinse their rocks.

"So, if we're not going to get them from the dorm, then what do we do?" Karl said. He stood a bit back from the water, clamping his hands around himself, staring out over the mist. The bell tower of the main chapel protruded from above the buildings on top of the hill.

"We wait until the workers start going home, and then we'll try to get the Shepherd's attention. He's a strong man and I'm sure he can run. I presume they follow that path over there to the house."

Roald nodded. "Yes, they go that way, and then up the hill and between the vineyards to the back of the main building. There is a chicken pen there, and they have ducks. The geese don't live near that part of the building. I think they don't like the ducks. Oh, and there is also a donkey, but it's not very friendly. You have to be careful, because it kicks."

"What time do they go back to the building?"

"Usually when it goes dark."

That meant a long wait. It also meant that even after they freed the men, they might have to stay out here overnight because it might be too dark to cross the river.

The thought of staying here overnight gave her the chills.

CHAPTER 18

THERE WAS NO COVER closer to the house, so they had to wait in the forest. Roald stretched out on the grass and was soon asleep, but Johanna felt uneasy. She spent a good while studying the shapes in the water. If she squinted, she could see them bleeding into the pool over the edge of the waterfall and re-forming once they were in the pond. She walked a little way back where she could see the cloudy water run out of the pit that the monks used to cool the iron. A stream of particularly milky water flowed out of a clay pipe that came from the deeper hole.

At regular intervals, a monk would come up the ramp out of that hole with a wheelbarrow full of black stuff. As Roald had said, his face was black as soot, and this made his eyes look oddly bright. He would wheel his load to the furnace, tip it over and go back down.

The water mill creaked, the huge bellows made a "whoomp" noise every time the air was pressed out into the furnace. Sometimes, fire would blow out of little air holes on the side.

Shepherd Carolus was still stacking the iron shapes. A cart had arrived with two huge horses and he was loading the iron pieces onto the tray. Whenever he stopped for a rest, one of the overseers would yell. This was the only time that the horses would twitch or turn their heads. They were *very* huge, with long fetlocks and big, fat rumps. She wondered if Roald knew these horses, too.

She counted at least fifteen men in the clearing and under the shelter, but there might be more in the hole where she couldn't see them. Some of those men would be supervisors, like the one with the embroidered key on his robe, the Burovian prince, but others looked like workers or, more correctly, prisoners.

The sun came through, its light weak through the mist, and then sank towards the horizon.

They sat between the trees and ate. The bread they had brought was dry and hard to swallow.

Karl looked really nervous, and when Johanna asked him why he was so jumpy, he only said that, "Strange things happen here at night." He wouldn't elaborate on what those things were, at which Roald started reciting a dissertation about *ghosts and other things unnatural*, written, he assured Johanna and Karl, by a priest of the Belaman Church. Strangely enough, it did nothing help Karl's nerves.

As dusk slid over the land, a few lights came on in the windows of the main building, but the whoomping of the bellows kept going and no one in the hole or in the shed with the furnace was preparing to stop work. Did these people go to sleep at all?

The Moon rose over the horizon like a giant orange orb and spread an eerie pale glow over the fields. In it, and the rising mist, shapes swirled over the surface of the water.

The thumping and creaking in the forest clearing continued unabated. A second cart approached over the main road from the main farm buildings.

"They're using Selmus," Roald whispered next to Johanna while they watched the two horses pull the cart at leisurely pace towards the forest. The cart did not come back, nor did the one that was already there.

"Do you know where they take those iron shapes?" Johanna asked.

Roald said, "A place down the river that's called Willow Bend. It's the abbot's summer residence. It's quite close to Aroden."

"And what do they do with them there?"

"Make machines."

"But whatever for?" Also, she had come up that river, but had not seen the abbot's summer residence, unless it had been around the bend from where the bandits had captured them.

Maybe . . . her thoughts whirled.

Maybe the abbot hadn't *wanted* anyone to see whatever happened at his summer residence and maybe that was the real reason they had been captured.

If that was the case, then it made sense that the men who had travelled down the river had never reached Saardam.

But there was no time to contemplate it further, because something was happening at the main building now.

A door had opened in the wall that faced the forest and a group of men came out, walking in a long line over the path. There were at least twenty of them, all dressed in robes. The first few in the group carried something between them that looked suspiciously like a body on a stretcher. Several of the men in the tail of the procession held candles, and the glow from the flames was reminiscent of fireflies: little pinpricks of light that did little to dispel the darkness.

When they had reached the end of the path between the vineyards, the stretcher-bearers turned towards the pond.

Lying on her belly on the ground, Johanna shuffled backwards so that they wouldn't see her. She sensed Roald and Karl behind her.

The line came closer and stopped at the edge of the pool, where the group gathered around their leader. He spoke, but his words were drowned out by the water rushing over the ledge and falling into the pond below. The mist that rose from the pond was rendered almost luminous by the moonlight.

They group shuffled aside to let the men with the stretcher to the water's edge. The thing under the cloth was definitely a body. The shape of the toes and the head pushed up the fabric.

Two other men dropped two planks of wood across two rows of stones that protruded from the water. The stretcher-bearers walked across these and lowered the stretcher into the water. One of the men pulled the cloth away.

The dead man's pale gown glowed in the moonlight. His skin was waxy pale and bore darker scars and spots as if he'd died of pox. Johanna shivered. Father had told her of the ravages of the pox epidemics in Estland and Gelre. For some reason, the disease had never done much in Saardam, but that could easily change.

The monks on both sides pulled the stretcher out from under him.

The body floated.

A man stepped forward from the group of spectators. Whereas most of the monks wore grey robes, his cloak was very dark brown or black, but unadorned, so he was not the Burovian prince, who, she thought, was still at the shed in the forest.

While the others watched, he raised his hands and started some sort of incantation. From her position at the top of the waterfall, Johanna couldn't make out any of the words.

For a while, Johanna thought this was a ritual for a monk who had died. She thought that once they had cleansed the body, the men would cover it up, carry it away and bury it elsewhere.

And damn it, now she noticed how the clanking of the water wheel and the whoomping of the bellows behind her had stopped, and the voices of men rang through the forest. The work party was about to stop for the night. They would walk over the road to the main building and now it would be difficult to attract the attention of Shepherd Carolus and the two others, let alone allow them to escape, with all these people here.

"Look!" Karl whispered.

Because something happened in the pond as well.

Tendrils of mist rose from the water and enveloped the body until it was encased in a misty gown. Slowly, the body sank under the surface with sucking and wet crunching sounds as if some sea creature was chewing it up. But the water was perfectly still.

The dark-robed man continued to stand at the bank with his hands raised towards the heavens. The monks watched, silent sentinels to this macabre spectacle.

Johanna was feeling ill to the stomach.

The mist released the body which bobbed back up. After hearing those sounds, Johanna was half-surprised to see it intact.

The body kept rising and rising until it came free of the water and floated in the air. The black-robed man held his hands higher, as if pulling it up by invisible strings. His voice rose into a crescendo, but although the words were clear, the meaning of them was not. Johanna didn't even know what language he spoke.

The body *twitched*. Eyes opened. Hands jerked. The man sat up, looking out of hollow, empty eyes. His mouth opened and he sighed out a hissing breath, but no other sound came out.

Karl, on the ground next to her, let out a muffled squeak.

"Be quiet!" Johanna whispered.

The apparition floated away from the bank and until it hovered over the middle of the pond. Like Princess Celine, it didn't look ethereal enough to be a ghost, and the colours of the skin and hair were too washed-out for a real person.

The black-robed man asked a question. The apparition turned away from him.

The man asked the question again.

The apparition now floated to the other side of the pond, closest to Johanna, Karl and Roald. Its skin shone with pale luminous light.

Judging by his finely-made nightgown, the man had been someone of higher standing in real life. Someone who would have died suddenly of a hidden illness and whose family would have the means to allow magicians to experiment with trying to return him to life?

But this man wasn't alive, and he wasn't a ghost with unfinished business to take care of, like the ghosts of people who had been murdered or died violently.

The man in the dark robe was now yelling at him from the far edge of the pond, the volume and tone of his voice rising, but the apparition did acknowledge him in any way.

The robed man gave a roar of frustration, balling his fists at the sky. He kicked the water, grabbed a stick and whirled around. All the surrounding monks backed away. He whirled at the pond, lifting the stick above his head and slammed it into the water. A great spray of drops flew up, glittering in the moonlight.

The apparition turned around in an annoyed way. It hissed, the sound so soft that it was barely perceptible, but it made Johanna's hair stand up. A cold breeze tracked over the water, disturbing the mist. The black-robed man said something, the tone mocking. Johanna caught something about the meaning of magic. The other monks retreated even further. The robed man laughed at them. There was something eerily familiar about that laugh, but Johanna couldn't see into the shadow of his hood.

The ghostly apparition floated towards him. The robed man grabbed waved his stick in front of him. He was still laughing. The apparition lashed at him, but the stick sliced through the ghost and cut off one of its ethereal arms. It hung uselessly in the air. The ghost stared at it, as if surprised. The black-robed man took the moment of surprise to cut the ghost in half at the waist, distributing swirls of mist over the surface of the water.

The two halves of the apparition drifted down and bled into misty shapes that sank into the surface of the pond. They were absorbed by the water until there was nothing left.

Next to Johanna, Karl let out a relieved sigh.

But then the water started to churn and boil. Something long and thin broke the surface: an insect's leg the thickness of a human arm, with bristles over its surface. And then another leg and another. The creature that rose from the water was not the same as the one as she had seen earlier. It was bigger and had more legs, and as its long body emerged from the water, more and more legs appeared, like a giant centipede. It reared and reared, until its head faced Johanna.

Karl screamed and ran.

Roald hid behind a tree, leaving Johanna standing by herself on top of the waterfall. There was nowhere to go and she had nothing to defend herself. She scrambled on the forest floor for a stick of wood, but there was none.

Slowly, she retreated, step by step, never losing the creature from sight. It swayed and wriggled its legs. It would be deadly if it chose to attack.

The black-robed man yelled, his hands outstretched. The creature twisted its long and glistening body around, and hissed at the man, who didn't move. He kept his hands outstretched, and kept chanting his strange words. His voice echoed over the water, a strong sonorous sound.

The creature froze. The luminous mist that made up its body lost its glow. The trees on the other side of the pond showed through its ethereal form. Slowly, its legs became thinner and grew shorter. Its body dissolved in swirls of mist which thinned and merged with the regular mist that hung over the water, until it had disappeared completely.

Johanna stared at the moonlit mist where the creature had been. There was not a breath of wind, no sound except for the distant call of a bird. The group of monks still stood on the other side of the pond, staring at her.

Slowly, the black-robed man lowered his hood. His face was surprisingly young, freckled, and his chin had the hint of a beard. He wore his red curly hair tied at the nape of his neck. She knew that face, and had seen that hair before.

It was Kylian.

CHAPTER 19

THERE WAS NO further point in hiding. Kylian had seen Johanna, although he might not have seen Roald and Karl.

She took her time to pick her way down the incline to the edge of the pond. While she did this, she stole glances at the group of monks who had come with him. Most of them looked disturbed and were still staring at the water. Oh no, she didn't think that the apparition had been killed. Neither had the one that looked like Princess Celine been destroyed when Loesie fought it. They were just waiting under the surface to strike again at Kylian's command.

Kylian looked straight at her. "Finally we meet again, little princess. I've been looking forward to this."

"What are you doing here?" Her heart thudded. No, she didn't want him anywhere near her. He was dangerous.

He bowed his head in a mockery of courtesy. "I was waiting to see your pretty face."

Johanna's mouth seemed to have frozen up. All she could think of was how, when she'd attended the ball, he'd swept her up in a dance in the gallery behind the ballroom in the palace and how he'd kissed her.

Johanna wanted to scream that she didn't want him near her, that he was an evil magician.

She wanted to tell the monks about the bodies in the ice cellar, that Kylian was a necromancer, but they probably knew all this already, and saying it out loud would make him angry and more dangerous.

She wanted to run, but she didn't think that her legs would support her. It was her own fault this had happened. She should never have come here.

But now that she had come down to the water, she recognised the Shepherd Carolus as one of the onlookers behind the monks. His eyes were wide and mouth hung open. When their eyes met, his lips moved. "Johanna?"

Johanna resisted the urge to check over her shoulder to see if Roald and Karl were still hidden, but that would give her companions away, although Kylian might already know about them.

Kylian walked slowly around the pond until he faced her.

Johanna wanted to back away, to run from him as far as she could, but she kept her ground, her back straight. If anything, her stubbornness would give Roald enough time to flee, if he was smart enough.

Kylian was now very close. In the moonlight, his hair looked brown. He reached out a hand to her cheek.

Johanna stepped back. She didn't want the hands that had touched a dead body to touch her. She didn't want to give Roald a reason to come storming down that hill to yell for Kylian to *keep your hands off my women.*

He chuckled. "You don't trust me."

"That's an understatement. Why should I trust you? After this evil magic I just saw you perform?"

"I saved much of your beloved city." He put his hand inside his cloak, withdrew a large splinter of wood and held it out to her.

Johanna covered her hand with her cloak before taking it from him.

He chuckled. "I see you've learned."

"What's this?" She held up the splinter meeting his eyes over its pointy end.

"Touch it. You will see." His expression was intense.

She lowered her hand. "I don't think I will. I've already seen far too many things I never wished I had, starting with that night in Saardam. I have no desire to see more blood or more fire or more dead bodies."

She held the splinter out in the space between them and dropped it. It fell, point first, into the mud.

Did he flinch or was that her imagination?

"You don't want to know what I did to save much of your city?"

"No, because I don't believe you. You came to Saardam to take possession of it. You took Alexandre Trebuchet and then washed your hands of him. But in truth, though you and your family may not like him, he's your minion more than anyone else's."

"You should learn the facts before you accuse people. Did we not see the fire demons from the back of the palace? Did I not run from the garden to help fight them? I knew none of the locals had any aptitude with magic, so I went to fight it. Magic is drawn by magic, as you will well understand."

"I have no idea what you did."

"Then pick up that piece of wood, and it will show you."

Johanna glanced down, but couldn't see it in the grass. She hesitated. Should she look for it? But no, she didn't trust him. And wood showed things that happened in the place where it was part of a table or a door. It showed snatches of conversation, people walking past. It rarely added up to a coherent story, unless he'd carried this piece with him for the *purpose* of telling the story, in which case she definitely didn't trust him. "Anyway, why would you fight it? You weren't in your town."

"We were in Saardam as guests of the king. Royal families help each other, as you will probably still need to learn."

Was that an underhand jab?

Why was he even at the ball? The ties between the Baron, the royal family and this monastery that was a place for unruly royal sons were far from clear.

"What were you doing in the middle of the night at Duke Lothar's castle? What were you doing, trying to interrogate my maid, but clearing out before you could speak to me? If you were so helpful, you might have introduced yourself to the new king of Saarland."

"I was there on other business, visiting a mentor in an outlying town. I often go to the Duke's castle to stay overnight when I'm travelling. He's my uncle."

"He tried to murder your father."

He laughed. "Oh, you've heard that story."

"What's so funny about it?"

"It was a practical joke. My uncle and my father are not enemies at all."

That was not how she understood it.

"My uncle helps my father quite a bit. Seeing as you like to talk about how we all have court magicians, my uncle could be called my father's court magician."

And who had told him that she'd been talking about court magicians?

"I don't believe that at all. The Duke and his son were very clear about where they stand. Where is your father anyway and why won't he talk to any of us? Why do you keep people here against their will? What are you doing here in the middle of the night with dead bodies?" She had to stop to draw breath. There were so many more questions she could have asked.

But it didn't matter, because he wasn't going to reply anyway. He was just going to dance around the issue and play with her as a cat plays with a mouse. That mouse again. She glanced at Shepherd Carolus.

"I'm here to say that you won't need to put up with me much longer. We'll leave as soon as possible, something we should have done long ago. Whatever is going on in Saardam, and you're not telling us, is not going to be fought from here."

She turned away from him but took only one step before he grabbed her upper arm in a strong grip.

"Not so fast, princess, where do you think you're going?" He was close enough that she could see the moonlight glisten in his eyelashes. The light fell sideways into his eyes and brought out all the intricate bumps, flecks and veins in his irises.

"I'm going back to the *Lady Sara*. We're going home."

"You think you can handle fire magic now? Do you have that magician you were looking for so desperately?"

Seriously, had Magda told everyone in town? "No, but is battling him without magic any worse than sitting here until we die and then being consumed by ghosts? This land is rife with magic. None of our people can handle it, and it's like we're slowly being poisoned."

"How about I help you?"

"You?" She met his eyes and for a moment, wanted to say yes. Because he might not yet be fully versed in necromancy, but she knew no one near as powerful.

But what was his relationship with Alexandre?

"You're still distrusting? I told you then that I could help you and I'm telling you now."

"A lot has changed."

"Nothing has changed in the world of magic at all. Magic is attracted by magic. You can feel magic in me. You are attracted to me."

"You have far too high an opinion of yourself."

"Why did you marry the Idiot Prince? Why, when you should have come with me and received training in magic?"

"And then what? What are you anyway? How do I know that you don't have anything to do with Alexandre Trebuchet? How do I know that you didn't send him? How do I know what the lot of you want from us? I do not believe that Alexandre acted by himself of his own accord, and I don't believe that you don't know what is going on. Now let me go and keep your hands off me."

"All right, all right." He stepped back, holding up his hands.

Johanna rubbed her upper arm.

"Then don't believe me. I can't make you. After all, someone who believes in that hideous three-headed monster has clearly lost his mind. Go on being a happy little queen without an heir."

Something snapped inside her. She lashed out and hit Kylian in the face with a slap that echoed over the water. Several of the monks gasped.

Shepherd Carolus looked at her with wide eyes.

Kylian grabbed her wrist and pulled her close. "That's more

like it." He was so close that she could feel the warmth of his breath. It smelled nutty with a faint trace of liquor. "Keep up the anger. You can't fight without anger. One day I might even tell you why you don't yet have an heir."

His face hovered over hers. For a moment, she thought he was going to kiss her again, and there was nothing she could do to stop him. Already her magic was singing out to him and part of her wanted it. She was hoping the Roald would come down to the water and go into one of his rages about *his women* but he did not. Again, Roald was smarter than she thought. Or maybe he had been captured already.

She pulled her arm. "Can you let me go? I've come here to speak to the abbot about our Shepherd and the other two men you hold prisoner. I don't know why they are here, but I'd like to take them with me."

"You—what?" Kylian started laughing. Shepherd Carolus was shaking his head, his eyes wide. "You have the hide to come in here and ask—what?"

Johanna tried to gesture with her eyes. *Run, run!*

"Why were they taken? What are you doing with them? What are you doing in that hole in the ground?"

"You would like to know all that?" His fingertips dug into the soft flesh of her upper arm. He chuckled. "You would really like to know all that, eh?"

Johanna met his hard gaze, trying hard to maintain her uncompromising stance. But his magic ate at her. *Just give in*, it said. *There is no way you can fight him,* it said.

"I can tell you, but then I'd have to kill you." He trailed the finger of his free hand over her nose, leaving behind a trail of tingling where his skin had touched hers. Part of her wanted to say *Kill me tomorrow morning, and it will all have been worth it*. She shook her head to force those silly thoughts from her mind. He was evil, a dark magician of the worst kind.

He paused his finger at her chin. "Or I could tell you, and I'd have to kill that idiot of a husband of yours."

No, Roald. He knew Roald was here. Maybe his men had captured Roald already.

"Or I could take you up to the dining hall, order a nice

dinner of food grown on the farm and tell you over a good glass of wine. I get quite lonely. I'll let your hapless companions go in return, and I'll even tell you a secret or two that will help you to get rid of that useless oaf Alexandre."

Johanna met his brown eyes. She had to do whatever she could to distract him men so that Roald and Karl could escape. "You're kidding, right?"

"No, I'm not. The choice is not so difficult, is it?"

"Just dinner?"

"Just dinner."

Johanna took a deep breath. She didn't believe him for one moment. He was going to take advantage of her, show her horrible things, keep her prisoner. Already, his magic affected her. She found it hard to think clearly. "Let me witness you letting the Shepherd and the two scouts go. Let go of my arm. I'm not a child."

He laughed. "Why so suspicious? My word is good." But he did release her arm.

"I want to see those men being freed. I want to see them walk away from here. Otherwise, I'm not doing anything."

"All right." He said something and two monks came forward with the Shepherd between them. His face was pale with red welts across his cheeks. From where he'd been hit?

He pleaded. "Don't, Johanna. Please, don't give in to him. Your life is worth more than mine."

Johanna stepped close to him and whispered in the space between his shoulder and neck, "Go to the river. You'll find a boat there. Wait for me on the other side. Save Roald." The Shepherd nodded, his eyes wide.

Johanna stepped back. "Let him go. I will stay and hear what you have to say."

She kept her back straight and rubbed her arm where he had touched her. The skin was still tingling.

She watched the Shepherd and the two young scouts walk into the night down the path. She hoped that Roald and Karl were smart enough to follow.

Then Kylian put his hand across her back on her hip. "Let's go inside, shall we?"

CHAPTER 20

A FTER THE SHEPHERD had gone from sight, Kylian led her past the pond through the fields. Mist pooled in the valley turning the vineyards into ghostly shapes.

The monks accompanied them as silent sentinels. Johanna felt oddly calm inside. Somehow, ever since that dance at the palace, she had known that it would come to this meeting. Whatever attracted him to her, he needed to be disabused of the notion that she should come with him. She would calmly explain to him that she was committed to Saardam and Roald, and that it was neither shameful nor strange to love someone who wasn't normal.

They went up the lane that led to the house. From the field came the sound of honking geese.

One of the monks ran into the field waving a stick to chase them off.

"Those things are a menace," Kylian said, and it was the first thing he'd said since Shepherd Carolus had left.

"They're only geese," Johanna said. She thought of Roald's dislike for the birds, and hoped that Roald was crossing the river right now. Not sure. She could see parts of the silver ribbon of water between the trees.

Kylian lit a storm lamp at the steps.

They went into a wooden door which creaked badly and gave

545

access to a barn full of shovels, picks, hoes, rakes, wheelbarrows and other equipment that cast long, tangled shadows by the light from the lamp. Against the far wall, there were a couple of long tables covered with tiny grapes. For making raisins, she guessed. Mice rustled in dark places where she could not see them.

From that large room they went to another, this one a well-appointed farm kitchen with a large stove, an open fire and pots and pans on neat shelves. The air was heavy with the smell of smoke and food. A monk was kneading dough at the table and another was cutting onions. He greeted Kylian with a bow of the head.

Johanna's stomach rumbled.

Kylian spoke briefly to both men and they responded with polite nods. A young boy came into the hall with them, carrying a candle.

Kylian took Johanna into a lush sitting room where the boy lit a few oil lamps. A lusty fire burned in the hearth. He gestured for Johanna to sit down on one of the couches and sat down on the other.

He said, "Dinner will be served shortly."

"This doesn't look much like a monastery."

"It used to be one. Abbot Guenther was an uncle of mine and after his death he bequeathed this building and the surrounding land to me."

"So it's no longer a religious place?"

"The land and the house are mine, but the monks are welcome to stay for as long as they want."

As long as they worked in his projects. "Do you still provide services for wayward royal sons?"

"Is that what you think we are? A work farm?"

"That's what it looks like from where I'm standing. That's what Roald has told me."

Kylian snorted.

She warned him, "Call him an idiot and my promise is off."

He let out a single huff of air that was a combination of a chuckle and a sigh. "Why so defensive of the idiot king?"

"He's my husband."

"A marriage of convenience, certainly."

"I happen to like him quite a lot."

"You can't be serious."

"No? Why is that such a surprise to you? He's smart, he knows a lot, and he's just awkward around people."

"I would have thought a smart girl like you could find someone better than that."

"You would like a smart girl like me to be hopelessly infatuated with you?"

He sniffed and let a silence lapse. From elsewhere in the building came sounds of voices. Then the door opened and a monk came in wheeling a trolley.

He pushed it to the table and set out two plates, glasses, knives and then a couple of bowls.

"The fare is quite simple here, but it's good," Kylian said.

When the monk had finished, they say down at the table. Kylian took his position opposite her.

The presence of the table between them made Johanna feel a little bit more relaxed. She let him pour her a drink from the carafe.

"Wine from the vineyard out there." He glanced at the window, where the last rays of daylight coloured the western sky.

The liquid was clear and sparkled in the glass. It smelled of grapes. Johanna took a small sip. "It's nice."

He sipped, too, and set his glass down. "Let me serve you."

He took her plate and carved a few slices off the roast leg of some sort of bird.

"Goose?" Johanna asked.

"You wish." He grinned.

And that set the tone for pleasant banter while they ate. Talking about food was safe, and she got the impression that he hadn't lied about being lonely.

She thought about his half-cousin Sylvan, who was often alone but never appeared to be lonely.

He had been right and the food was good. Johanna thought about Nellie, who would be out of her mind with worry right now, and maybe Loesie was behaving strangely again, and it worried her that Kylian was trying to keep her here, and that she must be strong against any magic he would try to use on her.

She prodded with her shoes for where the table legs were. Better not touch any wood here, considering the way he'd been trying to give her that splinter that would probably have told her about horrible things that had happened at the farm or in that hole in the ground.

After she finished her wine, he poured her another glass. The warmth from the hearth took the chill off the autumn air. The food was filling and the wine had made her sleepy.

"All right, enough now about the pleasant talk. Let's get to business. It's important that you know about this, because it affects all the known lands." He rose from the table, went to the desk and brought a roll of parchment, which, when he unrolled it, turned out to be a map.

Johanna blinked her eyes and squinted at it. Stupid. She shouldn't have had that second glass of wine. She was not used to it.

The map showed her the familiar outline of Saarland, Burovia to the south all the way to the lands of the southern ocean where the coastline was drawn in rough, incomplete strokes and the map gave only names like *One Tree Island* scribbled in pen after the map was completed. Not places where people lived.

The land to the east of the Horn was left empty. No one knew how much land was there. In the ocean, the mapmaker had drawn a fanged, scaled creature with its mouth open, as if about to devour the ship that sailed there.

Kylian placed his index finger on that sea creature. "Danger is coming from this direction, and we must get ready to defend ourselves."

His voice sounded ominous, and he met her eyes squarely. He seemed to be quite sober, though he was swimming in and out of focus.

"How do you know that danger is coming?" she asked. Her tongue felt numb. Also, what did this danger have to do with the current situation in the low lands? If anything, the mess with Alexandre made the countries less able to defend themselves. "If you wanted to make us more defensible, wouldn't you want to unite all the countries, not wage war between them?"

"We need to use magic to defend ourselves," Kylian said. "These people who are coming are strong magicians."

Ah, now she understood. "And any church that prohibits magic is in the way, right? So you sent Alexandre?"

"We did not ask him to do what he did."

"But you were more than happy that he did it without your asking?"

"Many people have been unhappy about the influence of this church on our major sea port."

"So you killed the priests and burned the city."

"We rely on the cooperation of Saardam to supply us and to protect us from the menace. Saardam will be in the frontline. They will come over the sea."

And he thought that attacking Saardam was the way to do that? "You are not listening to anything I say, aren't you?"

"No, you are not listening to anything I say. I've seen the danger on the wind. They have ships that need no wind. They have dragons. We need to act, or they will overrun us."

"If it's our cooperation you want, you have a strange way of going about it." She wished her head would stop swimming.

"If you would just allow me to give you this piece of wood, you would see it for yourself, and you would see that it is no trivial matter." He held the splinter out on his flat palm. How did that thing come here? She had dropped it and she hadn't seen him pick it up.

Johanna hesitated. She had been adamant that she would not touch any wood in this building. "I still can't see why you can't just tell me." She ignored his outstretched hand with the splinter.

"No words exist for some of the things that threaten us. They must be seen to be believed." He held his hand closer.

But the more he insisted that she touch the wood, the more she didn't want to do it. That splinter of wood held some sort of trickery, she was sure of that.

She made no move to pick it up, and he put it on the table between their plates. "You really don't trust me, right?"

"Having seen the evil magic you can perform, give me a reason why I should."

He pushed himself up from the table and walked around to her side. She thought he was going to sit next to her or touch her. In fact, he walked so close that the air that whirled in his wake brushed her face. Johanna did her best not to flinch.

He went to a cupboard behind her and took out a carafe and two glasses. The fluid that sloshed against the glass was oily and bright green. *Absinthe*, the drink of demons and evil.

That was it.

"I think it is time for me to go." Johanna pushed herself up from her seat. Whoa, her head.

"Why the hurry?" He faced her.

A smile played across his lips. He said nothing, but that expression said enough. It said how he didn't think Roald was a worthy man for her. It said that for some reason he'd set his sights on her. It said that it was highly unlikely that she'd get out of this room with her dignity intact.

Johanna looked up into his face. Her heart was thudding. She saw his face as it had been on that first night in the palace, when he had danced with her, when he had kissed her.

"The people in the camp will be worried about me." Johanna's tongue wouldn't cooperate. Her cloak hung on a hook near the door.

"Such a pity," he said. "I'd have expected a bit more fire from you. But, alas. I'll walk you to the jetty." He retrieved her cloak from near the door.

All right, that was a lot easier than she had expected. Yet it didn't make sense. First he threatened to kill her or Roald, and now he was going to let her walk out of here, just like that?

"You seem disappointed," he said.

"That's not the word I'd use."

"But?"

"But what?"

"But you had expected me to be more insistent?" He trailed a finger over the skin in her neck. It gave her goose bumps.

"Something like that."

"I'm an honourable man." He held up the cloak and she slipped into it. His close presence gave her the shivers. He smelled of horse and smoke.

"I appreciate a beautiful woman." He ran his hand over her hair, running the flyaway curls through his fingers. "But I know that she can't be mine, although I would beg on my knees for just one more kiss." His face hovered over hers.

"No," Johanna said. "My men are waiting for me."

He growled. "Your men are fools." He pulled her into the envelope of his smell and closed his mouth over hers. Johanna struggled. She tried to push him away, but he slid both his hands down her sides, holding her so tight against him that she could feel the heat of his body through his clothes. The magic burned in him. It sang to her, it pleaded with her—

No, he was just trying to trick her.

"Hmmm!" She pushed him away, but he was too strong. He forced her back until her back hit the wall. Nowhere to go. "Hmmmm!"

There was a sharp stabbing pain in her neck and the trickle of blood running down her skin. "Hmmm!"

Black spots danced in her vision. She saw giant flying creatures flapping huge leathery wings back lit by moonlight. She saw them open their mouths a spew fire. She saw a magician yell foreign words at them. His eyes were black as the night and his face glistened with sweat.

She was vaguely aware that Kylian picked her up with one arm under her shoulders and the other under her knees.

She saw ships coming into a foreign harbour. They were big and chunky, and the sails were red. Sea creatures reared from the water. Their big bodies coiled around her. Johanna tried to scream, but couldn't. The creature pulled her under water. She clawed at its scaled surface, trying to push herself free of its coils. She kicked, she scratched, she pummelled the scaled skin with both her fists. It held onto her neck with needle-sharp fangs buried deep into the flesh. The coils had pushed up her dress and a different part of the serpent held her in an entirely different way. It rubbed her in a pleasant way. It went inside her. It roared.

Glass shattered. A cold wind blasted through the room. Johanna fell and landed hard on her knees.

The lights were out and the fire had died. Blood trickled

down her neck into her dress. She reached up. Her fingertips found the wooden splinter still buried in her skin. She pulled it out and stared at it by the light of the moon.

There was a sound nearby.

She wanted to whisper, "Who's there?" but her tongue was too dry. So she sat up and looked around her. Nothing. Where was Kylian? How long had she been out? Quite a while, she thought, judging by the stiffness of her muscles when she climbed to her feet. The floor was covered in grit, shards of porcelain and rubble. Her dress got caught under her feet, almost causing her to trip. The collar was wet from blood, but otherwise her clothing was intact. In the vision she had been *naked*. A shiver crawled over her back. The blood on her hands was starting to go sticky.

Footsteps in the corridor.

Johanna pressed herself against the wall.

Someone, no more than a ghostly shape, walked into the room. The glare of the moonlight showed only a light-coloured shirt. No one wore those, except . . .

"Roald?"

"Nobody touches my women," came Roald's voice out of the dark.

Johanna stumbled to the door. She didn't worry where Kylian was. Didn't care. She fell into Roald's arms. He'd been holding something—a broom or a shovel—which he dropped with a clang and held her awkwardly.

"You came back for me."

"I'm sorry we were late. We fell asleep. The Shepherd woke us up."

Magic. It was affecting them all. She should probably be angry that he hadn't obeyed her and hadn't left this side of the river, but for now, she was glad that he had come.

"I love you," she said into his chest.

"It's my task to say that."

She held him, feeling his warmth through the wetness of her clothes.

"We must get out of here quickly, Your Majesty." This voice

belonged to Shepherd Carolus, whose presence was nothing more than a huge grey shape in the hall.

Johanna pushed herself out of Roald's arms. "Yes, we must go, immediately." Before Kylian turned up, wherever he had gone. Then she thought of the shovel Roald had been holding, and felt ill with the thought that Kylian might be lying on the floor unconscious somewhere in the house. Part of her wanted to go and look for him, to see if he was all right. That was the magic affecting her and she must fight it. She wouldn't ask Roald or Shepherd Carolus about him, or at least not until they were safely out of here. Not until there was no way magic could sabotage their escape.

Karl and the two scouts waited in the moonlit courtyard with Selmus the stallion. Roald lifted Johanna onto his warm and hairy back. There was no saddle. "I don't know if I can ride like this," She protested weakly. She was feeling dizzy all of a sudden.

"Hold on with your legs. We won't be going fast."

From somewhere within one of the surrounding buildings came a squawking. "What is that sound?"

"We locked the geese in the chapel," Karl said and he chuckled. "Someone will have a nasty surprise when he comes in for prayer tomorrow morning."

And by the lightening of the sky along the eastern horizon, the morning wasn't all that far away.

Roald took Selmus by the reins. Oh, those first few steps were wobbly. Johanna was still feeling dizzy and there was nowhere to hold on except the mane, but didn't everyone always say never hold on to a horse's mane? But after a while she became used to the horse's movement. Selmus was clearly a workhorse having endured much worse treatment than someone clumsily trying to stay on his back.

They left the courtyard for the main road that ran from the jetty to the hilltop farmhouse. The road sloped into a shallow valley where milking cows stood looking forlorn in the pre-dawn mist that hung low over the grass.

As they passed, swirls of mist oozed from the creek, stretching long ethereal fingers towards the road.

Shepherd Carolus at the front of the column hesitated. Roald stopped behind him, holding the horse's headgear.

"What is that mist doing?" the Shepherd said.

"Yeah, I don't like this one bit," said one of the scouts. Johanna believed the man's name was Willem. "See how the cows have all gotten up and come to the fence?"

They stood in a row facing the road.

"I've seen this happen at the chapel, but never here," the other man said.

"We didn't go this way often," Willem said.

"True."

"Keep going," Johanna said, her voice low. "Ignore it."

"The queen knows all about magic," the Shepherd said, and that scared Johanna more than anything. She knew nothing, except one thing: trying to get out of here was infinitely better than staying.

Slowly, they continued along the low-lying section of the road. The excess of rain had made the path muddy, but this area was naturally wet. Reeds and watercress grew in the meadows on either side.

Karl walked so close to the horse that Johanna's leg brushed his arm.

The mist continued branching out towards the road, now covering half the meadow. It was clear that they weren't going to make it to the jetty without having to confront whatever apparition was going to come out of the mist.

"Go and cut me a willow branch," Johanna said to Karl.

"But . . ." he said in a squeak.

"That tree over there." Johanna pointed.

He trotted to the fence and came back not much later with a long and floppy branch. What sort of willow was this?

Johanna held the twig, which resembled a whip more than a weapon.

And still the mist oozed out of the hollows and marshy areas. This entire land bled magic. Every person who ever died on this land had a ghost in that mist somewhere, because who ever died with all their business taken care of?

Their voices whispered in Johanna's ears. It didn't look like

Roald of Karl could hear them, but they could definitely see the tendrils of mist that formed into human shapes, that crossed the meadow in the direction of the road, that reached emaciated, bony hands to the living humans. Many of them were apparitions, not senseless ghosts.

"Can we please go faster?" Karl's voice sounded high.

Roald urged the horse on. Whoa! That suddenly made the rocking worse. The horse's back was slippery with the animal's fine coat. Johanna squeezed her legs. She groped for the horse's mane. Never mind the horse wouldn't like it. Both Karl and Roald were almost running now. It was still a fair way to the jetty, and Johanna wasn't sure that she would be able to stay on. Her backside bumped onto the horse's back with each step it took.

"Wait, wait. Please stop. Let me down, I can walk—"

The road trembled. The gravel moved as if pushed up from underneath by a giant hand. A mount of dirt grew higher and higher until the top bloomed open. A hiss of cold air streamed out. Karl screamed. The horse reared. Johanna slid from its back into the mud.

Ouch. She sat in the wet grass while water seeped up her skirt. The two scouts were running to the jetty. Roald had grabbed Selmus' reins and was trying to calm the horse, but the white showed in the corners of the horse's eyes. Shepherd Carolus stood in the middle of the road chanting prayers. He held up his pendant with the sign of the Triune.

Where was the willow branch? She crawled on her hands and knees in the mud, her movements restricted by her wet clothes.

"Look, look!" Karl yelled.

Johanna didn't need to look to know that a ghost had emerged. The man's figure was brilliant white with flowing, curly hair. His face had strong cheekbones and intense, not too deep-set eyes. His chin was strong but not angular. His nose was straight without being sharp or thin. His lips were full. It was the most handsome man she had ever seen. It was a perfect version of Kylian.

What? "What did you do to him with that shovel?" she asked Roald.

"The idiot did nothing," Kylian said and laughed. "He

couldn't harm me if he tried. I am one of the few people who can transcend the borders between life and death at will."

No one could do that. It was a trick. It had to be.

"Keep away from her," Roald said, lifting the shovel. Johanna realised *It has a wooden handle*.

"Give that to me." She pulled at it.

"I will protect you."

"You can't protect me from magic and keep control of the horse at the same time. Take the horse and the others to safety." She managed to get hold of the handle—she saw a monk shovelling manure from the barn into a cart—and faced the apparition.

The men stared at her.

"No, Johanna!" Roald called.

Johanna shouted, "Run to the boat! Now. Go!"

They backed away, hesitantly.

The apparition said. "You have worked it out. We can be dispelled with a simple piece of wood. But that doesn't even come close to killing us. Nothing can kill us. We always come back bigger and more frightening." He reached out, and Johanna held the shovel before her.

He laughed, but backed away from the wood. "Run now, little princess. You will live a bit longer. There will be a day that you will come back to beg me for my help. That day may be sooner than you think."

His ghostly form dissolved. Ice-cold wind whooshed over her head.

CHAPTER 21

J OHANNA RAN.

Roald and Karl were already in the dinghy with the Shepherd and the two scouts still on the jetty. Roald was trying to reel in the sea cows' ropes, but the animals were nervous and kept tangling the gear. They clambered in the boat, which wobbled with the weight of all these people. Karl kept a nervous eye on the water level on the outside of the hull.

The sea cows were tugging at the harness. It was impossible to reel them in so they'd have to do that after casting off. Johanna unhooked the rope from the pylon and the animals took off with such speed that she almost fell overboard. They tore across the churning expanse of water.

A dense mist hung over the far bank, blanketing the camp. Even before the forms of the tents resolved from the mist, the sound of shouts drifted in the stillness.

A chill went over Johanna's back. "Did anything happen in the camp?"

No one knew the answer to that question.

Johanna peered through the mist.

People were running down the riverbank and up the jetty, men women and children, all bunching into a large group in front of the *Prosperity*'s gangplank.

A man yelled. "Oh, look, they're back!"

"They've got the Shepherd!"

"And Ko and Willem."

"Thank the heavens."

It looked like half the camp was there, and a lot of people carried bags, too.

Johanna tossed the rope up the jetty and climbed out of the boat. Many hands helped the men up. The young scouts both had family in the camp who greeted them with squeals of happiness. The Shepherd received a hero's welcome.

A man yelled, "Make room for the king and queen!"

People shuffled aside to form a path.

Johanna spotted Captain Arense. "What's going on?"

"The camp was overrun by ghosts this morning," he said. "They came out of the river and all the marsh areas and drifted between the tents. Some people tried to fight them with burning torches, and some tents caught fire. Some are still burning."

"Was anyone hurt?"

"Not badly, no. People panicked and came here. We decided that we're leaving. I don't know what we'll find downstream, but it can't be any worse than this."

Johanna nodded. She agreed.

There were a lot of people already crammed on board the *Prosperity* and more people continued to climb aboard. Her eyes met those of Johan Delacoeur across the crowd. He didn't sneer. In fact, his expression was haunted. It had taken a long time, but Johanna thought he finally believed her. He gave a barely perceptible nod. She nodded back at him. A tiny measure of respect.

There was a great splashing in the water, where a sea cow threshed its tail on the surface while the deck hand tried to reel in the ropes. The animals were nervous, too. They wouldn't come. They wormed themselves out of their harnesses. They tangled up the ropes.

Loesie and Nellie stood with Master Deim in the deck of the *Lady Sara*

"Get the animals!" Johanna called out to Loesie and Loesie ran to the front, hopefully to do as ordered.

On the other side of the jetty, Karl was leading people to the *Prosperity*. Men in the camp were still trying to put out the fires which burned in the hay stores and some of the primitive wooden constructions that served as outdoor kitchen or overflow housing. There was no sign of any ghosts, but the sun was rising and ghosts did not usually appear in sunlight. Who knew what the night would bring, though? They were downstream from the farm, and the murky, magic-infused water flowed right past the camp. She had always wondered why the Baron hadn't offered a field closer to town. Now she knew.

Captain Arense yelled that everyone should go down into the hold. Wives called for husbands or children. It was too dark down in the hold to recognise faces.

She called, "Anyone who can't find a spot, come to the *Lady Sara*."

A line of people started up the gangplank to the *Lady Sara*. Nellie guided them to the rear deck and to begin filling up the hold covers from the rear. Entire families dumped their bags, blankets and other meagre possessions onto the lids. Johanna hoped that there was going to be enough room for everyone. The part of the camp she could see was starting to look deserted. Some people had even taken down the tents and covered themselves and others with the canvas. Roald had taken care of a couple of young children. One of the girls carried a lamb.

She shouted to Captain Arense, "Do you think we have everyone?"

Everyone who wanted to come, at any rate. She hadn't seen either Ignatius Hemeldinck or Fleuris LaFontaine.

Whether the camp was empty or not, they were out of time. A couple of the Baron's men rode into the camp from the main road. Their horses moved in full gallop, manes and hair flying. The first one carried a banner.

Johanna panicked. *Kylian*.

People on the deck had seen them, too, and panicked talk spread over the deck.

"Get ready, we're out of here!" Johanna yelled at Loesie and Nellie.

She cast the first rope loose. Then she ran to the back deck and loosened the second one. The rope was rough and cut her hands when sliding around the post. While the horses came down the riverbank, the *Lady Sara* drifted away from the jetty. The horses tore over the wooden planks with a thundering of hooves. Johanna held her breath. The front rider rode a warhorse and carried a sword and crossbow. He wasn't going to jump, was he?

The gap between the jetty and the boat grew, but not fast enough for her liking.

Johanna bit her lip. *Come on, come on, come on.*

The horse came closer and closer—

And the rider pulled hard on the reins. The horse slid to a halt and reared with a screaming neigh. His comrades pulled up behind with a good amount of snorting and swearing.

The *Lady Sara* and *Prosperity* drifted away from the shore, with nothing but churning, magic-infused water separating them.

The leader yelled across the water. Obscenities, no doubt.

The current pulled hard at the ship. Loesie and Roald had managed to pull in the sea cows in their proper formation and gave them free rein to swim as fast as they could.

Behind them, a man's voice yelled, "Eeeeyup!" and there was the sharp sound of a stick being banged against the hull to frighten the animals into going faster. Johanna spotted Master Deim and Karl on the deck.

The Baron's men turned their horses away from the jetty and ran along the river bank, but slowed down in the marshy area of tangled branches where, just days ago, she and Master Deim had found Loesie. The horses found no easy path through this area, and they were left further and further behind.

The sounds of their angry yelling faded until the only thing left was the sound of sloshing water against the hull. The sun was just coming up over the misty landscape, edging the world in gold.

"We're going home," a man said behind her, in an incredulous voice.

"Yes, we're going home!" another shouted.

"Long live the King! Long live the Queen!"

Roald had been sitting on the hold covers with the young

children he had helped. The girl had handed him her lamb, which he held cradled in his lap. Johanna went to pull him up, and he rose, still holding the animal.

"You're going to have to behave in a kingly way," she said to him.

"No. That's why I have you." He put an arm around her waist.

So they stood amongst their citizens: a painfully shy and awkward king who liked frogs and ducklings, an inexperienced queen and a lamb that symbolised the child they desperately needed but that had still not shown any sign of appearing.

At least they were going home.

THANK you for reading the Ghostspeaker Chronicles books 1-3. The story Continues with book 4, Fire Wizard. Get Fire Wizard from your favourite retailer or find out more on Patty Jansen's website.

ABOUT THE AUTHOR

Patty Jansen lives in Sydney, Australia, where she spends most of her time writing Science Fiction and Fantasy.

Her story *This Peaceful State of War* placed first in the second quarter of the Writers of the Future contest and was published in their 27th anthology. She has also sold fiction to genre magazines such as Analog Science Fiction and Fact, Redstone SF and Aurealis.

Patty has written over twenty novels in both Science Fiction and Fantasy, including the *Icefire Trilogy* and the *Ambassador* series.

pattyjansen.com

BOOKS BY PATTY JANSEN

More information:
PATTYJANSEN.COM